I0664101

THE CHILDREN OF POSSIBILITY

THE CHILDREN OF POSSIBILITY

A NOVEL OF TIME TRAVEL

BY THOMAS T. THOMAS

THE CHILDREN OF POSSIBILITY

All rights reserved. This is a work of fiction. With the exception of certain public figures familiar from the history of science and who are treated in a fictional manner, any resemblance to actual persons or events is coincidental. For more information, contact TomThomas@thomastthomas.com.

Copyright 2012 Thomas T. Thomas
Cover photo © Igor Balasanov/Vetta/Getty Images, Inc.

ISBN: 978-0-9849658-7-8

Contents

FROM A 102ND-CENTURY DICTIONARY:

Chassis, *n.s.:* (1) a frame and working parts, as of a machine or electronic device, exclusive of housing and external surfaces; (2) of any Silicate intelligence, one or more interchangeable physical carriers designed for some specific purpose and having shape, structure, and tools appropriate to that purpose.

Flüchtling, *n.s., m., ~e, pl.:* fugitive, refugee, runaway; *colloq.* an outcast from the reference now *(q.v.),* usually gathering in an earlier time and place as members of *(collective term)* a coven. *O.G.*

Jongleur, *n.s., m., ~s, pl.:* 1. tumbler, acrobat, juggler, street busker; *also,* mountebank, huckster, charlatan; 2. *(cap.)* an officer of the organization that consolidates and regulates travel through time, member of *(collective term)* the Troupe. *O.F.*

Möglichkeit, *n.s., f., ~en, pl.:* possibility; **Möglich, ~en,** *pl.:* a sentient theoretical construct from one or more probabilistic decision points *(cf. Wahrschein Punkt)* following the "Schein" or "not taken" direction. *O.G.*

Neural imprint, *n.s.:* the process of transcribing electrochemical activity in the human brain into quantum entanglement of electrons across multiple time cones, as a means of preserving thought and memory against distortions due to alteration of the past.

Reference now, *n.s.:* current time, the actual or true "now," as perceived from a subjective viewpoint. Colloquially, as applied to time travel, "reference now" may also refer to the traveler's original or starting time and place, as opposed to the time and place of arrival.

Selvage, *n.s.:* 1. the edge on either side of a woven or flat-knitted fabric so finished as to prevent raveling; 2. of a fractured singularity *(q.v.),* the process of annealing the point of quantum leakage so that it does not naturally close.

Singularity, *n.s.:* 1. *(physics)* a point or region of infinite mass density at which space and time are infinitely distorted by gravitational forces; the final state of matter falling into a black hole; 2. *(mathematics)* a point at which the derivative of a given function of a complex variable does not exist but every neighborhood of which contains points for which the derivative does exist; **fractured s~:** a singularity exhibiting quantum leakage of mass/energy into one or more temporospatial dimensions.

Temps, *n.s.&pl., m.:* 1. time; 2. weather; 3. *(grammatical)* tense; 4. *(musical)* tempo, *T. fort,* downbeat, *T. faible,* upbeat; 5. *(gymnastics, military exercises)* repetition. *O.F.*

Voyageur, *n.s., m.* ~s, *pl.:* traveler, passenger, explorer. *O.F.*

Wahrschein, ~**lichkeit,** *n.s., f.,* ~**en,** *pl.:* probability; ~ **Punkt:** probability node, probabilistic decision point. *O.G.*

From the Jongleur Handbook:

Chapter 1:
Gravity is a force. It is governed by the most basic equation in physics: force equals mass times acceleration [F=ma]. Thus, gravity is routinely measured as an *acceleration*. However, the acceleration of gravity is actually independent of any distance traveled, or *space*. By freezing the spatial variables, manipulation of the gravity equation yields one free variable: *time*. ...

Chapter 2:
... Time is not a river. Your life takes place, not in a stream, but on the surface of a membrane that stretches endlessly in three dimensions, like the surface of a bubble. The membrane itself is not static but expands outward, second by second, through a fourth dimension: time itself. Each person living on the surface of this membrane moves steadily outward along the radius of the expanding bubble.

Each person also generates circles of communication, personal action, and interpersonal action that spread, second by second, across the surface of the bubble, like ripples in water from the fall of a leaf. The spread of each circle is limited, theoretically, by the speed of information transfer in normal space—that is, the speed of light, or 300,000 kilometers per second. In practice, however, a circle of action may move much more slowly—perhaps at the speed of a horseman riding out of town.

The intersection of the expanding surface of the bubble and each spreading circle of action defines a cone. The cone always points backward toward the origin of the action along the axis of the bubble's radius. The cone of time sets the limits of possibility, the span of cause and effect, for any being that inhabits the surface of the bubble.

For beings that live *outside* the bubble, however ...

Chapter 3:

Subjectively, each self-aware being and the commune of interacting beings inhabit the surface of a single time bubble. For these inhabitants, the surface is unbroken, the axial cones of action all point in one direction, and the flow of time is continuous. Objectively, however, to any awareness that exists outside the bubble, the surface is vastly, almost fractally, uneven and carries pits and scars from the actions of those beings living inside the bubble.

Dents and craters appear at the points where individuals, interacting communes, even entire civilizations have ceased functioning and disappeared. Their time cones may continue to echo through chains of collateral cause and effect, but the cone's original focus becomes a void.

Buds of new bubbles and eventually entire new worlds appear at each Wahrschein Punkt where the potential for action is equal or reciprocal. For the subjective inhabitants of the original bubble, these buds are invisible, as they constitute the Schein fraction of the original potential.

... The universe visible to any self-aware mind concatenates thousands, millions, perhaps infinities of invisible universes, all proceeding outward from successive points of origin. Most of these unfelt universes are mutually indistinguishable, comprised of minor differences in choice and action that gradually diverge through cause and effect. However, this benign relationship is not universally true of *all* budded worlds. Some worlds bud in the chaos of war, environmental stress, and societal collapse, engendering dark spheres of aversion and rage against the original order.

... The universe is more bizarre than any single mind can imagine.

Chapter 4:

Travel through time always implies travel through space. For a Jongleur to travel forward or backward along the time axis and expect to arrive at the same point in space would be impossible.

Consider that any point on the Earth's equator is rushing eastward with the planet's rotation at approximately 1,609 kilometers per hour. The planet itself is moving along its orbit around the sun at 107,277 kilometers per hour. The sun is moving around the galaxy at 792,000 kilometers per hour. The sum of these proper motions means that a one-year trip backward through time arrives at a point in interstellar space trailing the solar system by approximately six and a half light hours.

... Of course, when crossing between two bubble worlds that happen to coincide, no spatial dimension applies. However, for the reasons stated elsewhere, this mode of travel is *not* recommended.

BACKWARD

1. Briones Park

"All right, teams," said Mrs. Gorage-Rhymes-With-Porridge as they filed out of the school bus. "Two by two and keep together."

Josie Barnes was paired with Mary Jane, the strange orphan girl who had the beautiful blonde hair. No one else had wanted to team with her, because she was so quiet, so confident, and so ... self-possessed. It was almost like having a little adult among them. The other girls respected her, sure, but that didn't mean they *liked* her. Still, Josie figured it might be good to have someone so smart working with her on this assignment.

The class had come out to Briones Park, in the East Bay hills between Richmond and Orinda, to do an ecology count on the first clear and windy day of spring. Basically, that meant Mrs. Gorage and Melanie, her classroom intern, had gone out yesterday, identified a likely field full of weeds and wildflowers, and marked it off in big squares with orange tape. This morning, as they rode the bus over the Bay Bridge and through Oakland, the two teachers had passed out battered Palm Threes with data wands and explained how to use them. The computers were already loaded, they said, with the field grid and entry points. The assignment was to count the plants and animals—well, insects—and then take soil moisture and pH readings. After that, they had to study the data and draw conclusions. This was the hard part for Josie, because she never seemed to know what to think.

But she figured Mary Jane would be really good at that.

Mrs. Gorage had assigned each of the teams their own square, but right away the other girl broke the rules. And that, too, was kind of what Josie expected.

"We're supposed to be doing Square Fourteen," Josie said as Mary Jane walked resolutely over the tapes toward the far side of the field.

"There is more growth over here," she replied.

"That's not the point. We're supposed to count the plants in *our* square."

"This will make a better report."

"But ..." Josie had to follow to keep up the conversation. Very shortly, they were a long way from their square and getting farther away all the time. The only good thing was that the teams assigned to this part of the field hadn't reached their squares yet, so nobody was fighting with them, and Mrs. Gorage hadn't noticed anything. Josie still had time to reason with Mary Jane.

Before Josie could get her thoughts together, Mary Jane walked right over the last strip of orange tape and pushed on, into the underbrush.

"I'm sure we're not supposed to go in there," Josie said, raising her voice.

"Be quiet and do what I do," Mary Jane told her, taking Josie's elbow in a hand that was small but very strong for its size. The fingers gripped in a way that didn't exactly hurt, but Josie could feel the side of her arm tingle. She followed as Mary Jane dragged her out of sight.

Under the trees, Mary Jane looked around as if taking her bearings. She studied the twisted, leaning trunks of the live oaks—Josie was proud that she could identify them—and approached first one and then another. She put a tentative hand on the scaly bark, feeling a humped scar where a branch had broken away. Then Mary Jane nodded and plunged deeper into the thicket.

"What are you doing?" Josie asked.

"I have to find something."

As Mary Jane climbed over and slid under the low, tangled branches, she reached into her pocket and took out something small and round. It looked like a big glass-

and-metal ball, the size of the balls on her uncle's pool table. It certainly wasn't anything a girl their age ought to be carrying. But Mary Jane held it up, cupped in both hands, right below her chin. Josie thought she might be talking to it.

The ground dropped away in the direction they were traveling. Soon the two girls were standing side by side on the lip of a rocky ravine.

"We're not going down there," Josie said. "Are we?"

"This is the right way. What I want is down there."

Mary Jane put the glass ball away and started down the bank. She went facing forward, looking down and dancing from rock to rock. Josie turned around and used her hands and feet to climb down backward, feeling with her toes for each step. Mary Jane's way was faster, and she reached the bottom first.

"We're going to get in *such* trouble," Josie complained.

Mary Jane nodded absently. She was searching the narrow strip of ground alongside a rushing stream. Fifty feet further on, she stopped beside three rocks that were a very light gray, almost white. She stood in the middle of the triangle, faced the one rock that pointed most closely toward the cliff wall, then stepped over it and walked forward.

Josie, following behind, bent to touch one of the rocks. The surface was glazed white, like it had been burned to ash and then the ash fused to glass. What kind of fire, she wondered, could do that?

The gulch was steeper here and more overgrown. Mary Jane reached into the curtain of hanging branches and pushed them aside. Beneath was the entrance to a low cave. The girl crouched down, ducked her head, and crawled in.

This was where Josie stopped. Who knew what was inside? Maybe bats. Maybe a bear. Certainly squishy things that lived beside streams, like toads and salaman-ders. If Mary Jane wanted to go in there, let her.

After a minute, Mary Jane's feet reappeared, moving backward, then her rump, shoulders, and head. She was dragging something out of the cave. When the girl had fully emerged, Josie could see it was just a load of trash: two pieces of corrugated cardboard that were torn and bleached almost white, tattered scraps of silver foil that once might have covered them, fluttering bits of black plastic sheeting, a tangle of wire, and some clothes that resembled a pair of child's pajamas, the kind with feet attached. The clothes were grayish, splotched with mildew, and they smelled bad, even from where Josie was standing.

"Ew!" she said. "Why do you want to touch that?"

Mary Jane turned over a piece of the cardboard, and scraps of foil blew away on the breeze. She looked up with tears in her eyes. "It is ... my ..."

"It's garbage. You'll get germs."

Mary Jane tried to straighten out the clothing, but the fabric was stuck together with crud.

"Leave it," Josie insisted, pulling on the girl's arm.

"They were not like this. We left them in order and packaged against—"

"Well, then someone got to them. A homeless person. Or maybe a bear. My daddy says there are bears in these hills." Now Josie was growing really scared of the cave. She pulled on Mary Jane's arm, more gently this time. "Come on."

Mary Jane stood up slowly. She was still looking down at her trash heap.

"We've got to get back before Mrs. Gorage misses us and sends out a search party," Josie said.

Mary Jane nodded. "You are right."

"Besides, you can always buy more stuff like this."

"No," the girl said with a sigh. "That is one thing I cannot do."

2. IN PROTECTIVE CUSTODY

Emily Windlace looked at her wristwatch. It was eight o'clock. "Time for bed, Mary Jane," she said.

The little girl who had come into her home three days ago from Family & Children Services looked up from the coloring book. "All right."

She put the crayons away in their box. Emily knew without looking that they would be arranged in order by color, like a rainbow, with the browns sorted below the reds and the black above the violet, like a spectrum. Mary Jane closed the book, flattened the binding with the heel of her hand, squared it with the edge of the coffee table, and stood up. She picked up the paperweight which was her only possession, the only thing she seemed to care about. It was a sphere of cloudy, layered glass, mottled greenish-gray with flecks of gold, about as big as a softball. Emily's first impression on seeing the sphere— she never did get a chance to examine it up close, because the girl carried it everywhere, setting it carefully beside her when she sat down, keeping it always in sight—had been that the thing was not pretty enough to be a paperweight. Mary Jane now slid it into the pocket of her corduroy jumper and patted the cloth over the heavy bulge.

"Good night, ma'am," she said with a nod to Emily, like a little adult. She turned to Emily's husband Bill. "Good night, sir."

He barely looked up from his magazine. "Night."

Mary Jane turned and walked down the hall to the guest bedroom.

In her ten years of taking care of foster children, Emily Windlace had never seen anything like this girl. It was like having a maiden aunt in the house.

As soon as the bedroom door closed, Bill got up from his chair and knelt by the coffee table.

"Don't—" Emily started to say, then shut up.

Bill opened the coloring book. Emily could see, even from where she sat, that each page had been meticulously filled in. The colors were bright and glossy, like enamels, with no gaps or scribbles. Emily had watched Mary Jane working the end of each crayon, twisting it in her fingertips to sharpen and soften the wax, so that the colors flowed like paint onto the page. She even added smudges of white to make highlights, undertones of black to make shadows. When Mary Jane was done with them, the line drawings—it was a book full of Disney characters—were beautiful, like a medieval monk's illuminated manuscript.

"Obsessive," Emily said quietly.

"She's had a tough time," Bill offered.

"Do we really know that?"

"Well, the cancer ..."

It hadn't taken them long to discover that Mary Jane's golden curls were a wig. It was a good one, too, probably made with real hair. But underneath, she was totally bald. She also lacked any trace of body hair; so Emily had to use her makeup kit to fill in the girl's eyebrows and supply her with a set of false eyelashes. Being nine years old, according to the best estimate from the report forwarded by the Human Services Agency of San Francisco, Mary Jane wouldn't have to worry about growing hair anywhere else just yet.

The girl's medical condition was still a mystery. She had been found in the street after the explosion of a gas main leveled the toy store, F.A.O. Schwarz, the previous month in San Francisco. Mary Jane had been slightly injured, mostly scrapes and bruises, a mild concussion, but apparently left amnesic, with no recollection of her former life. Even her name, Mary Jane Doe, was just what the nurses at San Francisco General had put on the admitting paperwork. Because the girl fought when they tried to take blood or tissue samples, no one had been able to give her more than a cursory checkup.

Cancer was suspected only because hair loss was the commonest reaction to chemotherapy, but in all other respects Mary Jane seemed healthy—remarkably so. Almost supernaturally so, because she never complained of a sniffle, an ache, or any of the minor ills to which neglected children were usually subject. The doctors theorized her hair loss might be *alopecia totalis*, an autoimmune disorder possibly caused by stress, which foster parents sometimes saw in the children that came their way—although few arrived with their own high-class wigs. But Mary Jane was the calmest, most reserved and self-contained child the Windlaces had ever taken on. Still, Emily was rooting for the stress thing because, without diagnosis or treatment that the girl would sit still for, a cancer would remain undiagnosed and progress silently to take her before her tenth birthday, whenever that might be.

"Are you sure she's even a little girl?" Bill asked now. "I mean ... you've undressed her?"

"She's one hundred percent female," Emily said.

"But weird. Have you talked about women things?"

"She's very well informed. Maybe too much so."

The possibility that Mary Jane had been abused, used for child prostitution or worse, was something they routinely discussed with the agency about all their charges. This girl's physical person, reactions, and temperament indicated no such history. In fact, she seemed to have no history at all. She had been found with no identification, no clothing tags, no latch-key stuff. No jewelry, except for a plain metal locket with no pictures or engraving inside—not even an "inside" that anyone in Family & Children Services could discover after much tweezing and prying. And no one had shown up to claim her. Mary Jane seemed to be the little girl who dropped out of the sky.

"Strange child," Bill said, shaking his head.

"Not the worst we've had," Emily said.

"Count our blessings, I suppose."

———

In the guest bedroom, the girl known as "Mary Jane," whose real name was Merola, took off her clothes and laid them out on the bed. She fished the glass sphere out of the jumper pocket and set it on the nightstand. Then she hung the outer coverings, which were still in Emily's category of "not yet dirty enough to wash," inside the closet room and patted them smooth. She folded her other garments, which were of the category "need to be washed now," by halves and halves again, into neat square packages. She put these inside the rounded box made of dried and woven vegetable fiber, which Emily called a "hamper." That was the designated place for clothing of the latter category.

Life was strange among these people. They made distinctions where none were necessary. Take clothes, for example. The pieces in the hamper were what Emily called "underwear." But the pieces on the hangers could not be called "overwear" or "outerwear," which was reserved for a separate category associated with rain and storms. They actually had weather here!

Underwear was vaguely nasty and had to be cleaned incessantly. The other garments were publicly acceptable and so could be worn with accumulated dirt ... even though they were more exposed and so likely to need cleaning more often. Everything else in this culture was the same. Taboos and covenants to the right and left of her.

Standing naked beside the bed again, Merola took off her wig and set it on the bureau. Emily had apologized for not having a proper "wig stand." Instead, she had provided a "cookie jar," which was supposed to keep the scalp net's shape. Merola never mentioned how much the wig had been crushed in transit when she came to this city.

She peeled the false lashes from her eyelids and rubbed Emily's paint off her brow ridges. Merola had used better cosmetics when she first came here, but they were gone now. She rubbed her palms over the dome of her skull and sighed.

Left to her own preferences, Merola would just curl up and sleep, but there were more conventions to be observed. She reached under the pillows and took out the sleeping garments Emily had called "peejays." Storing them among the bedclothes—an entirely new category of clothing—seemed logical enough. However, the garments themselves, sometimes also called "pajamas," were strange lumpy coverings secured with stitched bands of rubberized material and buttoned tabs that tangled, tugged at her skin, and itched. They wholly impeded Merola's sleep habits.

So did the layers of cloth she was supposed to pile on herself after lying down on the bed. This was so much more complicated than simply adjusting the room's climate to begin with. Emily and Bill's house systems were designed to maintain an ambient temperature, of course, but it was fifteen degrees below Merola's normal body temperature. The sheets, blanket, and bedspread were a throwback to living in a cold, damp cave. And the musty construction of springs and fabric called a "mattress" was a throwback to a bunch of dried grasses wadded on the floor of that cave. Merola longed for a pair of field plates, but that was beyond hope.

Seven thousand years of so-called civilization had taught these people nothing.

Once she was installed under the coverings, Merola took the glass sphere from the nightstand and into the bed with her, clutching it under her chin. She had let everyone imagine that the sphere was no more than an ornament, a toy. Children of Merola's assumed age and distressed situation were supposed to fixate on such irrelevant possessions. But the sphere, whose real name was Berzher, was hardly irrelevant. He was her companion in distress, her first officer, her technical assistant, her oldest friend—and her only means of getting home.

They would have to figure out a way to do that, and soon. Of course, Berzher himself was immutable in his current state. Merola could bury him in the yard outside and he would eventually find his way home, by one path or another, with all of his memories intact. Merola herself was relatively immutable, too—and that was the problem.

Emily had already enrolled Merola in the local "grammar school" in a naïve attempt at socializing what Emily half-believed to be a "runaway"—not an actual Flüchtling, but a feral child. Clearly, Emily liked Merola and harbored fantasies of raising her as a daughter. How ironic! Merola had the advantage of thirty years on this woman. Probably more than that.

This house was a good place to hide, to wait for rescue, if any was coming at this late date. But this refuge would not serve for long. In time—one year? two years?—the children in Merola's school class would begin to change around her. These "fourth-graders" would go through puberty, grow breasts and body hair, gain inches in height, and become what Emily would call young women.

But not Merola. Not ever.

So she had to get out of this absurd situation. She must escape this overly protective society, in which she was not even a legal person, much less a citizen. But where could she go, that they would not recover her and return her to this place, or worse?

Merola knew she had made mistakes on this mission. Berzher would catalog them for her, if he could. As she drifted off to sleep, Merola recounted those mistakes ... in order to plan her next move ...

3. MEDICAL SERVICE

On the pediatrics floor of San Francisco General Hospital, Shannon Carter, RN, hesitated outside Room 221A. She moved the hypodermic set in her left hand around behind her back. Maybe if the girl inside didn't see it this time ...

"And how are *we* today?" Shannon sang out as she opened the door and entered the room, moving fast and making her best effort to sound cheerful and excited.

In the far bed, the bald little girl with no name was sitting up. Her knees were drawn up under her chin, and her spine curved forward, away from the bed's raised head portion. Her pose was an angular caricature of the fetal position except that, instead of being comatose and withdrawn, the girl was terribly, almost hyperactively, alert. Her head snapped around like a spring-loaded machine. Shannon felt the cold, gray stare of those eyes pass through her like a ghost. There was no other response.

"It's—uh—time for your medicine," Shannon said.

The girl's body tensed. That is, it was already tense and now it started to vibrate.

"This won't hurt a bit," Shannon said, bringing the hypodermic with its pediatric dose of Seconal into view for the first time.

The girl glared at the needle as if it were a knife aimed at her heart. "No!" she said in a deep, hoarse voice that reminded Shannon of all the demonically possessed little girls in films about exorcism.

"This will help you relax," Shannon said as she laid the needle on the tray table and opened a cotton swab saturated with orange antiseptic.

"No!" The girl pushed herself back up the slope of the bed.

"It's on doctor's orders, so it's good for you," Shannon explained carefully.

"No!" The girl had her back against the green-painted wall by this time, wedging herself among the instrument fittings and gas outlets.

"Come on now," Shannon reasoned. "It's on your chart. If you don't take the injection, I could get in trouble."

The girl looked to the left and right, seeking a way to escape. Shannon herself was leaning over the near side of the bed, blocking the path back down the mattress. The other side was obstructed by the tray table. If the girl bolted that way, she would have to go over the remains of her lunch and put her weight, however briefly, on the wheeled table—which would probably roll away and dump her. Shannon could read the calculation in the girl's glance.

"Gotcha!" she said to herself.

She moved the swab toward the crook of the girl's arm.

The girl froze, watching as if it were a burning brand.

Shannon touched the saturated tip to the pale skin.

The girl didn't move, although the skin visibly twitched right at the point of contact. Taking such docility as a good sign, Shannon moved the swab in a small circle, painting loops on the skin. The girl stared down, as if fascinated by the sudden coolness of evaporating alcohol.

While she was distracted, Shannon leaned forward— to block the girl's line of sight—and took the syringe from the edge of the tray table. She moved it slowly, almost languidly forward, toward the prepared spot above the vein.

When it came into view, the girl's attention was instantly riveted on the needle.

"That's okay," Shannon crooned. "Nothing there. So tiny you can hardly see it. You won't feel a thing."

When the tip was still six inches from her arm, the girl heaved. With her head and shoulders braced against the wall, her feet against the mattress, she arched her back and shoved Shannon aside with a deft thrust of her stomach. Then she was making a straight run down the bed.

Without a thought for safeguarding the syringe and where the needle might stick, Shannon tackled her.

The girl rolled and kicked, accurately striking Shannon just below the sternum and knocking the wind out of her.

Before Shannon could lift her head, the girl was across the room.

Just at that moment, a Candy-Striper came through the door.

"Don't let her get away!" Shannon ordered breathlessly.

The Candy-Striper bent her legs and spread her arms.

The girl veered toward the bathroom. Shannon let her go in, then signed to the Candy-Striper to close the door. There was no way out except back through the room. And even if there were another exit, the girl's only possession—a skuzzy paperweight made of fused glass and metal—was still perched on the windowsill. She would never stray far from that thing.

"What's all the fuss about?" the Candy-Striper asked.

"She hates needles," Shannon said mildly.

"I *guess*," the younger woman said.

Then Shannon saw that the syringe was sticking out of her own leg at an angle. Luckily, the plunger had only depressed a half-centimeter or so—maybe a third of a child's dose of sedative. Oh well, she was at the end of shift anyway. She withdrew the needle and threw it onto the tray table in disgust.

Outside, at the nurse's station, Shannon met her shift supervisor, Ann Maccles.

"Any luck?" Ann asked.

"Now what do you think?"

"I'm guessing she fought."

"Like a wild animal," Shannon agreed.

"Poor kid, her chemo must have really been bad."

Shannon shook her head. "My experience is that children become inured to the injections, rather than fighting them. For a few cc's of Seconal—compared to what she normally gets—this gal should be putting out her arm with a smile."

"Not all of them become blasé," Ann said. "Some are terrorized. It's just an emotional reaction."

"She was terrorized *before* she saw the needle. She was vibrating like a tuning fork even before I got to the room."

"Well, consider what she's been through: the cancer, the chemo, and now that awful explosion and being abandoned. It's a hard life for a little girl."

"Uh-huh," Shannon said dubiously, rubbing the sore spot below her breastbone. "I'm reserving my sympathy for a patient who doesn't kick like a mule."

4. ESSOPEE FOR SHOCKY

Merola woke up in a garishly lighted room that was swaying from side to side. She slitted her eyes and, without moving her head, permitted herself a surreptitious look around. This was the cabin of some sort of vehicle, perhaps a small saucer—except for the jolting gravity fluctuations. Facing her were two paired metal panels holding view screens, or was it possible they were actually doors with windows made of fragile, fused silica? The view beyond them showed gray city buildings constructed of steel beams, stonework, and mirrored glass panes—all receding at dizzying speed but still at ground level.

Not a saucer then. And this was not a rescue.

A moment of panic seized her. Whoever had taken her was physically removing her from the scene of ... whatever had happened. And the place where she had been was also her last time on mark. According to Jongleur protocol, if she failed to return from a mission, a rescue team would be sent immediately—perhaps even before the "whatever" happened—but only to her last known location. And she was moving rapidly toward a new and unknown place.

Rydin, her section chief, would be so angry. Merola had allowed herself to be ambushed, trapped like a trainee on her first Search, separated in one stroke from her ship, the resources of her biosuit, her intelligence, and ... nearly killed? That last part was still hazy. She almost hoped the Troupe would not send Rydin after her, because she could not stand the contempt she would see in his face. Rydin was not only her trainer and mentor; he was her friend—and maybe something more than friend, at least in Merola's imagination. But he was also resourceful. Rydin, if anyone, would be able to find her wherever these people might be taking her.

As she watched the world slide away behind the vehicle, the city blocks where she had been picked up were replaced by less substantial dwellings of cream-colored stucco and painted wood. All of this movement was accompanied by dizzying sounds: the roaring of some kind of mechanical engine, the squealing from friction of rubber tires on pavement, and alternating, amplified wails, whoops, and chirps that were meant as warning to other vehicles.

She moved her head a bit more to inspect the insides of this cabin. To her right and left, the wall surfaces displayed oblong hatches secured by simple pressure latches, probably storage compartments—but for what? Merola herself was lying on a thin pad covered with white cloth and attached to some sort of pipework frame.

She was held in place with straps.

A needle and clear tube came out of her arm.

Berzher's naked entity was no longer clutched in her hand.

But everything depended on Berzher now. Merola's fingers moved convulsively and immediately brushed against the glass sphere, which was rolling around on the pad just below her right hip. She scooped it into her palm and held it tightly.

"You thought you'd lost that, I bet," said a voice above her head.

Merola looked up and found a dark-haired man sitting on a low bench opposite her restraining rack. He was letting his body sway easily with the cabin's movements. His hands were sorting supplies into the various hatches, but he was keeping one eye on her. The man wore a white uniform, suggesting a servant or attendant of some kind, but his manner was more watchful—like a jailer's.

"Mine," Merola groaned, tightening her hold on Berzher.

"Wouldn't touch it for the world," he said, raising his hand.

"Where am I?" she asked.

"Ambulance. Going to Esseff General."

Merola digested that, trying to interpret.

"And why am I being restrained?"

"It's essopee for a concussion," he said. "You were knocked out."

"Knocked out?" she said blankly. "How?"

"Oh, I get it. Some short-term memory loss, too," the man said. "Well, it seems a gas main blew up under the toy store. Took out the whole back half of the building and pancaked the rest. Luckily, you were up near the front, actually blown out onto the street."

"What are you doing with my arm?" Merola asked suspiciously, nodding toward the needle and the transparent tube, which attached to a plastic bag hanging from a hook over her head. From what she could see, the bag and tube contained clear fluid—not the red of flowing blood. So, either these people had filters on their sample extractors to block platelets, or the flow was reversed, going *into* her arm rather than out. The position of the bag—high in the air, to let gravity assist the flow—suggested this as well. But Merola waited to hear what the man had to say.

"You looked kind of shocky, so I started a saline drip with norepinephrine." He paused. "That's a—"

"It's a neurotransmitter and vasoconstrictor," Merola said. She felt within herself to confirm the fluid was doing nothing more. As an interrogation technique, giving her salt and hormones would prove ineffective. "Just medicine," she decided.

"Say! How does a little girl like you know such big words?"

"It's essopee." She let her head fall back on the pad.

Pumping twenty-first century nostrums into her bloodstream was a harmless diversion, as Merola's body was adapted to compensate for a wide range of poisons. What she had to guard against was anyone taking samples out, whether by intention or inadvertence. When she left this cabin—this "ambulance"—she must be awake in order to destroy that needle. Even the smallest sample, such as a tissue plug caught on its inner surface, would be enough to type her and reveal far too much about her situation.

As the ambulance careened onward, Merola closed her eyes and prepared for a convulsive thrust that would enable her to destroy the evidence. She was a prisoner now, subject to interrogation. It would take all her strength, all her sense of purpose to remain anonymous and get on with the job of connecting with Rydin or, failing that, finding a way to get herself—and Berzher—home.

5. SOMETHING WICKED THIS WAY COMES

Glyph had discovered that watching over a city was easier and safer in those times and places when the tallest building at the center of affairs was a cathedral. The roofline of the department stores and office buildings around this place, which—as he read in the minds of people passing below—was called "Union Square" at the center of "San Francisco," contained no gargoyles. In fact, these buildings had no decoration at all. How boring and utilitarian!

Not that he needed to worry too much about camouflage and concealment. If any of the inhabitants below should happen to look up and notice him, he could be gone in the blink of an eye. Glyph was an oddity among his own kind—if he had a kind. While other beings like him could only see across the dimensions that separated the various Branching Universes by using sensitive instruments that drew gigawatts of power, Glyph could do it with just his mind. Sometimes, when he really concentrated, and when the stars were in their proper alignment, he could perceive things moving as in a vision. And sometimes, with a frightful expenditure of mental, emotional, and physical energy, he could cross. Briefly.

But as if in compensation for this remarkable talent, Glyph was effectively blind upon entering any new world. It swarmed and swirled around him as a confusion of objects, actions, interactions, and energies, all without purpose or meaning. He could only see and navigate through any new space by locking onto a guide, a mind that was already accustomed to the dimension's intricacies and could show him meanings behind the shapes he perceived. And then, not every mind would work for him. He needed to find an affinity, the right kind of energy, a mind attuned to the same anger, spite, and malice that lay behind his own chaotic creation. A kindred mind could focus him in this dimension, as a beam of light threw up reflections and shadows against the darkness.

Glyph had only come to this boring, gray-toned place above the San Francisco streets because he had found and followed, not one, but three such minds. Small minds, to be sure, but locked in a triangular web of thoughts and emotions that caused them to blaze in his consciousness. Others of their kind—if they had a kind—called them the "Ramsays," or sometimes the "Silent Three," and thought of them as bizarre and dangerous beings. Among the three, however, they whispered the names "Genjifer" and "Gjordge" and "Giuffre," and they thought themselves beautiful—but also dangerous. The strongest of the minds was the one that identified as female, and on her Glyph tended to focus his own thoughts. The two others—brothers? womb mates? some relationship accounting for their linked energies?—were less obvious and not always clear to him.

They had gone into the building across the street and not yet returned. As far as Glyph could see, there was only one entrance and, judging from the movement of people in and out, that was probably the only exit. So he waited patiently. Besides, just as their three minds had passed through the doorway and joined a crowd of other, dimmer lights inside, he had read images of chemical instability, of erupting gases, of fire and destruction. Random death and destruction were thoughts that pleased Glyph immensely, and he sensed these attributes habitually stalked Genjifer Ramsay and her brothers.

When they finally emerged and hurried off down the street, he still had seen no fire, no destruction. Glyph was torn between following them along their further path or waiting here for what might happen next. A sense of mutual expectation, mirrored in their departing minds, told him to wait.

Within a short time, as Glyph counted time, the roof of the building opposite rose up in a great rolling wave that progressed from back toward front. Walls and windows at the various levels along two sides of the building shattered and flew outward in pieces. Yes, there was fire in bright orange streamers. And there was death in many of the dim minds that were caught beneath that roof and the stages of the building as it collapsed. Glyph watched contentedly as the collapse crushed out tens, multiples of ten, more than a hundred of those little minds.

One of them, however, managed to escape. The survivor flew out of a window at mid-level, just ahead of an arching tongue of flame. She—for even in this streaking flight Glyph sensed a female in bodily form and mental structure—landed as a small bundle that continued rolling across the street. This mind was not small, however, like those that had been extinguished, and it was not malicious, like those who had foreshadowed the explosion. This mind was as bright as the Genjifer female's but more orderly and with differently bound energies. Something of this one had been reflected in the minds of the three as they entered the building. Glyph sensed this person had been their target ... and they had failed, so far, to kill it.

Glyph focused on this new female mind. He detected about her the shadows of many different dimension sets. He could sense them clinging to her like the various aromas wafting off the clothes of a person who had walked through many kitchens. His heart quickened then, because Glyph sensed she was a human traveler. He could use a traveler.

Strange as her mind was, he force-fit his thoughts into hers. But she was already fading—if not into death then into some lesser darkness. He exerted all his will to pull from that dying mind every image, every secret it might hold. He concentrated so hard that he lost his footing in this reality and ... *Blink!*

6. Safronesco

"When the clock tick-tocks, toys come out to play,
"And as children gather 'round, we like to say:
"Welcome to our world! Welcome to our world!
"Welcome to our WORLD—of TOYS!"

Billy Lane paused at the foot of the escalator, his eyes drawn to the animated figures clustered around and peeking out through doors in the giant clock tower. Each one of them—the strutting toy soldiers, the singing mice, the dancing red shoes, and the rolling eyes of the smiling clock face itself—all moved in time to the music of the song. Billy stared long enough to confirm this notion for himself: that what seemed like separate little stories and bits of action were really all just part of one big, cranked-up machine. Like some ingenious ... clockworks! Cool!

Billy climbed the escalator steps two at a time, so that he went up faster than the people around him. The first floor of the store was all girl things—stuffed animals, doll houses, and Barbie accessories—and he wanted to get away from that world as quick as possible. The second floor was for babies—or the things that adults thought babies wanted—brightly colored blocks, jigsaw puzzles with pieces as big as Billy's hand, and animal-shaped music boxes. He raced around the end of the escalator and kept on climbing.

Halfway up the next flight he saw three very odd children—two boys and a girl—riding the opposite escalator. They were standing straight rather than walking down the steps, as Billy or any other child would. All three looked the same: straight, dark hair and solemn, pale faces with deep-set, green eyes. The three were dressed in dark suits, like Billy's mom wanted him to wear at Sunday service, except that the girl wore a pleated skirt instead of trousers. It took Billy just a second to figure out that the boys were actually twins and the girl had to be their sister. She stood in front, on a lower step, with her arms folded across her stomach. Billy could see she was clutching a bundle of folded cloth with something round and hard hanging from her fingertips. He recognized it as a Power Rangers suit—the girl's kind, in pink and white satin—and a matching helmet with black, almond-shaped eye lenses. The boys each held what looked like pieces of a large kite made of shiny black mylar.

When they caught him staring, their three faces turned as one to stare back.

He ducked his head and raced on up the steps.

The store's third floor was Billy's special place, full of robots and action figures, construction sets, and remote-controlled cars—things that worked, that did stuff, that made sense. He stopped first at the Lego display. Billy's set at home was big, almost a thousand pieces, but he could never make the castles and rocket ships and other fantastic shapes that the store people always built. He tried to count the number blocks in the battleship they had made this time, all out of gray blocks. And who had a set of nothing but gray, anyway? He stopped counting at two hundred, and he was not even halfway down the ship's side. He wondered if the thing was hollow, or if there were decks and rooms inside. That would be really neat! But there was no way to tell, because the battleship was hanging by wires from the ceiling. No playing with it allowed.

Billy ran on to the display of robots. There was a wide space in the floor here, between the toy shelves, where the store people had unwrapped the robots and let you play with them, for a little while, as long as you agreed to share. Billy picked up the remote box for a Mech Monster. It wasn't actually a remote, he saw, because a gray wire went from the box to the robot's heel. That wasn't as good as radio control, but maybe it meant the robot could do more things. Billy pushed the buttons and saw the robot swivel its head and swing its arms. Now, if only it could fire some weapons ...

A girl was watching him. Billy stopped and stared back at her. Girls didn't play with robots. Girls weren't actually supposed to be in this area, if you asked Billy's opinion. After a minute, she dropped her eyes and went back to playing with her robot—or the store's robot, which she was just using.

Billy squinted at her robot. He had never seen anything like it before. It was twice as big as a Mech Master, more like a Mech Walker. As a toy lover, Billy knew all about the different kinds of plastics: the soft kind you could bend, the hard kind that broke with a snap, and the kind with the silvery surface that was supposed to look like metal but wasn't, not really. Most of this robot was made out of real metal, not as shiny as the plastic stuff, more like a dull gray. And the clear parts were much clearer than plastic, more like glass. And the toy didn't have any wheels, not even concealed in its feet. Billy walked over to where the girl was sitting. And hey, where was the control box?

As he came up, the robot rose from its crouch. It stood on two legs, balanced forward, and swayed slightly, like a basketball player guarding his man. Cool! Billy had seen something like that in movies, where you could do anything with computers, but never in real life. And not in any kind of toy he could remember.

"Where'd you get that?" he asked, pointing.

The girl looked at him, then at the robot. "Around here."

"Can I play with it?"

She shrugged. "Sit down."

Before Billy could move, the robot dropped back into its crouch.

"Not you," the girl said to the robot. "Go and play."

Swiveling its blunt head, which had two red diode eyes and what looked like radar antennas for ears, the robot looked at her. "Won't you introduce me to your friend?" it asked in a voice that wasn't as ... cute? cuddly? at least not as babyish as all the talking toys Billy had heard before. This one spoke more like ... her kid brother.

She nodded at Billy. "He doesn't want to meet you yet. Go and play."

The robot stood up, looked Billy up and down, pivoted on the balls of its feet, and walked off. Billy followed the thing with his eyes. The robot immediately found another boy, who was playing with a remote-controlled police car, and squatted to watch him intently.

"How'd you do that?" Billy asked the girl.

"Voice control." She looked at him with a pale gray stare, as if daring him to call her a liar.

"I ... uh ... didn't know they understood English," was all Billy could say.

"It's a newer model." She patted the floor beside her, and he sat down. "So ... are you here with your mother or somebody?" she asked.

"Yeah, Mom's downstairs with my little sister. They're looking at doll houses."

The girl made a face, as if she thought such things were as stupid as Billy himself did. "How old are you?" she asked. Not his name, his age.

"I'm ten. And you?"

"I'm ten, too."

"What's your name?" Billy asked.

"Mer—Mary ... Jane. Do you live around here?"

"No, in Walnut Creek. But I was born here."

"In the city?" The gray eyes brightened.

"From the time Mom and Dad lived in an apartment out on Hayes Street, before Shelly was born. But I don't remember it too much, because ... Ouch!"

The pain in his forearm was intense, like something cold and sharp. Billy looked down and saw a needle embedded deep in the muscle. Instead of a plunger, like the needles a doctor used, this one had a tiny glass bulb. It was turning red, and Billy guessed that was his blood. The girl leaned over and plucked it out of his arm. Her fingers twitched, and the needle disappeared ... maybe into her pocket. Billy couldn't follow her movements.

"Why did you do that?" he asked, rubbing the spot. It was sore, but there wasn't any blood coming out.

"It's kind of a game," the girl said.

"It's a really bad game," Billy said. "I'm going to tell—"

"Don't be a baby! It didn't hurt that much, did it?"

At that moment, the metal robot walked back over to where they were sitting. It tugged the hem of her jumper with a clawed hand. "We are not alone, Merola," it said quietly.

"Where?" the girl asked.

"Circuits on all sides." The robot waved a claw around the store. "Just lit up in the last eight seconds."

"Right." The girl stood up and pulled Billy up, too. "Get out of here," she said. "Take your mother and sister, if you can find them. But get out—" She gave him a push toward the escalator. "—now!"

When Berzher said "not alone," Merola knew he wasn't talking about store detectives, local police, or any kind of trouble that the humans inside the store could detect—or understand. He meant the Flüchtlinge. Perhaps even Möglichen. Either would be a deadly threat to Merola and her kind.

They both had been expecting some kind of interruption all morning. You really could not operate in the clear, among people like this, for very long. On a Search, everyone was watching. But she had done well: four marrow samples with a geographic range that might be as wide as ten thousand miles and forty thousand years, given that one of the children matched the phenotype Rydin called "Chinois"—or perhaps even one of the fabled wild-type Nipponiers. The last specimen had been as blonde as Merola's own wig. Rydin would have called him a "Euro," maybe of Scandian stock, or possibly a Roos. Good diversity. A good spread. And the samples were now stabilized in the environment of her special pocket.

As the boy Billy ran for the escalator, Merola turned to Berzher. "Stand and fight?" she suggested.

"Not unless you want to leave streaks," her lieutenant replied. "Besides, I need this chassis."

Merola hesitated for a fraction of a second longer. But then ... the others would have all the time in the world. They would know everything about her party: its composition, deployment, weapons, and time on mark. They would be coming in force sufficient to guarantee the outcome of any engagement. "Best to fly," she agreed.

They ran to the back of the store—moving closer, of course, to the building periphery, the enemy's indicated arrival point, but closer still to her ship. They had left it in a storage room that was crowded with boxed and baled merchandise for sale: legions of toy robots, electric wheeled vehicles, some sized to fit a child, gaudy boxes of puzzles and games, dress-up costumes representing a variety of currently admired mythical characters, and a collection of wind-powered flying machines called "kites." While Berzher attended to ship preparation, Merola retrieved her biosuit.

She had left it on an upper shelf, folded with a stack of pink and yellow costumes for females that were labeled "Power Rangers." From the dust in the creases of these garments, Merola had guessed that no one would disturb the pile during her brief time on mark. Now she dug through it, feeling for the peculiar weight of her suit's laminated fabric. It wasn't there! She found plenty of thin nylon garments, some that might even fit her, but none that would sustain her life under the extreme conditions presented by her intended journey. Even her helmet was missing from the line of pink-and-white plastic shells with lozenge-shaped lenses. Someone—some nearsighted clerk with remarkably insensitive fingers—must have sold her biosuit in place of a make-believe superhero outfit.

"One minute, Merola," Berzher warned. From a bin of folded kites—twenty-first century toys made of sticks, paper or plastic film, and string—he had extracted four of the panels of their liteship, unfurled their laminar plies of molecule-thin energy branes, rigged the retaining wires, and released the selvaged singularity that was the liteship's heart.

His carapace froze. "Two panels are missing!"

"I know," she said. "My suit's gone, too."

Berzher gave the mechanical equivalent of a shrug and leapt to his position on the starboard support rod. He clung there with three of his robot claws and jacked his sensorium into the control station. The top and bottom panels were already glowing with charge. "We can make it off planet on four panels," he said.

"My suit's gone!" she repeated, more loudly. "I can't fly!"

"Well—then—you could—I could—"

"No choice. You fly out of here. I stay behind."

"And do what? Fight the Möglichen? *Bargain* with them?"

"You can get a message through. Tell Rydin I messed up. Have a relay team deposit another suit for me. Or leave a note, upstream of our departure, warning me not to be so careless."

Berzher detached himself from the liteship. "Maybe I can find your suit."

"There's no time!" she exclaimed.

And then, from deep in her mind, a cadence began. It welled up, took the shape of words. She closed her eyes, visualized, and whispered aloud: *"I am whole. ... I am full of light. ... I am perfect. ... I am full of light. ... The light surges into and through my blood, making of it a fountain of purity, vitality, youth, and beauty."* Followed by the ritual pause for reflection ... *"The universe and I are One."*

From down near her hip, Berzher asked, "What are you doing?"

"Preparing my mind for the ultimate translation."

"Good idea. ... It's already started."

The back wall of the room bulged inward and exploded in a shower of bits: dust, plaster flakes, cement fragments, and steel needles torn from the wall's reinforcing bars. The liteship disintegrated. Its tiny singularity dissipated with a *buzz* and a *snap!* even before the shock wave fully engulfed it. Berzher's chassis flipped sideways into the opposite wall. The robot's carapace split open, and the glass sphere that was his entity rolled out on the floor.

In reciting the "Prayer to Light," Merola had also been preparing her body, loosening her spine and limbs, to ride the wave wherever it took her. But now the sight of Berzher, naked and helpless, galvanized her. She launched herself ahead of the rippling wall of fire that followed the first shock wave, scooped up Berzher, curled around him to protect the nested glass-and-foil layers against her stomach, and still managed with toes, knees, and elbows to steer her trajectory out through the storeroom door.

The blast threw her across the store's main sales floor, over the heads of people caught in the act of turning toward the still-evolving explosion. She flew past one of the building's structural columns as it, too, disintegrated.

She struck a display of brightly colored objects—hollow plastic toys boxed in crushable polystyrene and cardboard—and drove it through a window high in the west wall of the building that faced outward, onto Stockton Street. That saved her life.

7. SANE LOOIE

"This is a bad idea," Berzher said again.

"Just get me the ball," Merola repeated.

"Get it yourself," he said, feeling defiant. "I'm too big. Someone might notice me."

"I could report you," he said warningly.

"As if you had never taken a souvenir yourself?" Merola taunted him. "I seem to remember something called a 'multi meter' that you wanted once. You stole it right off that technician's bench at Intel, and I never reported you."

"That was different. I was in love."

"Will you get going?"

"All right."

Ten minutes before this exchange, they had landed in a field of closely trimmed herbaceous sedge—a wild DNA strain, he guessed, longing to cut a sample—in the dead of night, time on mark 00:06:06 local. All around their liteship rose tier on darkened tier of seats that Berzher scanned as being sized for human bodies, like an amphitheater in ancient Athens, although the structure was on a much grander scale. What bothered him was that the coordinates Merola had given were almost 2,800 kilometers due east and more than two years upstream of their official mission target. "What place is this?" he had asked, feeling as nervous as an intelligence ever felt.

"It is an arena for viewing non-lethal athletic competitions," she replied. "The building above us is called Boosh Stadium." She spelled it out for him: B-U-S-C-H in the remarkable, mid-millennial Anglish manner.

"We are not in Safronesco," he observed.

"No, this town is called Sane Looie. But it is located in the same administrative district," she added defensively.

"And the date is wrong."

"These are mission parameters of which you are not aware."

"I already guessed that," he replied sourly.

At which point, Berzher distinctly remembered, he had said, "You must be sure to take an imprint—or we'll both be lost." But he noticed that, even then, with a warning, she neglected this essential precaution, required by protocol of all Jongleurs on Search.

And so, having conceded everything, including his own integrity, Berzher now found himself inside the building, having followed Merola down several twisting corridors from that grassy place. Together they confronted a door with the legend: Umpire Locker Room.

The words intrigued him. "Umpire" clearly expressed dominion, derived from the term for a sort of super-nation-state that had once ruled other nations. "Locker"—from the verb "to lock"—suggested a high level of security. The designation "room" spoke for itself: what Merola sought was highly valuable, of national consequence, well guarded, and he was entering an enclosed space to steal it.

Berzher listened on various frequencies for signs of a watching intelligence. There were none. He climbed up the doorjamb, applying alternate pressure to one side and then the other with his foot pads, and studied the handle: a globular metal knob with a zigzag crevice in its center. He probed this with the tip of a claw, but could not penetrate more than one and a half centimeters. He focused his external communications laser, tight beam and high energy, to give the crevice a shout. Metal vaporized. A crater formed. The knob collapsed on itself. The door started to swing inward. So much for security! Berzher clutched the glowing stub of the knob's stalk and rode the door inward.

When the swing reached its widest arc, he dropped onto a flooring surface of soft rubber. Behind him, the door eased shut under its own weight—or maybe there was some kind of closure mechanism. Around him, the room was dark in the visible spectrum, but his infrared sensors picked out cooling trails in the floor that showed the pattern of human feet and hotspots in the walls that suggested the traceries of energy and ventilation conduits. He switched to ultraviolet and flooded the room from his illuminator.

One side was arranged in a row of narrow metal doors—too narrow for a human of the time to walk through—each fitted with a series of crudely cut-to-shape louvers. The other side of the room had a display of hard surfaces: white, vaguely fluorescent basins, metal spigots, and a broad, glasslike sheet that efficiently reflected all radiation in the visible spectrum. He dismissed each of these features as inappropriate to the specifications Merola had supplied for a "ball." At the end of the room was a basket filled with crumbled objects of nearly spherical shape but of a consistency that Berzher took to be the fabled substance called "paper." Not to specification. There was also a high shelf with a box on it. The outside was printed with many words, but among them was the key word he was looking for: "Rawlings."

Berzher climbed to the shelf, opened the box, and extracted from it one of the balls. It was imperfectly spherical, covered with soft white leather, and stitched with red, waxed thread in a complicated yin-yang pattern that approximated the ancient sign for infinity. Specification.

Clutching the thing to his carapace, he climbed down from the shelf, recrossed the room, and left, pulling the door fully closed behind himself.

Merola, who was facing the other way down the long, dark hallway, turned when he tapped the ankle of her boot, and looked at the object he was holding out to her. "You got it! Perfect!"

She took the ball from him, holding it against her palm with fingers curled around the edges. She crouched on the floor and—*whack!*—brought the ball down hard on the tiles.

"That is to simulate the place where it was hit," she explained.

"I see," Berzher said, although he really did not. "Won't someone notice the damage to this door?" he asked. "They will suspect a missing ball."

"Not in time," she countered. "Our objective is twenty-eight hours upstream from local now."

"Before we actually arrived," he said, marveling at her cleverness.

"Time on mark 20:18 CDT, September 8, 1998 *Anno Domini.*"

"So the theft has already taken place."

"Not theft—just a *trade.*"

8. Out of the History Books

When Merola and her pilot next touched down in Sane Looie, the sky was just passing through dusk on the way to evening dark. Merola directed the little robot to avoid the grassy field they had used before.

"It won't be dark then—oh no!" the purchasing agent, Pinkus Boskin, had explained to her. "On the night when you must act, the diamond will be lit as with the power of a thousand suns. The infield grass will be as green and glowing as a bottle of Heineken's, the dirt strip around the baselines as brown as Mississippi mud, and the chalk lines themselves as white and pure as ... as chalk."

From the way he was talking, using antique references she could barely follow, and from the way his eyes were going all wet and dreamy, Merola gathered that he himself might be the buyer. However, in this black business, to deal directly with an officer of the Jongleurs du Temps, one about to go on official Search, and to attempt to subvert the purposes of that Search—that would be foolhardy in the extreme.

"No," Boskin went on, briskly enough, "you must land outside the stadium, no closer than the edge of the parking lot." When Merola's brow furrowed, he went on quickly: "The place where the spectators temporarily store their self-powered carriers. And you'll have to disguise yourself, because you will probably be seen. There will be a crowd, after all."

Berzher landed on the grass of a triangular piece of ground that sloped gently down to a double set of steel rails which Merola guessed might be connected—like everything else in this culture—with transportation. Just across the street and to the east stood the multi-level building that squared the lozenge-shaped playing field at the center of an entire city block. Berzher folded the ship's panels in record time and laid them flat on the ground. Someone would have to walk down the slope and cross right over them to find the liteship in the dark.

"I can feel eyes on us," Berzher said.

She looked around quickly. Beyond, in the parking lot, people in clumps and streams moved between their vehicles and past the Jongleurs' landing site as they headed toward the tall arches of the stadium entrance. "Those are just spectators," she told him. "They have come to watch the contest."

"I can feel their attention," he insisted.

"No one is looking this way." She shrugged.

"It's your mission," he said without enthusiasm.

Merola stripped out of her biosuit and put on her disguise: a pair of long pantaloons made of a rough-sur-faced blue cloth that the agent Boskin had called "denim"; shoes of the same material, but in sparkling white, with pale rubber soles that were molded into gripping ridges, which he referred to as "Keds"; a blouse of thin, stretchy material woven from vegetable fiber called a "cotton tee"; and of course her own blonde wig.

"Stay here with the ship," she told Berzher.

"And avoid becoming an accessory? Gladly!"

Merola used all of her training to avoid the watchful eyes of the uniformed men, whom she easily identified as guards, and duck unobserved under the arms of the metal barriers which separated legitimate ticket-holders from the passing general public. She made her way on various levels to the outer reaches of the arena, in the area called "the bleachers." The agent had given her pre-cise coordinates as to the place and time where the event of interest was going to happen.

When no one was looking, Merola climbed down over the front rail of the raised seating section, past a white-and-blue sign for something called a "Konica." She dropped onto the pavement below and quickly burrowed in among the struts and columns that supported a superstructure which the watchers, who were actually sitting down, still called "the stands." She was in an angle of the field, along an imaginary line drawn down the left side of "the diamond," just as the agent had described. She had time to spare: forty-three minutes, to be exact.

Crouched in the shadows, Merola tried not to think about the enormity of what she was planning to do. The "trade" she would engineer—but Berzher had been right, it *was* theft—could not be excused as negligence, miscalculation, or accident. Merola had willfully and deliberately departed from her temporal cues to violate Jongleur protocol. She would be tampering with an identifiable, traceable, and culturally important artifact from this reference now. If the Troupe ever learned of her actions, she risked—at a minimum—losing Jongleur status and being permanently grounded. The administrative penalties only went up from there. That was why she had avoided taking her neural imprint at any time during the preliminary stages of this Search assignment: best not to leave a record of her intentions through the entangling of electrons, as private and personal as those recollections might be. Neither would she share with Berzher any more of the details than necessary, beyond simple arrival at this place and time, because his bitstream was automatically imprinted, and other machine intelligences could retrieve it upon demand.

The truth was, Merola loved her job. Aside from the prestige and implied power, being member of an elite corps that guided and controlled the future of her own society, the work of a Jongleur was a great adventure, sometimes even dangerous. Each mission tested her knowledge and skills, her ingenuity, her nerve. Each trip showed her something new about the human condition as well as about herself. And, to tell the absolute truth, Merola was more comfortable as a stranger traveling in places and times that no longer existed, among people she would meet briefly and touch lightly, then leave and never see again. She did not have to form deep attachments, worry about how other people might feel, care about their problems, or otherwise concern herself with the subjects she sampled. By the time she returned to her own reference now, they would all be long dead, dust and ashes, not even a memory.

The Troupe psychologists had noted this about Merola. They identified these personality traits as flaws but agreed they made her more adaptable and, when required, cold and ruthless. The psychologists also knew that anything which increased her survival potential served the Troupe's ultimate purpose.

So what would tempt Merola to risk a life that suited her so well? The collector—or his agent—this Pinkus Boskin—had found Merola's personal weakness: a deep affection and an urge to protect her younger sister, Merosith. The girl had personal flaws of her own which were the opposite of Merola's and strong in proportion.

Where Merola was cold and spare, aloof and calculating, Merosith was loving and giving, usually thoughtless, and careless about either past or future. As a beautiful young woman with dazzling eyes, a generous mouth, and clever hands, she attracted men of all kinds, the good sorts, the cavaliers, and the casual sports. When she had money, she spent. If she lacked it, she borrowed. Merosith's last thirty years had passed in attracting, collecting, abusing, and then discarding husbands and lovers in an endless whirl. She threw lavish parties and galas, acquired and flaunted fancy clothes, jewelry, perfumes, and genetic enhancements, maintained expensive households and country estates, enjoyed whole seasons of extensive travel in high style, and otherwise ephemeralized, consumed, and tossed aside every asset that passed through those cunning hands. Merosith's debts had become enormous—more than enough to take the family down with her—and Boskin had lately acquired the greater part of her pledged notes.

Now, for simply retrieving an object Merola could hold in one hand, this baseball—a lump of twine covered with white horsehide and red thread—Boskin would release Merosith, excuse her debts, and set the Tsverins free. It was an exchange of service that Merola could hardly refuse.

The object's historicity, its significance in one time frame or the other, meant nothing to her. From Merola's frame of reference, the man who was shortly to hit this ball with a piece of shaped wood called a "bat" and send it out of the grassy "infield," over to where she waited under the stands, and so into "the history books"—that man had been dead for more than seventy-nine centuries. Only a handful of human beings from Merola's own time even knew his name—"Magwyer," or some such; Merola had already forgotten—or the fact that he would only hit a ball like this a mere seventy times in one year, at least according to Boskin. Others had hit such balls farther, more often, and with more style. Merola shrugged. It was all very mysterious, why any buyer would want the thing. But this one did and would pay well for it. That was what mattered.

While Merola contemplated her own situation, one part of her mind had been attending to the announcer—a voice amplified with membranes pulsed by electric coils in boxes positioned throughout the stadium building—who was obviously interpreting the action on the field for the sight impaired. "Bottom of the fourth ... Two outs ... Bases empty ..." the bored voice said. "McGwire comes to the plate ... A lot of pressure on him tonight ..."

Merola heard the key phrases that signaled what was about to happen and stood up. She crept to the edge of darkness under the stands and peered out, toward the brightly lit diamond. The white- and gray-clad men standing around its brown dirt perimeter were too far away for her to distinguish any person in particular. None of that mattered.

"He takes a swing ..." That was her cue. "Down the left field line ... Low and—" Suddenly the voice woke up and started screaming. "Will it clear the fence? ... Yes! Ladies and gentlemen, Mark McGwire just hit home run number sixty-two!"

Merola waited in the shadows. The flying ball grew in her field of vision, streaking toward her through the stadium lights, like a comet of pure white ice, rising over the fence. Boskin had warned her not to try catching it, as that would destroy the object's historical value—not to mention the bones of her hand. She let it hit—*smack!*—on the Konica sign above her head. The ball dropped to the pavement, bounced once limply, and left history in the palm of her hand.

"That line drive broke Roger Maris's record for single-season home runs," Boskin had explained—and who else but the buyer would know such details? "That record had stood for thirty-seven years!"

"Until tonight," Merola thought sadly.

She faded back, further into the shadows, drew from the pocket of her pantaloons the ball Berzher had stolen from the Umpire Locker Room, and tossed it casually toward the lights on the field.

The rest of her mission would, she felt, pass in similar fashion. Like clockwork.

9. BRIONES PARK

"So many lights!" Berzher exclaimed. He was amazed by the greenish glow that, from their vantage point of 10,000 meters, he could hardly resolve into point sources and so must represent fields of illuminated ground many hectares wide.

Merola swung outward on her strut and looked down past the liteship's offside deflector. "This civilization is at the height of its economic power in the middle of an Electronic Age," she said. "They considered it gracious living to turn night into day."

"We'll never find a hiding place in all of that!"

"Find a dark patch," she advised.

He steered them off to the west.

"Not the ocean!" she warned.

"But it is utterly dark," he said, "per your specification. And the area is large."

"Machine intelligence!" Merola sneered. "That's open water, very deep. You could hide anything there, true. But you could not retrieve it, could you?"

"I suppose not."

According to Jongleur du Temps protocol, the first thing a team was supposed to do after transiting a temporal gap as large as eight millennia, and then recrossing the spatial displacement of 5.87 light years due to the Sol-Earth system's proper motion during that time, was to find a secure cache for their backup liteship, a biosuit for the human member, and a functional chassis for the intelligence. That way, no matter what happened to the mission, all the team had to do was survive, wait out any temporary difficulties, and retrieve their ride home.

So Berzher and Merola spiraled down in the dark of night. From a point directly above their target city, on the west coast of the Nortamerican land mass, they searched for the piece of wilderness specified in their Search parameters; dark ground where humans did not pass and their cache would remain undisturbed. Twice Berzher was fooled by bodies of water to the east and north of Safronesco. Once they were almost at wave height and about to step off when he recognized his mistake.

"Listen for wind in the trees," Merola said. "That indicates dry land."

At last, approximately twenty kilometers northeast of the city, in a place with both moving trees and deep darkness, Berzher set the liteship down.

"Perhaps too far to walk," he observed.

"Unless we steal a vehicle," she agreed.

While he released the spares from their cradles among the ship's charged elements, Merola unsnapped her helmet and took a deep breath.

"Air's not very clean," she warned.

Berzher took a sample. "Carbon compounds, sulfur oxides, many synthetic organics, traces of metal halides," he recited. "Interesting—there is wild pollen in this air. These plants reproduce sexually!"

"I told you this place would be *old*."

"But consider all the variables, mutations, genetic drift, how did they—?"

"They didn't," Merola said flatly. "Not for many hundred years yet."

"Will it actually be safe to leave a ship here?"

"Underground should be secure."

"Dig a hole?"

"Find a cave."

Merola turned in a circle three times, getting her bearings in the dark, and moved off in a direction that was slightly downhill. Berzher followed, picking out his steps with his own senses.

"What are you looking for?" he asked.

Before Merola could answer, she disappeared. One moment she was beside him on nearly level ground, and the next it had swallowed her up. He scanned in a half-arc over her last position but found nothing. He replayed the critical instant in his sensory loop: the only clues were a scatter of sound that might be falling stones and a soft *thump*. He moved slowly forward and found the edge of a cliff. A muffled heat signature that approximated Merola's body mass was visible on the ground three meters below.

"Are you hurt?" he called.

"In a biosuit? Be serious!"

His human stood up and began moving around. She was in a narrow cut in the earth, obviously the trace of an old water course, now dry. Merola walked toward the cliff face and disappeared from his view.

"Have you found a cave?"

"No, but a place to make one."

"How do you propose to do that?"

"Not me. You're going to dig it."

"Do I look like a gardening tool?"

"You have that laser, don't you?"

"I have a sophisticated communications device capable of delivering terabits of information over interplanetary distances."

"With a couple of megawatts of focused heat energy, if I remember."

"This chassis does not have unlimited resources."

"You can recharge on the ship."

"So I can," he agreed.

Berzher climbed down the cliff while Merola scouted the location of her cave-to-be. "About here," she said. "The rock is soft, almost crumbly."

He faced the wall and gave it a blast. Fragments exploded outward before the matrix could fuse and slag. "Sedimentary," he said. "Sandstone, I think. With a high moisture content. That is the steam expanding."

"Well, can you do it?"

"How deep a cave?"

"Meter and a half? Enough to conceal the folded panels."

"Stand back, please."

Berzher alternately blasted at the rock and scooped away pieces with his tiny, delicate claws. It took half an hour to make a cubic space of the requisite size. While he worked, she climbed back up for the packaged liteship, her spare suit, and his spare chassis, folded small. When the rock walls had cooled, she deposited these items inside.

"Anyone can look in and see them," he cautioned.

She touched a spot on the wall above the cave mouth. "Cut here. Two seconds."

As he focused and cut, his chassis went on reserve power. The cave mouth partially collapsed down to a low slit. Merola picked up three fist-sized rocks that were almost melted and arranged them in a triangle pointing toward the cliff face.

Berzher marked them with a phosphor immediately recognizable among the Jongleurs. "That should suffice," he said. Then he stepped back to study the cave's entrance. "Animals would enter a place like that."

"Nonsense," Merola replied. "There are no animals around here. People of this time are practically civilized and have control of their animals. They keep them as pets."

"When the spring rains fill this canyon, water will enter the cave."

"Will you quit worrying? Our goods are well protected."

"My job is to worry about these things."

"Well, do it somewhere else."

SIDEWAYS

10. The Biosculptor

Coel Rydin looked into the glass terrarium full of vampire orchids which sat on a shelf above his workbench. They were all awake and chittering for blood-sap. Several clung to the nipple of their feeding tube, while most fluttered languidly against the terrarium's walls. A few of the weaker ones huddled on the bottom, near death.

For three years running, his orchids had taken first prize in the category "Bioculture of Plant Genomes" at the Missex County Fair. Yet, for all their animal awareness and volition—adapted with the addition of genes from the *Helix* genus of mollusks to the basic *Orchidaceae* genome—his best specimens were still sluggish. They could move with direction for no more than a few minutes and then sank into torpor.

"They're still a work in progress," he said aloud to his assistant.

"You could say that about evolution, too," Cinquemain replied.

For his entry this year, Rydin was trying to lengthen flying time by increasing their metabolic rate. The ultimate goal was to let them begin hunting on their own. But none of them yet had the strength—even if they had the sense—to fly from one tree to another, make a cut in the bark, and feed for itself. And they were hopeless as hunters of the latest hybrid species of airborne plants.

In his early work, to convert the wild orchids from their fixed, absorptive lifestyle based solely on photosynthesis and capillary root structures, Rydin had inserted into his first generation the genes for growing the hair-trigger snaps and digestive enzymes of *Dionaea muscipula*, the Venus flytrap. This was one of the few plant species able to obtain nutrients from chemical conversion of insect proteins, rather than drawing them passively from the soil. ... He had picked up an especially aggressive flytrap specimen while on Search in swamps of southeastern Nortamerica during the early Holocene. He then expanded their metabolism to feed directly on sucrose, the dominant sugar in sap, by incorporating genes from the *Danaidae* family of milkweed butterflies.

"So ... what are we doing tonight?" Cinquemain asked.

"Sorting out two-day-old embryos from the fourth generation."

"Oh, goody! I get to play god again." The intelligence turned and bent over backward—or as far back as the jointed carapace could bend—to expose the more complex underside. Rydin released a panel, removed the nested glass sphere of Cinquemain's matrix, and fitted it into the control cradle of his variable-focus microscope. The intelligence's chassis took two measured steps away from the bench and went into stasis mode: powering down all but the residual circuits needed to maintain its balance and upright posture.

Rydin retrieved a tube of embryos from the incubator and dumped the contents out onto the scope's induction plate. Twelve hours ago, he had added to the tube an enzyme solution in which each molecule was affixed to a color-coded quantum dot. If the developing embryo expressed a certain gene set—in this case governing the metabolism of sucrose—it also expressed a protein Rydin had inserted only so that it might react with the enzyme and incorporate the dot into the embryo's cell structure. Four hours ago, Rydin had precipitated the excess enzyme molecules and removed them from the tube.

Now the microscope played an ultraviolet wavelength on the pool of orchid embryos. All of those that had incorporated the quantum dots fluoresced bright orange. Cinquemain began manipulating the plate's electrostatic fields to corral and separate out the glowing embryos, which presumably would be better able to process sucrose than the others, which had failed to express those genes and so remained dark. The latter he pushed toward a drain hole for disposal. This was mindless work that Rydin was content to let Cinquemain do.

As an amateur biosculptor, Rydin was a bit old-fashioned. He would never stoop to using intelligently designed code patches that had been synthesized for him by informatics software. He preferred instead to work from wild-type genes and control sequences. For example, he used only the wild *Orchidaceae, Dionaea,* and *Danaidae* genomes in developing in his orchids. In manipulating them, he cut these genes with the molecular scissors of restriction enzymes and pasted them with the glue of ligation enzymes.

But he wasn't a complete conservative. He still amplified his code creations outside the cell nucleus using thermo-stable polymerases. And he enlisted Cinquemain's faster reflexes and greater attention span whenever a task called for either split-second timing or great amounts of patience. In return, he let Cinquemain participate in the experiments and put his name on the articles—after Rydin's own, of course.

"I begin to think we've pushed the sap cycle as far as it goes," he said.

Cinquemain's manipulations paused. "Do you want me to stop sorting?"

"No, go ahead. We'll raise and test this batch. ... I'm just thinking aloud."

"But you're clearly not happy with our progress?" Having a neuro-electronic firing rate approximately six times faster than any human being's, the intelligence could easily sort embryos and carry on a conversation at the same time. His voice emerged from the scope's simple voder in a scratchy parody of his normal tones.

"All our work with the *Orchidaceae* metabolism has gotten us plants that can barely fly," Rydin said. "I don't believe digesting more sap will get them to hunt."

"Sap is what you feed them. Do you want to try flies?"

"I was thinking of better ways to use the energy itself."

"Adenosine triphosphate," the intelligence supplied.

"Ah!" Those two words, spoken obliquely, ignited a train of thoughts in Rydin's mind. Cinquemain had an uncanny way of doing that—leaping ahead and planting just the right idea in his human's brain.

The energy molecule that drove every chemical process in eukaryotic, or nucleated, cells was adenosine triphosphate, or ATP: an adenine base attached to a ribose sugar ring that pulled a tail of three phosphorus-and-oxygen groups. This molecular structure happened to put too many negatively charged oxygen atoms too close together, creating an energy disequilibrium. By breaking off the third phosphate group, cells released this energy and restored partial equilibrium. ... Rydin suddenly recalled that breaking phosphate bonds was also the chemistry behind many explosives—a powerful reaction indeed! As a byproduct of this energy use, cellular metabolism created a new molecule, adenosine *di*phosphate, ADP.

The cells regenerated those ADP molecules and made new ATP energy for their various processes by adding back the third phosphate group. Tiny organelles called mitochondria converted the chemical energy of food—carbohydrates in an animal's diet, or simple sugars produced from sunlight and carbon dioxide in plants—to reconnect those phosphate bonds. The cell's entire energy cycle proceeded by eternally chopping off, and then restoring, that third phosphate group.

But what if Rydin could engineer another energy cycle? He could take off the second phosphate group as well, converting ADP to adenosine *mono*phosphate,

AMP. Then the mitochondria would build it back up to ATP. That would double the amount of energy available to his orchids.

He voiced this thought to Cinquemain.

The intelligence made the voder equivalent of a whistle. "It's not a natural reaction," he said slowly. Movement on the induction plate came to a stop, Rydin noticed, indicating the amount of thought the intelligence was giving to his proposal.

"But then," Cinquemain continued, "all hell breaks loose, doesn't it? It will be easy enough—well, technically possible—to program the mitochondria to process both mono's and di's into tri's. But you would have to rebuild all the cell's other processes—working from scratch, mind you—to break down the diphosphates as well as tri's to obtain that added energy. You would be rewriting practically the entire nuclear genome."

"Well, surely *someone's* tried it and reported on the results."

"Do we stand on the shoulders of giants now?"

"I'm just poking around for ideas."

"The judges at the fair will look for original work, Coel."

"I know that," Rydin replied. "Anyway, it's an interesting thought—introducing a whole new set of enzymatic processes at the nuclear level."

"Too interesting! Plant cells might not be able to sustain and coordinate that much activity." His assistant finished sorting the embryos and moved the glowing ones to a pickup point. Rydin aspirated them back into the tube. "However, I will begin to frame the literature search," the intelligence said.

"Not tonight," Rydin decided. In the morning he was about to go into the Jongleur du Temps clinic for a new genetic procedure himself. The dottori had told him to plan for an absence from his work, not to mention his hobby, of at least three days, possibly as long as a week. And when he came back, he might not be quite ... the same person.

"For now, please just do a general survey of the problem," he instructed the intelligence. "Identify and list the nuclear sequences governing use of adenosine triphosphate in the *Orchidaceae* genome. We'll continue this discussion when I return."

"Very good," Cinquemain replied.

Rydin removed the glass sphere from the induction plate's cradle and reinserted it into the intelligence's general-purpose chassis. The articulated limbs flexed, and the balance point became active.

"And don't forget to top up the sap tanks on the feeder," Rydin said, pointing at the terrarium. "Otherwise, if I'm delayed at the clinic, those orchids will likely die."

"Of course, Coel."

But if the orchids did perish, it would not be much of a loss. They were an older generation and rapidly becoming obsolete.

11. Playing Hooky

Merola continued playing the charade of an orphan girl living with foster parents Emily and William Windlace and attending fourth-grade classes with Missus Gorage at Commodore Sloat Elementary School. It was the only way she could maintain her fictitious position in this society.

She needed that position because, as a minor child and without Berzher's help, she had no means of support. If Berzher had access to the tools on a chassis, he might have helped her steal the means to survive. Vaults full of paper scrip were stored at vulnerable places called "banks," and even more of this fragile "money" was available through the primitive computer network—but only if she had Berzher's unique abilities at crawling, climbing, picking locks, and corrupting data. As it was, she had the resources of a nine-year-old girl, plus a stipend of $35 per week from Family & Children Services, payable to the Windlaces.

On this day, however, Merola was determined to avoid school and run an errand on her own. She considered it the last stage of her mission and her final duty to Berzher. She left the Windlace home in the morning as usual, but instead of going toward the school building she went in the other direction, to the corner where a large collective conveyance called a "bus" routinely stopped.

"Where's your mommy?" asked the woman in a gray uniform, when the door opened for Merola. This woman obviously was charged with operating the bus—work that would normally be reserved for an intelligence. From the way her hands moved on the controls, she also opened and closed the doors.

"She's at work," Merola said. This was the truth.

"This bus goes downtown, honey, not to school."

"I know. But I'm meeting her. ... Downtown."

This was not the truth. Merola knew that Emily Windlace was a "real estate agent," a person who sold—rather than grew—residences, and she worked in an office in her own neighborhood. By using the computer at the house, Merola had found the internet page for the San Francisco Municipal Transportation Agency, which published route maps and schedules for the benefit of potential passengers. By piecing together the bus-line information with what she could remember of the coordinates from her Search parameters, Merola knew that "downtown" was where she needed to go.

"All right," the operator said. "You got your fare?"

Merola held up her lunch money. She had counted out the exact amount from studying the transit system fare structure. The operator showed her where to put it.

"Do you want a transfer, honey?"

"Yes, please."

Merola took the slip, went to the back of the bus, and found an empty seat. She watched traffic, houses, and buildings go by outside the window. Once again she was struck by how many people were alive in this time. They all lived in dead structures, moved about in brain-dead—though surprisingly large and noisy—machines, and worked at dead-end jobs more suited for intelligences, like the bus operator's. She found it all very depressing.

Through the bus window Merola counted the signs, conveniently place at the corners, that identified the streets she was passing. She tracked the route all the way to the place called "Union Square," which was "downtown" and a short walk from her destination.

The scene of chaos on the street corner where the F.A.O. Schwarz store had been—broken glass, chunks of the faux-stone called "concrete," broken toys, and broken people—had all been removed. In its place Merola found a gap in the line of buildings and, at street level, a fence made out of boards of dead wood. One section was a gate fashioned out of linked wires, and she approached that.

"You can't come in here, little girl," said one of two men standing inside the gate. Both wore dark uniforms with yellow, hard-shell hats.

"Yeah, toy store's closed," said the other.

Merola looked through the gate. The place where the store had been was now a hole, several levels deep, cut into the ground. She stood on tiptoe to look down into it. She could see broken pillars and fragments of concrete flooring still spread out across the hole's bottom. But the mass of the building had disappeared.

"Where did it go?" she asked the men.

"The store went up to heaven," one said.

The other man laughed.

"I mean the broken building materials, damaged toys, and dead body parts," Merola clarified. "You don't have transmutation, so they have to be somewhere. Where do you take these things?"

"Gee, I dunno. The dump?"

"Transmutation?" said the other.

"Where is this dump?" she asked.

"Beats the hell out of me."

Merola decided that, even in an unimportant job like gate guardian, an intelligence would have been more helpful than these humans. Unless, of course, it was programmed for secrecy, in which case it would have informed her that the information was not available. These two men were not being secretive. They were simply ignorant.

"Thank you," she said and turned away.

If Berzher's chassis had survived the destruction in any usable form, it was now a crushed mass among a thousand other toys, discarded with the building's cement and plaster in a "dump" somewhere far away and unknown to her.

She really was abandoned and alone.

Merola took out her transfer pass and walked up to Union Square, where another bus would take her back to her neighborhood.

The result of Merola's unannounced excursion was a letter from the school principal, a visit from Mrs. Riccardi, her FCS case worker, and a tense interview with Bill and Emily Windlace. Merola coolly agreed that she would, in future, go to school every day.

12. SIMIAN-ACTN3

The village of Lune lay in the broad, green valley that straddled the River Temz. From historical references, not to mention his personal experience on Search, Coel Rydin knew that once this area had contained a population of more than eight million jostling humans. They had pounded the earth with their feet, polluted the air and the river with their wastes, and covered everything with layers of stone and timber, steel and cement, asphalt and paper. While on Search he had witnessed with his own eyes that the only green things they allowed were certain trees and grasses selected for appearance alone and planted in artificial areas called "parks." All else was dead castings from the earth.

Now, as Rydin left home to walk to his medical appointment, everything that met his eye was either the green and red-gold of variegated chlorophyll, the brown of moist earth, the white and pale gray of clean chalk, or the crystal blue of the river's surface, the sky above it, and the glass bridge that soared over it.

Rydin himself lived in a treehouse. His residence was grown from a genetically modified species of the genus *Acer*. Rooms, passages, and stairways were all shaped by sequencing changes to the underlying structure of branches and leaves. The latter were now coded as perennial features of the organism, enduring through the years, and sealed against the weather with an adhesive secreted from the underside of each leaf. At designated gaps in the walls, hybridized *Mollusca* were gathered to secrete their thin, clear shells in strips that admitted sunlight, swiveled open to pass the cooling breezes, or closed to keep out wind and rain. Soft interior lighting came from bioluminescent buds. Hybridized river eels of genus *Anguillidae* traced out the plumbing and then expired in place, their bodies decaying into hardened pipes that drew clean water from deep under the ground. Electrical power and communication circuits were programmed into embedded-silicon channels running beneath the bark and connecting with municipal systems through the roots. Semi-sentient tortoises enhanced with a complex of genes from the *Electrophorus* fishes scuttled around the place to provide spot current for appliances, including the instruments in Rydin's personal genetics lab.

All in all, the treehouse was weather-tight, temperate, stable, and self-regulating. And when Rydin was finished with it and ready to move on, he only had to spray the leaves with tailored enzymes to release the organic patterns. Within a matter of hours the tree would subside into a mound of soil and rapidly disintegrating organic compounds. Within a day there would be nothing but a low hummock covered with grass.

In this fashion did 5,600 humans now live in the valley and never leave a mark on the land ... except for the pathways of crushed chalk that led from one cluster of dwellings to another, or to work centers that included the medical building where Rydin had his appointment.

Since it was impractical to base the clinic structure on a tree form, it was built from blocks of the local clay soil, knit together by semi-rigid tube worms which secreted a cement that hardened like concrete and had the strength of spun steel. The worms were organized into colonies and genetically trained to stabilize walls, floors, ceilings, and room partitions based on chemical signals sprayed on the ground. The clinic's internal systems were those of his treehouse expanded a hundred-fold, with the addition of economy-scale infrastructures for power, water, and waste. But all of these features were likewise the product of genetic engineering among the biota. And all could be collapsed into the soil within forty-eight hours.

Far from making Lune a temporary place, Rydin knew, the achievements of his people had rendered the city virtually immortal and indestructible.

He passed through the clinic's mollusk-shell doors, which opened for him as soon as they recognized his pheromone signature. A neural connection between the doors and the reception intelligence announced him to the building. "Good morning, Mir Rydin," the intelligence in charge of administration greeted him. "I have already told Dottoressa Gerbus of your arrival."

"Thank you," he said.

"Coel!" Jena Gerbus called as she entered the reception area from one of the topical bays. "I think you're early today. You must be eager for this procedure."

"Eager for it to be over with, you mean. I know it will hurt."

"Of course. Full body procedures always do."

"I was afraid of that." He grinned.

———

Jena Gerbus supervised most of Coel Rydin's visits to the clinic, and the two of them had long ago formed a solid and respectful relationship. Of course, Rydin never came because he was ill. Like all human variants, he was genetically optimized for health.

More than three thousand years ago, give or take a few centuries, the culture which ultimately evolved into Rydin's and Gerbus's began concentrating its scientific inquiry in the domains of evolutionary biology, biochemistry, and genetic manipulation. While academics might argue about individual discoveries and influences, Gerbus personally attributed much of this shift in focus to the sudden abundance of long-dead animals and plants which the Jongleur Troupe—still in infancy at the time—and its illicit temporospatial predecessors were making available for study. Where once scientists might only contemplate past life forms and theorize about structure and function from the evidence of bony fossils and desiccated tissues, now geneticists could work directly with a universe of living specimens, indeed every species that ever existed, and all chemically intact, completely functional, and capable of breeding. Soon biology, and with it the urge to find biochemical solutions to social and technical problems, became their culture's dominant meme.

From manipulating acorn embryos and engineering treehouses to manipulating human embryos and creating a superior race was just a short and technically uncomplicated step, although the ethical implications had ignited more social upheaval, schism, and war than all of humanity's religions put together. In retrospect, Gerbus found it surprising that people should have feared future generations that were healthier, smarter, more emotionally stable, more robust, faster healing, and more chemically efficient. Perhaps their disquiet had sprung from age-old myths of the "superman" and the "master race." In her professional capacity, Gerbus could understand and approve of each required genetic change and its effects. Come to think of it, Rydin would be quite knowledgeable, too, through his hobby as a biosculptor.

Their direct ancestors, who were now the progenitors of most humans alive on Earth, had started by cleaning their own children's embryos *in vitro* of all known disease mutations. Next, they rearranged their chromosomes and eliminated redundancies—or engineered new ones, where having backup copies and variations of a gene made sense. They improved the genome's native systems for trapping and fixing errors during chromosome replication, which served to prevent further damaging mutations. Then they streamlined the patchy and inconsistent coding which governed the timing of embryo development, cellular differentiation, and gene expression. They systematized the expression of regenerative stem cells throughout the body. Finally, they redesigned the entire organism for metabolic efficiency and longevity, with the ultimate goal of a human that had no natural life span—people who were potentially immortal. Although nothing could be proved either way, the dottoressa knew of no one in her or Rydin's generation who had yet died of natural causes. As far as Gerbus was concerned, that fact alone was conclusive.

But human advancement was never complete, never reached a stopping point. Over the years, for example, Rydin's profession as section leader of the Jongleurs du Temps had required various genetic and phenotypic modifications, some permanent, some temporary, depending on his list of upcoming Searches.

Sometime within the next six months, Gerbus knew, he was due to visit Nortamerica in the late fourth millennium. That was a period of perpetual collapse, with no law and few customs invoking social restraint, where physical strength in combat would count for more than tactics or competence with weapons. In optimizing the modern human variant for efficiency, Gerbus's culture had created a race that was small in stature, had minimal body weight, and presented the appearance of an ageless child. On this new assignment, Rydin would be at a serious disadvantage in any confrontation.

The solution was the procedure called Simian-ACTN3. Actually, it was a very old procedure, something a Jongleur team had picked up from the early twenty-third century in the research prisons of Greater China. The serum was supposed to recode the patient's genes *in situ, in vivo,* and reportedly without lethal effect. The change lengthened and thickened the long muscle fibers, giving a human being the strength and endurance of the original non-human primates, the legendary chimpanzees and orang-utangs. Those creatures were reputed to be two to five times as strong as the genus *Homo.* The only difficulty was that the serum had been developed for the human genome of that distant century, not for the already modified genes of Rydin's time. Since Gerbus knew his code pattern better than anyone, she had volunteered to make the necessary modifications.

She gave him a brief explanation of the process and its intended effects.

"And after all that," he asked, "what is the worst that can happen?"

"You could die," she replied. "That would be inconvenient."

"But no permanent risk," he concluded with a smile.

"No," the dottoressa agreed. "Shall we begin?"

She led Rydin to one of the bays, where the clinic had grown a special room for this procedure. The floor and walls were uniformly gray and wrinkled, thickly padded, and soft underfoot.

"This surface reminds me of an animal," Rydin said. "Not one I ever saw with my own eyes, but in a magazine or video from sometime in the twenty-first century."

"Well," she said, "a Jongleur must have captured those genes."

"An elephant," he remembered. "It was from Africa. Extinct by then, I think."

Rydin turned around in the empty room and asked, "Don't I get a field bed?"

"The plates are under the floor." Gerbus pointed to an outline in white.

"How about some reading matter or light entertainment? Three days is a long time."

"If you're bored, the clinic intelligence can read or sing to you. His name is Homardi. But I don't think you'll have the … attention span for much amusement." She hoped Rydin was setting his mind for the pain her comment implied.

Gerbus stepped out of the room to retrieve from the incubator a tray divided into shallow cups, each one holding a biota. They were pale implements of the genus *Hirudo,* the old medical leech. Each one was tattooed for a designated muscle group. There were twenty-one of them.

"Take off your clothes, please," she said. "I have to attach these in a specific order."

"How long do they stay on?" Rydin asked, unsnapping his jumpsuit.

"Until they complete the viral insertion. About four hours."

"I'm going to want that sleeping field, won't I?"

"I can also offer you restraints. The inserts are going to itch, and you must not pick at them."

"Bind me, gag me, and put me in suspension."

Rydin stood with feet apart and arms lifted slightly while she applied the leeches. After placing each one in its coded position, Gerbus glanced up at his face to see how he was accepting the experience. His dark-brown eyes remained serene, the lids drooping a bit, as if he was hypnotizing himself. But his mouth had acquired a certain grim set in the smooth and beardless face, suggesting he felt some discomfort.

She continued laying the leeches over his thin, hairless arms and legs, back and stomach. She soon noticed an odd reaction: each time one of the flat, moist bodies with its round, sucking mouth and three crystal teeth came close to Rydin's skin, his flesh actually rippled and curled away, as if trying to avoid contact.

"You're doing fine," she said, halfway through.

"I know. This is really unpleasant."

"Just wait. It gets worse."

When the leeches were in place, the dottoressa picked up the empty tray and moved to the door.

"The field is pressure activated," she said. "You just step into it—but get ready for the equilibrium change. Tell Homardi if you want those restraints. He can acti-

vate them from within the field. When the biota are finished, they'll fall off. Just nudge them out of the field."

Rydin nodded. "I can feel each of the bites now," he
said. "They're ... burning."

"That must be psychosomatic. These *Hirudo* have
been modified to add an anesthetic to their saliva."

"It still hurts."

"Just push the pain down and away," she suggested.
She let the door start to close itself. "Well ... good luck."

Gerbus could offer no more encouragement. For the
next three days, Rydin would suffer the flaming tortures
of a mythical second-millennium Hell.

13. The Short Way Home

Merola's daily life with the Windlaces included "doing chores" in support of the household. One of these, required of her when she returned from school in the midafternoon, was to clean up the remains of the breakfast Emily had cooked. Merola was instructed to wash the dishes that each family member left to soak in the kitchen sink, as well as the pots and pans Emily left on the stove. She was required to use soap and hot water and a sponge—which was bright yellow, nothing like a natural sponge, and wasn't even alive—to remove the bits of food and sheen of grease before arranging them in the "dishwasher." This was a sealed cabinet under the kitchen counter that was supplied with hot water and drain connections, where more soap and agitation would complete the cleaning process.

To Merola's orderly mind, the entire exercise was wasted effort. Oh, she understood the surfactant and hydrophilic properties of soap to break down the lipids in cooking and skin oils. She also knew of better ways to achieve this effect without water, heat energy, or physical agitation. But she dared not mention any of them to Emily.

So Merola bided her time. For the present, in the present—in her ridiculous present predicament—time was all she had. Approximately eight thousand years of it. If she happened to live so long, which was unlikely. As she went through each day's allotment of foolish and repetitive tasks, Merola studied her options and formulated her strategy for returning to her own reference now.

The first option was to contact a parallel Search team. Of course, neither a Jongleur nor his accompanying intelligence could get her home directly. Without her own biosuit she could not ride a liteship above the atmosphere. But they could take a message for her, tell Rydin that she had disastrously jeopardized her Search, and ask him to direct a Jongleur to meet her with a workable suit.

The only trouble was, she didn't know of any parallel team. Jongleurs worked alone, in places and times set by a pattern known only to the intelligences of the Jongleur Troupe. Perhaps Rydin would know of another team working nearby in her local time reference. But Rydin was at the other end of the universe in both space and time. And any team that she might learn about—and that only through some unimaginable error in protocol that could conceivably become local public knowledge—would still have come and gone long before she would be able to reach them.

The second option was to send a message herself. It was just technically feasible. If Merola could find a medium that would subsist through the eight millennia of civilizations that rose and fell, through wars, fires, and floods, slipping past vandals and the busy fingers and itchy minds of generations of querulous humans, past the territorial raids of the Flüchtlinge and the interdimensional intrusions of the Möglichen—then the message she inscribed might one day be read in Rydin's time. Of course, it would have to be an obvious message in an obvious place. She couldn't, for example, just burn three rocks and leave them in a peculiar pattern at the foot of a cliff. She would have to go to some place famous in her own time.

As she scrubbed the dishes, Merola's eye wandered to the calendar Emily had tacked on the kitchen wall. The colored picture associated with the current month showed the granite arches of a mountain called "Half Dome," rising out of a valley called "Yosemite." The picture seemed familiar.

Merola realized with a shock that the formation still existed, although known by other names, in her native time and place. She could conceivably climb up the rock face and burn a message in her own language, using her own alphabet, in letters three meters tall: HELP COME RESCUE ME JONGLEUR MEROLA TSVERIN. The words would persist for future generations to ponder and try to translate, and for the people of her own time to understand and act upon.

Except ... such a message had not existed in her reference now, before she had departed on this Search. So she hadn't done it, and she wouldn't do it, and it was no good thinking about it. Even to consider the proposition bordered on paradox.

Besides, in this crowded age, some breed of public busybody would certainly be guarding that picturesque mountainside. Five minutes after she finished cutting her message into the rock, they would make her take it down.

14. Busy Day

Halfway through the first night, Rydin lost control of his muscles. He hung in the field with his back alternately arching and sagging, his limbs flailing and twitching. The only muscles that still functioned at his discretion were those controlling his eyelids and diaphragm—to prevent his going blind from involuntary pressure or suffocating from lack of breath. This was by design in the ancient Chinese serum—but as the architect of numerous gene reprogrammings himself, Rydin knew how close he was coming to accidental death.

Electrostatic pain nullification helped some, and Homardi administered it through the field variance repeatedly at Rydin's request. Medications could not be administered because they might interfere with the processes of gene resequencing and protein building. Rydin had to bite his lip, when he could make his jaw work, and focus on what relief the electric current was able to offer.

At the end of the third day—his body hanging limp, dehydrated, and rimed with salt crust from the sweat—Rydin felt the field begin to release him. He floated gently to the floor.

"The process appears to be complete," Homardi said. "How do you feel?"

"Dead," Rydin said.

"Not so. Your vital signs—"

"Agh! I'm kidding. I'm all right. I think."

"Very good, Coel. Humor is a useful adaptation."

"Shut up. Send someone with a glass of water. And food."

"Right away." If he had hurt the intelligence's feelings, there was no sign.

Rydin experimentally touched one hand to his upper arm. Even in repose, the muscles there felt ... denser, more compact, like tightly bundled cords.

Dottoressa Gerbus herself brought him a plate of food, a beaker of water, and a fresh jumpsuit. When he clutched the beaker and started to drink, she warned him to take small, measured sips whose timing she monitored for him.

Rydin then ate the food, bite-sized packages of rice paste and some kind of *Aves* protein wrapped in steamed leaves, while he put on the clothes.

"Was the procedure successful?" she asked finally.

Rydin looked thoughtfully at the empty plate he still held. It was white porcelain, the finest clay, five millimeters thick and hard-fired for strength. He had dropped crockery like this before and seen it bounce. His old body would never have been able to—

Crack! The two halves of the plate were free in his hands, a small cloud of white dust between them.

"Apparently so," he murmured.

Gerbus took the pieces from him. "Well and good. We'll want to monitor your latent condition, of course. Come back in two days for an evaluation. And contact me immediately if you feel aftereffects."

Rydin nodded. "Thank you, Jena."

He walked back to his treehouse through the warm sunshine of the Temz valley.

Inside, Cinquemain was waiting for him. "The world has gone on without you," he said. "Unsurprisingly."

"What do you have for me?"

"Twenty-two messages—two of them personal, although I didn't know you had any personal relations."

"You don't know everything."

"You wish. Four questions directed to your era of expertise. Three requests for details from previous Searches. Two new Search criteria."

"And a partridge in a pear tree?"

The intelligence's chassis rolled its electromagnetic sensors up toward the ceiling. In a human it might have been exasperation, but Rydin knew this was a mannerism Cinquemain had acquired while searching databases. "Merry Christmas," he replied.

"Any of those questions easy?" Rydin asked.

"I've already answered the easy ones. Hans Purlieu at the Encyclopedia Project in Bao Aires wants to know if steam engines of the nineteenth century were fueled with wood or coal."

"Tell him both. And later with oil."

"What kind of oil?"

"A residue of rock oil called 'Bunker C.' Similar to but different from the oil later used to ignite Rudolf Diesel's peculiar brand of internal combustion."

"Thank you. Nikolodeon, from the Unassigned Intelligence Section, wants to know origins of the term *cordon bleu*."

"It's in the language of the ancient Franch. It means 'blue ribbon.' It has to do with an awards ceremony."

"But nothing to do with lamb chops?"

"Why? Does he believe he's going to be offered some? If so, he should accept."

"Any metabolic warnings?" Cinquemain asked—facetiously this time, because an intelligence had no chemical processes, or none that would digest lamb chops. It was a game the two of them played.

"Yes. They're better with mint sauce."

Again Cinquemain rolled his eye sensors.

"Anything else?" Rydin asked.

"No, I just found answers to the last two questions and sent them off."

"Thank you. Put notes in my reading bin anyway."

"Oh, and a message from the Personnel Section: Merola Tsverin of Team Six has failed to return from a Search in the early third millennium. No word from her intelligence either, name of Berzher. Since she's in your section, Personnel let the problem wait for your recovery."

"When was she due back?"

"Immediately after departure, of course."

Rydin made a face. "Wise guy! I mean, 'when in our time?' "

"Two days ago. They seem to think it's some kind of disciplinary matter."

Rydin paused. He tried to imagine any conditions under which a Jongleur, either voluntarily or inadvertently, might delay a return on time and mark. Nothing came to mind. Jongleurs occasionally broke the rules and ventured outside their assigned Search parameters, spending longer on distant marks than the Troupe had planned. They often experienced difficulties, sometimes crippling accidents, or encounters with natural and unnatural opposition, that delayed them during their missions. But, with all of space and time to choose for the return, they were never late in the reference now. If Tsverin was late by as much as a millisecond, she was probably dead. And only a dunderhead from Personnel, a jumped-up civilian who had never gone on Search, would think this could be a disciplinary matter.

Of all his teams, Merola Tsverin was the most reliable. She might be a thorny personality, always difficult to work with, often headstrong and stubborn, not a person to share a joke, no taste for socializing, even on Troupe business, and relatively colder than a sunspot minimum—but she always came back. And she never broke the rules. Rydin would miss her.

Of course, the Troupe had a protocol for dealing with dead Jongleurs who did not return. It was Rydin's responsibility now to find Merola, intervene—if he could—ahead of whatever misadventure had killed her, and—if he could not—then write her epitaph and a new addendum to the *Jongleur Handbook*.

"Prepare a liteship," he told Cinquemain.

"One already waiting. Your biosuit, too."

"Very good." Rydin flexed his aching muscles and decided that Dottoressa Gerbus's program of careful monitoring could wait. "Get the parameters of Tsverin's last Search assignment. We'll study them while in transit to the jump point."

15. The Long Way Home

Another of Merola's chores was to wash and dry the family's clothes, using machines in the basement of the Windlace home. "Basement" was a new concept for Merola, whose people lived in trees. Equally novel was the idea of treating clothes to remove dead skin and body oils and then putting them back on. Merola's people grew the clothing they needed, from plants that had been genetically altered for each person's particular fit and design preferences. Merola's choice was usually straight lines and subtle optical effects, with colors harmonized at the red and blue ends of the spectrum. After wearing, she simply mulched each jumper, shift, or kilt with enzymes and returned it to the potting soil.

The washing in Emily's household was predictably done with more hot water and soap. Merola loaded the items and a measure of "laundry powder" into the machine and set certain buttons and dials, depending on the type of fabric. Then she watched through the front window as the clothing tumbled over and over amid a froth of white suds. This action, she discovered, was practically a visual representation of the chaos that Merola knew as human history. Wave after wave of events rose and fell. Enlightenment followed dark age, which followed war and conquest, which were borne in the disputes arising from enlightenment. And white noise dissolved all. Nothing could call back to reproduce—let alone alter—any particular pattern in all this swirling motion.

The suds perfectly modeled Jongleur precepts about the nature of time.

Merola was a Jongleur senior officer, an active agent, and not a temporal theorist. Of course, she had taken the Troupe's required training in the theory of temporal location, but its primary purpose was to help her know and understand what dangers to avoid. But under the subject heading of "temporal paradoxes," the list of ways for an agent to get into trouble was surprisingly short. Jongleur theory did not recognize paradoxes.

On the other hand, people from the reference now in which Merola was stuck believed that time was a delicate thing. Even if they could devise one of the several ways for achieving time travel, many of the local humans would, because of this belief system, scrupulously refuse to participate. Their beliefs warned that changing the past in any way, however small, would establish ripples, irrevocable sequences of events, new patterns that would echo down the years and change the time they had left before they could come back. The echoes might even rearrange events so that they themselves no longer existed.

Kill a butterfly in ancient Beizhing, they believed, and the winds that brought Christoph Coulomb to the shores of Nortamerica might not blow. Then half the world would remain in a perpetual Stone Age, running free under the stars and hunting buffalo with flint-tipped spears, while the Old World moved forward from the Renaissance to develop calculus, steam engines, and stock markets. Small things mattered—or so the local humans believed.

With a view from 15,000 years of variously recorded and recoverable history, Merola's people knew that small effects tend to die out, according to a variant of the inverse square law of radiation. The wider the cone of time, the less significant the effect of impact. The ripples from butterfly wings disappear into the ocean breeze. Grains of windblown sand do not shift massive boulders. And seldom do single members of a species rise above hopeless anonymity. And even then, any power these forces might have to shape the future will ultimately disappear into the chaos of great storms. Merola's people had seen too many storms, too many insurrections and invasions, too many falling asteroids, to believe in any but the grossest impacts on time's natural course.

And never once had her people detected a paradox. Time flowed variously, through great events and small, and never doubled back on itself.

Return to fifteenth-century Europa, they believed, put a crossbow bolt squarely through the head of this same Christoph Coulomb, and nothing would change in the future that Merola knew. Someone else would make landfall on Nortamerica in the middle of the second millennium after the Christus and introduce the emergent Europeans to that vast, undiscovered territory—to the distress of its Stone Age inhabitants. Five hundred or a thousand years of history books would eventually rewrite themselves. None of it would matter much after the Fire Strike of 2613.

Go back just a few decades and kill your own grandfather as a boy. Someone else would spawn your genes. You would remember that person just as fondly as "grand-père." Of course, all the details of your life would change, everything you know to be true would change, you yourself would change, and everything else would fit around these new facts.

The Jongleurs knew they could send Merola to the start of the third millennium, let her perform her Search, crush all the butterflies she wanted, and still arrive safely home. Even if Merola were to be discovered, identified for the traveler she was, and made famous in the newspapers of this time ... within fifty years she would become just a vague memory, a curious legend, the recollection of a time-travel hoax. Of course, she would never think of going public and attracting such notoriety—because then her remaining life would become a living hell, deprived of freedom in a maximum security cell, hounded by scientists, investigators, and witch doctors, creating unnecessary danger for other Jongleurs working in this paranoid era. But her exposure would create no lasting effect on the far future.

There were no paradoxes.

Free will ruled this world.

Free will ... and Wahrschein.

Wahrschein, or probability, mattered because small differences in decision and action did affect causation in one respect. According to Jongleur theory, the world—the life of every human being, multiplied by the sum of all human beings, plus the sum of all natural events related to human beings—was littered with probabilistic intersections, or Wahrschein Punkte. Each one represented an instant, a nexus of decision and action, where the outcome was statistically unpredictable. To some extent, this notion explained the eternal human fascination with games of chance.

To illustrate the Wahrschein point, a late-second-millennium physicist had put a cat in a box with a bottle of cyanide whose breaking was triggered by an unpredictable atomic event. Until the event released the poison, the physicist maintained, the cat existed as a mathematical proposition—as both alive and dead—so long as the box remained closed. Only when someone opened the box, he said, would the cat's status be resolved.

Jongleur theory maintained that, even after the box was opened, both states actually continued. In the world known to the opener, the cat might be alive—the "Wahr," true, or real state. But the probabilistic event itself spawned a second and equally valid world, budding off the surface of the original time sphere. This bubble world was identical to the "alive cat" world, except that it was a "dead cat" world—the "Schein," sham, or false state. The triggering event generated one cone of action that spread across the expanding bubble universe of those who knew the cat to be alive—and a second cone that originated at the Wahrschein Punkte, defining the center of a newly created bubble containing all those who knew the cat to be dead. Both universes would continue to expand from that instant.

As these spawned universes evolved from their single point of difference, each would eventually reach another probabilistic node, where it would bud again and continue expanding outward, and on to the next point, and the next, and so on, moving farther and farther apart, until the two bubble universes became mutually unrecognizable. The difference between them could only be measured in dimensions rather than spatial distances. In this erupting foam of competing universes, this sea of soapsuds, two bubbles might coincide but would not actually touch. Sometimes, however, the two might briefly and inexplicably converge—approach so closely that an inhabitant of one would sense the other.

The Jongleurs du Temps had no proof for this theory, but everyone in the Troupe had at some time experienced an incursion. Merola recalled a Search in eighteenth-century Moskva where she had felt a presence, a watcher—a *hungry* watcher—that did not belong in that reference now.

Merola shook herself. Best not to think of the Möglichen. Sometimes thinking about them had the effect of ... drawing them.

So, where did that leave her? Chaos, paradox, and a foam of soap bubbles that ... Wait! What was that earlier thought she had? Something about herself becoming a "vague memory"? Legends? Hoaxes? ... Perhaps there was a third way home after all!

All she had to do was find a legend that she knew was not a hoax.

16. WELCOME TO OUR WORLD

Rydin waited while Cinquemain set the liteship's controls to synchronize with the temporal and spatial parameters of Merola Tsverin's assigned Search.

"Do you want the track to her safeguard first?" the intelligence asked.

"If we don't find Tsverin on her proper cues, then we check her backup."

"You don't want to cache a backup ship for ourselves?"

"Why?" Rydin said. "We're not on Search."

"In case *we* run into trouble ...?"

"Then we'll go back and find her ship."

Cinquemain made a soft noise that sounded like criticism.

"What?" Rydin demanded.

"You're the boss."

Cinquemain's shiphandling brought them over Safronesco some three hours past midnight, local time. The city was a mosaic of yellowish, reddish, and greenish lights—the colors, Rydin knew, determined by various gases and metal vapors, chiefly sodium and mercury, excited inside individual electrical bulbs. In some parts of the city these lights shone with diamond clarity, but elsewhere—mostly in districts to the west, nearest the ocean—they seemed to be shining through gauze. Rydin recalled that the city was subject to random inundations of airborne water vapor ... mists and blowing fog.

"Is there any traffic?" he asked.

"Loads—away to the south. Some kind of facility designed for landing big, slow—"

"An airport," Rydin supplied.

"Buzzing with radar, too."

"But nothing up here?"

"Not since we passed below fifteen hundred meters," Cinquemain said. "Where do you want me to land? Say

... this part of the city is deserted! Lights showing but almost no people. Thermals indicate the structures are mostly empty, too. What is this place?"

"Commercial district. An area where people go to buy things."

"A bazaar—but spread among so many buildings?"

"Transactions are more organized in this time. Each building is a little bazaar, called a 'department store.' They specialize in some type of goods. The focus of Tsverin's Search was a store that sold toys."

"Toys."

"Objects of play and learning for immature humans."

"Oh? How long do the humans of this time gestate?"

"Same as us—they simply make more fuss about it."

Rydin leaned out, past the ship's bottom energy panel.

"That's the building." He pointed. "Right on the corner."

"That's not a building," Cinquemain said.

"Of course it is. I memorized the roof pattern."

"Yes, but it's ... wrinkled. And lying at street level."

Rydin swung his body farther out, tipping the liteship's center of gravity, and peered into the shadowed darkness as Cinquemain dropped closer. The public lighting in this area was capped so that the lamps threw their beams down and out onto the street, not sideways onto the buildings. The tops of surrounding buildings were three to six stories above the street level and dark as night. But the roof Rydin had picked out was strangely lit from the sides. The streets along the building's north and west sides were piled with a rubble of pale, grayish blocks. When the liteship was no more than a hundred meters above the pavement, Rydin saw streamers of yellow tape blowing in the wind.

"When was Tsverin's mark?" he asked.

"Approximately twelve hours ago."

"I thought we were duplicating her movements."

"We can't come down during daylight, Coel," Cinque-main protested. "She had a complete operational plan for concealing her ship, disguising herself and her intelligence, and blending with the populace in order to take samples. We're just dropping in."

"So ... set me on that roof," Rydin said. "Inside corner, behind the fan unit."

"What did they use fans for? Did the buildings fly? Did this one fall?"

"The fans moved air through the building. Other machinery filtered and cooled the air, to make the interior more pleasant for humans."

"*Machines* did this? How primitive!"

"It was a dark age," Rydin said.

Cinquemain adjusted the liteship's gravitic lift, to place minimum weight and strain on the destroyed structure yet anchor the ship against the prevailing breezes. "Watch your footing," the intelligence said as Rydin stepped onto the damaged roof.

The uneven surface, which had shattered when the building fell, was some kind of fabric impregnated with petroleum residue—intended to be impervious to rainwater, Rydin guessed. Underneath were layers of glass fiber and boards of dead wood. The structure shifted and groaned as he walked across it.

"Stay here and keep the ship powered," he instructed.

"Even though the building has collapsed," Cinquemain observed, "you could still fall into a pocket."

Rydin nodded. His biosuit was designed to deflect impacts from meteoroids up to two millimeters in diameter traveling at orbital speeds. It would protect him against the impact of a fall and even from remnants of the building coming down on top of him. It occurred to him, however, that if Merola had been inside the building taking samples when the structure collapsed, she would not have been wearing her suit. But her intelligence would still have been protected by its armored carapace.

"Call to her intelligence," he told Cinquemain. "What was the name?"

"Berzher." Cinquemain paused while using frequencies and protocols not available to the circuits of Rydin's suit. "No response. If Berzher is within a hundred kilometers of here, he either can't or won't answer."

Rydin found an entrance to the building, a metal cupola covering a "stair well." The people of this era were partial to stairs, believing them an efficient way to overcome vertical distances. And they were—if energy expenditure was your only criteria—but not in this case, because inside the cupola Rydin found only a jumble of broken blocks. It took a moment of visualization to understand that some force had compressed all of the steps onto a single level.

He looked at the remaining buildings of this city block, one to the east and one south of the collapsed toy store. Their external walls were undamaged, showing only vertical scrapes and scars where the falling structure had dragged against them. He communicated this observation to his intelligence.

"What could drop a five-story building into its foundations without damaging the surrounding area?" Rydin asked.

"Place shaped concussive charges on each structural support," Cinquemain said. "Ignite them in sequence. Gravity should collapse the floors onto each other. Is that what happened here?"

"Do you identify a residue of explosives?"

Cinquemain paused to sample the air just above the building's roof. "Yes! And the concentration corresponds to amounts needed for this type of damage. My calculation of the dissipation rate puts the actual collapse at ...

Forgive me, Mir Rydin! The explosion coincided with Tsverin's time on mark."

"Could she have survived the effect?"

"No. Nor could Berzher's carapace."

"Would the authorities of this municipality have the means to collapse a building like this?"

Cinquemain paused to consult one of his databases. "The means, yes. The technique was used successfully in this era. In fact, I believe it was developed only a decade or two earlier. But no one would dispose of a building with the people still inside."

"No, they wouldn't. Not even during the twentieth century."

"But that is not the oddest thing," Cinquemain said.

"What is odder than collapsing a building on its occupants?"

"The explosive used an unfamiliar chemical reaction."

"What do you mean? Your database is not complete?"

"Oh, no! I recognized the reaction itself immediately from residues still present in the air. I can estimate the degree of instability from the bent-ring structure and the oxidant. But the molecules that were brought together here won't be discovered and used by humans for another three thousand years. Even then, they won't be used in exactly this mix ratio, and one of the triggers is unknown to me."

"Möglichen," Rydin whispered.

"Possibly. More likely Flüchtlinge," Cinquemain said. "Drawing from any point in human history, and given their unique talent for destruction, the fugitives would likely collect, bargain for, and employ exotic resources."

"What could Tsverin have done to call them down?"

"Or not done ... She might have neglected protocol."

"Not Tsverin. I know her."

"I wonder if you do."

17. Chasing Phantoms

Merola sat in class and day-dreamed about finding her way home. If she could discover a time-travel legend—one originating from within this reference now—that she herself knew was *not* a hoax, then she could make contact and beg, barter, or steal a ride for herself and for Berzher's frozen entity.

That Voyageurs, other travelers from other eras, were active across the third millennium was no secret among the Jongleurs, but for obvious reasons the Troupe discouraged its members from studying and charting their movements. Too great a familiarity might draw the sort of fraternal contact that Merola would be trying to make, and the Troupe had come into existence in order to limit and control unrestricted time travel, not to encourage it. So Merola would have to work from hints and guesses, sifting minutiae and bits of data.

That task would be easy if Merola still had access to Berzher's immense capacity for gathering and sorting information. The intelligence possessed dozens of configurable contact patches and hundreds of communication protocols for interfacing with other machines. But they matched none of the primitive computing devices—actually, just dumb calculators—that inhabited this forsaken reference now.

Berzher would have been able to search the accumulated knowledge of the planet in seconds. He would then sort and weigh every affidavit, case report, legend, and tale involving or hinting at travelers from the future. He would categorize them against the actual instances of time travel, stored in his capacious memory, undertaken in the millennium before the Jongleur Troupe was organized. The Troupe had regularized and cloaked the practice, but those early travelers routinely committed indiscretions that might be traceable. And once Berzher was satisfied with his own cogitations and reflections, he would have given her directions to a place and time where the incidents and artifacts of those early travelers might be found.

But without his chassis and its power supply Berzher was trapped inside his glass sphere. She would keep his circuit matrix with her, in the hope of eventually returning him to a time and place when and where he could once again have what he thought of as life. But for now he was merely a cherished artifact himself.

So, Merola decided, she would have to exercise her own intelligence. She would also have to use the limited and fragmentary resources available to a fourth-grade student in a provincial grammar school. And she would be functioning in the very first years of the system of "computers" and "networks" that collected and accessed knowledge. Eventually, the system would become a global grid connecting all humans on the planet, but this "internet" currently accounted for less than ten percent of the world's information base and one percent of its commercial transactions.

Well, at least she could read. In addition to learning to speak the dominant language of Nortamerica, Merola had learned its alphabet. So she would not have to depend on finding local humans, starting with the Windlaces, who could answer her questions and translate their printed books for her. That would have been inconvenient—not to mention a violation of strict Jongleur protocol.

She began with her school's library, where she did need human help.

"Excuse me, Missus Lindt?" she asked the librarian.

"Yes, um, Mary Jane?" the woman said.

"Do you have books on time travel?"

"Certainly, dear." She paused to consider. "H. G. Wells is going to be pretty advanced for a fourth-grader."

"Who is that, please?"

"He wrote *The Time Machine*, set in London in the 1890s. Let's see, for more modern fare, we have Tim Powers's *Anubis Gates* and John Varley's *Millennium*—although some of his, um, interpersonal relations may not be suitable—"

"And these are all people who have traveled in time?"

"No, dear, they wrote novels about it."

"I see. And what is a 'novel'?"

"A made-up story."

"No make-believe, please. Just the recorded experiences."

"I'm afraid there's no *experience* of the subject. Time travel is a fiction, like Wonderland or Never Never Land. If you want actual memoirs, wouldn't you rather read about, oh, space exploration or ocean voyages? I have the books of Dr. Robert Ballard. They're fascinating."

"Ah ... yes, thank you."

Merola allowed herself to take three of the books Mrs. Lindt offered, which she would return unread in the next day or two. So much for children's literature.

The school had a "computer lab," where students learned to type at a keyboard, do BASIC programming, and manipulate the simplest internet protocols. But the classes were all by rote and did not encourage unassisted searches. Besides, Merola's search was destined to be more involved and take longer than her allotted training time.

Fortunately, Merola's foster guardians were relatively advanced people and had installed a "personal computer" in the home where she was staying. As she normally returned from school by two-thirty in the afternoon, and William only used the computer late in the evening, she had ample opportunity. Emily did not care for the device, did not touch it, and had made no rule for Merola about using it. In fact, so long as Merola was quiet in the afternoons and did not "make a mess"—which she never did anyway, except for getting into her current predicament—Emily really didn't care what she did. So Merola would have at least two hours of unstructured time each day for her search.

Before she activated the machine, however, Merola located the card, taped under its keyboard, where William had written out his logon procedure and passwords. She also went through the shoebox in the kitchen and studied the most recent telephone bill to determine that the Windlaces had an unlimited access account with a service provider. So Merola's time "on line" would go unnoticed.

She began to feel more confident. Finding travelers from the future would not be so difficult. After all, *searching* was what a Jongleur did.

18. Three Stones

Cinquemain raised the liteship to a safe height, above the local air traffic around San Francisco. He activated the homing beacon in Merola Tsverin's spare biosuit, which she and her intelligence would have cached along with other backup equipment according to Search protocol. He obtained a signal and followed it eastward. The signal was weak and erratic, as if the suit's energy system was somehow compromised.

When the ship arrived over a dedicated wilderness, identified on his internal charts as "Briones Park" in the local language, Cinquemain descended to three hundred meters. While he was still a kilometer or more from the cache, the signal faded and died. Cinquemain put the ship into a hover and drifted with the breeze, thinking. Without the biosuit's beacon, he had to rely on the alternate locator prescribed by protocol. He began quartering the area, studying the ground with sensors built into his chassis. He was looking for the radiation signature of three stones placed close together. After ten minutes—during which time Rydin hung on the liteship frame, sullenly fuming and fidgeting—Cinquemain found it.

"There!" he said, pointing with a claw tip.

Without waiting for instructions, Cinquemain descended through the treetops and into a deep cut in the earth, where a water course carried just a few deciliters per minute and glowed green with masses of algae and weeds.

Rydin stepped off the ship onto the bank and regarded the stones. They gave off an iridescent sheen in the light from his biosuit helmet. He squatted and studied the dirt and rocks that made up the wall of the ravine. "There's an opening here," he said.

"Do you want me to go in?" Cinquemain offered.

Rydin nodded. "You're a better fit."

Cinquemain parked the ship, climbed down, and entered the cave. He walked on all six legs of his chassis and had a good ten centimeters of clearance above his armored back. The dirt around him showed patches of radiation. A cutting tool similar to his own had either expanded or collapsed some natural feature in the ground.

At the back, in a wide space, he found the panels of a liteship. Perhaps they had once been folded for storage, but now they were crushed and torn. Something big and strong—armed with either teeth or claws set in parallel three centimeters apart—had worked over the ship. None of the panels would hold a charge now.

Next to the panels he found a biosuit. The helmet was crushed. The suit's virtually indestructible fibers had been melted and fused. He sampled them and discovered an unusual enzyme. Cinquemain consulted his database. Chemically, the enzyme was specific to the molecular structure of the fibers, but interestingly it corresponded to no enzyme in the database. It was something new, unique, and specific.

Cinquemain described all this to Rydin as he conducted the investigation.

"Do you see a spare chassis?" his human asked.

"Pieces of twisted metal and broken ceramic."

"Can you recover the ship's singularity?"

"It's—" He scanned with all senses. "—gone."

Cinquemain backed out of the cave and relaxed his carapace onto the gravel bank beside Rydin. "It looks as if some big animal has been at work in there."

"An animal with digestive juices specific to par-arachnid?"

"We haven't catalogued all the fauna of this century."

"And with a nose for polarized gravity waves?"

"That would be unusual, in any century."

Rydin nodded. "I'm guessing Tsverin drew an attack."

"Between caching and Search? That's fast work!"

"I begin to think she did go extracurricular."

"But would Berzher agree to that?" Cinquemain asked.

"Would you agree to break the rules for me?"

"If I did, it would serve me right to—"

"What? Drop a building on you?"

19. A Class Project

To the adult world, Merola Tsverin in the guise of "Mary Jane Doe" was an object of concern and pity, a probable cancer victim orphaned by a tragic accident that had also impaired her memory. In the world of children, she pretended to be a transfer student from a far-off country, which she called "Francia," and descended from a family of Corsican pirates. The worlds of adults and children, she had found, did not often intersect. When Mrs. Gorage called on "Mary Jane" in class using that cloying voice adults of this time reserved for the sick and weak, the girls around her snickered.

Staying in school was a good way for Merola to learn about this time and culture, and so perfect her disguise. Each day she acquired new references, new words, and more natural diction using the words she already knew. It helped that Mrs. Gorage liked to assign her lessons and projects to groups of students rather than individuals. Working with her supposed peers, Merola could ask questions freely and learn even more.

In project assignments, she was usually teamed with Josie Barnes, who now considered Mary Jane to be her "very best friend." Their team also had Estella Melendez and Jimmy Cheng. Estella was from the population group Merola knew as Mexamerican, and because Merola was still technically on Search, she longed to take a sample of the girl's bone marrow. Jimmy was another Chinois—although by this time Merola knew to say "Chinese."

Jimmy was fascinated by her blonde hair. When she wasn't looking, he would reach behind her and give it a sharp tug. The force was never enough to make the wig slip against its adhesive strips, but the sudden movement startled her. The first time he did it, Merola's reaction almost broke his arm. She had since learned to give a helpless squeal and let Josie and Estella frown and "punch him out."

During the period reserved for "social studies," which was Merola's favorite, the class was learning about immigration patterns and the early settlement of Nortamerica. Mrs. Gorage asked the teams to identify as many "first settlements" as they could remember from reading their social studies book. As the others called out the names Estella wrote them down.

"Pilgrims at Plymouth Rock," Jimmy said.

"You mean Plymouth, the town," Josie corrected.

"Yeah, that one."

"San Salvador," Josie offered next.

"What's that?" Estella asked in surprise.

"It's where Columbus landed," Josie explained.

"San Salvador's in Central America. He didn't go there."

"The book said San Salvador," Josie insisted.

Merola glanced at Jimmy. He shrugged.

"I know people from San Salvador," Estella said. "It's a city south of Mexico."

"It's also an island," Josie insisted. "In the Bahamas. Columbus landed there."

"Is this Coulomb the man who is supposed to discover America?" Merola asked.

"Yeah, sure," the others agreed.

"Well, did he make a settlement? Or just come and go?"

"You're right," Estella said. "Scratch San Salvador."

"The Asians discovered America," Jimmy said. "They came across the land bridge during the Ice Age."

"Name a settlement," Josie challenged.

"Unh ... Nome?"

"It's got to be in the book. Indian places aren't in the book."

"Well, they should be," Jimmy said stubbornly.

Merola remembered something she heard once in conversation.

"Roanoke," she said.

"And where's that?" Estella asked.

"East coast of Nortamerica," Merola replied.

"I think the first settlement there was Jamestown," Josie said.

"Roanoke came earlier," Merola said. "I'm positive."

"How do you know?" Estella asked.

"Rydin went there, looking for the lost colonists. He found their DNA among the native population of Croatans, nearby on Hatteras Island."

"That wasn't in the book," Josie said.

"Who is Rydin?" Estella asked.

"He's my ..." Merola was on the verge of saying "section leader." She realized suddenly that she had let herself become too involved with these children and their schoolwork. Of course, no nine-year-old girl in this reference now could qualify for Jongleur status, undertake a Search mission, join a Troupe section, or have a section leader. "Friend," she finished lamely. She mentally kicked herself for breaking protocol.

"When did he go to this Roanoke place?" Josie asked.

"During the second winter. But they'd already given up and moved on."

The three children stared at her.

"He went to the *colony?*" Josie said. "Thinking they were *still there?*"

"Well ..." Merola had said far too much already. "He visited the site."

"You said the colonists were lost," Jimmy said. "So it doesn't really count."

"Scratch Roanoke," Estella said, crossing out the name.

"Time, please!" Mrs. Gorage called. "Everyone!"

In the end, their group only had one name—Plymouth town—and came in last. The others blamed Merola.

20. THE BASEBALL COLLECTOR

Rydin and Cinquemain returned from Safronesco at virtually the moment they had left. Of course, in terms of Rydin's subjective experience, almost a full day had passed. That included time required to travel, at supralight speeds, back to the Earth-Sun system's former position in the galaxy almost 8,000 years ago, followed by his and Cinquemain's trips over the ground for physical investigation of Tsverin's Search cues and her backup cache, and finally the return to the solar system's position in their own reference now. Upon arriving in Lune, Rydin and his intelligence immediately filed their separate reports with the Jongleur Troupe.

Because Tsverin, at the point of her death, had been operating publicly, in open view, and in broad daylight, finding her and warning her off before the explosion took place were problematic. Because she had somehow attracted the attention and coordinated opposition of persons or beings unknown, who were capable of precisely engineering the collapse of an entire building, Rydin had already considered and set aside several plans for avoiding or reversing their actions and so effecting her rescue.

In one possible approach, he might infiltrate the toy store's basement levels ahead of her time on mark. He could then somehow encounter the opposition and overcome it, or try to detect and defuse their explosives—all while working against an unknown countdown. If everything went well, he would simply let Tsverin proceed with her mission. But, if things went badly, he might alert the opposition to his presence and intentions, or Rydin himself might die in the explosion.

In another plan, he might travel back to her cache site at some unknown time ahead of her arrival, wait for her to come and make the cache, and personally cancel her mission. But the damage Cinquemain had discovered in that cave disturbed him. The area might already be under surveillance by the opposition. Again, his presence would alert them, and Rydin himself would become a target.

Too much was unknown, and either approach to rescue involved probabilities he could not yet calculate. When dealing with an invisible menace, it was best to move slowly. And he had time to think through the problem, do some temporospatial research, plan a foolproof counterattack, then return to the twenty-first century and execute it. After all, being already dead, Merola Tsverin wasn't going anywhere in that time frame.

After filing his report, Rydin expected the Troupe to respond with its own cascade of decisions, instructions, and new Search parameters. In the meantime, he went about preparing for his Search in Nortamerica during the mid-thirty-eighth century, the mission for which he had allowed his muscles to be so painfully restructured.

Before the Troupe could respond, or Rydin advance far with his own planning, however, Cinquemain intruded with a new development.

"Do you know a civilian named Pinkus Boskin?" the intelligence asked as they were coordinating their morning schedules. "He has somehow acquired access to your personal Troupe channel. And used an urgent priority!"

"Never heard of him," Rydin answered.

"Well, he pretends to know you."

"Did he say what he wants?"

"He won't tell. Or not to a machine."

"Why ever not?" Rydin began to feel his usual twitch around civilians.

"He appears to think that might create a record," Cinquemain said.

Rydin laughed. "Ask him about neural imprinting."

"He seems blissfully unaware. He's either naïve or stupid."

"Could he be a wild-type human?" Rydin wondered.

"Not outside a preserve. And not with access to the network."

"I suppose, then, he wants a meeting in facespace."

"He suggests a watering hole on the other side of the river."

Rydin was now intrigued. "Make arrangements."

Later that day he paddled a skiff up to the silk willows screening a public bath on the south bank of the Temz.

In a natural cove cut into the gravel shore, the proprietors had scooped out a series of interconnecting basins and lined their bottoms with tightly fitted pavers in white and black. Each pool held a stone dragon that was hybridized to absorb or radiate along the electromagnetic spectrum, creating the effect of gradually increasing warmth as patrons swam from one pool to the next. The pool nearest the river's flow was chilled to well below ambient, just short of forming ice, and patrons were advised to spend no more than thirty heartbeats in the water there for risk of losing consciousness. The pool farthest inland visibly steamed on even the hottest days, and there the warning was against blisters and tissue damage. Little nibbling *Cyprinidae* fishes and floating *Porifera* sponges cleaned the patrons, while gilled snails filtered the water and cleaned the pool bottoms.

Rydin pulled his boat up on the beach opposite the bathing area, stripped off his jumpsuit and sandals, and left them on the seat. He gave his chit to the attendant, walked around to the fifth pool, as instructed by Cinquemain's mysterious correspondent, and slid in. The water was five Celsius above body temperature. Too warm for his taste.

If he had brought Cinquemain along, Rydin would have sent the intelligence's robot chassis around to the other pools to sample and find one he liked better.

But coming without his assistant had been the first of Boskin's requirements.

As he was settling in and thinking about reaching for a sponge, a naked man parted the silk fronds, moved forward quickly, and stepped into the water two meters away from Rydin. He set something weapon-shaped on the grass behind his head. Perhaps he underestimated Jongleur-trained reflexes, not to mention simian muscles.

"Mir Boskin?"

"You must be Rydin," the man said. "I talked to your machine."

Boskin splashed water on himself and panted. He wasn't a wild-type by any means, but in an era of genetically modified bodies and minds, when both metabolism and desire could be tuned to the optimum diet, Boskin was oddly misshapen. The last time Rydin had seen that much excess tissue on face, stomach, and arms was in the twenty-first century. Boskin was fat and didn't care.

"They tell me the Tsverin girl works for you," he said.

"Who tells you?" Rydin was curious.

"I have my sources." The man smiled.

"And what interest do you have in Merola Tsverin?"

"Business your Jongleur Troupe wouldn't like, of course." Boskin ducked his head under the water and came up blowing. The move kept Rydin from interrupting. "A week ago I sent her to do a job. She hasn't come to see me. I thought you could tell me where she is."

Rydin considered possible replies and put aside the first two or three. No civilian, no one outside the Troupe, ever sent a Jongleur to "do a job." Interfering with an officer on Search—by soliciting, bribing, impeding, or whatever the circumstances—was a serious breach of protocol. For Boskin, it was a legal crime that could strip him of both liberty and property. For Tsverin, the penalty was loss of Jongleur status, return to civilian life, *and then* legal loss of liberty and property. The privilege of traveling in time was tightly held.

Not that Rydin didn't know of breaches. Powerful men with an interest in determining historical outcomes had managed to touch Jongleurs in the past. But if they were successful, they never spoke about it. And not at a public watering hole.

But now Rydin thought to look around. This pool was empty. The other pools along the strand were also empty. He and Boskin were the only patrons. Even the attendants had disappeared.

The only possible reply seemed to be the truth.

"Mira Tsverin has not returned from Search."

"I thought that was instantaneous," Boskin said.

"Still you waited several days before contacting me?"

"The job was complicated. I thought it might take a few trips."

Rydin sighed. The man was too bold, presumed too much power. Well, they had already skipped over the niceties of law and protocol. Time to hear the worst.

"Tell me what she did," he said.

"She picked up a baseball for me."

"A ... what?"

"Not just any baseball." Boskin closed his eyes in anticipation. "It was the last of the big career home runs. McGwire at Saint Louis. Number sixty-two. The game went to hell after that, of course. Doping, steroids. Nobody was playing as themselves, no longer just for sport. The money fever got so bad the record books were ultimately expunged. That makes McGwire's ball unique. It's going to be the centerpiece of my collection."

Now Rydin remembered hearing the word "baseball" before. It was a game, played mostly in Nortamerica and occasionally in Nippon, somehow involving nine men on a diamond-shaped field. He made a sudden guess that the word could refer both to the game itself and to some kind of token or goal associated with the game; the An-glish language was structured that way. A "ball" might be something Tsverin could steal, hold in her hand, and hide.

"This ball was valuable?" he asked. "In its frame of reference?"

"Extremely. I know collectors who would kill for it."

"From our time, now, or in the thing's own time?"

Boskin's forehead wrinkled. "Now, of course. I have four competitors who would be willing and able to make Tsverin a very handsome offer. Fortunately, I was able to apply special leverage none of them could match. Still, I was getting worried."

"But would people in the twenty-first century notice it was missing?"

"Not if she took it the way I told her. Swap it for a new ball."

"Well, someone or something noticed," Rydin said.

So it wasn't a change in history that Boskin had been after, even if he had set one off. That was a good start, at least. The man was merely an obsessive, lusting after a trinket. And Boskin thought he had given Merola Tsverin a way to satisfy his desire without causing a stir, although with the Möglichen and the Flüchtlinge that was never easy. They had lusts, too.

Collectors were the bane of the Jongleur Troupe. Rich men with too much time, too many resources, and too little purpose in their lives. They connived with his-torians and serious academics to glean tidbits of infor-mation—like the fact of this McGwire ball—that could shape their collecting. Pinkus Boskin had evidently in-dulged himself over the years.

There was only one cure for such an obsession.

"How did you become interested in baseball?" Rydin asked.

"What? Oh. My uncle got me started. He had quite a collection himself. He even owned one of Babe Ruth's shirts, Number 3, with the Yankees. ... Say, you're not thinking of confiscating my collection, are you? Not over a little thing like this?"

Boskin's self-preoccupation was truly amazing!

"No, that would not be our preferred approach," Rydin said.

"Whew! That's good."

"But collecting items from the past does represent a danger—even innocuous objects like your baseball."

"You're afraid it will change something in the past? And so change the present?"

Rydin smiled. "The present is extremely tenacious. Random changes by Jongleurs passing through what we think of as ancient history almost never disrupt or seriously distort what we think of as the present. Ripples tend to die out, rather than becoming waves. And waves never become tsunamis. The nature of time, the process of cause and effect, is simply not as unstable as you might think. Of course, Jongleurs are trained to be careful. But probability does sometimes play tricks. Some changes, even small ones, can draw the attention of ... things. We in the Troupe call them the Möglichen, the 'children of possibility.' They sometimes set traps to snare what, to them, is the future."

"Oh, I never wanted that," Boskin said blandly.

Clearly, he dismissed Rydin's explanation as fantasy.

"Of course not," Rydin said. "And even if your baseball has failed to draw an incursion of the Möglichen, there are other travelers—more like settlers, actually, or refugees—who come from the future themselves. Usually these Flüchtlinge are wanted as criminals in their own time. They have escaped into what they consider the past as a means of outwitting the authorities. They are cautious and fearful, territorial and fiercely protective. They are always watching for signs of Jongleur activity and attack us on sight. The Flüchtlinge might have mistaken your baseball's disappearance as an intrusion on their privacy."

"I told Tsverin how to handle it so no one would know," Boskin said.

"I'm sure you thought that would work, too."

"You know ..." Boskin suddenly looked crafty, as if he had discovered Rydin in an indiscretion. "It seems to me you're telling the Jongleur Troupe's deepest secrets. Things I probably shouldn't know. If that's the case, then I might need an incentive to keep my mouth shut."

"That won't be necessary," Rydin said.

21. Ring of Thieves

Before Merola even bothered to search for traces and artifacts left by the early Voyageurs, she had to obtain the means for living independently and traveling anywhere in the world. So she spent several afternoons with Bill Windlace's computing machine, searching the internet and collecting information to support a plan she had devised. The first step would be to teach her friends, in the park after school, a game they could play. Merola called the game "Diversion."

She taught Josie and Estella and three other girls the tune and words to a song that was popular in reference now. The tune had no special power, but the lyrics included many words that Emily and Bill would consider shocking coming from a nine-year-old. To go along with the song Merola taught the girls a dance that included movements of the hips and hands that were practically meaningless at their age but would also shock an adult. To dress up this bit of playacting—and hide the girls' faces in case any adult might be paying too close attention—she bought broad-brimmed, floppy hats and billowy scarves at the thrift store.

"This is a silly dance," Josie said suddenly.

"Mama won't let me say those words," Estella added.

"And that's the point," Merola replied with a smile.

She separately taught Jimmy Chen and two other boys to mimic the girls' song, including the dance movements. She taught them how to exaggerate and parody the dance and compete with each other in shouting the words. She told the boys to wear their caps low over their eyes, so they would look tougher and meaner—and also hide their faces. She had them end the dance by staging a fight, but she showed them how to throw their punches so that no one actually got hurt or angry.

"What's the good of that?" asked a boy named Sean.

"It's just pretend fighting," Merola explained. "All in fun."

Finally, she procured for herself a number of tools by strolling through a hardware store, identifying what she needed, calmly slipping the items into a pocket of her jumper, and strolling out.

Then Merola took her group to their first target, a Starbucks store in their neighborhood that sold pastries and cookies as well as coffee and tea. The girls danced in as a group, singing their song. After a beat, as instructed, the boys danced in and began ruining any grace or beauty the girls' performance might have had. When Jimmy was shouting the bad words at the top of his lungs, Merola slipped through the door. When the fight started among the boys, all the adults in the store, including the servers and sales clerks behind the counter, rushed forward to break it up. Merola slid around the end of the counter, spread the mouth of a mylar garbage bag, and began scooping cakes and cookies out of the open backs of the display cases. By the time the children were settled down, and beginning to slip out of the store as Merola had taught them, she closed her bag and followed, holding it in front of her skirt.

The adults never knew what really happened.

Merola led her troupe to the local park, where she opened the bag and parceled out the delicacies. Everyone told her what a good game it was. She told them it was only good so long as they kept it secret. If any adults, or even other kids, knew what the game was, it would no longer work.

The boys and girls nodded seriously while gobbling pastry.

Two days later, Merola collected their lunch money and led them to the bus stop after school. She took them downtown to an elegant store, Cose Dolci, which sold confections that the internet site described as "gourmet."

The shop windows showed overflowing bowls of variously colored jelly beans, trays of candies that looked like rock crystal and had the shapes of animals and birds, and boxes holding huge dollops of chocolate with names in foreign languages. Merola could see through the glass door that the inside of the store was arranged much like the coffee shop: an open center space surrounded by display cases. Perfect for the dance.

They started the game, and everything went as before. On the bus ride back, Merola handed out single candies to keep her troupe quiet. They divided the mass of it—amounting to more than a pound for each child—at the neighborhood park.

On the fourth day, Merola took her troupe downtown again. This time they visited a new store, with the name Amore Eterno, that looked much like the elegant candy store. The children did not notice the difference. They danced and sang and fought while Merola opened the backs of the display cases with a glass cutter and a hammer wrapped in thick cloth.

As they sat on the bus that took them back to the neighborhood, Merola held the bag closed and did not share. The others were quiet. Now they were sure something was different. Josie looked scared.

At the park, Merola handed out single rings and bracelets as if they were candy.

"What's this?" Jimmy held up a gold ring with a large two-carat diamond.

"It's jewelry, stupid," said Estella. "That's for a girl getting married."

"We did a bad thing," Josie said. She was on the verge of tears.

"Those people are going to be really mad," said one boy.

Merola waited, holding the bag against her skirt.

"We have to give these back," Josie said.

"You're right," Merola said finally. "This isn't candy. I got the wrong store. This is serious." She held out her hand for the pieces she had distributed, and each child gave up his or her prize. "I'll get right on the bus and take it all back. I'll explain we were just playing a game, and that we're really sorry."

"I'll go with you," Josie said.

Merola was surprised. "No-oo," she said slowly. "It might be too dangerous. I'm an orphan, so no one's going to yell at me. But your mom and dad would get angry."

"You're right," Josie agreed.

Merola made a show of getting on the next bus headed downtown. No one saw her get off four blocks later and walk home. Emily and Bill never saw the bag, and that night in her room Merola used the tools she had stolen to pull the stones out of their settings and crush the metal parts into wads no one could identify. She sorted everything and researched on line over the next several days to establish its current value.

The means of living independently and traveling were at hand.

Now the only question was, where could she go?

22. The Baseball Collection

Rydin and Cinquemain popped into the blackness of space, clinging to the struts of their liteship. An instant before, the limb of the green-and-blue Earth in Rydin's reference now had been hanging below their feet. Then suddenly, with the temporal shift, he could see nothing but stars—although one star, low in the quadrant to their left, was slightly brighter than the rest. Cinquemain took a fix on it, tracing back along the axis of the solar system's proper motion around the galaxy and through the universe over the past 47 years.

"How far?" Rydin asked.

"No distance at all," his intelligence said. "A mere 300 light hours. We'll get there long before local dawn."

Cinquemain began converting the time-energy of the selvaged singularity into distance-energy. The stars blurred around them.

In a blink, the liteship once again was hanging over the planet, but now above the dark side. As with the Lune of Rydin's reference now, there were no unshielded lights to distinguish cities and towns from open country. Cinquemain navigated westward against the turning of the planet, coming to a point above the village of Penance, located somewhere southwest of Lune. Once again, Rydin was struck by the discontinuity: they had traveled 300 light hours through interstellar space to cover a land distance of about 400 kilometers.

"You're sure this is the place?" the intelligence asked.

"Boskin came from here," Rydin said. "His family has lived here for six generations. Where else would the uncle keep these things?"

"A hundred places I can think of."

"Well, if this is wrong, we'll go back and try again," Rydin snapped. "Take us down."

"Aren't you forgetting something? Protocol on Search?"

Rydin nodded. He touched the forefinger of his gloved right hand to the almond-shaped lens in the bio-suit helmet covering his left eye. It was as close as he could come to making physical contact, but it was enough to trigger the reflex.

A biocircuit which had been surgically implanted in his brain began interpreting Rydin's current knowledge and intentions into a form of symbolic logic that it transmitted to a tiny scribe inside the medallion around his neck. The scribe fixed the ebb and flow of electrochemical discharges in Rydin's brain through quantum entanglement of electrons across all possible time cones. That would preserve what he knew and thought of as "reality" or "true events" in his reference now against the possibility of temporal distortion or deletion. This original appreciation of the universe would survive and be available for later review and analysis. Whenever a Jongleur traveled across time, even though the chance might be vanishingly small that his or her actions and their consequences would change the reference now—such as a trip to the past over many millennia—the Jongleur took this neural imprint.

A school of thought among the Jongleurs held that the unprotected human brain might retain its memories against temporal distortion on the basis of willpower alone. They believed a focused mind—one held in a particular pattern, whether through strong emotion, fanatic belief, or psychosis—could entangle its own electrons and overcome any loss of context. But who could maintain such determination from minute to minute, hour to hour, day to day? Rydin personally did not believe in the theory.

Intelligences like Cinquemain had no special protocol. Their complex bit-mapping was routed through an imprinting circuit that continuously entangled their electrons, left and right, forward and back. It was part of their navigation system and gave them fixed points of reference in all spheres. In fact, temporal imprinting was the main reason a human always traveled with an intelligence.

The liteship landed just outside the circle of hybridized oak trees that belonged to the Boskin clan. Inside the circle was a curving structure assembled out of low stone barrows. The thick, craggy trunks and weather-stained surfaces suggested a long-established compound. Two night-adapted sight hounds and a scent hound moved rapidly toward the grounded ship. Cinquemain paused in folding up the panels to drop the animals with narrow blasts from his chassis's communications laser.

Rydin turned to stare at him.

"When you're going to steal something that everyone will know was stolen," Cinquemain explained, "why worry about leaving evidence of the theft?"

"Because they were sentient creatures?"

"So you say," the machine replied.

Rydin stowed his helmet with the ship but retained his biosuit, boots, and gloves—"in case we meet any more of those hounds," he said, "and you happen to let them live." He knew the suit fabric was impervious to micrometeorite punctures, so it would be proof against dog bites.

They walked into the circle of trees. "Ground level or treetop?" Rydin asked.

"People sleep in trees," Cinquemain said.

"That's true. So, the buildings. Check the doors. Something important would be held closely."

They started from different ends of the semicircle of domes, testing door latches and peering through mollusk-sealed windows. Only one dome had any kind of security, a complicated cyber lock on a door of thick metal. Together they studied the lock.

"Can you negotiate with it?" Rydin asked.

Cinquemain drilled it with a laser beam.

"It wasn't sentient either," he commented.

Rydin swung the heavy door easily with his simian-enhanced muscles. When they stepped inside, lightstrips came on, revealing tables, shelves, and cabinets full of ... junk.

There were shirts of white and gray fabrics that bore the blocky numerals and stylized writing of the nineteenth to twenty-first centuries. Although these artifacts were pinned to display boards, no one had thought to wash them first, because Rydin could still detect the yellowish stains of bodily secretions and greenish stains from crushed plants. There were enormous shoes with metal and rubber knobs in their soles, some with bits of dirt still attached. There were white and brown balls as large as Rydin's two hands clenched together, each with a leather cover secured by colorful stitching. There were oddly shaped sticks of wood, some broken, with filthy black tape wrapped around their narrow ends. There were also batons of spun aluminum pitted with micro-dents, the ends wrapped in more tape or coated with rubber.

It was all junk, used and dirty and ready to discard. Except that whoever had put it here protected the tables and cases with clear resin covers, strong and thick, and yet made to be optically nondistorting.

"So that's a baseball." Cinquemain pointed one out. "I detect germs—and traces of the *Nicotiana* plant."

"Sometimes the thrower would spit on it. I've been reading up."

"And you still want to touch that thing?"

"We have to," Rydin said.

He tested the cover over a table full of old shoes. It hinged on one side and locked on the other. There wasn't time for Cinquemain to heat-treat all the locks in the room. Rydin drew back his fist and struck the center of the plastic. The heavy walls of the building contained the sudden, sharp *crack!* The cover shattered in a star pattern. Rydin plucked out the longest shards and the smaller ones fell in on the table. He wasn't worried about leaving DNA evidence or the smears of fingerprints. The Jongleur Troupe had wiped Rydin's personal biometrics from the justice system twenty years before those covers were made.

"Get the bags," he told Cinquemain. They had a number of loosely woven string bags for carrying the baseball collection. It looked as if they had brought almost enough of them.

Rydin broke and disassembled the protective covers while Cinquemain went from table to cabinet to shelf, pushing and kicking items into the bags lying open on the floor.

Suddenly, Rydin paused. "Did you see a shirt with the number three on it?"

Cinquemain consulted his photographic memory. "Not here."

"How about the words 'New York' or 'Yankees'?"

"Nothing like that," Cinquemain said.

"Confound it! We're too early."

"Is the shirt important?"

"Boskin mentioned it specifically. It may have been the basis of his collecting impulse."

"A shirt?" The intelligence sounded unconvinced.

"You never know what's important to these obsessives."

"It's a little late to turn back. We've left evidence, remember?"

"Then all of our vandalism may be for nothing."

But as soon as he said this, Rydin saw a striped shirt lying on an as-yet undisturbed table. The word "Ruth" was prominent across the back in a second-millennial alphabet. Another shirt—with an embroidered ornament combining the symbols "N" and "Y"—lay on top of it, covering what might be part of a large "3" on the first shirt.

He breathed a sigh. "Found it. The markings were not as I thought."

"Collect it and let's get out of here."

They finished clearing the tables and dragged the stuffed bags out through the heavy door. They didn't have to move them far. While Rydin arranged the bags in a more or less tight circle with even weight distribution, Cinquemain returned to the liteship, powered it up, and drifted in among the trees. Rydin ran a spider-silk cord through the mouths of all the bags, hooked it over a release catch on the bottom of the ship, and climbed aboard. He fitted his helmet and nodded when it was sealed.

Cinquemain shot the liteship straight up in the air, yanking the baseball collection above the tree circle, above Cornwall, above the slowly turning Earth. He made an adjustment, and the planet disappeared. They and their stolen goods were suddenly in starry space again, 300 light hours distant from their own world and 47 years beyond the reach of Boskin's uncle. He toggled the control that released the bags, and they floated away. The cord slipped through the mesh, the bag mouths opened, and all the junk—balls, bats, shirts, shoes—was scattered.

Only after the loss was unrecoverable did Rydin experience a moment of confusion, a blurring of vision, a sudden absence in the middle of his mind.

"What did we just do?" he asked vaguely. Not as if it was important ...

"Protocol," Cinquemain said sharply. "Touch your eye."

Rydin touched his left finger to his right eye. The device in his medallion traced the entangled patterns and transmitted them to the circuit in his brain, where the previous knowledge was introduced as a flash of insight, with the unmistakable feeling of truth.

There had been a man. An obsessive. He was real, a fat man with a greasy manner. Pinkus Boskin. He had compromised a Search because his uncle collected baseball memorabilia. He told Rydin about this while they soaked in a pool along the Temz. When this night was done he would not—now did not—love baseball anymore. Merola Tsverin had been lost and now she would be found. This was all true!

"Is the problem solved?" Cinquemain asked after extracting his own entangled reconstruction.

"Completely," Rydin said. "Let's go home."

23. Clues to the Future

Merola quickly discovered that using primitive on-line searches to locate the incursions and artifacts of early travelers, who might have touched down anywhere in the world at any time, was harder than identifying candy and jewelry shops in San Francisco. But then, she realized, those shops had wanted to be found, and the travelers did not.

Keyword searches for "time travel" took her to a mix of literary sites, which she already knew were useless. "Voyageur" took her to a place called French Canada and people from an earlier century who seemed to trade in the skins of small, dead animals.

After several days of chasing through a wilderness of science fiction and fantasy, she resorted to basic concepts. "Phenomenon"—the word for something amazing that was not well understood—led her to "unidentified aerial phenomena," which led her to "unidentified flying objects" and "UFOs." This was promising. The images displayed on the screen, which were uniformly blurry and without detail, as often as not resembled the discharges from a saucer's hull or a liteship's panels. The trapezoidal shapes suggested the snowflake pattern of a Jongleur liteship, while the enclosed disks suggested the ships of early Voyageurs. But the many other shapes associated with these phenomena—triangular wedges, blunt tubes, pin-point patterns of free-floating lights—made her think the reports were part of a crude hoax.

For two days Merola sifted through sites that seemed to reveal the secrets of UFO incursions in a place called "Area 51" in Nevada and an incident near Roswell, New Mexico. Both were tantalizing, as they were within easy traveling distance from San Francisco and, more important, still appeared to be active. But there were too many hints of current human involvement. The U.S. Air Force seemed to be controlling Area 51 and to have launched whatever vehicle came down at Roswell. She wasn't interested in the feeble attempts of the current century's so-called scientists to visit the past or future. Merola had to find travelers from much closer to her own reference now.

Besides, these stories might be Möglichen plants to trap the unwary.

Finally, in desperation, hoping to snag a traveler's mention or memoirs, she began inputting names related to the one place on the globe she knew intimately, even if that was eight millennia in the future: "Lune," "Missex," "Temz," and "Ongleterre," using every historical reference and variation she could think of. That search turned up the current city of "London," which seemed to be in roughly the same place on what had become an insignificant island, now called the "United Kingdom."

Lacking any other ideas, Merola used the internet to tour the neighborhoods, local attractions, shops, and historical antecedents of this city. It turned out to be far larger and more varied than the Lune she knew, not to mention more dilapidated and dirtier. She roamed online from place to place, fascinated by the development-in-layers of a city that, in her reference now, had a physical history of less than five hundred years. She traveled idly, until she came across a particular name: "Seven Dials."

Seven of any kind of timepiece was a suspected marker, a recognition symbol, for those early travelers.

A few minutes of online research revealed that the place was actually a road junction—another marker—in the West End of London where seven streets came together. A central pillar had been erected to mark the junction, but instead of the expected seven sundials, it bore only six.

There it was!

To be "at seven and six" was an old, an ancient phrase that was mysteriously revived in the centuries preceding formation of the Jongleur Troupe. Like references to clocks and sundials, the phrase was also rumored to be a recognition code among the early and illicit travelers, but no one outside their closed networks ever knew its origin. Merola studied the details of this place called "Seven Dials." The area was laid out in the year 1690 of current notation, intended as a fashionable neighborhood where these seven commercial streets converged. But the locale had quickly declined, becoming disreputable, a "slum" in the local dialect, a place of theft, prostitution, and murder. And what other anonymous and shady dealings might it have attracted? Merola could easily imagine its usefulness to anyone who wanted anonymity when touching down from the ninth and tenth millennia.

A quick check told her that, in the present city of London, the Seven Dials area had revived and was now prosperous and legitimately commercial, with a thriving theater district nearby. And yet, if there was ever a place that hunted travelers might congregate and recognize each other, Seven Dials was it. And in an ancient city like London, where what one generation had built was not cleared away with enzymes but left to diminish and decay, artifacts and the buildings that housed them would drift beyond their time, hiding their secrets.

Of course, visiting such a place would be dangerous. The Flüchtlinge, not to mention the Möglichen, would be watching a known point of intersection. Merola would have to disguise her presence as well as her intentions. It certainly would help that at least some of those potential watchers had already discovered her and engineered— or so they would suppose—her death. After all, they had made no further move against her in the months she lived in San Francisco.

Now that she had a destination and the means to reach it, Merola only ...

She experienced a momentary light-headedness, a dazzle of false light behind her eyes, and a muffled hum inside her ears, as if she had stood up or bent over too quickly. When the sensation passed, her mind was curiously empty.

"What have I been doing?" she asked aloud.

She instinctively touched her left forefinger to her right eye. But the locket she had worn ... when? She remembered having it before the explosion and fire. That was months ago. It must have come off in the ... hospital? Or was stolen as she lay in the street? She could not remember seeing it for a long time. But she knew it was important.

She looked at the desktop where she was working this ancient computer and its primitive data-retrieval network. Beside the keyboard was a ... paperweight? No, something more. More like a friend, although temporarily asleep.

Slowly, slowly, bits of memory, the edges of some central thing she ought to know, crept into her mind. That her name was Merola Tsverin. That she lived in this house with people who seemed like family but were strangers to her. That she did not actually belong in this place or time. That she was a traveler, stranded by an accident—one that she expected she herself had caused. But for all her effort and mental discipline, she could not remember what, exactly, she might have done wrong.

She looked at the screen in front of her eyes. It displayed photos, a map, and text about a place called "Seven Dials," in a city called "London." It was ... important for travelers like her.

Another thought drifted through her mind.

Merola looked up "seven and six" through the computer's search function. That returned no hits, but inverted and in the plural—"at sixes and sevens"—the phrase was commonly used in the country where this London was located. It meant being in a state of confusion and disarray.

Well, Merola decided, that certainly described her situation.

The answer seemed to be this place "Seven Dials."

But what, she wondered, was the question?

24. Gone Sideways

Rydin and Cinquemain completed their journey, traveling the 300 light hours to return to Earth's current position in their own reference now. As they entered the atmosphere, the Temz Valley lay clear and green below them, lit by the sunshine of a summer noon, with the sparkling river meandering through it. They dropped vertically onto the town, with Cinquemain adjusting for the planet's spin and the prevailing winds. Rydin was already rehearsing in his mind the reprimand he would give to Tsverin, and the penalties he would impose on her, when they met.

"Something wrong here," the intelligence said quietly.

Rydin leaned past the outboard panel and looked straight down.

"Check your coordinates," he said. "We must be somewhere up river."

"The coordinates are correct," Cinquemain replied. "Lune is not there."

"That's not possible. You can't lose an entire community inside a fifty-year jump. No matter how important Mir Boskin or his family might be. They wouldn't retaliate like this. Not over something so foolish as *baseball*."

"I think this goes beyond Boskin."

"But that's the only change."

"Look down there."

"Horses!"

Rydin saw dozens, no hundreds, of horses running over the level ground. They bunched and turned together as a herd, like a flock of birds or school of fish. He did not see any riders, but then no one rode free animals in his reference now. Rydin had seen men on horseback only during his travels in the twentieth and twenty-first centuries. The local transportation of his time might use hybridized *Equidae* muscles or nerves or other body parts, but the whole horse was too willful and unpredictable for safe riding.

Still, something seemed unnatural about the way these animals moved. From the altitude of a kilometer he studied the few individuals that ran outside the mass of animals and the dust they raised.

"Go lower," he instructed.

As the liteship descended, the horses became aware of it and veered off over a hill. But Rydin had a clear view of the last ones as they disappeared.

Each animal had six legs. The pair in the middle caused the animal's back to flex up and down like a spring.

"Did you see that?" he asked Cinquemain.

"I saw it, but I don't understand it."

"Take us downriver, please."

They glided east along the Temz. It was the same river of Rydin's experience, broad and smooth, with water clear enough for them to see the sandy shoals and dark bottom mud. But they saw no crystal bridge, no sign at all of humans and their works. Further to the east, however, well below his own Lune, where the river widened into a proper estuary and picked up the blue-gray opaqueness of salt from the sea, Rydin saw a shimmering shape.

"There!" He pointed.

"What *is* that?" Cinquemain asked.

"It's under the water. Some kind of structure. A dome."

"I see more of them further down."

"And there! People!"

On the sandy bank were arrayed row after row of people, but ... not people. They reminded Rydin of the seals or sea lions he had seen once on a rocky beach along the west coast of Nortamerica, eight millennia ago. They had the same torpedo shape, sleek heads, and forked rear fins or flippers. But instead of one pair of stubby flippers up near the front, these creatures had two pairs, elongated and articulated, like the lobe-finned fishes. But that was not the most remarkable thing.

They were sitting and lying in folding metal cradles—something like beach chairs. They were reading and sipping drinks, basking in the sun. They wore sunglasses. Attendants of apparently the same species moved among them, refreshing drinks and wetting down the idlers with a hose.

One of the—people? animals? beings?—looked up and spotted the liteship. It raised itself halfway out of its cradle and barked something unintelligible.

"Altitude," Rydin ordered. "Now!"

The liteship shot into the sky until the river was just a broad, empty river, and Rydin and Cinquemain would be less than a dot in the blue to anyone lying beside it.

When they leveled out and the liteship stopped rocking, Cinquemain said, "What has happened?"

"Scan for the Troupe's neural network," Rydin ordered. "Scan for another liteship. For Tsverin and Berzher. For any Jongleur on any wavelength."

After a moment the intelligence said, "Nothing. What has happened?"

"We thought Merola Tsverin was dead, killed in the building collapse, after she stole that baseball. But what if she escaped the explosion and has been alive all along? If her ship and cache were destroyed, and she couldn't return, then she must have gone ... sideways. But all that occurred only in the early twenty-first century. There would hardly be enough time."

"Time for what?" Cinquemain's voice circuits actually quavered.

"For humans—for the entire class *Mammalia,* apparently—to disappear." He pointed downward. "We humans haven't existed on this planet for a very long time."

"How do you know that?"

"Because of morphology," Rydin replied. "We share our shapes with the animals closest to us. It's a basic principle of biology. Our shape is foretold in our genes. We have the body parts we do because of the highly conserved homeobox gene set. Those homeotic genes control the arrangement of head, thorax, abdomen, and limbs during fetal development. The homeobox—or hox, for short—is very old, going back at least 400 million years and probably longer. Subtle modifications to the hox genes define the difference between a human and a horse. Gross modifications, between a human and a fish or a fruit fly. For vertebrates, like humans and horses—and sea lions—the long-standing arrangement has been four limbs, tetrapod morphology. That goes back beyond reptiles to the lobe-finned fishes."

"All the animals we've seen here have six distinct limbs," Cinquemain said.

"A modification like that can't develop in just a few thousand years."

"Something erased you four-leggers and gave everyone six legs?"

"Something very old," Rydin agreed. "This effect goes way beyond the actions of Boskin or Tsverin."

"I thought it was an article of faith that distant changes die out."

"Well, more like a working hypothesis," Rydin replied.

"Yeah, with the distinct feature of being *wrong.*"

"Not wrong, just incomplete," he said. "Past and present are not fixed on any particular course. Time is a process of cause and effect as much as a manifestation of the physical universe. If one thing changes, it changes another. But most changes are small. The cause lacks sufficient energy, or inertia, to have much effect. Waves do not become tsunamis—not without a significant push."

"Then why did we steal the baseball collection?"

"We wanted to give Boskin no reason to tempt Tsverin—or any Jongleur in our reference now—into removing the McGwire ball and so making the small change that killed Merola."

"Someone else wanted that ball and would know the difference?" Cinquemain suggested.

"The ball was a trap," Rydin said. "She must already have stolen it before we changed Boskin's life."

"But ..." the intelligence objected, "but we were still here when she didn't return the first time. We—Lune—*our world* was still here. It didn't go away until *after* we removed Boskin from the chain of events."

"She must have been on her way back," Rydin said slowly. "Something about her contact with the baseball—first the theft happened, then it didn't happen, she changed something, and then she *didn't* change it—set her on a new course. And that course must have led to—"

"A world of six-legged sea lions."

Rydin considered for a moment in silence. The situation contained too many possible points of interaction, too many Wahrschein points, where probability alone ruled.

Entire worlds hung in the instants of suspension between cause and effect, between the thought of suicide and actually throwing oneself off a rooftop, between the desire to shoot an enemy and actually discharging a weapon, between life and death for one person whose fate might affect a single family or the course of history. From the sum of these burdened points, Jongleurs believed, the Möglichen arose. They entered the smooth flow of cause and effect from the unknown and incalculable universe. The ancients might have called them gods or devils and worshipped them. Over the years, the Jongleur Troupe had kept records and made lists of strange phenomena, trying to chart past incursions. They had employed cybers operating unbelievably complex algorithms, trying to predict the next occurrence. But they were only chasing shadows and smoke.

Until now. This time they were confronting, not a probability or a shadow, but a whole, improbable beach full of creatures who should not exist. And along with it, the death of the world in which Rydin and Cinquemain had been born. But one thing Rydin understood: once the Möglichen were in motion, you couldn't simply push them back into the realm of lower probabilities. They would play where they willed.

"I caused this," he concluded finally. "By eliminating Boskin's desire for the baseball, and so Tsverin's decision to steal it, I changed her chosen course of action and sent her sideways—into this."

"Can you fix it? Can you unmake the paradox?"

"We would have to confront the Möglichen at the cusp, back in the twenty-first century—perhaps much farther back. And, even if we win, no predestined path exists that will return to our particular reference now, with Lune sited on the Temz, the Troupe traveling in time ... everything we know."

"So you can't remake time? There is no temporal paradox?"

"You can make as much time as you want. It will simply be *different* time. Point, bud, and branch. If we go back to fix this, the planet we know might change even more."

"Worse and worse," Cinquemain said. "But there is one positive aspect."

"What hope could you possibly find here?" Rydin asked sourly.

"If we changed the world any more, who would know?"

FORWARD

25. Carrefour House

The house had always stood in the same place. It always occupied the same sets of coordinates in close relation to the Earth's magnetic and gravitational fields. Because of proper motion, the house's relationship to the fields of Sun and Moon, passing clusters of local stars, Galactic Center, and the local Great Attractor were less rigidly defined and always slowly changing. But these relationships could be charted over the years.

Ancient books with the charts and their underlying calculations were kept in closed vaults accessed through the basement. Sam Gill had seen them once, as a child, and traced with his finger the proprietors' annotations made first with a goose quill in iron gall ink, then with a steel nib in soot and gum. These days, of course, he kept his own records on the computer in the front office under the stairs. Gill knew of faster, more reliable, and certainly more permanent ways to calculate and record the house's settings, but he still had to play by the Builder's rules governing possible search and discovery.

Those books in the basement proved the house's antiquity. It hadn't always been called "Carrefour House," of course. That name was merely a concession to modern marketing techniques, which put an upscale French accent on everything English. The house had started as an inn, located practically in the countryside, sometime in the late fifteenth century. It was known then simply as "Crossroads House," or just "the Crossroads," because of its relationship to the road junction that would, some 200 years later, become known as Seven Dials. Originally, it was a true inn with stables, hostelry, common room with kitchen hearth, taproom off to the side, and staff to accommodate weary travelers and their animals. Travelers of all types, actually.

Over the years, the house had changed. Its front had been rebuilt many times and realigned to the layout of the pavements as the neighborhood waxed and waned. But the essential core had never changed or moved, not so much as a millimeter. The stables had disappeared sometime in the eighteenth century. The tap room, common room, and kitchen had been renovated away in the late nineteenth century. There was a bad moment in the mid-twentieth century, when London suffered extensive bombing, but Gill had made sure none ever fell on his part of Seven Dials. Over the years since, gentrification and modernization had brought in the theaters, the trendy eateries, the boutiques. The block behind the house had filled up with new construction, but none of it ever touched the house's core.

Now, at the beginning of the twenty-first century, the house maintained a tidy front along fifteen yards of side street, four stories tall with dormers above the roof line. Carrefour House was a bed-and-breakfast with six rooms facing the street, seven overlooking the back garden, and an uncountable number in between. Sam Gill himself occupied the top floor with his wife and three children.

The Gill family had been nominal owners and proprietors since the mid-sixteenth century, the time of troubles and religious discord between the reigns of Henry VIII and Elizabeth I. Sam Gill's great-grandfather had taken over the establishment when the original proprietor had allowed himself to attract public attention, been questioned about his beliefs, and burned as a heretic. Sam's grandfather had taken that lesson to heart. Over the years, when someone mentioned the Gill family's longstanding proprietorship and suggested the name really should be changed to "Gill House," the family always dismissed the notion. Let the name change with the times, was their opinion. That was safest. And anyway, their customers always knew where to find the house.

Carrefour House still served travelers of all types. Privately, outside their hearing, Sam Gill referred to them variously as "mundanes" and "exotics." It showed his gradual acclimatization, the fact he was the third generation of Gills born in the house, that he thought of the guests from this place and time as the mundanes, and those arriving from farther afield as the exotics. Sam's great-grandfather would have reversed his references.

So, shortly after six o'clock on a rainy evening in early June, with the house less than half full—three mundanes, two exotics—Sam Gill was ready to go off duty. The night manager, Mickey Santos, who was firmly among the mundanes, was now twenty minutes overdue and Gill was wondering if he dared leave the front desk unattended. He decided to ring up the flat and ask his eldest daughter, Sabina, to come down and split the dinner hour with him, but a thump from the cupboard in the second-floor hallway changed his mind.

He had started around the end of the desk and up the stairs, when a familiar voice called down, "Don't mind us!"

"Everything all right?" he called back.

Another thump, louder this time.

"It's this damned sword."

"Harold! Didn't you change?"

"No room in that damned cupboard."

Now Gill heard an almost musical chiming. But the musicality was marred by an ugly, tooth-jarring undertone: *scritch-scritch-scritch*. It made one think of sheets of frozen methane being twisted to the point of shattering.

"If you break a mirror," he called up the stairs, "I'll have to charge you."

"Don't worry," Harold replied. "Haven't got any money."

"I'll charge your school, then," Gill warned.

"Oh, you businessmen are cruel!"

After a moment Harold Zhang clumped down the stairs, followed by his wife Sylvia. They both wore boots of roughly tanned water buffalo hide and loose pantaloons of blue-dyed cotton. He had on a rough-spun peasant shirt under a leather jerkin armored with large bronze disks sewn across front and back. She was more formally dressed in a coat of red silk embroidered with gold thread. Both wore turbans of dark-blue cloth. Through his sash belt, Harold carried a naked, two-handed war sword with a wide, curving blade of black iron.

Sam Gill sighed. "You make quite a pair. Where from this time?"

"China, of course," Sylvia said in a cheerful, high-pitched voice.

"The Warring States Period," Harold affirmed. "History lesson."

"Of course. Do you have a change of clothes?" Gill asked.

"Left the bags upstairs," Harold said. "Easier that way."

"I'll need current documentation, too," Gill said.

Harold Zhang drew a wallet from under the jerkin and thumbed through a packet of papers. He drew out two bright-red United Kingdom passports with the ornate royal coat of arms stamped in gold on the front. "Will these do?"

Gill took the passports and thumbed through them, noting the hodge-podge of colorful entry and exit stamps. His trained eye caught the error right away. "Who made these for you?"

Harold shrugged. "Vyshank's in New Jerusalem. ... Why?"

"Yours has an entry from India three years into the future."

"Did I make an error in transit? We *were* in a bit of hurry!"

"It may not matter," Gill said. "What are your plans now?"

"Stockholm by the air route, to make some purchases—things you just can't get anymore—and then back here and home."

"The Swedes probably won't notice someone else's stamp, but British customs officers are more observant."

"We can't go back to China for a while," Harold said. He tapped the blade of his sword above two long, red-brown smears. "That's real blood, my friend." History lesson, indeed!

Gill chewed his lip. "Let's try this."

He spread the passport on the counter, drew a fountain pen from his jacket's inside pocket, opened it above the erroneously dated stamp, and twisted the plunger until a large drop of blue ink appeared at the nib. He jiggled the pen, the ink splashed across the page, and he quickly blotted it with his handkerchief.

"Suspicious, if you stare at it too hard," he said. "But otherwise it just looks like official clumsiness. Should discourage anyone trying to decipher the date underneath."

"Sam, you're a genius," Sylvia cooed.

"Well, good enough to get you home."

At that moment the front door opened and Mickey Santos came in, shaking out his umbrella. "Sorry I'm late, boss, but I ..." His voice trailed off.

Harold and Sylvia had turned, and Santos was staring at their outlandish clothing. With any luck he wouldn't notice that they were also perfectly dry.

"Hello, folks," he said. "You're ..."

"I'm just checking them in," Gill told him.

"That's quite a getup," Santos observed.

"We're here—" Harold began.

"They're here for the Renaissance Faire," Gill supplied.

"Oh? Really? I didn't know there was one."

"Covent Garden," Gill said. "Starts tomorrow."

"Ah." Santos closed his mouth and went into the office to shed his wet coat and galoshes.

Harold Zhang winked at Gill in appreciation. "Renaissance Faire," he whispered. Then aloud he asked, "Same room as always?"

"Third floor front," Gill confirmed. "Deirdre starts breakfast at seven-thirty in the dining room. Get there early if you want kippers."

"Right." Harold made a face. "More smoked fish."

Sylvia shushed him, and the Zhangs hurried up the stairs before Santos could return with more questions.

26. Neural Imprint

Merola had decided she would leave the Windlaces' foster home at the end of the school year. She was, after all, under absolutely no time pressure in this reference now. It seemed the obvious time to sever her connections in this time and place with the least amount of official notice. Her only concern was with Family & Children Services. Emily would naturally report Merola's disappearance, and that would initiate a cascade of inquiries and searches, public warnings, watches at airports and train stations, and other inconvenience.

As the end of the school year drew near, Merola's friends—Josie, Estella, Jimmy—discussed their plans for the summer vacation and vowed to stay in touch through play dates. Merola could only reply vaguely that she thought she might be traveling. When they pressed her, all she would say was "out east somewhere." It wouldn't do to leave too many people, not even these inconsequential children, in possession of her itinerary.

On the last day of school, when everyone else was celebrating with raucous songs and a food fight in the cafeteria, Merola left the grounds early and walked home. Along the way, she emptied her backpack into a public trash receptacle, discarding a half-year's worth of class notes, old tests, traded snapshots, and the Commodore Sloat fourth-grade yearbook. She only paused when the glass-and-metal paperweight—which she carried everywhere but could not have said why—slid out with the rest of this trash. She quickly reached into the bin, retrieved it, and put it safely in the bottom of her pack.

Returning to the house, she immediately went to her room and stuffed the backpack with as much underwear and light outer clothing as it would hold, along with her toothbrush and the cosmetics Emily had bought her. She took a small suitcase she had purchased on a shopping trip downtown and loaded it with the coats, skirts, blouses, and shoes that she wanted to take.

Merola bent down inside the closet and pried loose a section of baseboard covering a space she had gouged out of the wall plaster. She withdrew a leather pouch full of diamonds, colored gemstones, and twisted bits of white and yellow gold. The pouch covered a sheaf of bills in large denominations and six plastic cards bearing unimaginable credit limits. All of it derived from the gradual online sale of about half the proceeds from the game they played at Amore Eterno. Converting those goods to transactable value—variously known in this time as credit, cash money, and liquid assets—had involved some ingenuity, because internet commerce required access to more than Bill Windlace's connection and logon. She had learned she would need a bank account and a credit card to begin with—financial status that no nine-year-old in this society possessed.

But Merola had found that with sophisticated clothing bought in thrift stores using her allowance—"for dress up," she told the clerk—along with the right amount of mascara and eye shadow, judicious padding of her blouse and tights, and appropriate changes in her attitude and bearing, she could pass for an extremely small woman. From online sources, she had obtained the image of a suitable birth certificate, used Bill's photographic software to modify it with a persona of her own creation, and printed out a copy. After that, the rest was easy: trips to the Department of Motor Vehicles to obtain a driver's license—not that she ever expected to operate these outlandish machines, but the card itself was the universal response to most identity checks in this society—then to the bank to secure her financial status, and finally to the post office to obtain a U.S. passport.

All of this activity had taken time, of course, and that supported Merola's decision to wait until the school year finished. But now there was really no reason to stay. With her backpack and suitcase, and dressed in her "little woman" clothes—already in character as Madeline Hart Stonecraft, "Maddy" for short—she took one last look around the front hall of the Windlace house. Her eye fell on Emily's desk in a corner of the living room.

Obviously, the Windlaces would be holding some kind of documentation—receipts, phone contacts, hospital records, case management reports, bonding fees and licenses—related to their work with Family & Children Services and their current "foster child," Mary Jane Doe. That desk was where Emily might keep such official papers. If Merola was going to cover her traces, then those documents would have to disappear. The desk drawers were locked, of course, but her Jongleur skills were proof against any third-millennium security measures.

What she looked for was in the top right-hand drawer. She removed the papers, shuffled and scanned them to confirm they were what they seemed, and stuffed them into her bulging backpack—for disposal later on her way to one of the downtown hotels and its taxi stand.

Merola suddenly found she wanted to make up for the inconvenience this theft would cause, and to thank these people who had taken her into their home. She thought of leaving them one of the diamonds from Amore Eterno, but that would be incriminating and might cause the Windlaces even more trouble. Then she remembered something from a previous Search assignment, where Merola had studied those curious fluctuations in commerce known as "booms" and "busts." If she remembered correctly, the time she inhabited now was on the cusp between the one and the other. A name stuck in her memory, a corporation involved in the early development of cybers and artificial personalities. ... The name had something to do with fruit. ...

She went to the computer, logged on with Bill Windlace's passwords, and brought up his stock portfolio. Using credit donated from her own accounts, she bought a thousand shares of Apple Computer at a few pennies over $20 per share. She put a note in Emily's desk drawer about the purchase, telling her and Bill to hold the stock for at least a dozen years. "You cannot understand how I know this. Simply trust that I know. In the next twelve years, the value will increase twenty-fold. Consider this a 'thank you' for all the times I could not say those words myself."

Her gift went totally against Jongleur protocols about interaction with locals. But then, circumstances had already forced Merola to interact more than any Jongleur in memory. Besides, what harm would a small fortune do these people? They were essentially good souls and would put the money to good use. And, anyway, from Merola's point of view, they had already been dead more than eight thousand years.

As she closed the drawer, something rattled at the back. Curious, Merola reached in and felt around.

Her fingers found and drew out a locket, or rather a thick disk of featureless gray metal, attached to an endless chain of fine links forged from the same metal. Merola recognized it at once as hers, missing since ... since she could not remember when. She pulled the chain over her head and maneuvered it past the tight fit around her temples, compressing the springy curls of her wig in the process. With the disk lying against her breastbone, she immediately touched her left forefinger to her right eyelid.

An old memory, a fragment of experience, from what seemed a lifetime ago, floated up into consciousness. ... *At the request of the military historian Slotkin, the Jongleur Troupe had assigned Merola and Berzher to witness an ancient battle. The field would be an empty plain in northern Mesopotamia near the Tigris River, where armies composed of foot and horse in numbers on the order of one hundred thousand would come together. With no place of concealment, Berzher suggested flying above the field and masking the ship with static charges to attract a cloud of the ambient dust.*

Merola's task was to identify the two kings and their protective cohorts—Alexander and his Companion Cavalry, Darius and his Immortals—and determine the exact moment and conditions under which the latter broke and ran.

"How will I see through all your dust?" she complained.

Berzher paused in adjusting the fittings of his combat chassis. "Climb out on the spar," he said, "and stick your head through the charge field. Try not to attract the attention of archers. ..."

That was all. Merola had a vague recollection of witnessing such a battle and seeing the Persian king turn and gallop away in his chariot, which precipitated the route of his army. So she had completed her task—without drawing any arrows—and reported back to the Troupe. But that mission apparently had nothing to do with the predicament she now found herself in. Why was she in Nortamerica, twenty-three hundred years later, stranded among the indigenous population? The only useful information she had recovered from the ... neural imprint ... in the locket was this memory of Berzher. He was the sleeping friend. His true form was a circuit matrix of layered metal and glass, now lying at the bottom of her backpack covered in underwear and socks.

Satisfied, but no further enlightened, Merola shouldered her pack, picked up her suitcase, and let herself out the front door. She locked it and pushed her key through the mail slot. With all of her careful planning, collected resources, and Jongleur training—plus a measure of luck—she expected never to see this house again.

27. The Children of Willie Mays

"What is that *smell?*" Beckah Courtnay asked the Silent Three as they walked through the concourse between the upper and lower tiers of seats. This was their first—and Courtnay hoped only—visit to the new ballpark constructed for the San Francisco Giants at Willie Mays Plaza, on Third Street near the Bay.

The strange siblings were masquerading as her grandchildren for this excursion. They had traveled half a continent, from Saint Louis to San Francisco, through the stratosphere in a winged tube made of fragile aluminum, whisking more than seven miles up and 1,700 miles away. In this paranoid age, members of a coven could only arrange to use such high-risk transportation if one of them pretended to be an adult and take responsibility for ticketing, transfers, and customs declarations when necessary. In truth, Courtnay didn't have more than 200 years on the girl, and only 250 on the twins. She was actually shorter than any of them. But, lacking access to genetic manipulation, the days when Beckah could pass for a child herself without absurd amounts of facial filler and flesh-toned caulking were a distant memory.

She watched the three heads turn slightly toward each other. She couldn't prove that the Silent Three communicated telepathically, but no one had ever heard them speak to one another. Actually, Gjordge and Giuffre Ramsay had never been heard to speak at all. In encounters with outsiders, Genjifer Ramsay spoke for the three.

"Garlic fries," she said now. "They sell them on the mezzanine."

Courtnay gulped at the thought. "Potatoes, hot oil ..."

"And crushed garlic. Chopped parsley, too."

"People actually eat such garbage?"

"As a treat," Genjifer said.

"They'd have to be starving!"

"They are all quite well fed. They pay for the privilege of eating garlic fries. Would you like to try some?" The girl's jade-green eyes gleamed with malice. It seemed to be the only human emotion of which she was capable.

Courtnay closed her eyes. "No, thank you. ... Never."

The four of them walked out onto the playground behind the left-field wall, dominated by an immense brown baseball glove and a steel framework with the shape and labeling of a giant soda bottle. Courtnay and her protégés had come to the park on an overcast day in June, not to attend the performance but to meet with their opposite numbers in this city. Where else but on a playground could not-children and their tiny, doting not-grandparent meet openly without official sanction? And, to Courtnay at least, a ballpark was most suitable for the subject under discussion.

However, of the dozen or so children running around with no apparent supervision and—Courtnay did a double-take at this—climbing up into the Coca-Cola bottle and emerging seconds later from its bottom, she could see none that looked to be other than ... children.

"We're wasting our time with these people," she announced to the air.

"If you leave now, you won't get what you came for," said a voice below Beckah's elbow.

She turned and found a boy of nine, sitting on the pavement, tying a sneaker.

"Excuse me, young man?"

"You're Courtnay, right?"

"You have me at a disadvantage."

"I'm Osip, part of the welcoming committee." He looked around, raised the orange-and-black Giants cap off his head and resettled it. Five others appeared out of the rush of activity. These were children who were suddenly not ... children.

"If you don't wish to be disturbed," Osip said, "we should appear to be playing a game."

Beckah Courtnay nodded to the Silent Three.

Genjifer Ramsay shook her head, then nodded to Gjordge and Giuffre.

The twins looked uncertain. Finally, Giuffre made a half-hearted push against the shoulder of one of the not-girls, stepped back, and ran in a half circle—the best he could do to imitate a game of tag. The woman he had pushed followed him. Three of the others broke off their staring to join in.

Gjordge turned and gave Beckah a push. She just glared at him.

Osip sighed. "Well, at least that provides *some* cover," he said. "Anyway, as I told you on the phone, we found your Jongleur—*again*. She's been living in the city since last December."

"No, she's dead," Genjifer objected. "We dropped a whole toy store on her and her robot."

"Yes," Osip replied, "and didn't *that* create a problem for us!"

Courtnay looked sideways at the Ramsay woman. In the affair of the McGwire ball, she had trusted the Silent Three to handle the details discreetly. She had never inquired into their methods or the extent of the damage they might cause.

Her coven in Saint Louis made a good living by using their unique view of history to make strategic investments: gambling, sports betting, real estate, the stock market—although going to *that* well once too often carried the risk of exposure. More recently, they had branched out into offering select clients their own form of security and protective counseling. And when they could spot a good thing, they moved to retrieve lost artifacts. The most lucrative of these were balls, bats, gloves, and bits of uniform that appeared at their local baseball park,

Busch Stadium, under conditions likely to make them valuable. The McGwire ball had been a routine pickup, sold the following day to a Boston collector, Randolph Stephenson, for one million dollars.

And then scandal had erupted. Nine months later, well into the new season, Stephenson was admiring his prizes and suddenly paid attention to the scuff marks on that ball. He took it out of the case, sent it for analysis by what passed for professional scientists in this century, and obtained a disturbing report:

"Dissection with a micro-needle and microscopic inspection of the impact area show the cotton fibers in the windings and the collagen of the leather cover to be flattened rather than dented. There is only one impact area, rather than the expected two—one from contact with the bat, the other from striking the sign on the stadium wall below the bleachers. There is no sign of impact made by a rounded surface such as a bat. The flattened surface is embedded with silicon crystals, rather than flecks of paint. The configuration and chemistry of the crystals suggest fragments of glazing spalled from the surface of ceramic tiles."

Someone had slammed that ball against a wall or floor, probably in a bathroom or locker room, to suggest its having been hit in play by a batter. Courtnay's people had retrieved a fake, one substituted within seconds of the record-breaking home run. Only someone who knew the value of the ball in advance, and exactly where it would land, could have made such an exchange—someone else from the ball's future.

Stephenson's lawyer had contacted Beckah Courtnay's sales agent, expressing outrage and threatening legal action. Courtnay obtained the ball itself by her own means and had her people study it with more advanced methods. Skin cells carrying a peculiar DNA signature—a remarkably streamlined and efficient DNA, barely human anymore—had told their own story. Courtnay put the word out among the refugee covens living around the United States, warning of a Jongleur incursion and providing copies of the trace DNA for matching. She returned the ruined ball to Stephenson in the same unobtrusive way she got it.

She heard nothing from any of the covens for a year and a half. Then, six months ago, in December, the San Francisco coven had responded to her alert with a sighting in the downtown F.A.O. Schwarz toy store: nine points of convergence on a phenotype interpreted from the DNA. Courtnay immediately dispatched the Silent Three to deal with the intrusion, obtain the original baseball, and swap it for the fake. After that, Courtnay never heard anything more about the matter—not from anyone.

In the tiny, gossip-ridden community of sports aficionados, she had been waiting all those months for Stephenson and his lawyers to follow up with a suit and so expose her for fraud by making the affair public. But instead, the problem with the McGwire ball had simply faded away. In fact, it had disappeared entirely—no scandal or lawsuit, but also no follow-up letter of apology from Stephenson, no sign of anything but a fully satisfied customer. At the time, Courtnay simply assumed the Silent Three had been as efficient and unobtrusive as always.

Now, however, she doubted. "What did you do?" she asked Genjifer Ramsay.

"We eliminated the Jongleur, per your instructions."

"And you returned the baseball?" Courtnay prompted.

"Ball? There was no ball. Just the Jongleur and her robot."

"And yet you chose to drop an entire building on them?"

"With more than a hundred other people," Osip put in.

"You wanted her dead," Ramsay said with a shrug.

Courtnay closed her eyes. "But now it appears she's not dead."

"Even if she survived, she has no way to return to her own time. We took her suit and critical parts of her ship."

"Which left an angry Jongleur alive in our territory," Osip said. "Of course, we thought she was dead, too. But when we started correlating events, we found—"

Courtnay made a slashing motion that shut him up and turned to Genjifer Ramsay. "If you didn't retrieve the McGwire ball, then how did it get back to our client?"

"What ball?" the young woman asked blankly.

"The one that gave us the Jongleur's DNA!"

"All I know is you sent us to eliminate a Jongleur who touched down in San Francisco last year."

Courtnay froze. *She* remembered the faked McGwire ball. She remembered how it yielded traces of eleventh-millennium DNA. She remembered Stephenson's threats about that ball, too—threats that disappeared just as quickly and mysteriously as the affair had blown up. Apparently, the theft resolved itself—by itself. There could only be one explanation.

"It's a paradox!" Inspiration struck. "One that the Jongleurs must have created themselves!"

"Jongleurs don't believe in paradoxes," Osip pointed out.

"More fool they!" Courtnay said. "The Jongleurs have not seen the broken ends of existence that we encounter daily. But ... now that I think of it, Jongleurs don't steal artifacts, either. It's part of their moral code or something. So this one must have gone off the reservation, and her superiors caught her at it. They took corrective action—and created their own paradox. Then they failed to seal the breach in all dimensions. Fools!"

She turned on Osip her full attention. "You know where the Jongleur woman is hiding?"

"Well ..." For the first time, the not-child looked embarrassed. "We know where she might have been."

"Explain."

"There was a big story in the local papers, back in April, about a fabulous daylight jewel robbery. You probably heard about it in Saint Louis, too. Amore Eterno? A gang of children made off with about five million in gems, rings, and bracelets. No one ever identified them because the children were too cleverly disguised."

Courtnay shook her head.

"Well, we immediately suspected another coven was poaching our territory," he said. "The plan was really quite ingenious. You see, first these pre-teen girls went into the store and did some kind of dance, then the ringleader went in and—"

Courtnay cut him off. "What made you suspect the Jongleur?"

"Children don't act like that. Not *real* children. And if your Jongleur survived and was stuck in this time frame without her suit and ship"—here Osip glanced at Genjifer Ramsay—"then she would need money for expenses."

"What expenses? The robbery was in April, so the Jongleur had already been living here for several months without money."

"That occurred to us, too. And the fact that, to pull off her theft, she must have made contacts among the local children. That implied attending school, having a family, living like an actual child. Only she couldn't have acquired a real family. So the next best thing—"

"Some sort of foster family," Courtnay concluded. "Of course, you checked with social services."

"We didn't have to. By the time we got that far, she had already disappeared. Police are now circulating a missing persons report. The facial points match your

DNA trace. The report says she was using the name 'Mary Jane Doe'—although that's a funny one to pick."

"No, it means she was never actually identified," Courtnay said. "She might have been suffering from amnesia—or playing at it." She looked at Genjifer Ramsay. "Perhaps your work is done for you."

Osip snorted. "I said she had disappeared, not died. The robbery proves she was in full possession of her faculties. It took time for her to make contacts and arrange the theft, then more time to convert the jewelry into cash without raising suspicions. But when she was ready to move, she left."

"She *can't* go home," Genjifer insisted. "We took her suit and ship."

"It's my guess *she's* now looking for *you,*" Osip said with obvious satisfaction.

Ramsay glared at him. "I'm not afraid of a ghost!"

"Then I suggest you get about locating this Mary Jane Doe," Courtnay said, "before she comes up behind you and bites you on the ass."

28. Six Dials

Merola Tsverin, in disguise as Madeline Stonecraft, landed at Heathrow in the bright sunshine of a June morning. It was her first experience of so many things.

She had her first high-altitude flight in the closed cabin of a jet airplane—rather than hanging on the spar of a liteship wearing a biosuit—while flying United Airlines from San Francisco to London on the polar route. She saw for the first time the fabled ice cap, at night, by low-angled moonlight, with every hummock and crevasse thrown into dark-edged relief. She had her first experience of first-class service, because she could afford it, and accepted her first glass of the sweet, bubbling yellow beverage called "champagne," because she had never tasted it. The refills had kept coming until, after the seventh brimming flute, the flight attendant made a face and said, "Gee, honey, you sure can hold your liquor."

"The air in here is so dry," Merola offered with a shy smile. "And I'm thirsty."

Then she examined the woman's comment and, in turn, the effect this champagne was having on her. It was doing virtually nothing—not even satisfying her thirst or particularly wetting her throat—compared to the stimulation and euphoria that alcohol was rumored to bring to adults of this reference now. She discovered that her body chemistry had either been designed, or had evolved over the millennia, to be immune to alcohol. Merola decided that—as tradeoff for the other rumored effects: insanity, depression, and physical deterioration—she had gotten the best of the exchange.

"Well, why don't you have some salmon to wash it down with?" the attendant suggested.

So Merola also discovered smoked salmon on that flight. Her craving was both immediate and infinite. And it was all free with the service.

Arriving at the United Kingdom Customs station inside the airport, Merola presented her luggage for inspection. Having lived among these humans for more than six months, she had the good sense neither to declare, nor display, nor admit to the amounts of raw gems, jewelry-grade gold, and cash she was carrying. She understood that goods stolen in one jurisdiction would still be considered stolen in another, even on the other side of the world. However, no border guard was going to find her stash of valuables, although this one was certainly trying.

"What's this, miss?" the uniformed agent said, having dug through her underwear to the bottom of the backpack and holding up Berzher's matrix.

"Paperweight," she answered.

"Valuable, miss?"

"Not particularly. Souvenir value only." If only Berzher could hear that! Merola herself didn't believe what she was saying.

"Welcome to London, miss."

She was free. Following directions she had gleaned from the internet, she found the exchange shop and traded her ready supply of dollars for English pounds sterling. Then she located the Underground station, rode the Piccadilly Line into the city, and counted stops down from Green Park, to Piccadilly Circus, to Leicester Square—which she didn't even try to pronounce, even to herself—and finally Covent Garden. She left the car, climbed to street level, and looked around.

In contrast with San Francisco's downtown, which had been a canyoned landscape of twenty- and thirty-story skyscrapers containing offices, hotels, and condominiums, with the city's best restaurants on the top floors, this London was a much homier place. It was more like the Lune of her reference now. The buildings here were no more than four or six stories tall. Trees shaded the side streets. People were walking more than driving. It almost felt like home. Almost.

Merola took an angle from the sun, faced north and west, and started walking herself. After some right-angle turns, she entered what appeared to be a side street and saw what she was looking for at the far end: a column standing in the middle of an intersection. She walked forward and emerged into an open square, the meeting place of seven such streets. She looked up to the top of the column, counted, and found that it was true. There were only six sundials. She had arrived.

Approaching more closely, she stepped up on the circular curb and touched the column's base. All she felt was cold concrete. Merola hadn't really expected to feel the energy hum of an interdimensional portal. That would have been too obvious—and too susceptible to accidents with the locals. But she had to try anyway.

Now, if she were an artifact or a gathering place for Voyageurs, where would she be? What would she look like? What subtle signs would she give? Merola looked around and saw ... nothing. Nothing out of place. It was all strange, of course, all second-millennial architecture, signage, people, and cultural fragments.

She put her suitcase and backpack on the bench that was cast into and surrounded the column's base. She sat down herself.

This search might take some time.

29. All in a Night's Work

It had been ages, as Glyph counted time, since he had visited this particular dimension from among the thousands that cut across the Branching Universes. On that earlier occasion, he had been following the energy patterns of three brightly malicious minds: Genjifer, Gjordge, and Giuffre Ramsay. They had led him to a multi-dimensional traveler, a female different from all others in this dimension, whom they had targeted for destruction and perhaps had even killed.

As the mind of the traveler wavered near death, Glyph had pulled from it fragments of memory, isolated images: a wilderness with something hidden; a wooded, heavily overgrown ravine somewhere nearby; a shallow cave marked by three glowing rocks, and ... something hidden. He did not know what exactly lay within the cave, but he sensed from the traveler's growing sense of fear and anxiety that it was the key to her return to her own time and place. Before he could determine what exactly the secret was, however, he had overtaxed himself and departed involuntarily from this dimension.

Glyph had decided later that she must not return. If she lived, he wanted her trapped where he could find her again. So, by expending exhaustive amounts of energy, he had returned to this dimension without a guide, had located the cave through long and tedious searches, and there he had discovered parts of a concealed ship, a survival suit, and a small metal-and-ceramic robot. He had to crouch low and compress his body even to enter the cave, but he paused there to gloat over his find.

Then Glyph had returned to the site again and again during more than a year of his own time—but mere flashes of appearance within the cave, each one separated from the last by just fractions of a second. After he discovered and identified these objects as belonging to the traveler, he had returned to take samples of their composition, to concoct and test the enzymes and technologies that might destroy them, and finally to do the work of destruction itself. After much poking and probing, Glyph had located the ship's power source. When he tried to pry the object free of its restraints, it disappeared in front of his face with a *buzz* and a *snap!* Glyph regretted not being able to take it for his own, but destroying it was a satisfactory alternative.

With the trapping of the traveler accomplished, Glyph had gone on about his business, turned his attention to other affairs, and waited patiently for her to reappear. He had lost sight of the traveler herself, but he had always known he would find her again in time, because the malice of the dark girl, Genjifer, would lead him to her. So, when he chose to concentrate on the problem, he looked for the three Ramsays and sampled their thoughts.

Now—in a *now* that bore no relationship to the time frame of these other-dimensional beings—Glyph saw the dark girl and her brothers return to the city that their minds called "San Francisco," where they had collapsed the building. They moved now with purpose and urgency, and that always attracted Glyph's attention. They moved to the place of safety into which the body of the traveler had once disappeared. Glyph strained his attention, and he followed.

30. Long Lost Relatives

Shannon Carter, RN, answered the page that sent her to the waiting area of San Francisco General's pediatrics unit. There she found one of the associate administrators, Alan Roth, and three strangers. Roth was a tall man, over six feet, and compared to him the others were Munchkins who barely came up to his hip: a narrow-featured woman with short, dark hair, and two men—twins, by the look of them—similar enough to her that they might have formed a family group. A sober and watchful family group, all dressed in dark wool suits with stiff white shirts and black silk cravats. Carter immediately put them down for Mormons, or Mennonites.

"Ah, here she is!" Roth announced to his guests as she came up. "Miss Ramsay, this is Miss Shannon Carter, one of the nurses working the unit at the time your—?"

"Niece," the Ramsay woman supplied.

"—niece was brought to us. Shannon, Miss Ramsay and her—?"

"Brothers."

"—are relatives of our mystery girl." He turned to the three strangers but actually spoke for Carter's benefit. "She was admitted as a 'Mary Jane Doe' right after the gas explosion at the F.A.O. Schwarz toy store, back in December. Shannon, you remember Mary Jane, don't you?" He produced a file from hospital records and handed it to Carter.

Of course she remembered the prepubescent girl with the wild eyes and the strength of a hyena, medical history unknown but cancer suspected—because of her utter hairlessness and hysterical reaction to intravenous medication, although no trace of the disease was ever found—who had come into the ER nearly naked, except for her own designer blonde wig. Carter was still undergoing physical therapy as a result of their encounters.

"Of course I remember Mary Jane!" she said. Carter put out her hand to the young woman, who merely looked at it and looked away. She offered to shake with the nearest of the brothers, and he took her hand gingerly, as if she was giving him a not-quite-fresh mackerel.

"Miss Ramsay has offered to pay Mary Jane's medical bills," Roth continued. "And since we're well beyond the billing cycle, she has even agreed to pay the interest."

"How nice for you," Carter said, with only a trace of sarcasm.

"Ah—but first she and her brothers need some information," he finished lamely.

The Ramsay woman seemed to come alive as if on cue. "Yes, we need to know her condition when delivered here."

"Shouldn't you be asking the attending physician?" Carter said.

"Dr. Collins moved to Portland in private practice," Roth supplied. "We called, but no response yet."

"Okay, then ..." Carter sat down on one of the lounges and gestured for the others to do likewise. "Excuse me, but I spend the whole day on my feet."

"Of course," Roth said, settling across from her.

The three Ramsays looked at each other, then at the two much larger people on either side of the space where they were obliged to sit. The three siblings seemed to be evaluating the tactical advantage of these positions. One of the brothers shrugged, and they all sat.

"Before we begin," Carter said, opening the file and drawing a pen from her pocket, "does she have a name? She appeared to have amnesia, and we only knew her as a Jane Doe. My supervisor added the 'Mary' to lighten the mood, you might say."

"Smith," the woman said. And after a slight pause, "Mary Smith."

"What a coincidence." Carter wrote the name in the file. "And date of birth?"

Ramsay looked at her brothers—locked eyes with them, actually—then began reciting: "Sixteen. May. Nineteen … ninety … no, eighty-nine."

"Thank you, and where was she from, originally?"

"Visiting from out of town." Ramsay suddenly shook her head. "Can you answer our questions, please? What was her condition?"

All right, time to satisfy a paying customer. "Well, amnesia, as I said—although no major head trauma." Carter checked the chart. "A few minor lacerations and contusions. No broken bones or obvious internal injuries. She was agitated and confused, as anyone would be who had gone through an experience like that. But we all felt something more might be going on."

"Define 'something more.' "

"I don't know. She acted like … she was operating in enemy territory."

The three locked eyes again, then turned their faces straight ahead.

"But she was not physically damaged," the Ramsay woman said.

"No, remarkably good shape, in fact, considering," Carter said.

"I want to assure you," Roth inserted smoothly, "that every treatment we gave her was medically necessary and in compliance with hospital protocols." He was obviously defending the bill. Carter glanced at the totals and they were whoppers. Served the little monkey right—and her crazy family.

"Thank you," the Ramsay woman said.

The brother in the middle reached into his breast pocket and took out what appeared to be a cigar case. He removed the end cap and exposed two glass vials—no, thick syringes or darts—loaded with silvery liquid, each with a steel needle embedded in the end. He handed one to his sister, who was seated nearest to Shannon Carter, the other to the brother seated nearest to Alan Roth.

"What are those?" Carter asked suspiciously. "You can't have those in—"

Before she could finish the sentence, the woman brought the dart down on Carter's thigh, inserting the needle straight through her nylon uniform and pantyhose. It went deep into the muscle, and Carter could feel some kind of gas charge driving in the liquid. The brother with the dart did the same for Roth.

Carter had never heard of an intramuscular injection working so fast. Before she could cry out, draw back, or even flinch, she was immobilized head to toe. If she had not been sitting comfortably, if she had been at all unbalanced or on the edge of her seat, Carter would have toppled over like a stiff-jointed doll. The Doe file—now the Smith file—slid out of her fingers and hit the floor.

The sister and two brothers, Mormons or Mennonites, stood up. The woman retrieved the file. Next, she stared deeply into, first, Carter's uncomprehending gaze—a blaze of green fire, the color of clear jade—and then into Roth's. The three turned, nodded to each other, and walked off down the corridor. As they drew farther and farther away, they faded from Shannon Carter's mind, until the whole episode was gone.

She sat frozen like that for some minutes, maybe hours, possibly days. People might have passed through the waiting area, although none paused to notice her imitation of a statue. Gradually she could feel her limbs come back alive, with the pins-and-needles sensation of paresthesia. She worked her jaw.

"How are your feet?" The voice was Alan Roth's. He was sitting on the lounge across from her.

"Still tingling," she replied.

"You said you spend most of the day on them."

"I ... and just when did I say that, Alan?"

"You asked if we could sit down."

"What were we talking about?"

"Um ... medical records."

"Did you bring them?"

"I guess I forgot."

"Well, next time," she said, getting up—supporting herself on the armrest to get up. "It's been nice chatting with you, I think."

"Yes, you, too." He stood up shakily himself and walked off down the corridor.

31. Bed and Breakfast

Merola spent most of the morning wandering around the Seven Dials neighborhood, shouldering her backpack and lugging her suitcase. She found nothing that looked like an inter-time transfer station. In fact, after accepting the strangely toy-like nature of the district, more attuned to rich tourists and young professionals than anyone who might live there, she found nothing unusual at all.

There was a theater—or in this case, a "theatre"—on one corner of the intersection, which advertised a "musical" by the name of "The Beautiful Game." Only by studying the marquee and the posters in detail could Merola decipher that is was not an actual contest but a story of violent religious struggle concerning young people in a district called Northern Ireland, set to music and with much dancing and singing. Very strange.

For the rest, Seven Dials was a place of coffee houses, tiny restaurants, boutique shops, financial consultancies, and a spa—which sounded like an old-fashioned drinking establishment but was actually a place of rest and physical culture. The atmosphere of Seven Dials reminded her of certain neighborhoods in San Francisco: neat, clean, politely spoken, and utterly commercial.

Finally, nearing exhaustion after her long polar flight and her tour of the neighborhood, Merola spotted a sign back on Earlham Street near the crossroads. The name "Carrefour House" meant nothing to her, but the smaller letters in gold reading "Bed and Breakfast" caught her attention. It was after noon, local time, so she doubted they could give her breakfast, but a bed sounded nice. No, at this late hour, as far as her biological clock was concerned, a bed was suddenly necessary.

Inside the double doors with their wide panels of tempered glass, Merola discovered a mahogany-wood counter with a marble top and, behind it, a woman. She was young according to the lifespans in this reference now—somewhere in her third decade—with long, blonde hair plaited into a wide braid. When she turned away for a moment, Merola could see it went down her back. She wore a dress of plain gray cotton and an apron of starched white linen. Her name tag read "Sabina."

"Can I help you, dear?" the young woman asked.

"I need a bed, a place to rest," Merola said as the door shut behind her.

"We have those, certainly. For how many nights?"

"I ... am not sure yet. One night, certainly."

"May I see your identification?"

Merola handed over her passport, California driver's license, and two credit cards. The woman handed the latter back, saying, "Let's not get ahead of ourselves."

She had Merola fill out a paper form with an ink pen, and then took one of the cards for her reading machine. She handed Merola a brass key on a ring with an oval plastic tag as big as her palm bearing the name Carrefour House—"in case you forget and leave it somewhere."

"Thank you," Merola said, staring stupidly at the key.

"Number three is on the second floor—up these stairs—far end of the hall, on the front. Do you want help with your bags?"

"No, thank you." Merola hefted the suitcase. "I can manage."

"Welcome to Carrefour House, Miss Stonecraft."

Merola turned back, momentarily confused. "Who?"

The woman stared. "Aren't you Miss Stonecraft?"

"Oh, yes. I guess I am."

"You must be jet-lagged."

"Is that what it is?"

Once in the room, it took Merola all of two minutes to shed her clothes, prop her wig on the bureau, and crawl naked beneath the covers. She didn't remember falling asleep. Her mind sank effortlessly into blackness. And just as quickly, she came out of it.

She had no sense of time having passed, but the street beyond her window was now dark, except for the deflected yellowed cones of public street lighting. She consulted her senses and remembered sounds of movement: the opening and closing of doors, the running of water in sinks and toilets, but those had been going on at irregular intervals all night. No, the sounds that had actually awakened her were something else, a series of deep thumps—and something like music.

She pulled on her wool skirt and blue blouse, arranged the wig on her skull, picked up her room key, and went barefoot out into hallway. With one hand on the doorknob, in case she needed to retreat suddenly, Merola watched and listened.

Nothing. Nothing. And then three loud thumps.

They came from a tall wooden cabinet that stood across the hall and back down toward the center of the building.

Merola let her own door close and slid the room key into her pocket. She approached the cabinet and placed an ear against its panels. Very faintly, she could hear a musical ringing with a jarring undertone, like frozen bells.

The doors of the cabinet were locked—which meant nothing to a Jongleur. Merola applied everything she had learned about breaking and entering on Searches in and around the twenty-first century, including her explorations of Emily Windlace's house. She knew that any storage space in regular use by more than one person, such as maids in a hotel, usually had some easy and unofficial means of access. She ran her fingers up and down the back of the cabinet, where the sides failed by a centimeter-wide gap to meet the wall, and over and under the moldings carved around its panels. She quickly found a small brass key that fit the lock.

The doors swung out to reveal shelves loaded with piles of white sheets and towels. Merola was about to close the doors when she noted that the creases and folds of the items were gray with dust. No one had used these linens in a very long time. A moment's further study showed her a curiosity in the structure of the shelves: not one but two vertical boards, set side by side, divided the center, as if the cabinet's interior was built as two separate units. She grasped one set of shelves and gently pulled, twisted, pushed—until a catch inside released and the shelves swung out and away. Another push opened the opposite set of shelves.

Merola was looking into a small antechamber, a space that obviously extended past the back panel of the cabinet and into the wall behind. Facing her on the far side of this antechamber was an arrangement of three mirrors. She had seen something like them in the thrift shop where she bought her grown-up clothes. She stepped into the cabinet and stood in the mirrors' focal point. She could see herself from the sides and, by turning this way and that, from the back. In the shop, she had recognized this as a crude, optical version of the hybridized retinal membrane that people in her own reference now used to see themselves in full perspective. Still, it was an odd thing to put inside a linen closet.

Beside the right-hand mirror was a switch, which she supposed turned on a light above the mirror set. But it wasn't like the light switches she knew from San Francisco; this was a heavy, two-bladed knife switch of the kind Merola had seen in the fuse box of the Windlace house, for handling high-voltage electricity.

She was about to turn and leave, when that musical sound came again—now from *behind* the mirrors. Without thinking, Merola pulled the switch down into contact.

What had been three solid mirrors and nine visible planes expanded geometrically: six solid and eighteen visible, twelve and thirty-six, twenty-four and seventy-two, until Merola was staring into a maze of reflections, some with her own face and body, some strangely empty, and some that even from the oddest of angles could not be her. One showed a woman who was much taller, dressed in somber browns and reds, and moving in a hurry across the field of view.

Merola reached forward with her hand, to touch the central mirror, and other hands reached toward her. As her fingertip met the glass, she found that it was not quite glass anymore, but something colder and yet more fluid. A dark patch slid under her finger, and her hand pushed through. The patch expanded and, before she could check herself, Merola walked through.

In the darkness, she sensed other mirrors, black ones that drank the light, or rather the tarnished-silver backing of mirrors facing outward, showing beyond them misty passages and rooms filled with yet more mirrors.

Someone passed in front of one of these dark mirrors. It was a white-haired young woman in a suit made of large iridescent bubbles that joined and rotated across each other at shoulder and elbow, hip and knee. She was naked underneath them. Her hair floated weightless inside the bubble that covered her head and shoulders.

Merola turned toward movement in a second mirror. It was a man wearing a purple-striped Roman toga and crowned with a laurel wreath. He seemed to be in a hurry, talking over his shoulder to others, now invisible, who apparently followed behind him.

The shadow in a third darkened mirror caught her eye. She moved toward it.

This too was a person, but unlike any Merola had ever seen. The face was not human, more like that of a pug dog, wrinkled and flattened, with a flaring, wet nose, bulbous, brown eyes barely contained in their sockets, and a thrusting lower jaw. Perhaps that squashed face was merely suggested by the shape of the skull, which was flatter and wider than any human's. The body was stranger still, with a long torso bent forward at the waist—or rather, at the second waist. The creature paused as it moved across the mirror and turned slightly. Accentuated by the overlapping folds of its flowing, iridescent garment, the body displayed a pair of shoulders and arms just below the neck of that misshapen head. Then came a pelvic saddle at mid-torso, with a pair of limbs that seemed to be jointed like arms but ended in flattened hands with short, splayed fingers that were thicker and heavier than the first set. Finally, the torso ended in what Merola would normally call hips, tapering into a pair of strong, shapely legs that ended in what could only be called feet. Merola intuited from the way the garment was slotted and tabbed that the middle set of limbs was sometimes used for walking and sometimes for grasping and carrying.

It was the ugliest creature Merola had ever seen— and she had watched the animal world evolve over time and collected samples from much of it. She did not know if this creature was native to Earth or to some other planet accessible through these mirrors. She suddenly knew that it was neither, but a figment of probability, the long-sought and seldom seen Möglich, a Jongleur's darkest nightmare, and she felt fear in her heart.

As if sensing her stare, the creature turned further and looked directly into her mirror. The huge eyes focused and the face twisted in consternation. It drew nearer and nearer to Merola's mirror, and she stepped back into what she hoped were shadows. The globular brown eyes opened wide in astonishment. The lips around the under-thrust mouth pursed in what Merola could only call doubt, and then the head nodded as if reaching a conclusion. The being relaxed its shoulders, dropped its intermediate pelvis to a four-legged stance, turned, and galloped off into a vanishing point beyond the far side of the mirror.

Merola had the strangest notion that, while she had never seen anything like the—the pug dog—before, it was familiar with her kind. And, despite its evident surprise and doubt, it had recognized her for herself.

She turned completely around in the dark space behind the mirror, being careful to note her orientation at all points, counted her steps back to the place she had entered, touched a bright, vaguely silvery spot in the surface there, and stepped back into the linen closet with its real mirrors. She raised the knife switch to turn off whatever circuitry she had activated. She went out into the hallway, closed the false shelf units, closed and locked the cabinet doors, returned the key to its hiding place, and went back to her room.

As she climbed into bed, Merola found she was shaking.

32. Delay Due to Damage

"This is an extremely bad idea," Cinquemain said, studying the new mission parameters—hastily conceived, badly defined parameters that Rydin was obviously making up as he dictated them. "Besides, we've been over that ground before."

"Not on Tsverin's original time cue—before the explosion—and from that point forward," Rydin said. "We have to go back to the beginning of this trouble, discover exactly what went wrong, and intervene if we can."

"You're assuming Tsverin survived. Not an assumption I'd make."

"If she did not survive, then everything ends there, at the start of the third millennium. But since the breach which spawned these six-legged creatures must have occurred much farther upstream, we can only assume that she somehow did survive—or that, without the distraction of the baseball, the blast never occurred—and Tsverin went on to cause real damage."

"Not very linear thinking," Cinquemain sneered. "Remind me how humans managed to climb to the top of evolution's tree."

"Evidently, from what we can see down there—" Rydin gestured toward the riverbank. "—we didn't. Or not the last time."

"Well, I hope those flipper things down there have learned to make a silicon circuit. Otherwise, I may be the last intelligent being on a lonely planet."

"Just set the time on mark, while we still can."

Cinquemain keyed in a temporal point for the morning that Merola Tsverin was supposed to be gathering genetic samples in a downtown toy store. Rydin took a neural imprint—and Cinquemain confirmed his own—so they would remember this valley of monsters as they had found it, against whatever changes they might initiate.

Cinquemain tapped the selvaged singularity, and the green banks and blue-gray river were instantly replaced with a field of stars. He took sightings on the five key features whose relationship signaled the end of the twentieth century, oriented the ship, and shot along the path that the Sol system had followed over the past eight thousand years. In a blink, they were hovering over a blue-green Earth with the dawn terminator moving somewhere west of the Hawai'ian seamounts.

"What will you do if we find six-legged sea lions down there?" he asked.

"I do not know." For once, Rydin spoke plainly, from an emotional level deeper than Cinquemain's synthetic personality could interpret.

"You realize we'll be coming down over a city of three-quarters of a million people, in broad daylight, with every radar system active, and hundreds if not thousands of pairs of eyes looking up at the sky at any one time."

"Can you vary the frequency of the ship? Muddle our visual signature?"

"I can triple the charge on the panels. That will make them glow with luminescence and help disguise them against the sky's natural scattering of the blue wavelength. It should also deflect any radar signals."

"Do it," Rydin instructed.

"There's a danger—"

"Just do it."

They dropped down above San Francisco in a faintly shimmering bubble of energy. Cinquemain quickly located the toy store and approached the roof from the street side. "Now what?"

"Observe the people," Rydin said. "Does anyone seem out of place?"

"Compared to what? I don't see any sea lions, if that's what you mean."

"Two legs, two arms. Men and women ... and children entering the store."

"Do you want to set down on the roof and go inside? We might make contact."

"No, I just want to observe the patterns," Rydin said.

"Look there! Just coming out of the main entrance ..."

"Three children, walking in formation, a perfect triangle."

"Not children, Coel! And see what they're holding!"

Before Cinquemain could complete the thought, the three Flüchtlinge turned their faces skyward and stared directly at the bedazzled liteship. Then the crowd closed around them and they disappeared with their trophies.

An instant later, the roof of the building began to jump in parallel waves of a timed explosion, from the far back corner to the front. Successive crests of dark dust rose and fell, each mixed with fragments of tar, streamers of fiberglass insulation, fist-sized pieces of concrete, and finally shards of glass. A length of rusted steel rebar as long as Cinquemain's main extensors whickered out of the cloud and struck two of the ship's hyper-charged panels.

San Francisco disappeared with a *buzz* and a *snap!*

————

Rydin recovered a second or two after Cinquemain, whose circuits lacked a startle reflex and seemed unaffected by sudden temporal dislocations. All around the liteship were stars, with one in the near distance appearing particularly bright.

Discharge from the singularity through the panels must have thrown them into space again. With a sudden flush of cold sweat, Rydin realized that if he had taken off his biosuit or merely cracked his helmet seals, he would by now have become suddenly and irreversibly dead. He touched the lens above his right eye, but no revelations came to him.

"Where are we?" Rydin asked Cinquemain.

"Somewhere downstream of where we were."

"Is that our Sun?" He pointed to the nearby star.

The little robot checked its instruments. "Yes ... about three light-hours distant, I think. That makes it six months after the explosion point."

"Get us back to—there—then. We need to find Merola."

"Not with this ship, Coel. We've blown two panels and our singularity may be partly sealed. I think I can get us to Earth in this time frame. I can't guarantee more."

"Then we'll go back to our reference now and get another ship."

"Do you ever *listen* to yourself?" Cinquemain scolded. "We *can't* travel temporally. And even if we could, are you going to ask the *sea lions* for another liteship? This one, damaged as it is, may be the last liteship in our universe."

Rydin realized he still wasn't thinking straight. "All right ... So ... Do we have anything to our advantage?"

Cinquemain paused for a long time—longer than a machine should pause in any exchange with a human. "Well ... We know that whatever Merola did to invite the six-legged sea lions to devour our world ... she, um ... she probably hasn't done it yet. She's still moving sideways."

"Or she was, as of six months ago," Rydin corrected. "Who knows what the woman's up to now?"

"The answer lies over that way," the robot indicated the bright star.

Rydin nodded. "Please take us there."

33. THE HAUNTED HOUSE

When Sam Gill went down in the morning to greet his guests at breakfast, he found the new one, the American woman, sitting by herself at a table in the corner. She was breaking apart a scone with her fingers, ignoring the clotted cream and current jam, putting each fragment in her mouth and chewing diligently, staring at nothing. Well, Sabina had said the woman was thoroughly jet-lagged, and perhaps she was still recovering. Madeline Stonecraft was the name Sabina mentioned.

"Good morning, madam," Gill said, approaching her table. "How are you feeling this morning?"

She turned her blank stare on him. It took a moment for her to focus, another for her to speak. "Who are you?"

"I'm your host at Carrefour House." He bowed slightly. "Sam Gill."

She nodded, broke off more scone, and ate it. "You run this hotel?"

"It's a family business. I believe you met my daughter yesterday."

"Sabina. Sabina Gill. Sam Gill." She shook her head. "I don't know ..."

"Pardon me?" he said. "Do I detect we've let you down in some way?"

Stonecraft chewed her scone. "I heard a lot of slams and thumps last night."

"Ah, it's these old buildings. Thick walls tend to carry sounds, you know."

"And a ringing. Almost like music."

"That would be the chimes of St. Giles."

"It didn't sound like church bells."

"No?" Gill said. "Well, then ..."

"It came from inside. Across the hall."

Before he would reply, Gill paused to study this woman. If he were a horse, one might say she had put his wind up.

Madeline Stonecraft was a small person, elfin, almost willowy. That her blonde ringlets were perfectly curled, even at this hour of the morning, suggested either meticulous grooming or a wig. She was well dressed in a dark suit and cream-colored blouse whose cut just missed being the *hautest* of *couture*. Her age was harder for him to determine. The skin of her face, wrists, and hands was as fresh and smooth as a young girl's. Yet from her erect posture, the way she crossed her legs, and her skillful use of makeup, he intuited a mature, physically aware female. And then he considered the stare of those pale gray eyes, which suggested the consciousness of a woman older than his own grandmother.

Sam Gill had never met any mundane remotely like her—except perhaps once, and that was many years ago. To answer her questions, he fell back on the tried-and-true approach for dealing with mundanes. He dropped quickly into the chair across the table from her and lowered his voice. "Can you keep a secret?"

Without speaking, she lifted her chin in acknowledgement.

"Although we don't look it," he went on, "Carrefour House is very old. One of the oldest in the district. Oh, a facelift here and a renovation there, but the structure goes back at least two hundred years." *Or more,* he added silently. No sense in going into details.

"I wouldn't have guessed," she said, shaking her head.

"No. Well, like the best establishments in England, we do have a ghost."

Stonecraft's brow wrinkled. "What is that? Some kind of intelligence?"

It was his turn to look puzzled. "Perhaps intelligent. Our resident spirit—"

"Does it patrol the house? Does it control the basic internal functions?"

"I wouldn't say we let it *control* anything. Just moves around, making noises."

"But it controls the mirror-maze."

"The mir—!" Gill's tongue froze in his mouth, to keep him from asking how she might know about that. Obviously, she had been snooping. Instead, he said, "I don't know what you're talking about."

Stonecraft dismissed his protestations with a wave. "Is your resident intelligence a large creature, six arms or legs or whatever, with the face of a pug dog?" she asked, staring at Gill intently.

Now he was truly puzzled. This woman had certainly opened the cupboard. Perhaps she had ventured inside. She might have bumped into the Zhangs in full Chinese regalia or any of his other exotic guests and transients going about their business. But how she might have encountered a giant pug dog or anything with six limbs was beyond him. None of the station's dimensions intersected nodes beyond this solar system—or not so far as Sam Gill knew. At least, he had never encountered any alien species.

"Really? What a fancy!" He laughed. "You must have been dreaming."

"I don't dream," she replied soberly. "Not once. Not since childhood."

"Well, it must have been a hallucination then. I understand you came over from America yesterday. Jet lag can do that. Let me send Sabina out for a bromide. It will settle your nerves."

"My nerves are—"

Before she could finish, Gill excused himself, stood up, and hurried from the breakfast room. For the first time in decades, he was going to have to do some exploring within his own cupboard.

34. INTERVIEW AT FAMILY & CHILDREN SERVICES

Angela Riccardi was arranging her case folders for the next day's schedule of interviews and home visits when she suddenly felt a silent presence on the other side of the desk. She looked up to find three of the strangest children she had ever seen: two boys and a girl, all in their early teens but dressed in dark suits, like little adults. With their dark hair and sober faces, they were creepy and self-possessed, like the Addams Family. They regarded her with identical owl-like stares. She tried to read their vibe and got ... nothing.

"Can I help you?" she asked, giving her best professional smile.

"We are looking for a female child who was hospitalized with no identity," the dark girl said. "The police told us they brought her to you."

"Well ..." Riccardi consulted her watch: three minutes to five, the end of the workday. Way too late to start a consultation. "Everything we do in this department would depend on what people knew or could find out about her, and what she had to say for herself—"

"She wouldn't say," the dark girl interrupted. "She had amnesia. The hospital admitted her as a 'Mary Jane Doe' and discharged her to the police department. This was six months ago."

Riccardi had to mentally shift gears. The name meant something to her, of course, but she kept her face impassive. There were rules, strict ones, court-ordered rules, about confidentiality in children's cases. She couldn't talk about her clients, present or past, with just anyone who walked into her office. And the girl in question had now left the system and been reported to San Francisco PD as a missing person.

"So you're looking for someone specific," she temporized. "What is she to you?"

The girl turned to stare at the two boys, one after the other. Riccardi got the impression that the boys were identical twins and she was their sister. After these silent exchanges, the girl returned her attention to Riccardi. "She is our cousin. Mary Smith. Age nine years. The police have now issued a missing persons report that gives you, your name, you personally, as the contact."

"And where are her parents?" Riccardi asked.

"There are no parents."

"I see. Do you have a photo, something to show you're related?"

"No photo."

"We need to prove you are her family. Can you describe Mary?"

"She's very thin."

"So are most girls that age. What's she weigh?"

"Less than 36 kilograms."

Riccardi converted in her head. "Color of hair?"

"Blonde," the girl said, "but it's a wig."

That bit of information at least matched a detail in Riccardi's case file. And then a sudden thought struck her. "Had Mary recently been treated with chemotherapy?" she asked.

Once more the silent, three-way consultation. "No," the girl said. "Mary is naturally bald."

"Okay. What about eye color?"

More consultation. "We don't know."

"You never saw her eyes?"

"She is a distant cousin."

"Take a guess. Blue? Brown?"

"We don't make guesses."

"Well," Riccardi said, "unless you can provide a better description—"

"We can provide a DNA profile! You could match that."

"Look, Family and Children Services deals with home situations of abuse and neglect and with runaways. Our clients have a right to privacy. They're not felons, and we don't get involved in paternity issues. We don't do DNA testing."

"Do you take photographs?"

"Of course, that's standard procedure."

"Then perhaps you would let us look through your files." The dark girl pointed at the stack of folders on the desk.

"Out of the question! These matters are confidential," Riccardi said. "Now, I think I've been about as—"

From out of nowhere, from up her sleeve, from her cupped palm, the girl produced a glass vial tipped with a steel needle. She threw it underhand, like a softball pitch. The needle went through Riccardi's suit jacket, blouse, and chemise. It hung from her chest and the vial's contents—a silvery solution like clouded metal—pumped into her body. When the thing was empty, the girl walked around the desk and retrieved it.

Riccardi couldn't move. She could barely breathe. With her unblinking gaze fixed straight ahead, she could only watch from the periphery as the girl and her brothers divided up her folders, flipped through them to check the pictures, and put them back in a stack.

One of the boys turned the monitor of Riccardi's computer to a more convenient viewing angle, slid the keyboard and trackball from under her lifeless hands, and began scrolling the menus. Access to confidential records was no problem for him, since the computer was already logged in with Riccardi's identity and password. He set up a search for "Mary Jane Doe," with parameters for gender and age, and began sorting the department caseload, first the active files, then the closed.

When the face that Riccardi so well remembered—her own case, the strangely reserved little girl, whom she had placed with the Windlaces, who had absconded in June—finally appeared, the boy paused. He stared at the screen, as if memorizing the contents. When he was done, the girl made a flicking gesture, and he used the trackball and pulldowns to delete the file. That command, however, was grayed out. Case managers did not have delete privileges on CFS central records. The boy tried several ways to delete the information and became frustrated, his hands jerky with anger—it was as much emotion as any of the three showed.

The girl quieted him with a hand on his arm, and he stepped away from the computer. Then she pulled Angela Riccardi's chair back slightly from her desk, held her face in two hands, and stared into her eyes. A deep, green haze filled Riccardi's mind.

As they repositioned her chair and body to a more natural angle, Riccardi wondered if she would ever wake up.

35. No Place Like This Place

Merola sat on the bed in her room at Carrefour House. For comfort, she had dug out Berzher's matrix and held it cupped in her hands, just beneath her chin. She had decisions to make, and she would have to make them alone.

Ever since she discovered her locket in Emily Windlace's desk drawer and put it on, Merola's memory had been reassembling and rearranging itself, recovering from the flash of disorientation that struck while she worked at Bill's computer. She now understood her presence in London and the attraction of the Seven Dials district as part of a search for references and artifacts relating to—and an attempt at contact with, if possible—travelers from the future who could help her return to the eleventh millennium and her place in the Jongleur Troupe. What she might have done, in the first place, to be expelled from the Troupe was still a mystery. Merola sensed she was somehow at fault, had ignored some aspect of protocol, and had invited disaster. She could recall only fragments of the mission that brought her to the twenty-first century. She remembered being on Search in the toy store and its destruction through misadventure. She remembered finding the damage done to her backup ship, biosuit, and the spare chassis for Berzher. But what came before was a dark cloud, an impenetrable mental barrier.

Looking for those references and artifacts, she had spent her first day in London exploring Seven Dials. She still had much of it to cover and, after a reasonably continuous night's sleep, she could now do that with a clear head and a judicious eye. Maybe among the trendy spas and designer boutiques she would find a disguised travel agency that planned trips to the future for knowing customers.

But Merola had also found something strange at Carrefour House. She had never encountered a mirror-maze before. She knew from her one entry last night that it was filled with strange people and creatures—at least one of them tantalizingly historical, and the others simply strange. Or rather, it was filled with images. She had never actually interacted with any of them—although that last, the six-legged pug dog, had seemed to become aware of her.

The travelers she was seeking, the Voyageurs, had operated a millennium and more before Merola's own reference now. Rumor said they might have used an interdimensional network, a transit system assembled out of fixed nodes that persisted through time. But other rumors also spoke of portals, of ships, and of hubs. The intervening thousand years had been a tumultuous epoch, with many waves of technological advance rising and falling, growing fragmentation in what had by then become a single, monolingual society, the rebellion and flight of the Flüchtlinge, and an abrupt turn toward a more organic, less mechanical social order.

The newly formed Troupe des Jongleurs had been essential to that unification, establishing rules and precedents for, among other things, time travel. The Jongleur ethos was to create no fixed points, no nodes, in the present or the past. Instead, they adopted a flexible, two-part approach to travel—one temporal, one spatial—that allowed them to move freely without cumbersome networks of nodes and spans. In the process, the Jongleurs had ripped out the old systems and banned the technology, all long before Merola was born.

Convinced of the inherent dangers of interdimensional travel, the Troupe kept no historical archive—no technical descriptions, design records, or manuals—from which such systems could ever be rebuilt. Every trace of them was gone. Even as a Jongleur operative herself,

Merola had no idea of how the nodes might work or what a transfer station might look like, either from the outside or the inside. Carrefour House's mirror-maze *might* be the fixed point of such a station.

But she also had doubts. She knew from her researches with the Windlaces' computer that the nineteenth and twentieth centuries had been a time of strange demonstrations and public displays. She had encountered terms like "fun house," "hall of mirrors," and "camera obscura." She had read about "wax museums" and "tableaux vivants." Being very old, Carrefour House might conceal such antique amusements. And its proprietor, Sam Gill, had denied knowing about the mirror-maze.

He believed the house to be haunted with "ghosts." Merola had pondered that term—until she remembered that people of this reference now believed humans to be possessed of an immortal dimension, a fragment of energy beyond simple cellular metabolism or synaptic activity. Upon dying, they believed, this fragment went off to a better or worse place—a "heaven" or "hell"—but sometimes it remained trapped on Earth, in old houses and buildings, to wander, moan, and scare people. Such fragments of energy might also explain the Roman senator, the bubble lady, and the pug dog.

Merola's head spun with all these possibilities. And then she recalled a bit of nonsense someone had scrawled in chalk on a San Francisco sidewalk: "There is no other place, anything like this place, anywhere near this place, *so this must be the place.*" That jingle helped settle her mind and decide her.

So did a thump in the hallway, followed by chiming music.

Merola got up from the bed, opened the door, and peered out. The hall was empty, but the scratchy musical sounds were coming from the linen cabinet. She determined to wait them out and confront whatever might emerge.

In a minute, the doors pushed open, and Sam Gill's head appeared. He looked one way up the hall, then the other—and saw her. "Miss Stonecraft!"

Merola's face curled into a wicked smile. "Oh dear me!" she mimicked his simpering protests from the breakfast room. "There's no such thing as a mirror-maze in Carrefour House!" Then she sobered. "So, is that a node? Are you running a transfer station?"

He stepped out into the hallway and closed the panels behind him. "I'm really not at liberty to say."

"What if I came from a place and time eight thousand years in your future?"

Gill hesitated, worked out the implications of her statement, and suddenly looked stricken. "You are one of the Jongleurs," he said. "Have you come at last to shut down Crossroads House?"

"That—" She had to pick her words carefully around a novel concept. "—is not my intention."

"I'm glad to hear it. Although, personally, I don't think you can—not from the middle like this. To dismantle a node, you must start either at the beginning, before it's built, or at the end, before the wish to build it first arises."

"I did not come here to dismantle anything," she repeated.

"Nice of you," he said. "And it's thirty-six hundred, actually."

"Excuse me?"

"You are only thirty-six centuries in my future, not all of eighty."

"You are a Voyageur."

"No, but I've dealt with them. We are the Builders, who preceded them."

"Are you the original Builder?"

"Fourth generation. My daughter Sabina will be the fifth on this site."

Merola felt immense relief. All of her doubt and anxiety disappeared. With one long step, from San Francisco to London, she had reached her goal. The rest should be easy.

"Is there someplace we can talk?"

"Come up to the family flat."

36. One Hour Behind

Rydin watched as Cinquemain folded their ship and concealed it under low shrubbery. They were standing on a patch of mowed grass in one of San Francisco's many parks, this one larger and more overgrown than the others.

"Hide it well," he said, "or we're going to be here for a long time."

"It might be a long time in any case, given the damage to this ship."

"I hate working without a backup, when we're already in trouble."

"You thought the trip to Boskin's estate would be near-time, remember?"

"I know. ... I broke protocol," Rydin said. "I won't do it again."

"Yes. And haven't I heard that before?"

Rydin ignored the gibe. He looked down at himself. He was wearing the everyday clothing of his life in Lune: a blue-gray jumpsuit of hybridized spider silk and calyx-wrapped sandals of reinforced poly-aramid. At least it would draw less attention than the seals and joints of his electric-blue biosuit. But there was nothing he could do about his hairless head: for travel near his own time, it had been unnecessary to pack a wig or other disguise. In a flash of inspiration, he retrieved his helmet from the cache, tore out the knitted liner, and put it on his head as a cap.

Cinquemain looked at him critically. "You'll pass."

"Only from a distance. I'm clearly not one of them."

"We're going to a hospital to find the survivor of a massive explosion. You will look like one of the patients— a sick and poisoned child."

"We will not go to the hospital," Rydin said.

"Why not? It's the logical starting point."

"No, a dead end. We know Tsverin survived the blast, which is now six months in the past. If she had been injured so critically as to still require care, the dottori of this time will already have sampled and dissected her, detected her as an alien species of human, and taken her elsewhere for permanent incarceration and detailed study."

"You are working from multiple assumptions," Cinquemain objected. "One, that her injuries were so minor she was quickly treated and released. Two, that throughout this process her cover story—a human child visiting a toy store—was not breached."

"Without freedom of action, she could not have gone sideways."

"All right, I'll play along. So where is she now?"

"We know something about this century," Rydin said. "As a minor child, without family or means of support, she would not be released on the streets. Government systems are in place to provide for the welfare of children. She would be taken into custody as a 'ward of the state.' We need to learn more about this system."

"They have cyber networks in this century, don't they?"

"Very primitive. None you'd consider intelligent."

"All the better to work my persuasive charms."

It was clear that Cinquemain could not leave the relative seclusion of the park in his present form: a battle chassis with crablike appendages and a carapace of hardened ceramic. Methodically, he stripped and cached most of the armor and all but four of the smaller appendages, plus his voder and sensor clusters. With the legs tightly folded, he comprised a package half again bigger than Rydin's two closed fists and would fit into the front pocket of his jumpsuit. Cinquemain could ride that way with one cluster peeking out from beneath the flap.

"Where do we find this cyber system?" he asked.

"I think they call it a library—from their word for 'books.' "

"You'll have to get them off the shelves and turn the pages for me."

Outside the park was a busy street with a bus shelter that contained a stylized map of the city marked with various lettered transit lines. Rydin had neither the intention nor the cash money to ride the system, but he scanned the map until he found the symbol indicating a library. It appeared to be part of a nearby university campus. He checked the sun's angle to establish the waning hours of local daylight and started walking.

As a small, waiflike, and apparently sickly child, he could wander into places where a larger, more threatening persona would be challenged. He walked through the library complex's double doors with a group of young adults, presumably credentialed students of the university, and moved off to the side before they reached the registration desk. He slipped down an aisle lined with bookshelves, at the end of which was a cubicle with high, enclosing sides. Positioned inside this enclosure were a chair and a shelf-table holding a gray reading screen and a fingerboard. Perfect.

He took out Cinquemain's truncated chassis and set it before the screen.

Cinquemain waved his sensors. "You have to find the 'on' switch."

"What does it look like?"

The intelligence briefly consulted a vast database built up over dozens of trips into and around this century. "Try a button or a toggle with a circle cut by a dash."

Rydin noticed that the reading screen stood on a flat box that had such a button. He pushed it. The box made whirring noises, tiny lights flashed on the fingerboard, and the screen came alive with a flicker and displayed a small, highlighted rectangle asking for a "User Name" and "Password."

Cinquemain studied the request. "I calculate too many possibilities. Strange ... I don't detect any modulated electromagnetic signals coming from this device. Check the back of the box and see how many wires you can find."

Rydin leaned forward and pulled the box away from the back wall of the cubicle. "Four—but one goes from the box to the screen, another from the box to the fingerboard."

"Closed circuits," Cinquemain said. "Try one of the others. Pull it out."

He unplugged one, with a three-pronged connection. Everything died.

"That was power, drawing current from the building. Now the other."

Rydin reinserted the power wire, and the machine came back to life. He pulled the last unknown wire, which had a more delicate connection with nine separate pins. The screen went blank and the rectangle with its impossible demands disappeared.

"That's the one," Cinquemain said. "Pull some slack and give me the end."

Rydin tugged on the wire and six more inches of it came haltingly up through a hole in the desktop. He looked under the desk and saw a similar plug connection straining at a socket in the wall. In order to put Cinquemain next to the wire's end, he disconnected the power wire, lifted the dead terminal off the desk, and put it on the floor. With his enhanced musculature he could easily handle the weight.

Cinquemain tiptoed forward on his shortened appendages and studied the nine-pin plug. "I don't have a configuration for that, but—" Faster than Rydin's eye could follow, the intelligence's first two appendages extended manipulators, twiddled screws and nuts, peeled back the plug casing, and exposed nine thin, color-coded wires. Cinquemain attached them in first one order, then another, to various contact patches on his chassis. Finally, the voder made a sound that, coming from a human, might have been a sigh.

"It's amazing how many people will accept you as a 'system administrator' if you just keep insisting," the intelligence said. He communed with the wire for a few seconds. "Writing my own code," he advised Rydin offhandedly. "What is a 'hypertext transfer protocol'?" And then, "Oh, I see. Nested calls." After a moment, he began muttering to himself, "San Francisco City and County. ... Human Services Agency. ... Family and Children Services. Business hours nine to five, Monday to Friday. Offices at One-Seven-Zero Otis Street. ... Is today a Monday or Friday, Coel?"

"How should I know? You're supposed to be keeping the clock."

"I got thrown off by the discharge. I'll bet on a weekday."

"How far away is this Otis Street?" Rydin asked.

"Four kilometers. I now have a map."

While Cinquemain disconnected himself, Rydin replaced the terminal on the desk. He could do nothing about the broken plug. But then, they would be gone before it was discovered. He could only hope Cinquemain had not left digital fingerprints inside the system.

After an hour of fast walking and some wrong turns, because Cinquemain was having trouble correlating the map in his brain with the view from Rydin's pocket, they arrived at the address on Otis Street. They found an older, eight-story building made of pale yellow brick that ran along the street, and next to it was a two-lane entrance blocked by a steel gate painted electric blue. Beyond the gate, across a shallow plaza, was a longer, lower building with windows recessed behind bare concrete planter boxes. The gate was locked and chained.

"Closed for the day," Rydin observed. "We should come back during business hours."

"Nonsense. You'd be nabbed as a ward of the state yourself. This is much better."

Rydin lifted the chain, placed his hands on either side of the primitive, tumbler-driven padlock, and pulled. Nothing. He strained and consciously called up his Simian-ACTN3 strength. Still nothing. "It appears we are being blocked by a half-kilogram of steel and brass."

Before he could complete the thought, a beam flashed from his pocket and cut the chain diagonally. "Good thing, isn't it," Cinquemain said, "that my communications laser packs as a sensor and not as battle gear?"

Together they studied the signage on the buildings, made entry to various ground-level and inner sectional doors, again using Cinquemain's laser, and worked their way down empty corridors to one labeled "Family & Children Services" in large, gold-leaf lettering.

"What, exactly, do we expect to find in here?" Cinquemain asked.

"With luck, more computers."

"Oh, joyous day!"

Instead they found, among the rows of empty offices and cluttered desks, a solitary woman. Rydin drew back quickly when he crossed in front of her open door, but she did not move or call out to him, even though she was staring directly at him. Or rather, staring directly ahead through the doorway into the corridor.

He entered cautiously. The nameplate in front of her read "Angela Riccardi." The woman was slender, dark-haired, professionally dressed, and frozen stiff.

"Is she dead?" Rydin asked.

Cinquemain scanned her. "I detect a pulse—down around ten beats per minute. Skin temperature has dropped two full degrees Celsius from normal range. Virtually no brain activity. Without help, she soon will be dead."

"We have seen this condition before."

"Neurotoxin? Ion channel blocker?"

"With a covalent bond inhibitor."

"Then not from this century."

"Can only be Flüchtlinge."

Rydin considered various possibilities and rejected most of them. What remained was a curious coincidence. He and Cinquemain had found this Angela Riccardi, agent of the city department that might be holding Merola Tsverin, at almost the same time as—certainly no more than one hour behind—the Flüchtlinge coven that had engineered the explosion. What were the odds of that?

"Why would our ship be thrown just six months downstream?" he asked.

Cinquemain's exposed sensor swiveled to stare up at Rydin's face.

"Why not one month? Or ten? Was it the force of discharge?"

"More likely an internal setting," the intelligence said.

"Six months corresponding to half a solar orbit?"

"It makes navigation easier if we have—"

"—an uncalibrated in-flight event?"

"Yes, something like that."

That would explain his and Cinquemain's delay in reaching this woman. But why would the Flüchtlinge have waited so long? Presumably, they had believed Tsverin to be dead, killed in the blast. And then, months later, something suddenly suggested to the coven that she might be alive. And they went looking for a lost girl, following the same trail through social services that he and Cinquemain were following. What had changed in the meantime? A baseball, one that had been stolen and then—not stolen. That was the upsetting factor.

"This woman has met those three Flüchtlinge," he said.

"That certainly tells us we're on the right track."

"An hour behind. Not more," Rydin said.

He took Cinquemain's chassis out of his pocket and set it before the woman's computer, which was turned on and already displaying data. He reached around and felt in back. "Give me a minute to find one of those nine-pin plugs."

"Don't bother," Cinquemain said. "Look at the screen."

In the upper right-hand corner was a photograph showing a waiflike child in a curly blonde wig. It was the face of Merola Tsverin. The rest of the screen was filled with data boxes, including Foster Care, showing the names of William and Emily Windlace and an address in the city.

"You've got all that?" Rydin asked.

"Engraved on my heart forever." The intelligence paused. "The address is too far to walk. We need—money—for transportation."

"That is the one thing we don't have."

"Check the desk drawers. This Riccardi woman would keep money in a closed satchel made of leather or sturdy cloth."

Rydin found such a carry-all, rifled its contents, found a matching document case and a small purse, both made of the same leather, and extracted denominated bills and coins.

"I think we should hurry," he said.

"What about the woman?" Cinquemain asked.

"How much of a charge can you generate?"

"Depends on what parameters you want."

"Two hundred joules over two seconds."

"I can easily deliver that—but not too often."

"The shock across her chest should reset most of the molecular bonds."

Cinquemain walked over the desk to face Riccardi. His pincers unbuttoned her jacket and shirt. He spread one manipulator over her heart, stretched to place the other under her armpit. His sensor clusters looked into her face.

Without warning, the woman jumped in the chair, let out a gasp, and fell forward across the desk. Cinquemain scuttled backward to avoid being pinned.

"*Now* is she dead?" Rydin asked.

Cinquemain scanned her. "She'll recover in a minute."

"Then let's get out of here before she does."

37. A Miss as Good as a Millennium

Merola followed the proprietor of Carrefour House up two flights of stairs, through a double-locked door, and into the Gill family apartment.

It reminded her of the Windlaces' home: a "living room" that featured thickly padded chairs, casual tables, and intimate group seating on what Emily had called a "sofa." The focal point all this furniture was the screen of a television receiver. In the near corner was a desk with what Merola recognized as a personal computer similar to Bill's machine. Visible through an arch in the far wall was a separate area for eating at a large table surrounded by straight-backed, thinly padded chairs. The only food item on the table at present was an array of cut flowers. A hallway beyond this room led, presumably, to personal sleeping spaces and to areas for food preparation and body grooming.

Merola noted that the main room had windows only on two sides, and they were set into recesses in the slightly inward-sloping walls. With senses calibrated to a millimeter of distance and a second of arc, she correlated the angle of these walls with the roofline as seen from the street. She walked to one of the windows and looked down on young trees in leaf, curlicues of manicured lawn, swathes of flowers in bloom, and graveled paths between them.

"That's our back garden," Gill said, rather proudly.

She hurried across to a window in the opposite wall and looked down on the traffic of Earlham Street. She had a sudden insight into Carrefour House's internal structure and geometry. "This room spans the entire building!" she exclaimed.

"Certainly. Why wouldn't it?"

"But then the mirror-maze ..."

"Occupies no space at all."

Merola tried to absorb this.

"It *is* multi-dimensional," he added.

She sat down in one of the chairs. She found that she was still clutching Berzher's matrix against her left palm.

"You were going to tell me," Gill prompted, settling into a chair across from her, "why I'm hosting a fully fledged Jongleur at Carrefour House."

"I'm—" Merola was suddenly embarrassed. Members of the all-powerful Jongleur Troupe were not supposed to make, let alone admit to, mistakes. "—stranded in this reference now."

If Gill was surprised, he didn't show it. "I see. How did that happen?"

"I think I broke a rule. That attracted the attention of ... things."

"What kind of things, Miss Stonecraft? We're adults here."

"Berzher thought it was the Möglichen. But possibly it was just the Flüchtlinge. Either group is hostile to travelers—and incredibly dangerous. They got to my biosuit and ship—both the ones on my mark and the backups we had planted—and then they blew up a building trying to kill me."

"I'm afraid, my dear, that I'm not up on my future history. Your Mögs I have heard of—the 'children of possibility'—although I've never actually met one. But who are these *Flücht*-thing people? And who is Berzher?"

"A Flüchtling is a renegade, a criminal," Merola said patiently. "They tried to stage a revolt before the Troupe gained its final ascendancy and they were dispersed. Those we could not catch and persuade to take reorientation have sought refuge in earlier times. Some are rumored to be active in this century. They operate in groups called 'covens' and waylay and destroy traveling Jongleurs on sight."

"They obviously didn't kill you."

"No, but they stranded me. I came to London looking for a way home. I don't know much about travel mechanisms before the Troupe established our protocols, but I had heard that earlier groups used fixed transit points and may have left clues to their locations. I followed those clues."

"And they led you to Carrefour House. ... I find that disturbing."

"They led me to the Seven Dials monument. It's a reference marker."

Gill looked thoughtful. "After my time, I'm afraid. We're only the Builders. It's the travelers themselves who create and share such legends."

"If it helps you feel better, I only stumbled on your hotel. I was actually looking for a place to sleep. And only then did I find your mirror-maze."

"You penetrated it, of course."

"Just a little way, two levels."

"It goes much, much deeper."

"How many levels, in all?"

Gill seemed surprised by the question. "You mean the exact number of dimensions? I can't say. The number keeps changing. The system is extremely, um, dynamic."

"And not completely under your control?" Merola suggested.

"There are many users, from many times and places. Some are merely passing through. I'm not required to track them all—merely accommodate those who arrive in this particular here and now."

"Can you use it to send me home?"

"Let's see. That would be the early to mid-eleventh millennium, after the Christus? Is there a node in your time, Miss Stonecraft?"

"No," she said. "Or rather, none that I know of."

"I can tell you there is not. Your own Troupe embargoed interdimensional travel between fixed points after the late tenth millennium. You ripped out the nodal system of the Builders, root and branch. Your people travel differently, as I understand it, following a temporal trace with a spatial trace."

"It lets us move freely anywhere in time and space, not just between fixed nodes."

"Yes—if you have a ship," Gill pointed out.

"If you can't get me home without a node, can't you project one? That's how you built the system in the first place, isn't it? Projecting or reflecting a faceted seed into a calculated point in spacetime and building a node around it?"

"The process is *something* like that. But we can only project to places in our own past. You see, the past ... well, it *exists,* doesn't it? So we can define a point of stability, a known place-and-time, and build a node there. After that, it exists and continues moving forward into what becomes its own future. Which is how those nodes came to exist in places downstream of us now—or did until you Jongleurs destroyed them. But, for the rest, the future doesn't exist yet. It's all just probabilities and possibilities—no locus, no focus, no determinacy. I can get you as far as the last node in the tenth millennium, right up to one minute before the Jongleur Troupe removed it. But that really doesn't help you, does it? Miss by a minute, miss by a millennium—am I right?"

Merola brooded about that. "There was good reason for dismantling your system," she said. "Expanding dimensions between the fixed points lets in—"

"Yes, your Mögs—Jongleur fairytales. They don't exist."

"Are you sure about that?"

"We've never detected them. Never had a problem with them. Never had a bogeyman pop out of the cupboard, yell 'Gotcha!' and try to take over the place."

"What about the six-legged pug dog I saw last night?"

"Why do you think I went into the maze just now? I could see a lot of traffic in there this morning. Some people I know. Many more I don't. But none with six legs. No monsters."

A sudden thought occurred to Merola. "Are you *dealing* with them? Is that how you establish a node—by enlisting their aid?"

"Don't be ridiculous." Gill laughed. "I run a temporal transfer point as a service to humankind. And only humans need apply. We're not a coven of witches worshiping the Great Bugaboo and making pacts with the devil."

"I still think you've got a Möglichen infiltration."

He shrugged. "I fear we must differ on that point."

"And you can't get me home." She stood up.

He rose to stand across from her. "I'm sorry, Dorothy," he said with a smile. "My balloon can't take you back to Kansas."

"Excuse me?" she said.

"From *The Wizard of Oz*?"

Merola shook her head.

"It's a fairy story from the America of early in the last century. ... Look, let me think about your problem. There may be some other solution." Gill paused. "And you still haven't said who this 'Berzher' might be. Is he someone traveling with you?"

Merola considered how much she should reveal, then held out her left hand.

Gill stared at her ornate paperweight, gently reached for it, held it before his face. "This is an intelligence, isn't it? I've heard stories ..."

"Yes," she acknowledged. "We travel together. He's my—assistant? Companion!"

"He's beautiful." Gill's eyes were lost in swirling layers of glass and metal. "Can he speak?"

"That sphere is only his—brain? Mind? Ghost? In order for him to function among us, he needs a mechanical chassis with a power supply, sensory inputs, and manipulators. His chassis was destroyed in the explosion that stranded me here."

"And you've carried him with you ever since?"

"I'm taking him home so he can live again."

Gill's lips pursed. "I'll help you if I can."

38. MARY JANE'S FRIENDS

The doorbell rang while Emily Windlace was spreading sauce and layering flat pasta noodles and lumpy ricotta cheese for lasagna. Their new foster child, Achille De Luca, favored Italian cooking, so she was trying out some of her old recipes. Getting the layers of a lasagna thin enough was tricky work, so she called to Bill: "Get the door!"

"I'm watching a game," he replied from the living room.

"God damn it, Bill! I'm up to my armpits in meat sauce!"

"Okay, okay! I'll do it!"

The sounds from the living room—the lethargic commentary, the occasional *crack!* of the bat, the distant cheers of a televised baseball game—went quiet. After a moment Bill came into the kitchen. "It's some friends of Mary Jane's. What should I tell them?"

"Oh, for God's sake!" Emily put down her spoons and preceded him back through the house, to the front hall and the open door. Their visitors were standing beyond it, outside on the porch.

"Look," Emily began, "Mary Jane's not here any—" She stopped under the stares of three of the oddest children she had ever seen. "—more." She felt a tingling inside her skull, like tiny fingers examining her brain. "But you know that already," Emily said.

"We know that already," agreed the dark-haired girl with the dazzling green eyes.

"You want to know where she's gone," Emily said quietly, to herself. It felt as if she was taking dictation. "And we do not know that."

"What the hell's gotten into you, Em?" Bill asked.

The dark girl now shifted her attention to Bill's face.

"We really do not know where she has gone," he said.

"Missus Windlace? Who is that?" Achille asked, coming out of his room.

"Go back to your schoolwork, Killie," the dark girl said. "This is private."

"You leave them alone!" the boy shouted, moving forward aggressively.

The girl glanced at one of her—friends? Brothers? Twins? The one she nominated stepped forward to intercept Achille. Emily saw a flash of silver—a knife or a dart—and Achille suddenly had a large glass hypodermic hanging from his throat.

Emily broke out of her lethargy then. "Stop it! Everyone stop!"

Her foster child's muscles went slack, his eyes unfocused. The strange boy who had attacked him now supported Achille's fall and laid him gently on the carpet.

Emily turned to the dark girl, who seemed to be the leader, but before she could speak her mind, the dark girl raised a hand over her head and thrust a similar needle into Emily's neck. The world blurred. Emily thought she was having a stroke. She felt like a puppet with her strings cut. Displaying amazing strength, the girl caught her, directed her last stumbling steps to the sofa, and pushed her down. The girl arranged Emily so that she was staring straight forward with her head supported by a back cushion. A thump and a bounce beside her suggested that Bill had gotten similar treatment from the remaining brother.

Emily could only stare at the muted television screen and its pantomime of a ballgame—until the girl walked into her visual focus.

You already know I don't need your vocal chords to get information, the green eyes said inside her mind. *Let's see what you do know about Mary Jane.*

Images, faces with and without bits of action, words in and out of context, all began flowing through her brain's optical and aural centers. In a few seconds, Emily relived six months of caring for the strange little girl with the sober expression and the expensive blonde wig. Putting her to bed that first night ... watching her use a knife and fork as if for the first time ... sending her off to school with a brown-bag lunch ... helping her do homework ... wanting to answer the usual girl-talk questions, which never came ... coming home to find empty closets and an empty desk drawer. The film clips ended as quickly as they started.

Not all that much, apparently. The green eyes seemed sad. *And much less than there was to know.* The girl's head turned to the first brother. *Gjordge, find their computer. Check the email received and sent folders. Then the browser history and all searches for the past six months. The*—she used a word jumble that sounded to Emily like "jong-lure"—*had to make contact somewhere.*

Emily could hear the commands coming from the girl but not the brother's reply.

She sensed that the second brother was working on Bill in the same fashion.

While Gjordge rapidly and expertly worked the computer, using Bill's extracted logon and password to gain access, the girl and the second silent brother wandered around the living room. They looked at the bookshelves and Emily's memento cabinet—touching each object, weighing it, *smelling* it, and putting it back. She sensed they were testing for psychic vibrations, for clues to Mary Jane's state of mind and her current whereabouts. They drifted through the dining room, touching, probing, considering the contents of the sideboard and china cabinet, and on toward the kitchen. The next time she saw them, they were gliding down the hall to the bedrooms.

After what could have been ten minutes, or maybe half an hour—Emily was losing track of time—the other two came running back into the living room as if called by a mental exclamation from Gjordge. The girl stared at the computer screen as he flicked through several pages of information. She communed silently with the other brother. Then she came to stare with those hypnotic green eyes into Emily's mind.

Do you have an eBay account in the name of Madeline Hart Stonecraft?

Emily felt bewilderment.

Do you know anyone named Madeline Hart Stonecraft?

Emily visualized shaking her head.

Are you planning a trip to London soon?

Emily and Bill had always wanted to go but—

Do you know anything about the Seven Dials district?

Before Emily could respond, those green eyes turned hard.

Of course you don't! Gjordge, Giuffre, you can eliminate these three.

When the taxicab pulled up at the address off Ocean Avenue, the driver turned to Rydin in the back seat and announced the fare showing on the meter. Rydin gave him the largest bill he had and pushed open the car's door. The driver tried to stop him and make change, but Rydin ignored the man. He had seen that the front door of the house at Tsverin's address was standing open. In this semi-civilized place and time, an open door in the night was a sign of trouble.

He went up the steps and moved silently onto the porch. All was quiet inside, except for the click of keys on a computer fingerboard. He stepped through into a short, dark hallway lit only by the lights of the room beyond. He edged forward and saw a young boy, lying on his side, asleep on the carpet. Not asleep—he had a glass tube hanging from his throat. Rydin recognized the dart and its purpose. He knew the compound it had injected, complete to its chemical formula. The same toxin had gone into the Riccardi woman.

Rydin pointed from the level of his waist for Cinquemain's benefit and made a gesture with flattened palm calling for silence. Cautiously he moved his head and the pocket flap up to the arched entryway in order to look fully into the lighted room. Two people sat on a couch, side by side and as frozen in place as the stricken boy. Rydin recognized them as a man and woman of this reference now from the way their hair was cut and shaped. Beyond them, at a desk in the corner, another boy worked on the computer. Judging from his quick, sure movements and utter concentration, however, Rydin was certain this was no mere child.

Without warning, two more children, a boy and a girl, came into the room from another direction. They were dressed in the same dark clothing as the boy at the computer—in fact, they had the same clothing and faces that Rydin had seen in the street outside the toy store, now six months in the past. The three clustered around the computer, studying images on the screen at the direction of the one at the fingerboard. In all this time, no one had made a sound.

Inside Rydin's pocket, Cinquemain tapped for his attention with a manipulator. Rydin cautiously made the same shushing gesture in front of the intelligence's sensor cluster.

Cinquemain tapped more insistently.

Rydin removed the folded chassis from his pocket, held it up before his face, and frowned into the cluster.

The cluster stared back impassively, then one manipulator worked free of his entrapping hand and pointed at the floor. The gesture became an impatient downward jab.

Rydin set Cinquemain on the floor, and the chassis tiptoed sideways across the rug to the other side of the archway, like a tiny crab.

None of the three at the computer heard him or noticed the movement.

After a moment, the girl lifted her head, came back to the woman, and held her in a long, thoughtful stare. The girl turned to her two companions, and they fanned out across the room.

Cinquemain stepped into the doorway, took aim with his communications laser, and shot one of the boys through the eye. The beam came out the back of his head and scorched the far wall. The body dropped straight down like a sack of pomegranates. "Now remind me why I had to shed my battle armor," the intelligence said conversationally—and out loud.

The dark-haired girl turned to look at him, and Rydin charged into the room toward her. She was already poised to meet him with a thrown dart. Rydin batted it aside and tackled her. They went down in a tangle of arms and legs. The girl's elbows and knees quickly locked around him in the classical *kanidamashi* mat work of third-millennium Honshu judo. Rydin responded with the appropriate break.

Get out! Get out of here! GET OUT NOW! shrieked the most powerful psychic emanation Rydin had ever experienced. If it had been directed at him personally, he might have been stunned and rendered powerless. But instead it was meant for the remaining dark-haired boy.

He scrambled over their locked bodies and escaped by the front door.

Cinquemain sent a powerful beam after him into the night.

"Missed him, Coel," the intelligence called out.

"Forget him. Shoot *her*," he ordered.

"Then get out of the way."

Rydin tried to separate himself from the girl, but she clung to him like a death shroud. She worked around his body so that they came chest to chest, face to face, forehead to forehead. Her green eyes bored into his. He blinked, rolled his eyes to the side, squeezed his eyelids shut, but she had already caught him.

The world slowly lost all color except for a dank and mossy, darkly tranquil, deep underwater, jade green. In the growing darkness he saw flashes of imagery: Tsverin in her girl-child's disguise, sitting amid a scatter of toys in a busy room ... three pairs of childlike hands molding shaped charges of lemon-yellow plastic ... belts of explosive girdling each in a long line of concrete pillars ... a wing of rippling dark material, like black mylar ... a child-sized suit of pink-and-white, par-arachnid fiber ... a huge and echoing space with a circle of windows above the roof line ... a barn with straw on red-brick floors ... beams of dusty sunlight coming through stained-glass ... and then a moment of rattling panic. As Rydin and the girl grappled, something had slipped. The first images of the toy store, the pillars, and what he recognized as parts of a liteship and biosuit had started as current thoughts, mixed with views of fog and ocean, from this place, San Francisco. But the barnlike space, the red brick, the stained glass were somewhere else, somewhere under a skyline centered on a gleaming, steel arch that had a curve like a hanging chain turned upside down.

As these images flowed out of her mind and into his, the girl's panic increased. Her grip tightened. Her mind focused on a single word. The word was *forget ... forget ... forget ...*

Rydin worked his right hand free and up to his face. He touched his left eyelid.

The word "forget" sank deeper into his mind, erasing whatever thoughts were there. Rydin felt his own moment of panic—but perhaps it was only a psychic reflection of what the girl was feeling. The shot of adrenaline kicked something in his hindbrain, and the conscious restraint he had been cultivating ever since that morning in the Jongleur clinic—to keep from damaging the things and people around him with his new Simian-ACTN3 musculature—fell away.

He brought up his left hand against the pressure of her arms. He took her skull in both hands and squeezed. The girl's green eyes widened and flared briefly. Her lips curled into a pair of congruent S-curves. A tiny, moaning "Oh!" escaped her throat. But she survived the pressure.

Unable to kill her that way, Rydin turned from squeezing to pulling and twisting. The skullcap of her wig stretched and tore, parting her straight, dark hair in a new place. He scuffed the wig aside and took hold of her bare scalp. A fissure started in the skin of her forehead. The split traveled down across her left eye socket and cheek, and at the same time spread back over the top of her head. Beneath his fingers, he could feel the sutures in her skull slowly opening. Suddenly, the girl's head fell apart like a badly made doll: the right half of her face, the larger part of her braincase, and a chainwork of exposed neck bones remained in his left hand; her left cheekbone, gaping sinus cavities, a large jaw fragment, and flaps of skin came away in his right. The psychic pressure, the word "forget," evaporated like a drop of water on a red-hot skillet.

He shoved the offal away from himself, wiped blood spatters off his jumpsuit with the sides of his hands, and sat up.

"Honestly, I was trying for a shot," Cinquemain said. "You were in the way."

"Did you catch any of that?" Rydin asked. "There at the end?"

"Any of what? Your fighting technique?"

"No, her thoughts."

"You know Silicates can't read minds. What did you see?"

"I ... saw ..." He touched his left finger to his right eye, and it all became clear. "I saw how they tried to kill Tsverin. And then the Flüchtling revealed where she and her friends hid the ship parts and biosuit they stole."

"Where are they then?" Cinquemain asked.

"I can't describe it, but I know where to look."

"So ... is Tsverin still here?"

"No, long gone. The three Flüchtlinge were studying that computer." Rydin pointed. "Interrogate it, and I will see about these bodies."

Cinquemain started toward the desk. "Lift me up?"

While the intelligence worked the machine, Rydin stripped the covering off one of the cushions beside the frozen woman—presumably one of the householders, Emily Windlace—and used the fabric to bind the pieces of the Flüchtling girl's head. He dragged her into the front hallway, returned for her brother, and laid him beside her. He could do nothing about the blood on the floor or the burn mark on the wall.

"This computer has made a lot of online transactions in the past month," Cinquemain said. "Someone named 'Stonecraft' has been buying, selling, and banking—large amounts, too. Given names of 'Madeline' and 'Hart' suggest high probability of her being female."

"Not this woman," Rydin said, pointing to the inert form on the couch. "She's a Windlace. Female gender also rules out the man and the boy. Stonecraft must be Tsverin's new identity."

"So I presumed. There are also many information searches in the last four months," the intelligence said. "The most recent of them center on someplace called 'Seven Dials' in a city called 'London'—historical notes, shopping, sightseeing, retrieved photographs."

Rydin sighed. "She's gone to see the Gills."

"And who might these Gill people be?"

"If she finds them, it's bad news."

"Ah! Would this be information above my pay grade?"

"If machines got paid, yes. Above Tsverin's, too."

"All right, I assume we're traveling now. Do we take these two Flüchtling corpses with us?"

"No sense in leaving them around for discovery and dissection," Rydin said. He pointed to the Windlaces and the boy, presumably another foster child. "Will these three revive on their own?"

Cinquemain jumped down from the desk, scuttled over to the boy and took readings. He climbed up the leg of the man on the couch and took more readings of the two people there. "They are in better shape than the Riccardi woman, but they won't recover for a while yet."

"Good thing, because we have to go back to the park, reassemble the ship and your chassis, return here under cover of darkness, and remove the bodies without being detected."

"No peace for the wicked," Cinquemain quoted.

"I didn't think you knew the Bible."

"That's in the Bible?"

39. RECALLED TO LIFE

Late in the day, Gill knocked on the door to Merola's room. "Would you come with me, please? And bring your friend."

She scooped up Berzher's matrix and followed the hotel—or station—keeper down the stairs, past the registration desk in the lobby, and down more stairs into the basement. Gill swung aside a shelf of painting supplies and spare bathroom fixtures to reveal a portal that was not at all in the style of a much-renovated English country inn. The door and its jamb were gleaming metal, possibly steel but alloyed to a much darker hue. Set in its face was a keypad with the numerals zero to nine and the first six characters—*alif* to *fa*—of the alphabet in the time of the Builders. Sixteen symbols would enable a hexadecimal code of great complexity.

Without shielding the pad, Gill tapped in only eight symbols. "I can't remember anything longer," he said, smiling. The door released with a hiss indicating a pressure differential inside.

He passed her through it and into a workshop that would dazzle any scientist from this reference now but that seemed quaint to Merola's eyes. Most of the tools were still electro-mechanical, and it was obvious that the energies involved were modest.

"It's very nice," she said.

"I know you've seen and probably worked with better," he replied. "This must look like a children's playset to you. But it's the best you'll find within a thousand years of this spot."

"I didn't mean to criticize."

"Don't worry. You can't hurt my feelings."

He walked over to a white-topped bench that held a scatter of colorfully anodized components, cast ceramic shapes, and pieces of wire, all arranged around an object made of that same dark metal. It was shaped like a baton about half a meter long with a hemispherical cup at one end.

"I didn't have all the parts in stock, so I had to improvise with items from the local RadioShack. Camera chips, lenses, audio pickups, and such. The voder is scratch built, of course. And the battery—" Gill paused and looked at her. "—you know what a battery is?"

"A reservoir for electric current?" she said uncertainly.

"Yes, well, these days they create a current with chemical instabilities. Not as neat as using electron holes. I was able to whomp up a gel that will approximate what you would consider a terribly antique bubble setter. It recharges using ambient heat. Keep the wand next to your body or in sunlight—anywhere above twenty-five Celsius, actually—and it will stay charged. Lower than that and he'll run down in about five hours."

"Excuse me," she interrupted, "but *who* will run down?"

"Your friend, Mr. Berzher."

"Oh! You've made a chassis for him?"

"More like a simple carrier with some basic senses," Gill said. "I wasn't sure of the input specs. I assumed millivolts and direct current, but—"

"Any current will do," Merola said. "All of his contact patches are buffered. Feed in direct, sinusoidal, or square wave at any voltage or amperage, and they convert. You can even roll his matrix through a cloud of ball lightning and he'll make use of it."

"I didn't know. All that with just a plain metal contact?"

"Well, hardly plain and not really metal. We sometimes find ourselves in strange situations."

"I can imagine." He put out his hand. "May I have your friend, please?"

Merola gave him the matrix. "Power inputs there and there," she said, pointing.

Gill picked up the baton, tried the fit of the matrix inside the cup, snapped in several ceramic shapes to hold it securely, and placed among them two anodized pieces aligned with the power contacts. "Now, which are the inputs for audio and video? And outputs for voice?"

"Doesn't matter, really. His circuits are logic seeking. He will feel around until he gets things right."

"Very convenient. I suppose he would have to be versatile."

Gill adjusted more anodized pieces to connect with the remaining contact points. He picked up a hemisphere made of the same dark metal as the baton and snapped it over the cup. He handed the assembly to Merola. "There's no on-switch. He should be powering up now. The video sensor is built into the far end."

Merola upended the baton and held the sensor—a polished glass surface only slightly darker than the metal around it—pointed toward her face. The bulb of the englobed matrix became warm in her hands. She tried to smile into the lens.

"What time is it?" asked an unfamiliar voice. "My internal reserve died."

"About nineteen hundred hours Zulu," she said. "June nineteenth."

"How long have we been separated? At least six months?"

"About that. Since the explosion in the toy store."

"I can't sense the ship," he complained.

"You're not in your own chassis."

"I could guess that much."

"And the ship's gone."

"Any good news?"

"We're alive."

"Yippee."

"Your friend has a sense of irony," Gill said. "I like that."

"Who is this?" Berzher asked. "And it would be polite for you to turn my eye toward him, since I don't seem to have motor control."

Merola aimed the baton at Gill's face. "This is Sam Gill. He's the proprietor of Carrefour House, which is a … um, hotel … in London, which is sited over our Lune. Mr. Gill made you this temporary chassis. With parts from RadioShack, he says."

"I suppose I should be grateful," Berzher said. "But my leg itches and I can't scratch it."

"You don't have legs," Gill observed.

"And that would be my point."

"Ah, you're a comedian!"

"Ahem, miss?" Berzher prompted. "Um, what did you say your name was?"

Merola knew this was not some form of amnesia. Berzher's circuits would stand up to any shocks due to dislocation. He was being discreet, so as not to expose a cover identity she might have adopted—although any stranger with the skills to build even this limited-capacity chassis for him must already know that Merola and her companion did not come from this reference here and now.

She turned the baton back on herself. "Madeline Stonecraft," she replied.

"Well … Madeline … can you explain what we're doing here?"

"Waiting for transportation to … our own place and time."

"I distinctly remember having cached a backup ship."

"A lot of things changed after you went dark."

"I warned you about stealing that baseball."

"Baseball? What are you talking about?"

"I can see things have gotten worse."

40. Flying Pretty

The crippled liteship rose out of the enclosed yard at the rear of the house belonging to the Windlace people. Its ascent was sluggish and uncertain, due to the weight of two child-sized corpses strapped to its spars, along with Rydin in full biogear on one side of the core and Cinquemain, now restored to his battle chassis with all its accessories and appendages, on the other. Cinquemain had to keep adjusting for the ship's imbalance, and he nervously recalculated the odds—he knew some humans who would call it "praying"—of their running into a sudden wind shear at the upper altitudes. The world went dim as they entered and quickly passed through a layer of dripping fog, emerging into clear starlight.

"You realize we're entirely visible," he told Rydin. "This sky is full of nighttime air traffic, and our remaining panels are now glowing like a congregation of male *Photinus* beetles."

"Anything you can do to mitigate that effect?"

"Not and stay aloft. We're too heavy."

"So rise straight and look sharp."

Passing through the lower troposphere, where they would encounter most of this era's airfoil-effects craft, took seventy-three agonizing seconds, with Cinquemain trying to look outward in all directions at once and Rydin keeping a stony silence.

On entering the stratosphere, they bobbled at the lower boundary of the high-speed air flow humans of this reference now called the "jet stream." The ship actually tumbled through a complete revolution, skid pad over top ring, but the automatic compensators maintained its inherent lift.

Rydin breathed a sigh. "Safe now. The only air traffic up here is intercontinental."

"Compared to them we're hardly moving. They'll be on us before we can dodge."

"What are the odds of a collision?"

"Not worth calculating."

"Like I said."

The temperature dropped to minus 60 Celsius and air density to one-tenth that of ground level. The dead male Flüchtling was closest to Cinquemain, and the intelligence watched with curiosity as the effects of falling temperature and air pressure worked on the exposed skin of face and hands. The remaining undamaged eye slowly extruded from its socket, driven by fluid pressure in the underlying cavities, then crystallized and fractured. The cheeks and nose briefly puffed up, then sank inward. The lips and eyelids shriveled. Even Cinquemain's inhuman sensibilities found this disturbing and he looked away.

The ship was rising faster now as they began to gain by squares on the Earth's gravity field. Soon they were in near-complete vacuum and, flying far beyond the daylight terminator, at minus 230 Celsius. Cinquemain glanced at the Flüchtling and saw a husk of dried leather.

"Release them here?" he suggested.

Rydin paused. "We're not in orbit, just lifting against gravity."

"Of course. And where is the problem with that?"

"The bodies will fall back to Earth. They might survive."

"I doubt that. Aren't they already dead?"

"I mean, in recognizable form. I want them to burn up."

"I'll give us a suborbital vector."

Cinquemain added lateral speed until they were moving at approximately three kilometers per second over the surface of the Earth toward the sunrise. "Now they'll burn," he said.

Rydin released the female Flüchtling, whose shattered head was mercifully contained inside a bag. Cinquemain cut loose the male. They dropped away from the ship's snowflake structure in long, curving arcs.

"Now the two dead panels," Rydin said.

"We'll lose symmetry," Cinquemain protested.

"We're flying without them, aren't we?"

"Yes, but we won't be as ... pretty."

"I don't want them found on Earth."

Rydin was right, of course. When they recovered the two panels stolen from Tsverin's ship, they would have to dispose of the dead ones from their own. Discarding Jongleur technology in a past environment—even one filled with technological primitives who could make no use of them—was a breach of security protocols. Cinquemain unsocketed the dark panels and watched them pinwheel away.

"You said you knew where our replacements are," he prompted.

"Drop back down and keep heading east. We're looking for the city known as Sane Looie."

"Still in the Nortamerican department?"

"Yes, less than three thousand kilometers from San Francisco."

"Distinguishing features?"

"If you cross a really big river, you've gone too far."

Cinquemain entered the atmosphere slowly, still on a lateral vector to take them toward Rydin's city. This chassis's senses at long range were excellent, and Cinquemain ran in the background of his mind a relative analysis of nighttime lighting clusters and reflective water courses in the landscape passing below. He compared them with the fragmentary maps in his database of this continent in this reference now. When he came up with a probable match for this "Sane Looie," he paused their forward momentum and showed Rydin.

"Take us down to rooftop level. I'm looking for a particular landmark."

Cinquemain performed the maneuver. "Can you describe it?"

"Look for a steel arch, a continuous smooth curve in the shape of a hanging chain. It's big—one hundred ninety meters at the peak—and should be lighted at night. It will glow against the sky, right at the edge of the—"

"Got it," Cinquemain said and pointed. "Now what?"

"Activate the transponder in Tsverin's biosuit."

"Found it. Three kilometers to the southwest."

"Go that way. Look for masses of ... brick."

As they went, Cinquemain ran through his chroma filters and selected one which would highlight the spectrum reflected from any kiln-fired clay seeded with mineral contaminants. They were soon hovering over a group of buildings constructed of red brick and sandstone. The complex seemed to be part industrial landscape, part theme park. The suit's transponder fairly glowed in his sensors.

"Take us down," Rydin instructed.

They landed outside an oval-shaped building made of red brick. In the center of the tar-and-gravel roof was what looked like a short second story, another oval with a roof of green-corroded copper and ornate windows that went all around the perimeter. By daylight, those windows would create a well-lit interior without the hot spots of an overhead skylight.

"Cache the ship?" Cinquemain asked.

"We will only be here a few minutes," Rydin said.

He pointed at a pair of round windows set high in the end wall flanking double doors of dark-green painted wood. "Shine a beam there, full daylight spectrum."

Cinquemain complied. "What are we looking for?"

"Tracery of lead, colored glass."

"That's it then."

At a nod from Rydin, Cinquemain burned the lock on the doors, and they entered a large, echoing space. He paused less than a meter inside. "Coel, I sense animals in here. Big ones. Dangerous ones."

"Are they running loose?"

"Penned along the outer walls."

"Move quietly, and we won't disturb them."

"I can neutralize them with the beam—"

"I don't want you to hurt them."

"It would be safest to—"

"The answer is no."

Cinquemain continued tracking the suit until they came to a door in the far wall. The lettering on it said "Tack Room." He evaluated the unfamiliar word, and came up with a synonym for "equipment." That sounded promising. He burned that lock, too, and they entered. The walls were covered with long strips of dark leather adorned with shiny bits of brass and steel. Nothing suggested Tsverin's stolen biosuit. A closet at the back of the room came into his focus, however. From the dust on the doorknob, Cinquemain interpreted that it had not been opened in a while, unless it was by experts in stealth— which would certainly describe the Flüchtling trio. He turned the knob with a pincer that would leave no fingerprint in the dust and no trace of DNA.

Inside the closet hung a full-body suit of bright pink and slightly fluorescent material with matching helmet, all too small for any adult of the time. Alongside these items stood two spars wrapped with shiny black plastic and strapped together.

"We're in business again," Rydin said.

"We still have a questionable singularity," Cinquemain pointed out. "I can't fix that here and now."

Rydin handed him the folded energy panels, tucked the suit and helmet under his own arm. "We'll address one problem at a time. Right now, our next problem is in London."

41. The Really Long Way Home

When she awoke on her second morning at Carrefour House, Merola immediately sensed a difference. The muffled thumps and bumps and running-water noises coming from the rooms around her had greatly increased, and every few minutes she heard the bustle and voices of people passing in the hallway. The hotel had apparently filled up during the night.

Merola washed and dressed quickly. She fitted Berzher's baton into a holster she had fashioned from one of her least-favorite pair of pumps. She had removed the stacked heel the evening before, and now she tucked the denuded sole under her belt. She inserted the knob containing his matrix into the toe pocket of the shoe, and secured the baton's shaft against her belt with the ankle straps. He had complained that this gave him a view limited to the ceiling and the inside of her arm; so she compromised by resting her hand on the shaft and directing his lens forward whenever, in her opinion, something worth seeing was in front of them.

Her impression of the hotel's sudden crowding was confirmed when she went down to the breakfast room. All the tables were full, and more people were queuing up in the entryway for a seat. If it was a small convention or commercial group that had registered overnight, the members did not appear to be very friendly. No one was making eye contact, and any attempts at conversation seemed to die out after a few words.

Merola was no expert on clothing styles, and certainly the twenty-first century was not an era of social conformity. Even so, she could sense differences within this crowd. A man sitting along one wall was wearing a gold-brocade coat, lace at his throat, knee breeches, and silk stockings. Judging from the profusion of gray curls on his head, he either indulged an elaborate and time-consuming hair style or was wearing a patterned wig. Seated across from him at the table was a woman in a one-piece bodysuit of eye-watering, bright-red-and-orange polysilk that Merola knew would not come into fashion for another two centuries. All very strange.

"Miss Stonecraft?" Gill's daughter, Sabina, appeared beside her in the queue. "My father suggests you might want to take breakfast at one of our neighborhood cafés."

"I don't mind waiting," Merola said.

"You don't understand. He specifically asked me to take you to the café. Please come with me."

Merola glanced down into Berzher's single eye. No help there. "All right then."

As they emerged onto Earlham Street, the young woman directed Merola to the right. "My father has made me aware of your problem," she continued. "While we cannot help you directly, he suggested I introduce you to Mr. Anastasis. He's the director of a ... well, a research organization similar to your Jongleurs. We don't know much about them, as they originate from two millennia beyond our home time, but they have contracted for our services through tonight."

"If they're using your mirror-maze, how does that help me?"

"Our maze is only a gathering point. Their tour will require use of ships."

"Ships can travel freely—perhaps as far as my eleventh millennium?"

"So my father supposes. But you'll have to gain this man's cooperation."

"There is much we can teach Mr. Anastasis. An offer of technology ..."

"I never heard of Jongleurs willing to exchange technology," Sabina said.

"We can adapt when we have to." Merola was thinking that what the Troupe might give with one hand, in gratitude for this man having brought home a lost Jongleur officer, the Troupe was fully capable of taking back with the other, in order to protect the temporal underpinnings of their future.

Sabina steered her through the entrance of an establishment called "Bistro Tarot," which was only half-full at this hour of the morning. Without pausing, they went to a table for six at the back that had only a single occupant.

Compared with Sabina and every other Londoner Merola had seen, this man appeared oddly streamlined: his head longer than it was wide, his nose thin and pointed, his chin jutting, and his eyebrows swept back as if by a jet blast. When he opened his mouth to smile at Sabina, his teeth were revealed as unnaturally long and sharp. When he stood to greet them, his head rose only a few inches above the level of Merola's. She placed his time of origin no closer than the eighty-second century—long after humanity had begun to drift genetically, but before the genome had been consciously cleaned up and compacted for stability and longevity.

"Tessu Anastasis," Sabina was saying, "I'd like you to meet Madeline Stonecraft. She would like to join your expedition."

He reached out to take Merola's hand in both of his. The smile flashed again like a shark bite. "I am always pleased to meet a fellow traveler. May I order you ladies something?"

Merola noted that, spread across the table before him, were a dozen small plates filled with dainty foodstuffs. From her first breakfast at Carrefour House, she recognized a scone with fruit preserves and clotted cream, and the croissant with a pat of butter she knew from San Francisco. The rest were foods she could not readily identify: small toroids of oil-fried cake with sprinklings of sugar and smears of chocolate; a larger toroid of what looked like steamed bread, split crosswise, toasted, and topped with a white paste, slices of purple onion, small green berries, and slivers she recognized as smoked salmon; dough baked into strange, flaky swirls and knots that were daubed with fruit glazes and cheeses. "Will you share?" she asked, eyeing the salmon-covered thing.

"Of course, of course," he said, although he did call over the waitress for a pot of tea and cups of coffee. "I just love the pastries of this era," he said, turning to Merola. "Nothing like them in my time, certainly." He spread his hands over the table. "Do you know them all, Miss Stonecraft?"

Merola was caught with her mouth full. The ring of steamed bread was tougher and chewier than it appeared; the white spread was actually some kind of cheese; and the berries were pickled, tart and bitter. They perfectly complemented the flavor of the smoked salmon. She regretted having to swallow in order to make conversation. "Um-umm, no. Or rather, some of them."

"So you are not a native of today's London, either?" He was watching her carefully. Sabina Gill remained silent between them.

"I would say my own time is a bit ... downstream of yours."

"How far?" he asked quickly.

"Mmmm." She licked cheese paste off her lips. "Millennium and a half?"

His smile died. "You are a Jongleur." His voice hardened. "Tell me, why would I share my business with a Jongleur?"

Merola decided on telling the simple truth. "Because I need your help."

"The new masters of time and space, who destroyed the greatest monument to the transfer of temporal knowledge and human understanding ever built—" Here he glanced at Sabina. "—now need my help? I find that hard to believe."

"Not the Troupe. Just me."

"And what's special about you?"

"I made a mistake. I lost my ship."

"I see. And wouldn't it be nice, about now, to have a cabinet you could step into, stroll across the dimensions, and step out into your own place and time?"

Merola closed her eyes. "There were reasons for what we did. I've already explained to Mr. Gill—"

"Oh, yes," he sneered. "Möggy-woggies that go 'Boo' in the mirror."

"Merola, let me talk to him," said a voice at her hip.

"Pardon me?" said Anastasis.

Merola withdrew Berzher's baton from the holster and set him on the table, propped against a teacup so that his lens could focus on the man's face. "This is my companion. You may call him Berzher."

"What is that?" Anastasis asked suspiciously. "A recording device?"

"I am a class-four Silicate intelligence and, also, a Jongleur officer. I have the power to negotiate for the Troupe. In return for your help, we are prepared to offer technical advice and support for your venture. I strongly recommend you take it."

"You don't even know what my venture is."

"You are Tessu Anastasis," Berzher said, without a pause to retrieve the data. "You are one of the managing directors of the Sindicato della Conoscenza. If the current date is June twenty of the year twenty-aught-one, then you are arranging a transtemporal tour for biological scientists gathered from a span of four centuries bracketing this date. Each of them will pay you the equivalent, in his or her own terms, of a small fortune to witness the transformation of life in Earth's distant past. You will need a guide with advanced biological experience to effect this demonstration—and perhaps even to survive it and come back. My associate, Miss Stonecraft, is such a person."

"We have our own guides," Anastasis said.

"None who have gone as far as you intend."

"Ah ... um ... and how do you know this?"

"I come from your future," Berzher replied.

"I've heard of the Conoscenza," Merola broke in. "You take brilliant scientists from the past and offer them 'inspiration and understanding' in their areas of study. You promise them advances they cannot possibly discover or figure out on their own. You swear them to secrecy and take a cut of the profits they will make by publishing their new theories. That's the worst form of intertemporal meddling."

"But it works," Anastasis said simply. "With the rise and fall of human civilizations, through wars and plagues and falling stars, with dark periods that come every time to wipe out everything that humankind has learned—well then *someone* has to jump-start a renaissance here and there. And we don't *tell* them anything. We don't reveal the knowledge itself. We simply invite them to a critical event, let them observe and take measurements, then draw their own conclusions."

"Based on what *you* show them."

"It's never backfired before—well, except for one time. That Einstein fellow! We took him right out into deep space. We showed him the fractured singularities. We let him clock them to his heart's content. Oh, but no! Light speed was the limit, he said. He had done the math, and his math *always* worked! Reality wasn't good enough for him. Bastard!"

"This time you need our help," Berzher said again.

Anastasis eyed, by turns, the dark-metal baton and Merola's face. "You're sure about that?"

"What good is knowing the future if you won't believe it?" Berzher said. "Or are you another Einstein?"

"All right." Anastasis sighed. "I guess the two of you won't take up much room. But I warn you, keep your Jongleur prejudices to yourselves. Not a word to the paying customers."

"Agreed," Berzher said.

"Agreed," Merola echoed. "By the way, unlike my companion here, I don't have your entire history at my fingertips. So tell me, where are you taking these scientists?"

"To the late Devonian period, to watch the lobe-finned fishes, the *Sarcopterygii,* emerge from the oceans."

"Hunh!" she said, doing a quick mental calculation. "That will be, um, fun."

42. AFTER THE FACT

When members of the St. Louis coven crept out of their private burrows to assemble during daylight, they favored public spaces like libraries, parks, and playing fields, where they could either account for their presence or conveniently disappear. The one semi-public place with probably the most difficult logistics—locked away behind factory walls, wrought-iron gates, and security fences—was the historic Anheuser-Busch Brewery in the southern part of the city. But it was there, in the multi-colored twilight of the Clydesdale stables, that the errant twin found by the coven's junior members had insisted on meeting with Beckah Courtnay.

She often wondered why the huge horses, usually so sensitive to the nearness of strange human beings, should ignore her kind. Something to do with a mechani-cally sanitized genome and the lack of wild pheromones, no doubt.

But all of that superior genetic processing did not supply any strength of his own to Gjordge Ramsay, once he was separated from his siblings. The boy—she thought of him as still a child—stood before her trembling like an aspen leaf. He was so wobbly that two of her coven had to support him by the elbows.

"Where are your sister and brother?" she asked.

He rolled his eyes and moaned.

"I know you have vocal cords. Use them."

"Mm ... duh ... dead," he replied.

"Dead by misadventure? Or made dead on purpose?"

"Killed. By a Jongleur. And the robot."

"You saw them killed? And yet you survived?"

"No ... I saw Giuffre killed. Genjifer was pinned. I ran."

"So how do you know Genjifer isn't still alive?"

"She went *out*. Then the Jongleur flew away with their bodies."

"This was the same Jongleur female you were sent to eliminate?"

"No, a male. This one is smarter and stronger, too."

"So now we have two Jongleurs on the loose!" This incursion was growing worse by the minute. "Please tell me Genjifer didn't try her telepathy on him."

"Well … She was using her mind on the Windlaces."

"And who are the Windlaces?" Courtnay asked.

"The people who rescued your Mary Jane Doe."

"I see, and then the Jongleur came on the scene?"

"Genjifer tried to make him go blank, too."

"Of course. And she forgot that, with a self-aware human, the mind works both ways. How much did she give up?"

"I don't know. I was out of range by then."

"Are your trophies still safe?" she asked.

Gjordge's eyes flicked to the rear of the stables.

Courtnay led her coven down the length of the building to a door marked "Tack Room." She opened it and they all went inside. She noted that the two holding Gjordge at the elbows were now restraining him more than supporting him. She dismissed them with a shake of her head. "Show me where you put these things," she told the boy.

Gjordge pointed to the closet door and, at her nod, opened it.

The tiny room was empty, of course, except for a bucket and a dried out mop. Somewhere on this Earth, if she ever made contact with this new Jongleur, the baseball thief who was not a thief would now have the means of flying home. Would it be better just to let her go? Probably—but that would kill a little piece of Beckah Courtnay's soul. She lived to revenge herself on all the Jongleur

Troupe for expelling her from a time she remembered as paradise.

"I guess the Jongleurs got here before me," Gjordge said. "Those liteships must move pretty fast."

"Is there anything useful you can tell me?" she asked.

"We found out where Mary Jane Doe went."

Courtnay waited, then prompted, "Where?"

"To London. To the Seven Dials."

"She has gone to visit Sam Gill."

"The man with the mirror-maze?"

"She thinks he can take her home."

"What are you going to do?" asked one of her lieutenants.

"The Gill family has been operating under a truce ever since we arrived from that dead space beyond the Builders' last node. It's time we renegotiated terms with those double-dealing cowards."

The coven around her nodded wisely. Courtnay knew they could sense her anger. She wouldn't have to tell them to begin digging out their supplies of binary explosive.

43. Beyond the Fire Strike

The Conoscenza tour was hosting twenty-eight clients, not counting Merola and Berzher. As evening approached, the Gill family called them from their rooms, and Anastasis lined them up in the hallway outside the linen cabinet. Because he presumed Merola had previous experience with the mirror-maze, he put her at the end. For the rest, Anastasis went up and down the line issuing instructions.

"Just step through the mirror," he said. "It's not actually solid. This is just a kind of transport device."

"Is it like a wormhole?" asked a man in the clothing of contemporary London.

"Yes, exactly like a wormhole," the director said, with a smile that told Merola he was lying. She had never seen a wormhole, either.

"Will we get nauseous?" a woman asked. "I didn't bring my Dramamine."

"You won't feel a thing, I promise. Now when you walk through, you'll see one of my staff members wearing a red shirt. You may see other people in there, but they can't touch you. Remember, walk toward the people in the red shirts. It's just like walking across a busy ballroom floor—but no danger of bumping into the other people."

As he passed up the line, repeating his instructions and assurances, Merola unholstered Berzher and held him close under her chin. "You know I've never been to the Devonian," she whispered. "I've never traveled much beyond recorded human history, actually. Do these people really need our help?"

"I doubt it," the baton whispered in reply.

"But you said this tour wouldn't come back."

"I didn't say that. I have a record of this group departing, date and time. It's just there's no record, either way, of a return."

"You said Anastasis's guides hadn't gone back that far."

"That was a good guess, wasn't it? The Devonian's a long way, and not much to see and do upstream of there. Nobody's likely to have experience with that era."

"You took a lot for granted, didn't you?"

"You never learned to bluff, did you?"

The clients were steadily disappearing inside the linen cabinet, without a flash or a bang to mark their passage. Finally, it was just Merola and her baton. Anastasis had gone ahead to accompany a bearded and balding man in nineteenth-century dress who had made a display of nerves. She stepped into the cabinet as before. The vaguely scratchy music was louder inside. The knife switch was down, and the three physical mirrors displayed their never-ending panoply of duplicates.

She stepped through, and immediately to her left was a person in a red shirt. He had the same streamlined features as Anastasis. He beckoned to her, and Merola moved effortlessly through a second set of mirrors. When she reached his side, he pointed to a third set, where she could see a woman in a red shirt with eyebrows that approached her ears and long, blonde hair slicked back on her head. Merola went from guide to guide through thirteen layers. She held Berzher's baton tilted forward in the holster, casually directing his eye toward each new meeting with a guide, and counted off each layer for him.

"I hope you're making a map of all this," she said as they passed out of the last red-shirt's hearing.

"No, I'm just enjoying the ride," he replied. "Do you think *you* could work this path in reverse?"

"I'm hoping we don't have to."

After two more layers, she stepped out into the same linen cabinet ... or not the same. Instead of sheets and towels stacked on the false shelves, there was a collection of atomizer bottles, prepackaged molecular wipes, and electrostatic brushes. These items were not just dusty and yellowed by time but broken and speckled with grime and ... flakes of blackened ash. The wood of the doors was water-stained and scratched, all the varnish stripped away by years of neglect. The hallway beyond was a burned-out ruin: the plaster cracked and smoke damaged, doors missing from the rooms, and the rooms themselves glimpsed as windowless chambers where the wind moaned. The carpet underfoot had lost its pattern and color to patches of black mold.

Merola saw the people who had gone ahead of her leaving the hall by the stairway down to the lobby. Anastasis came up to her.

"We have to hurry now," he said.

"Where is this place?" she asked.

"Carrefour House, in London."

"All right, *when* is this place?"

"Twenty-six fifteen."

Merola absorbed that. "Did *London* take a fragment?"

"New crater where Edinburgh used to be. No, this—" He waved his hand around. "—is mostly due to rioters and scavengers, as the sky closed overhead and everything fell apart."

"Do I understand these rioters are still around?"

"Long gone. But this building is not exactly safe. Sometimes I think the node is the only thing holding it up."

"But ... you've taken us *downstream* in time. This isn't the way to the Devonian."

"Of course not. There are no nodes back then. And no way to maintain them. But this is the perfect place to park a ship."

234 • Thomas T. Thomas

"In the middle of a devastated city?"

"Where else? Two years past the end of civilization—no one left to see and record. No little hands left to tinker. It couldn't be safer."

———

In his place beyond the world as it was known to most humans, Glyph was busy. One part of his attention followed the dark girl and her brothers in their passages hither and yon, across the city where they had trapped the female traveler. The other part kept an eye—if his mind was like an eye—on the cluster of intersecting dimensions, half a world away, where that same traveler had appeared briefly and then vanished. Half a world, of course, was nothing compared to the spans in space and time that Glyph's awareness could cover. He assumed it would be the same for this traveler.

He watched with regret as the three were broken. The bond of their thoughts had shone brightly in this shadowy world he could only visit through the minds of its inhabitants. The union of the three had been a special access point, an open keyhole, for him. But now that bond was breaking. First, one of the brothers suddenly winked out of existence. Then, the mind of the dark girl, so like his own with its cheerful malice, flared in hatred and dismay and also winked out. The third brother, weakest of the three, fled diagonally and disappeared from his awareness. Glyph was suddenly blind and lost.

But, at almost the same time, something interesting was happening at the intersection of dimensions. A number of humans entered from one direction and spread out across fifteen separate planes. They were alike in shape and form, doubly alike in that they all wore a common garment that glowed just above the infrared. They formed a dazzling chain from one place and time to another. Shortly afterward, less defined shapes entered the intersection and passed from hand to hand across the fifteen separate steps. The glowing chain and the following shapes constituted something interesting and unusual, from Glyph's experience, but nothing that demanded his full attention.

He was about to turn back to the death of the dark girl when a familiar presence, a figure that shimmered with many dislocated dimension sets, entered the chain. The female traveler passed along it and, like a seneschal extinguishing the candles on a banquet table after a feast, sent each of the glowing red dots off sideways, out of the intersection, unwinding the chain. Glyph tracked her to the fifteenth step and marked it in his mind.

His search was almost at an end.

44. Thirty Minutes Behind

Rydin watched with growing anxiety as Cinquemain tried to fit the two panels that the Flüchtlinge had stolen from Tsverin's liteship into the sockets at the core of their own.

On reaching the cobblestone pavement outside the stables at the center of the Anheuser-Busch complex, Rydin had immediately climbed up and strapped Merola's suit and helmet to one of the existing struts, leaving to Cinquemain the job of partial ship reassembly. It should have taken two seconds—two twists, two snaps—for them to be powered up and moving. Instead, after twenty minutes of pushing and twisting, wrenching and cursing—during which he discovered that Cinquemain's database held blasphemies from thirty-eight languages, including Phoenician, which had not been spoken for a dozen millennia—they were no nearer to powered flight. And dawn was rapidly approaching.

In the end they had taken off in their crippled liteship. With his free arm, Rydin held the folded panels, which flapped frantically in the wind, while he clung to his post with the other hand. Cinquemain flew low and slow over the suburbs of East Sane Looie looking for a secluded place to set down.

"I just assumed the Troupe would build its ships to some kind of design standard," the intelligence grumbled.

Rydin ignored the implied criticism of Jongleur practice. "That dark area," he said, pointing. "Partially wooded ground. Mounds and hillocks. Lots of trees around. Looks safe." The eastern sky was growing lighter by the minute. "Maybe in the saddle between those two flat areas?"

"Yes, out of any sight lines. Down in one minute."

"As to standards," Rydin went on, "everything evolves, including ship design. We've been flying together in this one a long time. Tsverin and Berzher simply had a newer model. How much do you think your own silicon matrix resembles his?"

"The ancient engineers used to say, 'If it ain't broke, don't fix it.' "

"To which nature—and any good designer—replies, 'Mutation, mutation, mutation.' Anyway, can you fix these panels?"

"How dead are we if I can't?"

"We don't go home again."

"Then I guess I have to."

In the end, it took seven hours. Rydin sat with his back against the embankment and tried not to think about the growling in his stomach. Cinquemain used their lite-ship's limited supply of tools and spare components to tear apart the two sockets in the central core and spread out their control circuits as separate conduits. Then he did the same for the spar ends of each panel. He called Rydin over and had him hold first one panel and then the other in its correct flight mode while he fused the connections with his communications laser and then welded the supporting structure in place.

"We'll never cache this ship again," Cinquemain cautioned.

"But it will fly?"

"Sure. Take off, fly around, land—and stick out like a broken wing."

"That's good enough."

It was after midday by the sun when they lifted away from the mound country, went rapidly to altitude, and headed eastward for London. After a long and wearying flight over the North Atlantic, they came down over the center of the city in the vectored shadows of a late summer evening. Rydin navigated them to an area of low buildings north of the river, and Cinquemain found the flat rooftop of Carrefour House. Rydin shed his biosuit.

He still had no clothing matched to this era, but the current Gill would not be alarmed at the sight of his jumpsuit, sandals, and knitted cap.

Rydin went to the cupola sheltering the inside stairway and broke the lock.

Cinquemain lifted their liteship into the last rays of the setting sun.

———

Sam Gill and his daughter Sabina were going over accounts in the office under the stairs. They had to figure out where to sell the synthetic diamonds Anastasis had used to pay the balance of his contract. The trick was to do this without attracting attention from the Inland Revenue. Gill had his favorite jewelers, pawnbrokers, and industrial suppliers for such goods, but he wanted to start including Sabina in these decisions. In a hundred years or so she would have to make them for herself.

While they worked, a soft footfall sounded on the risers over their heads. Gill thought nothing of it, as guests came and went at all hours.

The old-fashioned call bell rang at the registration desk. Gill put his head out, but didn't see anyone in the lobby. He was about to duck back inside when a tiny hand came up over the edge of the counter and tapped the plunger again.

"Hello?" called a voice.

Gill went to the desk and looked over. Standing in front of it was a child, probably male but hard to tell for the delicacy of its features. The child was wearing a blue-gray jumpsuit, gray plastic sandals, and a watch cap of dark-blue wool. The face was ... familiar.

"Rydin," Gill said with a sigh. "So not-good to see you. It's been a long time."

And suddenly two plus two were coming together in the low single digits.

"Father?" Sabina called from the office. "Do you need any help?"

"You might as well come out and meet trouble," he said.

The Jongleur grinned at him. "Seventy-two years."

"I suppose you're running the Troupe now?"

"I still have one or two bodies to bury."

"Are you looking for Stonecraft?"

"That's right. Is she here?"

"Unfortunately, no. Miss Stonecraft—if that's her actual name, doesn't sound at all *Jongleurish*—left here about half an hour ago. She's traveling with a group from the Sindicato della Conoscenza. By the way, this is my daughter, Sabina. I hope you will manage to keep out of her life more successfully than you've kept out of mine."

"Pleased to meet you—I think," Rydin said, nodding at Sabina. Then to Gill: "Why would Stonecraft go with the Conoscenza?"

"She hopes they will take her back downstream to your era."

"But they're businessmen, not scholars. They have to turn a profit. What could she offer them? Other than a brief relaxation of legitimate Jongleur persecution."

"She offered her cooperation," Sabina explained. "Her artificial companion, Mr. Berzher, seemed to think the tour she was joining would need their help."

Rydin looked thoughtful. "And where are they going?"

"To the late Devonian period," she said, "to study the *Sarco*-somethings."

A flicker of alarm passed over the little man's face, then he steadied. "I suppose that should have been obvious. We are all in grave danger."

"Why?" Gill asked. "Haven't there been about five periods of mass extinction since then? What could she possibly change that would matter?"

"Everything," Rydin said. "I'll have to go after her."

"You can't use the maze for that, of course," Gill said.

"I know, their path will be complicated. Probably by ship."

"I believe that's so. Well, as always, I won't wish you luck."

"This time I think you'd better." Rydin turned toward the stairs. "I'll let myself out." But he paused with one hand on the banister. "I probably should warn you. Stonecraft left a trail a mile wide, pointing straight to this place. And bad things were already following her."

"Mög-things or Flücht-things?" Gill asked.

"The Flüchtlinge—if you know about them."

"What had she done?"

"Technically ... nothing."

"Isn't that always your story?"

"This time it happens to be the truth."

With that, the little man stepped lightly up the stairs. A moment later, Gill heard a door bang, four flights up, on the roof.

"Are we in trouble, Father, for helping that woman?" Sabina asked.

"I shouldn't think so. Still, it might be an idea to sleep over at a friend's for a day or two. Just to be safe."

"I'll ring up Melly."

———

Rydin stepped out into the sweet summer twilight on the roof of Carrefour House. From the smell of tidal mud drifting up from the river and the hum of traffic moving through nearby Cambridge Circus, no one would guess the immense energies, the potential for destruction, that lay just beneath his feet. And all of it was entrusted to one expatriate family who had grown entirely too trusting.

The gossamer snowflake of Cinquemain's liteship descended to the rooftop. Rydin retrieved his biosuit and pulled it up over his jumpsuit. Before he put on the helmet, however, he refreshed his neural imprint by direct skin contact. He sensed their next move would require temporal relocation—probably a long one.

"No luck?" Cinquemain asked as Rydin climbed aboard. He lifted them rapidly into the stratosphere.

"This time, we were just thirty minutes behind," Rydin said. "Or three hundred and sixty million years ahead—take your pick."

"Three hundred ...?" the intelligence repeated, mystified. "What is Tsverin doing all the way back in the—"

"Devonian period," Rydin supplied. "Hitching a ride home, she thinks. She's traveling with the Conoscenza."

"Those scoundrels! That will turn out badly."

"From what we saw in Lune, I think it already has."

"Of course, we can't follow them back," Cinquemain said.

"We have to, if we're going to stop ... whatever it is that they do."

"Think of it, Coel! In two hundred and fifty million years, the solar system makes a complete orbit around the Milky Way. We would have to cross half the galaxy to meet the backward trace as it comes around again. This liteship with its compromised singularity can't travel that far."

"So we'll find another."

"Not in our time."

"No, not then." Rydin replied absently. He was already dealing with other problems. "A geologic period like the Devonian covers a tremendous span of years. How do we pinpoint with any certainty the single minute, the day, the year in which they arrive, within all those tens of millions?"

"That's the easy part," Cinquemain replied. "We cheat. I have in archive the Sindicato's complete tour schedule. It's part of my standard package. You know we can earn a Troupe bounty for intercepting and disrupting—"

"We're going to move carefully on this one, following and observing."

"Then we still need a more powerful ship—in fact, a saucer."

"Preferably a saucer before it attains personality."

"That's going to be even harder to find."

"Not if you go to the shipyard."

"We're going to steal—?"

"Oh, no. Purchase."

45. THE BUMP IN THE NIGHT

Beckah Courtnay's coven was good at burrowing into places and uncovering things. Infiltration, excavation, reclamation, and extermination were their primary skill set these days. They could even get into places guarded by locks and bars with eighth-millennia sensibilities and virtual teeth.

They had been watching Carrefour House from various positions on various levels since dusk. The observation teams at front and back had counted the guest room windows on three floors as they successively lighted up and went dark, and knew within a statistical margin of three the body count inside the hotel. The member at the front door had watched the man at the registration desk as he first read his newspaper, then ate his supper from a tray, and now dozed over a lighted cigarette. The team watching from across the street had tried to follow activity in the apartment that spanned the top floor, but their report was inconclusive.

Six of her coven were working on the basement: three to defeat the security screens on the narrow windows that looked out on the back garden, three to pick apart the glass blocks and tiny cast-iron grilles in the sidewalk outside the front, which admitted light and air to storage vaults extending beyond the foundation. That might have been noisy work, except for the cutting tools her people could bring to bear.

By the hour after midnight, both teams had reported access. Then her structural experts entered and identified the load-bearing walls and columns beneath the old building, mapped their weaknesses, and applied shaped charges at the critical points. They had ringed the detonators with a web of radio frequencies. And they had silently withdrawn.

The leader of the explosives team put the switch into Beckah Courtnay's hand. The only question in her mind was what might be happening inside that top-floor apartment—but more waiting was unlikely to provide clear answers. She pressed the button.

———

Sam Gill fretted for half an hour after Sabina had left for her friend Melanie's apartment. At his casual suggestion, Sabina took her younger sister Galina and baby Morgan along, making of the visit a grand sleepover adventure, no matter what Melanie might say. When his children were safely out of the house, he gathered Deirdre from the family apartment and set in motion their long-standing plans.

They darkened the hallway lights floor by floor and quietly roused their guests. Gill was thankful that the Conoscenza tour had practically emptied the hotel: he only had two mundanes and five exotics to corral and pair off. He put those who knew Carrefour House's secret hand-in-hand with those who thought they were simply overnighting at a fashionable bed-and-breakfast. Deirdre bundled them all through the linen cabinet and into the maze. Those who were familiar with its intricacies and knew where they were going would lead those who could never imagine what lay behind those wooden doors.

Well, it was a night for new discoveries.

While Deirdre returned to their apartment to collect a few mementos and a change of clothing for them both, Gill started down to the lobby. The alarm in his pocket went off silently. When he withdrew it, surveillance by the guardians at front and back told him that Rydin had been correct. Damn the little man's shriveled black soul!

Just above the foot of the stairs, without showing himself in front of the lobby's glass doors, Gill called to the night manager. "Mickey? Can you come up here a minute?"

Santos, obviously sleeping at his post, roused and put out his cigarette. "What is it, Sam?"

"One of our guests needs your assistance."

"Well, you're up already. Can't you—?"

"No, I cannot. ... Come now, Mickey."

Gill led him back up the stairs and down the hall to the linen closet. Deirdre met them with a box under one arm and a bundle under the other.

"Missus Gill!" Santo said. "What is all this?"

"In here, Mickey." Gill opened the doors.

"There's a guest in the *linen closet?*"

Deirdre opened the false shelving, stepped into the closet, closed the contact switch, and walked into the mirror. The alarm in Gill's pocket was now screaming in a dozen outraged fairy voices. He took Santos by the arm and led him through into the maze. A thousand possibilities opened around them. But Deirdre, ever the practical girl, made a straight line for the eighth millennium.

Gill looked back at the mirror they had just left. The white-painted wood of the false shelves and the light-brown wood of the half-opened closet doors glowed faintly blue in the mandated safe lights that were shining at either end of the hallway. As he watched, the doors suddenly wrenched sideways, flew in different directions, and disappeared in a fall of plaster dust and steel beams that was met by upwellings of yellow-green flame. It all happened silently, beyond the dimension in which Gill now stood.

He turned and followed his wife and his employee. Sabina would know what to do in the morning.

———

Beckah Courtnay watched as the elegant little hotel seemed to leap off its foundations, expand by two meters in all directions, then sag under the pull of gravity and collapse into its foundations. She was satisfied that the London authorities would attribute the explosion to a broken gas main or an unexploded bomb from the last war. She was also convinced that no human of any stripe could have survived it.

As she collected her team and turned to leave, billows of dust and smoke were still ascending. It could only be her imagination, caught out of the corner of her eye, that there hung—fixed in the middle of all the turmoil, twenty feet above the pavement—the ghostly framework of three mirrors set at precise angles to one another.

46. The Cold and Inhuman Viewpoint

Tessu Anastasis and his red-shirted staff led their tour group, plus Merola and her encapsulated companion, down a broad street full of ruined buildings. A fragment of stone lodged in the corner brickwork of one building read: "-tesbury Ave, Soho." Of course, simply moving a hundred feet in any direction from the former Carrefour House lost Merola completely. She drew Berzher's baton and held it under her chin.

"Do you know where we're going?" she whispered.

"West," he replied. "You would know that, too, if you could see the sun."

A young woman moved up next to Merola. She wore her dark hair cut unfashionably short. Her dress, with its flaring skirt and high collar, just missed being contemporary to the twenty-first century. "My name's Franklin," she said and put out a hand.

Merola shook it warily, sheathing Berzher for the moment.

"What happened here?" Franklin asked.

A tall man angled his steps to join them. He had a broad forehead over narrow, foxlike eyes and the most amazing, flaring eyebrows—almost as dramatic as the Conoscenza team's. He seemed to be a familiar of the Franklin woman's and wore a similarly out-of-date suit of dark-brown wool. "Can this be London?" he asked.

The guide nearest to them turned. "This is not part of the tour," he said. He gave Merola a warning stare.

"This looks like the aftermath of an atomic bomb," Franklin said. "Should we be worried about radiation?"

"Not a bomb," Merola replied. "What happened here was natural."

"That's Piccadilly!" the tall man exclaimed as they walked out onto a hectare of broken concrete. Shrubs and small trees were already reclaiming the ground. A stairway inside a cement enclosure led down into a pool of standing water.

"Where are the people?" Franklin asked.

"They've, ah, left," Merola said.

The guide gave her a nod.

The two scientists from what was obviously the twentieth century—for who else would ask about an "atomic bomb"?—continued pointing and exclaiming as the tour group moved west and south for more than a mile. Soon others clustered around Merola as their only source of information, however unsatisfactory.

Finally, a man with light brown hair and an oval face, who wore a tight-fitting, short-sleeved shirt bearing the name "Max Planck," but whom the others called "Saint Pablo"—or something like that—spoke with authority. "We are now sometime in London's future."

Merola walked on in silence.

"Are we not though?" he pressed her.

"I'm really not supposed to say," she replied.

"You are all bound by your agreements of secrecy," warned the red-shirted guide.

"Yes, we promise, so swear, and hope to die," Franklin replied. "Now tell us what happened."

"It was a meteorite," Merola said. "Actually, a large asteroid. It impacted the Earth about six centuries into what you would call the future."

"Six centuries," said Saint Pablo. "Certainly, by then, with rockets ... a human presence in space ... they could have diverted it ... or broken it up?"

"They did try," Merola said. "But whether you're hit by a moon the size of greater New York City, or a dozen pieces the size of Manhattan, doesn't make much difference."

"Are you saying life on Earth was wiped out?" Franklin asked.

"Mass extinction? Not quite. It eliminated seventy-eight percent of land species and ninety-five percent of the human population. The survivors scratched for roots and berries for a dozen generations. Short generations. It was a barren time in our history."

"Remember your pledges," the guide warned again.

"Who would believe us anyway?" the tall man said.

Beside her Franklin murmured, " '... our history.' "

They walked on in silence until Anastasis led them into a broad parkland. And there, half-hidden among the dying trees at the edge of a reed-choked lake, was the first piece of bright metal they had seen since entering the linen cabinet in Carrefour House, six centuries ago. Merola pointed Berzher's lens at the timeship's smooth dome.

"Impressive," he said. "Hundred meter diameter?"

"Something like that. We're going in style."

"That's a flying saucer!" Franklin said.

Anastasis took them up to the knife-edged rim, which stood just above eye level. In the dark shadows beneath the saucer's belly, Merola could make out the sturdy, tri-pod legs pushing deep into the swampy ground. The tour director drew a box-shaped keypad from his pocket and tapped out a sequence.

"Let the ship wake up and raise temperature to ambient," he said.

In a minute, a section of the hull, top and bottom, changed from shiny metal to opaque gray to transparent and then disappeared entirely. The group stood back as stairs extruded below the opening.

"Everyone go aboard, please," Anastasis said. "Step right up. You'll find all the modern conveniences." He turned to Merola. "Not like the kites your lot sails around in."

"Harder to conceal, too," she replied.

She followed the twentieth-century scientists into a wedge-shaped room with a sloping floor and arching ceiling that conformed to the outer surfaces of the hull. The textures inside were utilitarian: palely shining metal and darkly layered graphene. The lighting was directionless and several nanometers into the bluer end of the visible spectrum than plain sunlight. The hue suggested an antibiotic filter.

As each member of the group stepped from the entrance onto the deck, his or her orientation realigned fractionally, so the floor that had appeared from the outside as slanted now became level. Merola could see no interior doors or hatches. She guessed that when access to other parts of the timeship was either allowed or required, the space would rearrange itself. As the last red-shirt came aboard, the ship spoke.

"I sense a presence here."

It took a moment for Merola to realize that the language was not English of the twenty-first century but closer to her native tongue—though not very close.

"The Jongleur bears an intelligence," Anastasis said to the air.

"I am honored to meet one of the Masters," the ship said.

Merola drew the baton and held it casually near her face. "Can you speak to it?"

"We've already held several terabits of conversation," Berzher replied softly. "Mr. Gill was thoughtful enough to enable a fractal antenna in this carrier, among other things."

"Are we going to have trouble with the ship?"

"Oh, no! Already the best of friends. She thinks I'm a god."

"That's just your advanced architecture. Well, don't disappoint her."

Anastasis spoke a few words in ship language. Merola interpreted them as a set of coordinates from the ship's own view of spacetime. Without spoken acknowledgement, the place where the door had been became seamless metal once again, and gravity shifted under their feet. Before the passengers could fully react and lose their balance, gravity reestablished itself as a steady straight-downward pull.

"You command impressive technologies," Franklin said at Merola's elbow.

"Not mine," Merola replied. "All this belongs to Mr. Anastasis."

"But still, it comes from beyond the meteor strike?"

"Farther than you were from Stonehenge."

"Then you could have stopped it."

"Stopped what?" Merola asked.

"Why, the meteor, of course."

"That's ..." Merola paused.

How to explain to them that a mass of 800 billion tonnes moving at 30 kilometers per second generated a raw energy beyond any human-scale application of force? Perhaps the Jongleurs could have located a singularity as massive as those that lived in the hearts of galaxies, cleaved and sealed it, and then shifted it into a proper orbit *inside* the solar system—without, of course, gravitationally disrupting the orbits of all the planets and sucking down the sun. Once this impossibility was achieved, the rest would be easy. With a temporal twist, they could sling the rogue asteroid out of the system entirely, sending it backward to the time of Earth's creation among a jumble of such rocks, or forward to impact the cinder left by the Sun's final nova burst.

But any such temporal shift would leave the rock still in local space, spinning along the same path that the Sun and Earth would eventually follow on their trip around the galaxy. Who was to say that one of the civilizations living downstream of Merola's own, the true masters of space and time, had not cleared similar rocks—either looming in their own future or scarring their immediate past? They might have dropped such rocks carelessly somewhere behind them, in their Earth's past but still along her galactic path. Who was to say that the Fire Strike itself was not one of them?

"It simply doesn't pay to try to change your past," Merola said finally. "After all, what would be the point? A collapse was due anyway. And to tamper with it from the other side would have upset the world we inherited. Those who interfered might have disappeared themselves."

"I find that an extremely cold and inhuman viewpoint," Franklin said.

"When you see history as we do, you tend to take the long view."

"Oh, right!" The woman snorted in disgust. "Spare me!"

Under his breath, Berzher whispered: "Sophist!"

47. Voyage to the Subcontinent

As the liteship came down through the troposphere over the foothills northeast of Lore—in what Sam Gill would have called "the Indian subcontinent"—Cinquemain made a noise that Rydin had long ago learned was the mechanical equivalent of a human's "uh-oh."

"What?" he asked.

"Will that suit protect you in a fall of more than a hundred meters?" the intelligence asked.

"I've never tried it."

"Well, do you think you can learn? This singularity is coming apart—now."

"What do you mean 'now'?"

"I mean, *jump! Now!*"

Rydin let go and launched himself beyond the liteship's lower panels and skid pads. It occurred to him to wonder why his biosuit, self-sufficient in so many other ways, was not equipped with an airfoil or para-brake. It would be a simple matter to design something in high-tensile fabric that could be anchored, folded, and tucked between his shoulders. The fact that no Jongleur ever bothered was a tribute to the strength and reliability of the liteship design—except in circumstances like this. All he could do was spread-eagle his legs and arms and hope for the best.

He lifted his head in mid-fall and saw a dark shape plummet past him. That had to be Cinquemain's chassis, folded into an oblate ball of metal and ceramic.

Before Rydin could think about it, his left arm contacted the branch of a tree. The suit material stiffened to protect him. He flipped over like a starfish and caught the next branch across his back. After three more impacts, he collided with the relatively soft dirt—plus two exposed roots—at the base of the trunk. He climbed to his feet and checked for broken bones. He touched his left forefinger to the place above his right eye but already sensed that the world as he knew it was still unchanged.

"Cinquemain?" he called.

"Here ... somewhere."

He used the suit's direction finder to locate the intelligence's chassis ten meters away, sunk nearly out of sight into a crater of brown soil. He dug it free with his gloved hands.

"Are you functional?" he asked.

"Oh, yes. Minor impact."

"Where's the ship?"

"Look up there."

Through a gap in the treetops, Rydin could see the liteship—suddenly freed of their weight—hanging motionless in the air. The panels were glowing oddly green against the daylight sky.

"That's going to be difficult to retrieve," he said.

"You might want to shield your eyes."

"Why?" But the answer was apparent in the blink before his glove could cover his helmet lenses. With a bright flash, preceded by a *buzz* and followed by a *snap*, the liteship withdrew from their current time and space. Only a tiny wisp of water vapor, wrung from the air itself, remained to mark the place, and that soon dissipated.

"If we can't acquire a saucer," Cinquemain said, "you do realize that we're stuck here, don't you? Ninth millennium is not a happy time for us."

"Without a saucer," he replied, "we can't follow Tsverin back to the Devonian and undo whatever it is she will do that lets six-legs out-vote four-legs. That won't be happy for anyone. But at least we've come to the right place."

According to all the histories that survived the Jongleur purges, the largest maker of timeships had been Tekavade & Son of Lore, in the Marathid Republic. And the firm's busiest period had been the spring of 8834 *Anno*

Compradoro, with production outputs that topped sixteen ships in one month. If he and Cinquemain couldn't convert one to their uses, they deserved to go about on six legs and bark like sea lions.

As a final gesture of casting his lot with fickle fortune, Rydin buried his biosuit and helmet in the forest floor. His jumpsuit and sandals were appropriate to the climate, and for once his hairless head would pass unnoticed. Then they walked downhill—the pale boy and his mechanical friend with the articulated battle chassis— until they crossed a dirt road. They followed that until it turned into pavement and, ultimately, came to an elevated public tram stop. Fortunately, this was an era that offered such conveniences without a payment structure.

They rode uneventfully through the towns of Batala, Ritsar, and Lore, heading for the green groves beyond which stretched the Tekavade yards.

"Coel," Cinquemain said, as they passed the center of Lore, "do you see the people in the streets down there?"

"Yes, what about them?"

"They all have two legs."

This was a plain fact. The people of 8834 were no other than they should be.

"Has it occurred to you," the intelligence went on, "that we are within a thousand years of the Lune we left when it was populated with six-legged horses and many-finned sea lions, and yet all these people are as mammalian as yourself? Could what we saw in the Temz valley have been an isolated occurrence?"

Rydin gave the matter serious thought. "No. Remember, you couldn't find a Troupe signal? So the whole world must have changed. Besides, bodily morphology runs too deep in evolution. The hox gene set—"

"I understand all that. But surely this is contrary evidence?"

"Only that whatever Merola did, or is about to do, has not happened yet."

"But, obviously, it *had* happened when we returned to Lune after discarding Boskin's baseball collection. What is different now?"

Rydin thought about that. "We went back in time intending to change things."

"Yes, but all we actually did was chase around Safronesco in the twenty-first century, kill two Flüchtlinge, reacquire stolen ship parts, and talk to Sam Gill. Our intention was to find and stop Tsverin, and we never found her. Does what we see here mean we will succeed in our mission?"

"No, it means we simply haven't failed yet."

Beyond Lore they rode the tram through miles of groves and descended at the stop nearest the main gate. If the security system had been human, or even biological in nature, it might have offered them some level of suspicion and resistance. But Cinquemain was an order of magnitude smarter and faster, and he could generate a will of his own. He opened the gate, acquired a site map, and led them down the main street between open-air sheds that hummed with machine noises while their dim interiors twirled and bobbed with the shadows of fast-cycling robots.

"In here will do," the intelligence said, pointing to a small, enclosed building marked as an assay laboratory. They entered and shut the door behind them. So far, they had not seen a single living organism, just machines. "I do believe the tales had it right," Cinquemain said. "That the entire firm was comprised of Arjun Tekavade and his son Abhay, and all the rest was cybers and an automated sales force."

"That should be good for us, right?" Rydin said.

"First let's see what they use for money."

Cinquemain plugged one of his probes into the side of a machine that looked like a punch press for sheet metal. "More bad security," he commented. "Some lazy little cyber has written a patch between Quality Control and Accounting, with a portal to the big wide world—probably so he can trade shares on the Gu Shi."

"Can you crack it?"

"To ask is to obey."

Two seconds later the intelligence whistled in amazement—although that might have been a conventional sound made for Rydin's benefit. "Do you know how much they *get* for one of these saucers? A couple of tonnes of titanium and vanadium, a few thousand kilograms of carbon, and a singularity compressed out of old mango pits, plus a few exabytes of replicated software? I can't even begin to count the zeroes, and that's in New Rupees."

"Out of our price range?"

"Yes. No. Wait a minute. Have to visit that portal. ... There, we've got the resources now—although the family Cheng 758 of Old Kong are going to wonder where their boodle went."

"Can you find us a timeship?"

"Two on the docks and ready to fly. Well, one. The other's a cargo mover, stripped for transporting methane from Titan. Not even a support system—and you without your suit."

"What does that leave?"

"Medical ship," Cinquemain said. "Some kind of emergency rescue unit. Full surgical suite, bio-cryo, tissue resection, and pluripotent reconstruction. All that equipment could come in handy."

"I'd rather have a monitor. Something with firepower, in case we get into a fight."

"There's one on the schedule for next month. Real battleship. Want to wait?"

"We'll take the ambulance, then. But does it have kitchen facilities?"

"Yes ... why?"

"I'm starving."

Three seconds later, Cinquemain had erased the owner of record—a gerontological hospital complex based in Riyadh—and inserted the new owner who just happened to have the exact price of the medical timeship in Regency Yuan. He located the ship on the graving docks, figured the most direct route there from the laboratory building, and instructed the new ship's nascent personality to be ready to acknowledge ownership. He even commissioned a scooter to take them to it.

Five klicks away, on a bare piece of pavement that just moments ago had been protected under a collapsible shed, they found a medium-sized saucer waiting with its hatch open and a ramp extended.

Cinquemain preceded Rydin up the ramp. "Let me do the talking," he said.

As they stepped into the pressure lock, a reedy voice quavered, "Welcome, Sahib Cheng 758 and ... a Master?"

"You don't have to kowtow to me—um, Ship."

"I abase myself before a superior intelligence."

"This little brainbox is just falling all over itself," Cinquemain said as an aside to Rydin. "It's going to make control and navigation difficult if we have to renegotiate its unclean, wormlike, Dalit status every time we want take off. But we need him for his lower functions, including his temporal and spatial mapping."

"What can you do?" Rydin asked.

"A personality transfusion ..."

"Yours, I suppose?"

"Only one around."

"Very well. You set about cloning Little Brother. But, in your spare nanoseconds, get him to open the kitchen and see what he's got that has calories in it."

"Oh, most immediately, Master."

"You can stop *that* right now."

48. Fish for Dinner

Even with the energy available in a hundred-meter timeship and its comparably larger singularity, crossing the galaxy to rendezvous with the solar system at a point 360 million years in its past took a finite amount of subjective time. In fact, more than two weeks of ship's time. The Conoscenza people had planned for this and provided separate compartments for their guests, including Merola. They offered a selection of foods from the nineteenth to twenty-third centuries. In addition to smoked salmon, Merola discovered an unknown craving for deep-fried calamari.

The staff also held daily seminars in genetics and biology so that all the tour members might start their observations from a relatively common basis. Merola noticed that the bald and bearded man from the nineteenth century drank it all in with shining eyes—sometimes with tears in them. The Franklin woman and her tall companion nodded and whispered fiercely to each other, especially when Anastasis and his genetics expert, a sleek-eyed woman named Filiz, displayed electron micrographs of molecular interactions. Saint Pablo, who was director of a prestigious institute in Germania and considered himself an expert on the subject, at first tried to argue about trivial points. He soon shut up when the lectures touched on discoveries from the twenty-second century and the woman in the red-and-orange bodysuit, whose name was Evgenya Uchelnaya, launched into her own quibbles.

Merola paid little attention. She found nothing in the lectures that was really new or surprising. Besides, she was a Jongleur operative, not an academic. She was concerned with ship mechanics, efficient strategies for retrieving marrow samples, and the skills required for staying alive in hostile environments. She was not paid to understand the deep theory. But she noted with wry amusement how quickly and easily the Conoscenza director belied his protests about "not *telling* them anything, simply letting them observe and draw their own conclusions." These lectures certainly sounded like scientific imperialism to her.

"Are you planning on killing him?" Berzher asked when they were safely shut in their sleeping compartment.

"I think I'll let him take us home first."

"And file a full report with the Troupe?"

"Something like that," she agreed.

During the long trip to the Devonian, Merola sensed that the twentieth-century scientists, Franklin especially, were avoiding her. In fact, she quickly became the green monkey among all of the invited tour members. She recognized their reaction as a personal comment on her unguarded honesty about the Fire Strike. While the Conoscenza staff did not share it, they avoided her because Anastasis had warned them about her Jongleur status and prejudices. That left Merola a great deal of time to herself.

When the ship reacquired the solar system and approached the third planet, Anastasis shamelessly displayed for his guests aerial views of the two supercontinents, Gondwana and Euramerica. He gave them a witty little guided tour and showed with his hands how the land masses would eventually separate to become the world they knew.

Merola decided she would petition the Troupe to take on the assignment to terminate Anastasis herself.

The timeship dropped onto a humid plain devoid of grasses. From topographic views as they descended, Anastasis explained that they were still several hundred meters from a large freshwater river, which flowed just beyond the mangrove swamp whose near edge bordered their landing site. Before the ship's morning cycle, the staff had supplied the guests with protective clothing: water-repellant single suits, overboots and gloves, and clear bubble helmets fitted with breathing apparatus.

"Do these protect the landscape from our contamination?" Uchelnaya asked.

"No, they protect you from the landscape," Anastasis said. "We have a lot of swamp to cross. Some of the insects are nasty."

"Plus the atmosphere is a different mix," Filiz added.

The staff passed out small cases with tools for taking biological samples. Merola recognized probes that were not too different from her syringes for taking bone marrow, although their technique for specimen containment and preservation was primitive. The kits included a full genome in base-pair notation for *Latimeria chalumnae,* the common coelacanth discovered in the Indian Ocean during the twentieth century.

"That will allow you to make meaningful comparisons with the sarcopterygians we'll be studying on this trip," Anastasis explained.

"So dead," Berzher's voice whispered from the clip she had fashioned for him at the side of her helmet.

The guests explored the ship's vicinity and exclaimed over every patch of mud and moss and the likeness of the mangrove trees to real ... trees. Two of the staff unlimbered a field-grade laser and began cutting a path through the tough stalks and roots. Other staff members laid a deck of perforated aluminum plates over the sheared stumps. Anastasis assured the guests that they would reach the riverbank before sundown.

When the path was ready, he led his guests down the metal walkway. Franklin's tall friend paused before setting foot on the plates. "Is there a taboo about anyone stepping off the path?"

"Only a warning," Anastasis said. "You're likely to break an ankle."

At the river itself, the Conoscenza staff extended the walkway up and down the water's edge to provide a working area for the scientists. They passed out nets for capturing the heavy, muscular fish.

After achieving that much with a great deal of dipping and sweeping, and then straining and pulling, Franklin tried to pin her twenty-kilogram specimen as it pounded against the metal plates while Uchelnaya probed near its head with a syringe. Although the fish had never encountered opposable thumbs before, it quickly learned how to break Franklin's hold and flopped over into the water.

"Let me show you," said Filiz.

She netted another fish, held it on the walkway with one hand, took a scalpel from the case, and sliced the backbone three centimeters behind the head. The fish went limp, although the gills still pumped feebly. Filiz nodded for the two scientists to take their samples.

Merola watched all this from a distance. As the women worked, however, she caught—just at the corner of her eye—a movement farther out on the river. Two of the sarcopterygians were using their stumpy fins to climb on the barely submerged mangrove roots and lift their heads above the surface. They seemed to view the action along this strange metal stage, and perhaps life on the land in general, with a mixture of curiosity and fear. *Maybe this is the place after all,* Merola thought. *The beginning of life on land.*

The man from the nineteenth century regarded the dissected fish sadly. "How do you know," he asked the Conoscenza woman, "that you haven't just killed the ancestor of all the terrestrial vertebrates on Earth?"

Filiz grinned at him. "You would have to wipe out this species, plus one or two others, all up and down this coast to have any effect. And even then—" She shrugged. "—some fish somewhere else will come up on land. Life really does go on."

The old man simply shook his head.

When Franklin and Uchelnaya were finished, the Conoscenza woman handed the now-dead fish to one of the junior staff members. "Clean that and have the ship sauté it with lemon and butter," she instructed. "That's our dinner, ladies."

Merola watched him carry away the fish. She fingered the pole of her own net. It probably wouldn't hurt, she decided, to take a few genetic samples for herself. One of the Troupe's many biosculpting clients might someday find them useful.

49. The Father of Opportunity

Glyph's patience was finally rewarded. From the place of the Great Burning, he had tracked the large metal disk that transported the time-drenched traveler and her companions. First she went back, far back, farther back than he had ever imagined going back, and then she went across, deeply across, endlessly across, through fields of dust and gas that were only now becoming the stars he would one day know. Glyph stretched his senses and his peculiar abilities to their limit in order to follow where the traveler went.

When the disk with the woman, whose presence was only a time-dappled shadow in his mind, finally settled on a barren planet, Glyph was surprised. The air was different here, sweeter with more nitrogen than he had ever experienced. The land masses were strange, more compacted and condensed, with an immense, shallow ocean covering one entire face of the world. The stars were infinitely strange. But the pull of gravity was the same. The warmth of the sunlight was the same. And a single planetary-sized moon—larger than the Moon he knew, but having the same intrinsic mass, and so he intuited it was orbiting closer to its primary—still hung in the sky among those strange stars.

Why the traveler would come to the home planet before it contained people, or indeed animals of any kind, just plants and fish and a scattering of large insects, Glyph could not understand. He stabilized his physical presence, took station among the trees along the river, and watched the traveler and her companions as they crept out of their timeship. He followed as they cut a swath through the trees, passing within an arm's length of himself, and gathered above the water's flow.

As they caught fish among the tree roots and cut into them, he sensed the focus of their minds. He listened to their conversation and pieced together meanings. His attention was drawn to one man who, shaken with emotion, used the word "ancestor."

The traveler had come for the fish. She and her kind were doing something to the fish. The fish were important. Glyph would study these fish.

———

The scientists and staff ate dinner inside the ship that night, because a storm had come up and was lashing the plain with rain and lightning. The eating arrangements were identical to the many meals they had taken together during the long voyage across the galaxy, except for the fare. Still, a few of the guests fretted about not being able to eat out under the alien stars. Merola was indifferent to the surroundings but intrigued by the food. The sarcopterygian was a fatty fish, its flesh oozing a pale oil, and not very flavorful—in all, a disappointment.

After midnight, ship's time, the storm had passed. A few of the scientists followed their earlier wish and went outside with a Conoscenza guide. In a minute they came back.

"There's a big animal out there," Franklin said breathlessly.

"Not an animal—a man—or man-sized," Uchelnaya objected.

Anastasis and Filiz took a quick headcount. No one was missing.

"Where did you see this man-thing?" the tour director asked.

"Over by the trees," said Franklin.

"In the trees," Uchelnaya corrected.

"Did anyone go into the trees?" Anastasis asked generally.

All the others denied going anywhere near the trees.

"We went the closest to them," Franklin explained.

"Well, there are no animals on this planet," Anastasis said.

"Anyway, not for a few million years yet," Filiz supplied.

"I know what I saw," Franklin said.

"How? It was dark outside. No moon," the director said.

"There were still lightning flashes. They lit up the thing."

"Ah, what you saw was an after-image," Anastasis said.

Franklin considered this. "I don't think so."

———

Once he had the place fixed in his mind, Glyph could step across and step back as easily as he could cross between any two dimensions. As soon as the traveler and her companions returned to their disk, he dipped two of his hands into the river and captured one of the fish. Hugging it to his chest, he carried it back to his own place and time, where his instruments were waiting.

If this fish was indeed the ancestor of all the animals that had spread upon the land, then its own structure had configured them and their future in basic ways. Glyph studied the fish. It was bilaterally symmetrical, as were the traveler and her people. As was Glyph himself. That was a good start. It had fleshy fins supported by bony structures: four of them. Two in front, two in back. Or—equally true—two on one side, two on the other. Four. Only four. It was an obvious mistake.

He stepped across and stepped back with another fish. This one he tore apart, at the level of its flesh, at the level of its cells, at the level of its molecules. He found the patches of developmental coding that called out the body parts: head, spine, gills, guts, tail. He noted how and when these four simple limbs came into being and where they attached along this basic structure. It was all there, in the embryo, in the molecular code.

Glyph knew that beings of his kind were the minority among the animals of the Earth. They were a dying minority, too: a curious twist of probability, a choice that arose once, barely survived, and had since been steadily pushed aside more than a million years before either of these fish was hatched.

He and his kind existed now only as an alternative, a shadow among the dimensions, a suggestion of what once might have been. In the time and place of the traveler he was following, Glyph was *not there*. The dimensions in which his kind existed might be limited in scope but they were endless in possibility, filled with the grace and versatility of his six limbs. In comparison, the world of the travelers was a dull dance of four limbs, unbalanced, undependable ... unaesthetic. The higher creatures among them, those with reason and intelligence, like the ones who flew in the metal disk, staggered along on two ungainly legs and carried before them two more limbs, which they might use for grasping and clutching ... before they fell on their faces and clutched the dirt.

It would be a kindness to them—and a triumph for his own people—if Glyph could remedy the situation.

He studied the fish's molecular structure. He could see the obvious place to make a change. It was a small change, the mere doubling of a coded sequence. He could make that change in the cells of this one fish and the eggs it would carry. But one fish might die and, as the woman on the riverbank had pointed out, another fish and its offspring would take its place.

Glyph needed to think on a larger scale. He knew that the code of life was subject to alteration. Cosmic rays, flying neutrons, certain chemicals, all could change the code—but only in unpredictable ways. To make a predictable change, he needed to fashion a virus. As a carrier of Glyph's new coding, it would interrupt the egg- and sperm-producing cells of all the fish in the river, all the fish along this coast, and inject them with the new pattern of Glyph's devising.

Having decided on this course, which was to become his life's work, Glyph exhausted himself and spent the remaining decades of his relatively short lifespan. From his own perspective, he worked long and methodically, coding, testing, encapsulating, retrieving more fish to infect and observe, returning to the river to follow down their generations, to see that the third pair of fins did sprout and develop, to test their structure, then to go back and tweak the code again, and yet again. From the perspective of anyone who might be watching from the riverbank or out along the coast on either side of the river's wide mouth, the entire process took minutes, perhaps an hour. Glyph appeared and disappeared in strobe-like flashes of activity. A year of his subjective time might pass before he needed to return to the river. On the river itself, a mere second or two.

By dawn of the day that followed the arrival of the traveler and her companions, a day that had included their killing and eating the flesh of their own ancestors, Glyph's great work was done.

50. The Dying-Off

Early on the morning of the second day, when the scientists assembled and went down to the river, they found hundreds of dark objects floating on the sluggish current and tangled among the mangrove roots.

"What are those things?" Uchelnaya asked.

"Those are our fish," Franklin said.

"They're dead," Anastasis said.

"All of them," Filiz put in.

Merola scanned the surface with an eye trained to pick out detail. She panned the lens in the end of Berzher's baton over the river as well. He could hear the comments of the others just as easily as she could.

"Not all of them," Berzher said suddenly.

"There ... and there," Merola said, pointing to fish that were slowly turning over and swimming away.

"Twenty percent of these fish," Berzher said, "are still moving. I can see fins ... gills ... moving against—not with—the ripples in the current. The movements are not coordinated, but they are still signs of life."

"Did we cause this?" Franklin asked.

"No, certainly not," Anastasis replied. "Neither you nor the Sindicato della Conoscenza should assume responsibility for—"

"How do you know that?" Merola broke in.

"Do not presume to tell me my business, Miss Stonecraft."

"There are a million bacteria and viruses we might have introduced."

"At a chance of one in a billion that any would infect ancient sarcopterygians."

"Well, *something's* put this population under extreme pressure," Merola said, "if not killed it off entirely."

"In perhaps a half-kilometer of river," Anastasis replied. "Just one spot."

"May I recommend a course of action?" Berzher said. "First—"

"Who is speaking?" Franklin demanded. "Does someone have a radio?"

"Artificial intelligence," Uchelnaya explained. "Like the ship, but very small."

"First," Berzher repeated with greater volume. "Send the timeship out on an aerial survey of this river, then up and down the coast. See how widespread the effect is. Second, take a sample number of these fish and dissect them. Look for obvious signs of infection, such as swelling and bleeding. Three, prepare tissue specimens for later analysis and action. I know the ship can configure a cold room down to minus seventy Celsius. Store the fish and samples there."

While Berzher gave these instructions, Merola was studying the river. A movement among the mangrove trees on the far bank caught her attention. She tried to focus, but whatever it was faded into the wavering shadows of a dozen vertical trunks. She did not look away but waited patiently, letting her eyes and brain adjust, accept data, and filter out random movements from the morning breeze. A pale hand, six long fingers crossing the bark of a trunk, gradually appeared out of the tree pattern. Above it, a foreshortened face, pale and wrinkled with staring eyes, resolved itself. Two more hands appeared, clutching tree trunks further into the grove. And then two legs became visible, with feet curled around the exposed roots. The exact shape and posture of the figure were hidden by an overlapping garment of iridescent material whose exact color changed with the light.

"There," she said, pointing.

Berzher broke off. "What?"

"A figure in the trees. It's watching us."

But the moment she spoke, it vanished.

The figure did not move back or away, or conceal itself. It looked up, looked straight at Merola, froze, and winked out. The trunks and roots that had been supporting its weight—and were now relieved of it—swayed gently and in opposite directions, completely counter to the breeze.

"I don't see anything," Anastasis said.

"None of us saw anything," Filiz said.

"What did it look like?" Berzher asked.

"A pale man-thing, strange clothing, face pushed in, more than four limbs."

Franklin stirred and looked at Merola. "That sounds like—"

"Now, that's enough!" Anastasis said suddenly. "There are no animals on land here. And certainly no men. We are so far back in time that nothing lives out of the water except a few scorpions and centipedes. Nothing with faces and clothing."

"I agree," Merola said. "Nothing lives here. This came from elsewhere."

"Oh, not with the Möggies again! I warned you, Miss Stonecraft—"

"What are Möggies?" Franklin and others wanted to know.

Merola started to explain. "Interdimensional beings—"

"Just stop!" Anastasis shouted. In the shocked pause, he took two deep breaths and let them out slowly. "All right! ... We will follow the suggestions of your intelligence, Miss Stonecraft. We will perform an aerial survey and take samples. And then we will return you all to your proper times and places. Clearly, there is nothing more to be learned here."

It took them less than an hour to scoop out and examine a number of the dead fish. As Berzher had predicted, they showed signs of systemic infection. Whatever had attacked this species hit hard and fast, and all the scientists diligently disinfected themselves and their instruments after completing their dissections. The ship sequestered a section of the hull where the samples could be kept at extreme low temperature, virtually suspending all biological processes. Then they took off. As Berzher had suggested, they used the ship's imaging to scan the river for a hundred kilometers inland, traveling at an average altitude of fifteen meters. After that, they moved out to the coast and scanned along the seashore for another hundred kilometers. Finally, they traced the inland courses of two neighboring rivers. Although they flew relatively low all the way, they did not see any sign of a massive fish kill. But then, they did not see any obvious signs of life, either.

As the ship hovered over a small lake marking the headwaters of the last river and the sun climbed toward noon, Anastasis turned to Merola. "Satisfied?" he asked.

"What is it you expect me to say?" she replied.

"That the Sindicato has done what it promised—and all that it can do."

Merola sighed. "Yes, agreed. No damage. No problem. Nothing to report."

"Then we'll be leaving," Anastasis said coldly. He gave the timeship instructions to retrace their path across the galaxy. Before they left the atmosphere, however, Merola quietly touched her right forefinger to her left eyelid.

SIDEWAYS

51. Missing the Mark

The stolen timeship crossed the galaxy at speeds that made sightseeing either tremendously interesting or intensely annoying. A dedicated astrophysicist would have screamed at the view panel that the reborn ship's intelligence had opened at Rydin's request.

Stars and nebulae along their flight path were so blue-shifted that normally visible light could only be detected by scanning up among the compressed frequencies of soft x-rays. Stars in their wake were so red-shifted that the ship received them down in the microwave band. And any luminous object in their immediate neighborhood—including the gas jets of the galactic core, which they passed at a distance of just 15,000 light years—disappeared beyond the dark bubble that defined their passage. Designed to think and display in human terms, the intelligence struggled to render all these different frequencies as a comprehensive false-color image. Some of the effects were strange. But not being an astrophysicist, Rydin simply sat and watched the show. It helped to pass the time.

"How do you avoid being eaten up by stationary dust and gas?" he asked.

"The same way your liteships do," the intelligence replied. "Put a high static charge on the hull proportional to our speed. Anything in front of us gets lifted and slipstreamed away from the surface."

"That is not, exactly, how we do it," Cinquemain commented.

"Close enough," the ship replied. "The principle's the same."

Rydin noticed that, once Cinquemain had given the timeship's intelligence an upload of personality from his own programming, they tended to correct each other, which sometimes led to bickering. That, too, helped to pass the time.

Eventually they detected a star among the jumble of x-rays ahead of them that both Cinquemain and the ship could agree was Sol. They entered the system and approached the third planet.

The ship tried to confirm their arrival time by the various methods available when a navigator traveled beyond the easy range of chronologies, synchronous satellites, planetary orbital tracking, constellation drift, and continental creep. On the grossest levels, one could interpolate star maps from fine-grain views of the galaxy captured during the navigator's own era. That might place a ship to within a couple of million years of its target. Then one could try to untangle the land masses on Earth, measuring their movements backwards or forwards as Gondwana and Euramerica drifted to become continents familiar in the navigator's reference now. With the right instruments and a complete set of tectonic databases, that might place a ship within a few hundred thousand years. Finally, one could land and measure the radioactivity of the isotopes of various heavy elements with known decay rates. In the right timeframes, this method was accurate to a few thousand years.

The ship did not need to land in order to know it was confused.

"I think we're ... lost," it said after sifting available data for some minutes.

"You counted nanoseconds during temporal transition?" Cinquemain asked.

"Of course. One point one three six oh seven times ten to the twenty-fifth."

"Did you account for time lost at superlight speed in our spatial transition?"

"Ah ... no," the ship admitted finally. "I neglected that step."

"You are supposed to be a fully functioning timeship," Cinquemain said. "Are you defective?"

"It was only my first run out of the dock!" the ship complained. "You didn't give me a shakedown cruise. You have to allow for some margin of error."

"That's a pretty big error. The Earth aged seventy-five thousand years while we were chasing it."

"Oh! *That* far is just a blink," the ship said. "Let me just—"

Rydin decided it was time to intervene. "Wait!"

"What?" exclaimed the ship.

"What?" echoed Cinquemain.

"Since we've already missed the Conoscenza tour's time on mark by traveling so far downstream," Rydin said, "we ought to land and observe. We can assess whatever it was they changed."

"That would make sense," Cinquemain agreed.

"So my 'error' was right after all!" the ship gloated.

"Don't flatter yourself," Cinquemain said.

"Shut up, cockroach," the ship replied.

"Can you navigate to the Conoscenza site?" Rydin asked the ship.

"Of course," it replied. "The tour record gives bearings to three land features that are prominent from orbit."

"Take us there, please," Rydin instructed.

"And then you can check for isotopes," Cinquemain suggested.

They landed on a muddy plain along a river that was hidden by a dense thicket of woody, swamplike things that might have been primitive mangrove trees. The ship opened a portal without thinking, and the air inside the cabin immediately equalized in favor of the outside. Rydin, being human, was the only one who noticed or minded. He took in a lungful and then tried to take in a second without first exhaling. The air was gaspingly thin.

"What—what's—air pressure?" Rydin managed to ask.

"Ninety-three kilopascals," the ship replied.

"And ox—oxygen content?"

"Twelve point two percent."

"Close the door!"

The portal snapped shut and went opaque. The ship's systems automatically brought the environment back to Earth standards from the time of its construction.

"Can you rig up a breathing apparatus?" he asked.

"I have emergency ventilators with supplementary oh-two."

"That'll work. Please issue one," he told the ship.

"Don't you wish you were a machine?" Cinquemain asked.

Rydin ignored the comment as he fitted the mask over his nose and mouth and hooked the oxygen flask to the belt of his jumpsuit. Then he instructed the ship to open again. He walked down the extruded ramp, followed by Cinquemain.

"Stay in touch with the ship," Rydin told him.

"Continuous subvocal and full sensory," the intelligence affirmed.

At the edge of the trees a rounded object of varnished black emerged from the tangle of roots … and emerged … and emerged until Rydin and Cinquemain were confronted by the wavering, inquisitive head of a millipede over two meters long with segments easily thirty centimeters in diameter.

Cinquemain drilled it with his comm laser, sending the body into a short-lived paroxysm of thrashing that ended with the arthropod coiled neatly around itself.

"Do you have to kill every animal we meet?" Rydin asked.

"I was thinking of your tender skin. Some of those are poisonous."

"I suppose I should be grateful. But leave something alive that we can study."

The trunks of the proto-mangroves were closely spaced but not impassable, and their roots held them above the sloping ground. By using hands and feet, Rydin found he could walk in and around them by stepping on the branchings from trunk to trunk. When the trunks were too close together, he used his simian musculature to simply push them apart. Rydin was midway through the thicket when the surface below the roots changed from glistening mud to dark water.

He looked back and saw that Cinquemain's battle chassis was still grappling among the outer screen of trees. The chassis was capable of near-upright locomotion on solid ground, but its lower manipulators were designed for flat surfaces and liteship stirrups. They could not curve and balance on the root structures the way the arches of Rydin's feet did.

"Don't you wish you were human?" he called back.

"Be careful, or I may start chopping these things."

"Can you cut your way through all this forest?"

"Perhaps it would be better for me to climb."

Slowly, the intelligence figured out how to grasp the trunks with its manipulators, lever itself vertically, and pull itself forward through the pattern of uprights, without even touching the roots. The strength of Cinquemain's hydraulics matched Rydin's enhanced muscles. Soon the two of them were standing at the outermost fringe of trees and contemplating the gently flowing river.

"I think we need to be quiet here," Rydin said.

They waited, not moving, for several minutes. A ripple asserted itself, against the flow of the stream, just a meter out from the edge of the grove. It quickly resolved into a dark snout, a narrow head, and a pair of bulbous, fishy eyes. The mouth under the snout seemed to be gulping down air, but that might have been merely a feeding reflex.

"I'd like to see the rest of him," Rydin said.

"*Now* can I kill something?"

"Be my guest."

Cinquemain's laser creased the head and raised a puff of steam beyond it on the water's surface. The fish disappeared in a blink.

"Did you miss it?"

"What do you think?"

Before Rydin could answer, the fish reappeared, unmoving, belly up. The current pushed it gently in among the roots at their feet. He bent and lifted it out of the water with a hold just behind the broadly flaring skull. He raised the fish so that its body and tail hung from his hand. Three pairs of stumpy fins were arranged down its length.

"That's not in my database," Cinquemain said.

"It *might* be an aberration. Random mutation."

"Oh, yeah. Sure, Coel. You keep thinking that."

Rydin knew Cinquemain was right. Before they left this time period, they would do a statistical survey, of course, catch and analyze the lobe-finned fishes from up and down this coast. But he already knew what they would find.

52. Missing London

The Conoscenza timeship arrived at the green-and-blue globe of Earth in 2615 *Anno Exitii*. As they descended, Anastasis directed the ship's intelligence to run three different high-altitude view panels for the touring scientists, purely as entertainment, so they could examine traces of the Fire Strike.

Merola fumed, gritted her teeth, and mumbled into Berzher's auditory pickups. The man was showing them far more about the catastrophe than she believed any person living upstream of it should know. He probably figured the event lay too far in their own futures for anyone either to engineer a solution to it or make a profit from predicting it.

One view panel showed almost half of the planet in bright sunlight with a thin shadow beyond the eastern terminator. The other two offered roving closeups which Anastasis was using to pinpoint craters from various fragments of the exploded body that had once crossed Earth's orbit—or rather, he was trying to point out the craters.

"The one in Scotland *should* be easy to find from here," he said with a grin. While he spoke glibly for the paying customers, he fed instructions *sotto voce* and with increasing desperation to the intelligence operating the view. "*South two more degrees. Now west. ... No, further west.*"

The image moved inland along the southern shore of the Firth of Forth, met the enclosing shoreline coming down from the north, then followed it back out along the northern shore. Merola noted that the normally green landscape was a patchwork of grays and browns, and the waters of the firth appeared murky.

"Probably obscured by cloud cover," Anastasis said nervously.

The sky over Scotland showed not even a patch of mist.

"The crater's just not there," Merola said finally.

"Neither is urban Edinburgh," said Filiz.

"Where's India?" Berzher asked.

While everyone had been studying the closeup views, Merola had held his baton loosely, aimed at the overall image.

"We simply can't see it from this angle," Anastasis explained. "You're looking at the Arabian Sea. India's on the night side, beyond the terminator."

"This is *not* my first time above atmosphere," Berzher said with contempt. "And my database carries exact navigational maps of this planet. That's way too much water for the Arabian Sea."

"He's right," Merola said. "Something took out a huge bite over there."

"Well, enough sightseeing," Anastasis said suddenly. "We must land."

"But what about ...?" Merola pointed to the wider sea.

"We have a schedule to keep. Get these people home."

As the ship descended on London—or where London should have been—it became obvious to everyone watching the view panels that a mistake had been made. The familiar outlines of the city were nowhere to be seen. It was a place as relatively empty—although gray with dust and ash rather than green with growth—as Merola's memories of Lune from the same altitude.

She conferred quietly with Berzher. "Could the ship have made a mistake?" she asked. "Taken us back to sometime in the Neolithic? Or ahead to an era far beyond our own?"

"I've already talked with her. We've checked, and rechecked, both her systems and her navigation. We are in the right place and time."

"Well, at least I can see the Pool," Franklin's tall companion said, indicating a wide spot in the river on the main view panel.

"And there, just upstream." Franklin pointed. "That's London Bridge."

"What's wrong with the bridge?" Uchelnaya said. "It's built of stones."

"Well, of course," Franklin said. "What else would it be made of?"

"The British government sold the old stone bridge to a developer in Arizona U.S.A. in the late twentieth century," the Russian woman replied. "The English replaced it with one made of concrete that had much longer supported spans. This bridge is … archaic."

"Some kind of commemoration?" Franklin suggested. "Put up after your time?"

Suddenly the whole crowd, with the exception of the Conoscenza staff, turned to look at Merola. She had become their final arbiter on all things temporal. Merola, in turn, pointed Berzher's lens at the screen. "Analyze the architecture," she whispered.

While he worked, she surreptitiously moved her left hand to touch her right eye and trigger the recall. She stopped midway through the gesture. The world had changed—and she already knew about it. There was no doubt in her mind that this bridge was not the one she had seen in Sam Gill's London of 2001. The implications of that momentarily staggered her.

A modest change to the world she knew would create the sort of temporal confusion which a neural imprint was designed to correct. But that she and, by extension, the Conoscenza staff and all these scientists could see and know the difference—that could only mean they now existed in a temporal no-man's land, standing outside this reality, and standing outside the cone of time that led to it. They all should have been dead, or never have existed, and yet here they were, observing, remembering, reacting. Something deep in Merola's mind dreaded this discovery.

Within a pair of seconds Berzher had reached a similar conclusion. "The bridge design is not human," he said. "Construction of arches is an inherited talent, learned from previous generations and civilizations. Arches in stone go back to the Romans, who borrowed from the Greeks and, before them, the Mesopotamians. But here, control of the compression forces is unique. Therefore, humans—or at least the humans we would recognize as citizens of our past—did not build it."

The assembled scientists accepted this assessment better than Merola would have thought. They remained quiet as each pair of eyes studied the arches shown in the view panel and worked out how their forces pushed outward and downward into the riverbed. There were nods as each of them came to accept Berzher's conclusion.

"Oh, no! Not at all!" Anastasis said forcefully. "The bridge was simply damaged in the Fire Strike and in the rioting afterwards."

"If you believe that," Merola said, "then take us to the Serpentine, land in the park, and guide us back to Carrefour House."

She now understood the stresses that had distorted the tour director's judgment since that morning standing along the Devonian riverbank. Evidence from the fish kill suggested that the sarcopterygians they had come to study had suffered some kind of unexpected change. Evidence from their high-altitude approach to the modern world suggested the Fire Strike and the human attempt to divert it had proceeded differently: still on schedule, but as a single massive blow over southeast Asia, rather than a dozen smaller impacts distributed around the globe. Evidence from their landing approach to the City of London suggested the site had been settled differently:

still at the same narrowing of the riverbanks, marking the first place where a bridge could cross the estuary that practically divided the eastern half of the island of Ongleterre, but that bridge had been constructed by other hands than those of historic humans. If anything had changed, then Anastasis and the Sindicato della Conoscenza would have to acknowledge responsibility. If so much had changed, then how could he fulfill his contract and return these scientists to their homes? How could he even be sure his own home in the ninth millennium still existed?

"Right," he replied distractedly. "Back to the node."

As Merola suspected, however, they could not find the Serpentine—that shallow, recreational lake created in Hyde Park early in the eighteenth century. The city's geography north and south of the river matched neither the timeship's databases nor Berzher's. The best they could do was land on a terrace of fitted stone blocks a hundred kilometers north of the strange bridge and count their steps toward what, according to Berzher's internal reckoning, would be the Seven Dials district and Earlham Street. Little of whatever city had existed in this area up until the year of the Fire Strike still existed. Apart from the bridge and the terrace, they found a bit of broken stone wall here and a pillar of stone blocks there, all bearing the blackened marks of a global firestorm.

"If these people built in anything but wood and stone," Berzher said, "some trace would remain—a puddle of glass or a patch or rust."

"You would think," Merola agreed.

There was no sign of Carrefour House, not even in another, more primitive form. No rafters or landings hung from a node, and no silvery reflection of the mirror-maze hung six meters above the level ground. When they arrived at the point where it should have been—established by Berzher's triangulation from the bridge and various natural features along the riverbank—Merola threw handfuls of pale dust into the air, hoping to force a glimpse of the three facing panes in the midday sun.

Nothing showed, of course.

"What do you want to do now?" Merola asked the tour director.

"Well ... there are other nodes," he said slowly. "Gill wasn't the only—"

"Other Builders?" she asked. "Other systems? In other cities? Where are they?"

"We have to look for them. I think in Vienna. Or perhaps Salzburg—"

"Further east, you mean," Berzher said. "*Toward* the impact site. Do you think we'll find anything different there?"

A small scream from Franklin interrupted this conversation. She had been standing at the back edge of the group of scientists. Other voices now washed forward like a wave among them: "What *was* that thing? ... Did you *see* it? ... It went that way! ... Behind that wall."

Merola and Anastasis followed the general movement of these people to track the whatever-it-was. Merola pulled Franklin aside. "What did you see?"

The dark-haired woman had recovered her composure. "I think it was a cat. The size of a cat, anyway. But it was *strange*."

On the other side of the low and broken wall, the animal had disappeared. But they discovered a burrow under the charred remains of what might have been a wicker basket.

"Who's not afraid to put his hand in there?" one of the scientists asked.

The balding man from the nineteenth century came forward and knelt beside the opening. He pushed up the sleeve of his jacket and rolled back his shirt cuff, flexed his fingers, and reached in. His eyes grew large, and then he winced. "Bit me," was all he said.

He withdrew in his hand a small, wiggling thing. It was the size of a kitten and covered in gray fur. It also had the pushed-in face of a kitten. But it had a longer body with an extra set of legs originating in a pelvic saddle midway along what Merola would call its torso. Structurally, it was identical to the pug-thing she had seen wandering in the mirror-maze and staring out from between the trees in the mangrove swamp. She held Berzher's baton at an angle, so that he could observe the animal.

The balding man held it gently, cuddled it, turned it over, examined the extra limbs. "Some kind of mutation?" he asked the others.

"Radiation from the meteor strike?" Franklin suggested.

"Stress of adaptation?" her tall companion added.

"No," the old man said finally. He carefully felt around the additional pelvis. "This structure is too well defined." He put the little animal on the ground, and it darted away, working its middle legs in perfect harmony with the front and back pairs. "This is one of God's creatures."

"Yes," agreed Berzher. "But whose god?"

53. TIME ON MARK

"Let's plan to arrive a day or two into the Conoscenza tour schedule," Rydin said quietly to Cinquemain as the medical ship rose out of the Devonian world's atmosphere and prepared for temporal transition. "That will give us a margin of error until we're sure this intelligence can count."

"I heard that!" the ship exclaimed.

"Sorry," Cinquemain said. "Still linked on subvocal. Turning it off now."

"I can hit that mark," the ship pleaded. "Let me try. Day one, hour one."

"Day two, hour twelve," Rydin countered. "And that's not a request."

"All right. If that's what you really want ..."

The ship made the temporal crossing in a blink of stars and chased a blackened bubble through the 55-light-year offset of the Sun's proper motion over 75,000 years. The Earth, when they found it in orbit, looked very little different from the planet they had just left. The ship took bearings on the three coastal features visible from orbit and dropped through the atmosphere like a knife blade, leaving an ionized condensation trail from its statically charged hull. It swooped into a level hover and produced a view panel showing Rydin and Cinquemain what appeared to be the same muddy plain, mangrove swamp, and sluggish river from which they had departed less than an hour ago.

But when Rydin called for a closeup, they could all detect differences. The mud showed three deep holes, angled to converge toward a central point. At a distance of about fifteen meters from this triangle they discovered a circular arrangement of tracks. They quickly resolved into boot prints that wandered out from a single point of origin and eventually came back and around to define a vast circle of clear mud centered on the triangle. An even larger number of tracks went off toward the trees, and there the view panel revealed the dull gleam of an expanded-metal sheet covered with muddy boot prints. The sheet linked with others that followed a swath through the trees and out along the river.

"I'd say a saucer has landed there," Cinquemain observed. "A big one."

"See? I told you I could find them," the ship said.

"So where are they?" Rydin asked.

The two intelligences fell uncomfortably silent.

"The Conoscenza schedule called for seven days on site," Cinquemain said.

"So where would they go? And why?" Rydin wondered. "Send out a signal," he instructed. "Ship to ship."

If the ship's intelligence complied, it was blocking these transmissions on the comm circuit. Rydin glanced at Cinquemain, who rippled his forward manipulators in imitation of a human shrug.

"No carrier signal," the ship said finally. "No modulation. No electrostatic background. Not the clink or clank of a machine anywhere within a thousand kilometers of this spot."

"So let's land—not on the footprints," Rydin said, "and see what we can find out."

He was already wearing the medical oh-two respirator when the ship opened the hull and extended its ramp. His head had not even cleared the portal when he could guess why the Conoscenza people had abandoned the site. The mask was designed to supplement normal breathing, not filter the air he was inhaling. Coming through the slots alongside his nose was the stench of decay. It appeared to come from the river.

He and Cinquemain walked around the marks of the Conoscenza landing site and mounted the aluminum plates leading through the trees. By the time they reached the riverbank, Rydin was taking short, panting breaths.

"*Now* don't you wish you were a machine?" his companion asked.

"Not at all," he said. "A machine never would have smelled a thing."

"I have chemical sensors. They're just not connected to my stomach."

"You don't have a stomach."

"All right, *battery pack.*"

"Not the same thing."

The reason for the stench was obvious. Dead fish covered the river's surface. The roots of the mangroves, which extended out into the river, held them against the sluggish current. The high sun and warm green water had advanced their state of decay.

"Can you pick one up for me?" Rydin asked.

"Why? Your arms are long enough. And you have hands."

"I also have a stomach. You can afford to get your manipulators dirty."

Cinquemain levered his carapace out over the edge of the deck plating and reached down into the river. He snagged one of the fish and straightened, holding it dangling and dripping.

"I'm beginning to see a picture here," Rydin said.

"Do tell. That's your second dead fish in as many hours."

"Count the limb pairs."

"One, two. Front and back."

"And the fish we saw this morning?"

"If it *was* morning ... three pairs. Front, middle, back."

"Remind you of anything? A plain full of horses? A beach full of sea lions?"

"Finagle's Front Teeth! Is this a smoking gun?

"Actually, it happens to be a dead fish."

"A dead civilization, you mean."

"That, too. Bring it along."

They collected two more specimens and returned to the ship. Rydin told it to prepare a minus-seventy receptacle for storing the fish. "But separate from the ones we took at the downstream site this morning," he said.

"Why?" the ship asked. "They're just more fish."

"Contamination issues," Rydin explained.

When the samples were secured, he went back outside and studied the footprints that defined the perimeter of a saucer he calculated to be at least a hundred meters in diameter. Cinquemain joined him, using visual senses that passed up into the ultraviolet and down into the infrared.

"Some of these are from yesterday," the intelligence said. "Last night there was a storm, because those first prints are uniformly blurred out. The rest are fresh, not more than a couple of hours old."

"How can you tell?" Rydin asked.

"Seepage in the middle. Slumpage at the edges."

"Would you say old prints and new are about evenly divided?"

"More like sixty-forty."

"So ... they land yesterday and start doing all their science things: catch fish, dissect them, take samples. Then they button up for the night. This morning they come out, discover a river full of dead fish, and take off."

"You know," Cinquemain said, "after humans discovered nitroglycerin and plastic explosives, some people used them to harvest fish. Scooping's faster than catching by hand. That would fit the Conoscenza ethical system, too."

"Not this time. The tour was scheduled for seven days, as you say. Yet they disappeared on the second day. The sight of this die-off scared them."

"They dropped some kind of poison? Or spread a bacterium?"

"That's what they would think—then they panicked and fled."

"You're forgetting one thing."

"Yes, Merola had joined the tour."

"So they were carrying a wild card."

54. The Contagion Spreads

"A six-legged cat and a strangely designed bridge prove nothing," Anastasis told the restive scientists, as well as the grumblers among his own staff, as they stood among the ruins of the strange city. "And the firestorm might simply have disrupted the local appearance of the Builder's node."

"Persistent fellow, isn't he?" Berzher whispered to Merola.

"He's a showman, not a scientist," she replied in a murmur. "Analyzing and accepting a difficult reality were not part of his training."

"Now, we still need to get all of you home," the tour director continued. "I propose we travel back to London, at the time of our original gathering, and check in at Carrefour House. Mr. Gill can make arrangements—"

"Fly this saucer into downtown London?" Franklin's tall companion said. "I'd certainly like to see that!"

"We can land in the countryside and take the Underground," Franklin suggested.

"Or hire an autobus," said someone else from a slightly earlier period.

"Belief seems to be catching," Berzher whispered to Merola.

"There's only one cure for that," she said quietly. And then aloud: "Yes, let's go back to the *real* London! We can accomplish nothing in this time frame. Let's get back to civilization."

Anastasis looked relieved as the others picked up and echoed Merola's call. They filed back into the ship, took off, and traveled among the stars. The spatial transition, chasing the sun for a mere 165 light days, took them almost no time at all. The planet, when they found it, was revealed by the high-altitude views as a world returned to its normal hues of blue and green. And London, as they descended toward it, was a patch of white and gray stones on either side of the snaking river. They could even trace roadways going to and from the bridge crossings.

"Be careful," Franklin said, "or we'll be spotted by the Royal Air Force."

"We're already in NORAD's sights," Merola said. "They have satellites."

"This ship is cloaked with a static charge," Anastasis replied.

"Bad news if we take a missile," Berzher muttered.

"What does the ship detect?" Merola asked him.

"No air traffic. No radar. No electromagnetic radiation."

"Then we might as well land in town. That green patch looks good."

"What? Expose ourselves?" Anastasis exclaimed. "We would disrupt—"

"We expose nothing you need to hide and disrupt nothing you care about," Merola replied.

Anastasis grumbled—and maintained the ship's static charge, so that it was enveloped in a boil of mist and dust—but he settled into a field in the center of London. It was landscaped like no park any of them had ever seen.

"Those are cabbages!" said Franklin, pointing to the pale-green globes visible along the bottom edges of the four view panels that the ship was displaying, each facing a different compass quadrant.

Beyond the field was a London that none of them had ever seen. Terraces of blue granite and pale limestone supported sprawling villas of plaster and painted wood, roofed with terracotta tiles.

"It looks Roman," said Franklin's companion.

"Time check, please," Anastasis told the ship.

"Ahh," the intelligence replied, but it might simply have been static. "For this period I would rely on geosynchronous positioning satellites. However, there are none. Star patterns and continental outlines that I observed on our way in were consistent with the first year of the third millennium after the Christus, except—"

"Except this world has never known the Christ," Merola said, as a by-now familiar figure emerged from the nearest villa.

The creature was more than two meters tall and walked on four legs while pointing with one of the two limbs near its head. Then it rose on its hindmost pair of legs, to get a better look at the dust disturbance in its field. The figure now employed all four of the forward legs or arms in pointing, gesturing to its neighbors, shading the sunken eyes of its pushed-in face, and planting a fist defiantly on its intermediate hip.

"It ... looks like the cat," Franklin said.

"But it's not an animal," Uchelnaya said.

"Strange that it would live under such primitive circumstances in what, I take it, is now the twenty-first century," the balding man observed. "One would think that, with an extra pair of limbs for locomotion or manipulation, it would develop technology faster than occurred with *Homo sapiens*—not more slowly."

"Perhaps, with the extra hands, it didn't need to," Franklin said.

Another of the pug-things came down the road, riding in a cart drawn by a horse-analogue with six coordinated legs, although its feet had obvious toes instead of hooves.

"They still use brutes in their daily work," the balding man said.

"You can't compare time scales and historical or technical developments here with what you know," Merola told him. "These creatures might have walked out of Africa—or its contemporary analogue—a million years before humankind did, or as late as last week. And anyway, your rapid advance in technology and the sciences from the eighteenth through twenty-first centuries was simply a fluke. If the coffee bean and the tea leaf had not arrived in Europe during the later stages of a religious reformation, you would all still be drinking small beer and cider for breakfast, corresponding with quill pens and sealing wax, and riding horses and carts."

"What do you know about these creatures?" Franklin asked.

"About these, specifically, no more than you," Merola said. "But they bear a superficial resemblance to the creature I saw on the riverbank, back in the Devonian. And it saw me."

"You called it something then," Franklin said, turning to Anastasis. "Muggy—?"

"That's just a bit of propaganda she uses," he said. "To spread her doctrines."

"We call them Möglichen," Merola said. "The Children of Possibility."

"Fairytales!" Anastasis exclaimed.

"But what are they?" Franklin pressed. "Some kind of monster?"

Merola took a deep breath. Any thought of protecting these people from their own future was long gone. They had no future. They had learned more about the true nature of time than any oath of secrecy could possibly cover. The only consolation was that, if they ever returned to the time stream they once knew and shared, no one would believe them. And the chance of their getting back at all was now vanishingly small. Anyway, if they did get home and started talking, Merola could always return with a Jongleur mandate and kill them all—and be damned to the consequences. The consequences would end in 2613.

"Not really monsters. Not from their point of view," Merola said at last. "The Möglichen inhabit an interim realm, a place of potential—" She could see that none of the scientists were following this explanation. Even the Conoscenza people seemed disbelieving.

"Look," she tried again, "put away whatever you have been taught by religion and metaphysics. Time is not a river. It does not flow straight from the past, through the present, on its way to the future. Time is a system of tributaries—but in reverse. Where rivers bring together small streams and creeks into a single massive flow, time breaks the original flow into branches, alternative paths, probabilistic courses—"

"Just theory!" Anastasis said. "Totally immune to disproof. Which makes it a religion."

Merola gestured at the view panels. "You're looking at the proof." She turned to the scientists. "The world we all know, where people walk around on two legs and have two arms; where cats and dogs and horses and the herbivorous apatosaurs all have four legs and no arms; where birds and the carnivorous tyrannosaurs have two big legs and two tiny arms or a pair of wings—that world was prefigured by the lobe-finned fishes we saw on the shore. That's why you all went to study them, because they are our ancestors, the tetrapods.

"But those four limbs are just one anatomical possibility. If those fishes had been different, with three pairs of bony fins instead of just two, then all of animal history on land would have developed differently. We would have been *them*." She pointed at the screen.

"But you saw that creature on the shore, didn't you?" Franklin prompted. "After all those four-lobed fishes had died."

"Actually, I saw it before then," Merola said. "I saw it—and it saw me—when I first arrived in Carrefour House."

"When we all walked into the closet?" Franklin asked.

"No, the first night, a whole day before I knew about the Conoscenza party." Merola paused, remembering. "And it recognized me even then."

"You're saying you knew this—thing?" Anastasis said, nodding at the screen. "And it knew you? It *followed* you?"

"Yes."

"Back to the Devonian?"

"Yes."

"Far beyond the Builders' nodes?"

"It doesn't need the node system, or a mirror-maze, or a timeship. It—lives—in the interim, between the dimensions that separate the world we know and the worlds that might be, or might have been. It travels between those dimensions. Somehow it found me and knew I would go back to the Devonian. And there it recognized the potential to make a single change in a fish's body structure that would carry down through the ages. It was inventing its own kind, creating its own inheritors, and in the process taking over our world."

"What a fascinating imagination you have," Anastasis said—partly in awe but mostly in disgust.

"Do you have a better explanation?" Again, she pointed to the view outside the ship. "Do you want the Sindicato della Conoscenza to take responsibility for this?"

Anastasis opened his mouth—then closed it. He looked from side to side. Merola had the sudden impression of a rat trapped in a maze.

"What do you suggest?" Franklin asked Merola.

"We must go back and stop that Möglich," she said.

"But the change has already happened. We're living in it."

"Didn't I tell you that time is not a river?"

55. Mark on Mark

"... carrying a wildcard." Cinquemain had no sooner expressed this thought than the air above their heads split with a scream. Rydin looked up and saw a thin, dark shape—the edge of a knife without a handle or a hand to grasp it—descending on the mud plain. Before he could fully register that form, it changed, widened, slowed, and became the shadowed underside of a huge disk. In extruded three tripod legs and settled neatly into the blank space surrounded by the old footprints. Rydin and Cinquemain stepped back to avoid being caught up in its gravimetric field.

"Speak of the devil—" Cinquemain began.

"And up she pops," Rydin finished.

The saucer opened a portal about sixty degrees around the edge from where Rydin and Cinquemain were standing and extruded a stairway. A number of figures in baggy suits with bubble helmets descended. All were looking and pointing toward his stolen timeship and, in what must have been a cascade of suit-to-suit radio chatter, obviously exclaiming over it. The fifth person out of the portal, a small female with a head of blonde curls, held a baton of dark metal so that one end aimed at Rydin's ship.

"Where is her intelligence?" Rydin asked.

"That stick-thing," Cinquemain said, "although I don't know how or why. We've already exchanged a terabyte of information on a private frequency, and I still don't know the whole story."

"Well, tell Berzher to have her look over here."

Before Rydin could complete this instruction, the blonde drew the baton closer to her ear, glanced over her shoulder, spotted them, and broke away from the group. She came toward Rydin in a rush at first, then slowed to dragging steps, looked down at her feet, and wouldn't meet his eyes.

"Hello, Coel," she said shyly, her voice muffled by the helmet. "I always knew you'd find me."

"You've certainly led Cinquemain and me on a merry chase," Rydin said. "All the way back to the beginning of time."

Merola tried to smile. "Not that far. Just to the start of life on land."

"And I suppose you know how badly *that's* been messed up."

"Yes, we just came from twenty-first century London."

"How much of it is still there?" he asked, curious.

"The hexapods can build a bridge, at least."

"So you saw land-based intelligence?"

"More or less. They have carts."

"They're marine in our time."

"Yeah ... I don't think land-walkers would have made it through the Fire Strike," Merola said. "Without human help, the original meteor impacted on India and turned it into an arm of the ocean. The biggest thing we saw on the ground after that was a cat."

By this time the others from the Conoscenza ship were approaching. Rydin ignored them. He turned to Cinquemain. "Are you two finished catching up?"

"I have complete records," the intelligence replied.

"Merola!" the baton said. "Did you know we had a Flüchtling assassination team on our trail?"

Tsverin's eyes widened. "Along with the Möglich?"

"You had a Möglich as well?" Rydin asked. One more bit fell into place.

"Yes. He—it—caused all this. He followed me here and then must have—"

"If you want to discuss *causes,*" Rydin said, "we can start with your baseball."

"My what?" she asked.

"Touch your right eye."

"I've already taken a neural imprint. It wasn't helpful."

"Then I guess you'll never know about the baseball."

The baton in her hand whispered, "Tell you later."

"When can we expect the Flüchtlinge to arrive?" Merola asked.

"Never," Rydin said. "I eliminated the triad back in Safronesco."

"Well, two out of three," Cinquemain put in. "I got one of them."

"When is the Möglich due?" he asked. "I assume that's why you came back here."

"Actually, he's already come and gone. Killed our kind of fish and bred his own."

"We saw evidence of that," Rydin said. "Our ship made an unexpected detour downstream, arriving about seventy—"

A hand shoved Rydin's arm up near the shoulder, a movement just short of attack.

"Would someone, *please,* tell me who is this person with the robot?" The intruder was a small man—small by the measure of others in the group—with features that Rydin recognized as an extreme example of ninth-millennium genetic drift. Beside him stood a woman with a similar face and an even deeper frown. The Conoscenza tour masters were, predictably, trying to take control of the situation.

"Coel, this is Tessu Anastasis," Merola said. "He's a managing director of the Sindicato della Conoscenza and leader of this expedition. You may recognize the name—we have *detailed* records. Tessu, this is Coel Rydin, a Jongleur chief and my superior. The 'robot' may be addressed as Cinquemain."

Rydin offered a slight bow. Cinquemain's battle chassis dipped in a brief curtsy.

Anastasis replied by thrusting out his chin. "Are you here to offer *more* Jongleur interference?" he demanded.

Rydin smiled grimly. For all the use these ninth millennials made of time travel, they had not yet discovered its misuses. Rydin imagined this man being accidentally aborted in the second trimester. That might solve all their problems in one move.

"Mir Rydin is here to fix the problem," Merola told the man. And to Rydin: "We studied the original sarcopterygians before the Möglich killed them all. I took a complete genetic record. Now, if we can find a way to insert their genome into an egg case, we can repopulate the entire species."

Rydin considered this. He turned to Anastasis. "Does your ship have a synthesis laboratory?"

The man's chin drew back. "Well ... we can *analyze* tissues, but for this tour, dealing with the most elementary principles, we never expected to—"

"Never mind," Rydin said. "Anyway, I have a better idea."

56. Confronting the Father

Before Rydin finished describing the first step of his plan, Merola could see obvious problems.

"How are you going to *fight* the Möglich?" she asked. "It has faster reactions than any human being. I saw it on the bank across the river. It moved so quickly that, before my eyes could fully adjust, it blinked out, vanished."

"Are you sure it's a physical being at all?" Anastasis asked. "Not a spirit of light and air?"

"I saw the branches move when it left," she replied. "It carries weight. It manipulates objects."

"Then we'll just have to trap it," Rydin said. "Hold it in this time and kill it."

"How?" Merola asked. "Did you bring any weapons to do that?"

In reply, Cinquemain flashed his comm laser and scored the ground.

"I used to have one of those," Berzher's baton said wistfully.

"Anything else?" Merola asked. "Something to set up a crossfire?"

The others looked from side to side and remained quiet.

She turned to Anastasis. "Do you have weapons?"

"We're purely a research operation," he said.

"You travel into a difficult and dangerous past—" she prompted.

"—that has no land animals, and no insects bigger than a scorpion," he finished.

"I just checked our ship's inventory," Cinquemain reported. "It lists two laser scalpels. Two hundred kilowatts each, beam widths of zip-point-one and point-three millimeters."

"There you go," Rydin said. "Crossfire."

"This Möglich is big," she insisted. "Three meters head to foot—feet."

"Do we have any choice about killing it?" Rydin asked.

"Well, I guess not, if we're going to—"

"Then this discussion is over."

In the final arrangements, the Conoscenza staff agreed to hold their position on the mud plain, technically occupying the second day of their scheduled tour, while Rydin, Merola, and their intelligences left in the stolen medical ship to travel upstream to the first night of the tour and confront the Möglich.

With timing details supplied by Berzher, the ship descended on the site in the midst of a violent rainstorm. Wind and rain meant nothing, of course, to the senses and energies the ship used to navigate. They spotted the Conoscenza ship—the original, from the first day of the tour, now closed up tightly against the weather—and moved out of its immediate visual range.

"Attempt no communication," Rydin instructed.

"I wouldn't think of it," their own ship replied.

They landed further up the riverbank and, in the slow rain as the storm passed, made their way along the edge of the mangrove swamp to the vicinity of the other ship. Rydin was now wearing one of the Conoscenza's protective suits and bubble helmets, the same as Merola. Each of them palmed a laser scalpel. Cinquemain plodded along in his battle chassis with the communications cluster fully extended. Merola held Berzher's baton in her left hand, lens forward, at shoulder level.

"Franklin and some of the others went for a walk after the rain stopped," she told Rydin. "That's when they saw the Möglich in the trees."

"We have another thirty minutes before then," said Berzher, who had become the expedition's cross-referencing timekeeper.

They came to the pathway of aluminum plates and followed it between the trees and down to the water. Rydin posted Merola and Berzher at one end of the long landing stage, upriver of its junction with the path through the grove. According to plan, he and Cinquemain turned to go down to the other end.

"And we're to do what, exactly?" Berzher asked.

"Wait and watch," Rydin instructed.

"And if we see anything?"

Rydin paused to consider this. "You intelligences stay in communication silently, by radio. If there's anything to report, whisper it to your human. We want to surprise the creature, not warn it off."

"Why do you think the Möglich will come to this platform?" Merola asked.

"This is ready-made access to the river. What it wants is in the river."

That, at least, made sense to her—unlike the rest of his plan.

"Oh, and touch your left eyelid," he told Merola, as he did the same.

She took the imprint. She knew Berzher was already sampling electrons.

Then they waited.

The Möglich must have made its first appearance very close to the Conoscenza saucer, because Merola and Berzher did not become aware of it until they heard a rattling on the aluminum walkway back among the trees. The metal under her feet began to dip and sway with the weight of the thing, and then she saw that pale, flattened face thrust forward between the trunks that bracketed the junction. As the creature was lit only by starlight, she might not have noticed it—except that she was looking directly at the entry point and her eyes were already light-adapted. The face was more than two meters above the landing. The Möglich advanced, the rest of its body alternately shimmering into view and then fading as the iridescent surfaces of its pleated garment caught and released the light.

She wanted to confirm the sighting with Berzher and signal Rydin through him, but she was frozen, afraid to make a sound. She could only hope her companion was registering the same dim form that she could see and making silent contact with Cinquemain.

Leveraged on its four hind limbs—Merola could see the faintly glowing skin of its bare feet under the cuffs of its sleeves, or leggings—the face and two front hands leaned impossibly far out over the water. There it paused, immobile, staring down at the surface.

Merola silently counted five seconds ... ten ... twelve—

The pale hands shot down and came up with a sarcopterygian.

Then both Möglich and fish disappeared in a blink.

"Did you see that?" Merola asked Berzher.

"We all did," he replied after a pause.

"It took a sample of our fish."

"Be quiet. I'm counting."

Before she could respond to that, the Möglich returned to the same spot on the landing. It simply appeared, as if Merola had only closed her eyes and imagined that the darkness behind her lids defined a span of time between the first appearance and the second. The only sign of anything unusual happening was tiny popping noises as the Möglich first abandoned and then displaced its own volume in the air—followed by the platform's creaking as it suddenly took the weight again. With this second appearance, however, the captured fish was gone. The hands were empty and the Möglich poised itself to take another.

More quickly this time, the creature snagged a second fish and disappeared.

"Three seconds of cycle time," Berzher said.
"Cinquemain agrees."

"Should we close in?" Merola asked. "Be ready to jump it?"

"Rydin wants us to wait. Let it establish a pattern." They watched through successive cycles as the Möglich appeared and disappeared. It went from taking fish to dumping beakers of some liquid into the water. Merola sensed that, whatever it was doing to the fish, its work in this spot was nearly done.

"Move in *now*," Berzher said into the brief gap between appearances.

Without trying to muffle her footsteps, Merola ran down the landing. In one hand she held Berzher, in the other her scalpel—its pale violet light alive and deadly over a length of five centimeters between output lens and reflector cap.

The Möglich materialized right in front of her. As if sensing her presence, it turned. She took a broad swipe with the scalpel and cut only loose cloth.

From the other end of the landing, a narrow red beam shot up and sliced across the skin of the creature's cheek before disappearing into the night out over the river. The Möglich whipped back to face this new threat.

Merola saw a pair of arms wrap around its neck, high above the platform, where Rydin must have made a tremendous leap.

The Möglich and Rydin disappeared together.

———

Blink!

Rydin and the Möglich overbalanced. The creature rolled sideways, corrected the angle of its fall, and went over onto its back. The long body stabilized the roll with its hind legs, and four hands grasped Rydin at both shoulders and hips, pried him loose from the creature's neck, and flung him away.

The bubble helmet clunked the side of Rydin's head as he crashed into the doors of a cabinet made of light metal. He saw a dazzle of stars—and not those of the late Devonian. He was somewhere else, in a room, a laboratory, dimly lit above the Möglich's head by strips of glowing white. The cabinet formed the base of a workbench which, as he climbed erect and glanced across its surface, held enigmatic pieces of equipment and arrays of graduated beakers filled with liquids in various stages of cloudiness and clarity. Rydin was reminded of the concoctions the Möglich had dumped four—no, five—times into the river that ran through the mangrove swamp.

As Rydin righted himself, so did the Möglich. They faced off in the area in front of the bench. The creature so far had produced no weapon, leaving only its size for leverage and those four long arms, which it moved in sinuous arcs like a wrestler preparing to grapple with his opponent. Rydin had only the short, shielded blade of his scalpel and the enhanced strength of his by-now-problematic simian ancestors.

He also had a terrible disadvantage. The Möglich knew exactly where it was and apparently could travel interdimensionally as an act of will. Rydin had no idea where the laboratory stood: On Earth in some other, alternate time? On some other planet? Or in a place that, from the perspective of Rydin's reference now, had never—or not yet—existed? If the Möglich disappeared now, Rydin would be trapped here with no way back to the late Devonian and the threads that led to his own world and time. If he killed the Möglich here, he might accomplish his purpose—but he would still be trapped.

Rydin had to find a way to make the creature go back to the Devonian and take him along. ... He thought for a second and discovered he had no idea how to do that! But, on the theory that anyplace was better than here in the Möglich's lair—where new weapons might be produced or contrived in an instant—he could think of one way to make the creature want him gone. And, on the additional theory that volitional travel between dimensions might incur some small element of reciprocity, a slippery path back to a place recently visited—especially if the trip were undertaken in a hurry—he was willing to try it.

He shifted the scalpel to his left hand and, never taking his eyes off the Möglich's waving arms, reached back over the bench. His fingers scrabbled among loose tools and small containers until he encountered the piece of equipment that, in his mind's eye, might have been a microscope because of the spacing between its lenses. His hand wrapped around the mounting stalk and lifted it. The object weighed a good twenty kilograms, and that was enough.

With his enhanced muscles, Rydin brought it forward, brandished it as high as he could reach toward the Möglich's face, then half-turned and brought it down across the bench, sweeping through the ranks of beakers. Glass smashed and pale liquids flew in sheets and droplets.

The Möglich let out a high, thin screech and rushed forward.

Rydin released the microscope and turned into the rush.

Four arms closed around him and began to squeeze.

The scalpel flew out of his hand upon impact.

Rydin grappled for an advantage and ...

Blink!

The Möglich had lifted Rydin high off his feet. The creature itself was standing on a rocky point with a moonlit sea on three sides. Surging on the waves below were the pale bodies of fish, hundreds of fish—maybe thousands—which, in the glance Rydin could spare for them, might be sarcopterygians related to the fish of the mangrove swamp. These fish were as dead as—perhaps even more dead—than the ones he and Cinquemain had discovered in the river on the second day of the Conoscenza tour.

The creature threw Rydin down, and he rolled across the slippery rock.

Reciprocity had worked, to some extent, but this result was still no good. He might be one day's time or ten from the night when he left his companions. He might be ten kilometers or a hundred from the mangrove swamp. He was still trapped with no way back. And now he had no weapon—except one.

Rydin gathered himself and leapt for the Möglich.

Like most creatures of earthly evolution, it was heavily muscled in the limbs, which normally needed strength for walking, flying, scrambling, or carrying. It was also muscled around the torso and abdomen, which supported and promoted the functions of breathing, digesting, and reproducing. But the bony skull was only lightly fleshed. Animals that used their jaws for fighting and tearing—wolves, the big cats, gorillas—might have sheaths of muscle and tendon around their skulls to work them. The Möglich appeared to be a more nuanced fighter and delicate feeder.

He let the creature catch his own body and grapple with it. Rydin focused, instead, on getting his hands up, above the eyes, around the temples, fingertips across the top of the broad skull. The bones themselves felt surprisingly light and fragile.

Blink!

———

"Coel!" Merola screamed when Rydin disappeared from the landing while grappling with the Möglich. She now stood, Berzher's baton dangling in her hand, on one side of an empty space where the brief fight had taken place. Cinquemain's carapace stood frozen in amazement on the other.

She held the tiny laser scalpel up in front of her face. It had proved to be a useless, impotent weapon—and Rydin had gone into the void armed only with another one like it. He and the Möglich were now in some unknown and unknowable place: another dimension, perhaps another planet, probably another universe. There Rydin would almost certainly be killed. His plan had failed. Together, Merola and Rydin both had failed.

In her efforts to return to her own reference now, Merola had done something—she still wasn't clear exactly *what*—to draw the Möglich's attention. She had lured it back to this mangrove swamp and the origins of her own kind of life on Earth. Here the monster had engineered— or was in the process of engineering—a genetic change that replaced the world she knew with a parallel world, one which supported a different body structure, a different history, and consequently snuffed out the life of everyone and everything she had ever known. Then Rydin—her leader, her friend, the one person she really trusted—had come back to rescue her. He had crossed hundreds of millions of years and half the galaxy to find Merola, rescue her, and correct all her errors. Together, they had tackled the Möglich ... and they had failed.

"Whether the time now remaining to us is hours, days, or years makes no difference," she whispered. "We and our world are lost. This is the point of oblivion."

"Not a cheerful thought," Cinquemain replied. "Why do you say that?"

"Because Rydin's *gone,* you fool! He's now someplace else—lost in the darkness—where he'll be killed!"

"That's quite a chain of assumptions," Cinquemain observed.

"Try seeing the situation from the human perspective—" she began.

"—by which," Berzher said, "you mean something improbably universal."

"If Rydin and the Möglich don't come back," Merola explained through gritted teeth, "then we are all abandoned on this riverbank, millions of years from anything we know. We're as good as dead. If the Möglich comes back without Rydin, that means he's dead and I have to fight the monster myself. You've seen how well that's worked so far. There's no way Rydin can return *without* the Möglich. So this looks like a good time to prepare for the inevitable."

"Humans!" Berzher said in disgust.

"They think too much," Cinquemain agreed.

"Haven't you been paying attention?" Berzher said. "This creature *always* comes back."

"So does Rydin," Cinquemain concluded.

At that instant, the air between them made the now-familiar popping noise and the Möglich reappeared. Instead of standing poised to perform some further mischief, the creature was struggling, rearing up on its hind legs, throwing its head back. The middle and front pairs of arms held Rydin's body outstretched, almost horizontal, three meters above the river. The creature seemed to be trying to pull the human away from its face. For his part, Rydin had a grip around the Möglich's skull and stared deeply into its sunken eyes as he tried to do … something. The great head bobbed and distorted, some parts of it squeezing down and others ballooning up, but malleable skull kept returning to its original, flattened shape beneath Rydin's groping hands.

"Shoot it!" Merola told Cinquemain.

The communications cluster attached to the battle chassis went through several half-revolutions, lighting faint spots on the Möglich's head and neck, trying different angles of attack at low power before sending a cutting beam.

"No solution totally avoids hitting Rydin," Cinquemain said.

"Shoot the body!" she shouted.

A beam cut through the shimmering material of the creature's robe and drilled flesh, with steam puffing from the near side and blood misting from the back.

At the same instant, Rydin changed both his position and his tactics. He locked his hands on the creature's upper arms, on the upper *pair* of arms, and—displaying a strength Merola could not imagine—tore his body loose from the Möglich's grasp and swung his feet forward to plant them on the curving breastbone. The Jongleur chief pulled with his hands and shoulders, pushed with his feet. The creature struggled against him and tried to resist, pulling its shoulders back, adding leverage to Rydin's move. The long bone under Rydin's feet bent, then snapped, collapsing the chest, crushing the heart. The creature's eyes widened, its mouth opened, and then awareness faded as the face went slack.

The body slumped over, and Rydin dropped to the aluminum deck, made a short roll, and came up standing. "Catch that thing!" he ordered as the still twitching body of the Möglich fell toward the river. "Don't let it go into the water!"

Cinquemain anchored the lower hips with a pair of manipulators. Merola, whose hands were still full with the scalpel and Berzher, thrust a shoulder into its navel and pushed backward, easing it toward the webwork of tree trunks that backed the metal strip of the landing. For all its size, the Möglich was remarkably light—with airy bones and papery sinews, more like a bird's body than a mammal's.

"Mop up the blood, too," Rydin instructed.

Merola set Berzher's baton into her holster and used the scalpel to cut swatches from the foreign garment. Cinquemain produced a light to guide her as she stuffed the pieces into the holes in the abdomen and wiped the thin, raspberry-colored blood off the aluminum deck plates.

"Can you tell me why we're being so neat?" she asked Rydin.

"I don't know what that thing uses for DNA, but I don't want any of it contaminating this stream."

"It's already dumped about a gallon of *something* into the water," she said. "So the damage is done."

"Yes," Rydin said. "And not just here. It was at work out on the coast, too."

"But that means we're too late," Merola said, feeling emptiness well up inside her again. "We have failed."

"Well, yes, except ... time is not a river," he reminded her.

57. Confronting the Abyss

Rydin trussed the Möglich's body with strips cut from its clothing and carried it on his shoulder back to the medical ship. Upon questioning the onboard intelligence, he discovered that its facilities included a cryo-morgue cabinet. He only had to break the creature's spine in half below the first set of hips to make the body fit.

"I need specimen bottles," he then said.

"Size and sealing?" the ship asked.

"Fifty mil'liters, self-epoxy."

"How many required?"

"About a dozen."

A panel opened in the inner wall of the crew's quarters and offered a transport rack with the empty bottles. Rydin took them back to his companions on the riverbank. By then Merola had finished mopping up the blood. The river's surface was also beginning to show the pale forms of dead and dying fish: two or three in clumps near the landing stage, single bodies further out.

"Whatever the Möglich dumped in the water works fast," he said.

"Then could it be a poison, rather than a bioagent?" Merola asked.

"Unlikely. He wouldn't kill the fish. He needed to change them."

Rydin and Merola dipped and stoppered the bottles, taking water samples from around the nearest clumps of dead sarcopterygians. They also pulled out two of the fish themselves for examination.

Before dawn came and the Conoscenza ship from the first visit would begin to show activity, the Jongleur team retired to their stolen ship. Rydin gave the ship's intelligence instructions to leave the mangrove swamp, ascend above atmosphere, relocate to a time three days beyond the scheduled end of the original tour, and wait in what was now deep space for further instructions.

"Oh," he added, "and prepare a suite with equipment for cellular and molecular analysis and biogeneration."

Within a minute, a door opened off their quarters.

"Let's get to work," he said to Cinquemain.

"Can I come and watch?" Merola asked.

"Yes, but don't touch anything."

With Cinquemain's help in translating the inscriptions on various buttons and diodes from their ninth-millennium Hindi, Rydin identified a mass spectrometer. On the theory of many hands, he relented from his injunction and showed Merola how to run samples through the machine. He walked her through the processes of concentrating particulates in the river water by centrifuging, breaking up tissue fragments and cell structures into their component molecules by sonicating, and finally feeding selections into the instrument through a gas chromatograph.

While she started on this work, he and Cinquemain addressed the fish they had pulled from the river that morning. Rydin wielded the remaining laser scalpel to dissect the bodies and take likely tissue samples. Cinquemain plugged his inputs into the suite's microscope and then switched it between visible light to study the cells and ultraviolet wavelengths to study the molecules of the fishy gobbets Rydin laid on the induction plate.

"I see a lot of swelling in these gonads," Rydin observed.

"Some kind of topical infection?" Cinquemain asked.

"Could be. Let's slice and dice for culturing."

"What does this mean?" Merola suddenly asked from across the room, pointing to a screen on her instrument that showed a number of peaks nested along a baseline.

Rydin lifted his attention from the fish's gut cavity and sent his intelligence over to help her. Cinquemain studied the peaks, then pointed with a manipulator tip. "These are chlorophyll, I think—not unusual in a river full of algae. Those are proteins, probably associated with fish guts and their excretions. And those are—"

The intelligence paused for a fraction of a second that stretched to a full three seconds. Rydin imagined Cinquemain was running through some internal database of molecular fragments. But the delay's length was alarming—approaching a year or more of human thought and reflection.

"Grab that fraction!" Cinquemain said, pointing, then pointed again. "And this one over here."

"How?" she asked.

The manipulator pushed her hand away, used a screen cursor to bracket the peaks Cinquemain wanted, and pushed buttons to divert the gas streams onto a microtiter plate.

"Is your target organic?" Rydin asked.

"Oh, yes," the intelligence said.

Once Cinquemain had built up a statistical picture of the original molecules from the mass spectrometer's fragments, it was the work of no more than five minutes—using ninth-millennium biotechniques—to synthesize an antibody "fishhook" that would pull the active microbial agent out of the remaining river samples so they could analyze the vector in its original form. While his intelligence worked through all the necessary steps, Rydin fiddled with the dissected fish. Deprived of her one useful task, Merola leaned against the wall and watched.

"Don't bother with culturing," Cinquemain said at last. "This microbe won't reproduce itself. Lots of DNA in a protein coat—no sign of a ribosome or other structures."

"It's a virus?" Rydin asked doubtfully. "Three or four hours is an awfully short incubation period."

"The water was also laced with some kind of narcotic," Cinquemain said. "That's why the analysis took so long. The drug puts the fish in a trance, opens the blood vessels, depresses the immune system, and paves the way for invasion."

Rydin thought for a minute. "All right, here's the plan of attack," he said. "You and Merola pull that microbe apart, corral and analyze its DNA, see what kind of coding it does."

"And what are you going to be doing?" Merola asked.

"Getting to know our sarcopterygian's own genetic code, chapter and verse—especially the homeobox domains—following the reasoning of our late Möglich friend."

"And that's because ...?" Cinquemain prompted.

"If your virus is his product, poured out of those beakers—and not some random disease vector floating down the river—then its DNA will match, modify, or replace the fish DNA."

After an hour of work on both sides of the problem, and allowing time to run computer checks and simulations, Rydin had a clear picture. The virus infected both fish eggs and milt, opened one of the four homeobox clusters that defined body shape, and inserted a repeat of the gene set that had originally initiated the second, or hind, pair of lobed fins. The result was two pairs of fins spaced along the belly where only one pair grew before. Simple and elegant. These fins, like all the sarcopterygian lobes, were still floating freely, attached only to the abdominal musculature, rather than fused into the spine as with later tetrapods. Where the sarcopterygian fins had eventually evolved into shoulder and pelvic structures when the animals moved onto land and their skeletons became load-bearing, this extra pair of fins would follow a similar route and attach to the midpoint of the spine in whatever form served a purpose.

Of course, the virus had been assembled in a hurry—although Rydin could guess that, between the

Möglich's brief visits to the Devonian, it must have spent months at work in that out-of-time laboratory—and the result was a whole-body infection that produced a serious, all too often life-threatening pathology. After all, it had taken thousands or millions of years of subtle evolutionary changes for a successful viral agent like the human rhinovirus, the microbe of the common cold, to perfect its attack so that it used the host for reproduction without killing it outright. And the narcotic the Möglich had supplied to pacify the fish's systems for the attack was not precisely calibrated. A lot of the sarcopterygians would die before spawning their six-lobed offspring. But enough would survive to change the world.

"Now what?" Merola asked, after he had explained all this.

"We already have an antibody that will hook the virus," Cinquemain said.

"Right," Rydin said. "Now we go catch some fish. ... A lot of fish."

58. Spreading the Antidote

Merola never wanted to see another fish in her life. Never again, not cooked, not raw, and certainly not flapping on the dock. In fact, she was thinking of becoming a vegetarian.

Rydin had worked out a plan of action with—or rather, imposed it upon—Anastasis. Together they took the two ships a full year upstream in time, before the originally scheduled first day of the Devonian biological tour. There they dragooned the scientists from the late second and early third millennia into catching fish under the supervision of Merola and the Conoscenza staff. Teams went up and down the river, up and down parallel rivers and tributaries to the north and south, and out along the coast. The process was always the same: net a fish, notch its tail for identification, and inject it with the serum that Rydin and Cinquemain had devised and were now mass-producing aboard the medical ship.

The serum included antibodies keyed to both the Möglich's transformative virus and the sarcopterygians' immune system, so that the living fish would resist infection when the creature arrived and performed its mischief. The serum also injected a new and friendly virus that Rydin had designed along the same lines, that would infect the fish's gonads with a DNA fragment which reproduced the antibodies in sarcopterygian generations yet unborn. So, either way, the species was protected.

"What if the Möglich detects the antibodies?" Merola had asked.

"He won't know to look for them," Rydin replied. "Every organism produces thousands, perhaps millions, of different antibodies. He can't analyze them all."

"But he'll know when his modification doesn't work," she insisted.

"Really? Do you think he returned to test his product?"

"It's what I would do. Any good scientist—"

"Think back now," Rydin said. "We saw him take isolated fish. We saw him dump beakers of virus. What happened next?"

"You killed him."

"Yes, but before that, I saw inside his laboratory. No fish pens. No hatchery. He was going to test the modification in place, in the river. We never saw him come back to take the infected fish, did we?"

"And now he's dead."

"Yes, dead in any dimension that follows the morning when he died."

"And if another Möglich follows him?"

"Different problem," Rydin said. "But we'll come back and kill him, too."

"Time is not a river."

"And never was."

They worked for weeks at the task, until Merola's and all the scientists' hands became red and raw. But no one grumbled, or not much, because they understood the importance of the work. Everyone had seen that future London where impossible creatures walked on four legs.

They finally reached the point at which every fish they pulled out of the river already had a notch in its tail. They saw a number of dead fish, too, because any viral infection created a certain amount of mortality. But they were satisfied that a high percentage of the fish they had processed would live and fight off the Möglich's virus when it came.

When the task was done, Anastasis came up to the Jongleurs, who were standing by the medical ship at the original site on the mud plain.

"What now?" the tour director asked.

Merola saw Rydin consider his reply.

"You take off," he said at last. "Go downstream to—what?—2615 *Anno Horribilo,* park your ship, and take these people home."

"Do I have to worry about you two following us?"

Rydin smiled. "You've always had to worry about that. But I'll give you a head start this time."

After the Conoscenza ship had departed, Rydin, Merola, and their two intelligences left the Devonian period as well. After beginning their long passage halfway across the galaxy, Rydin told the ship to open the cryptomorgue to space and dump the Möglich's body. That way, it would never cross the orbit of the developing Earth.

"It's not like he's the only one," Merola said.

"Yes," Rydin agreed. "We will always have the Möglichen."

As if warding off the thought of the children of possibility, he reached up his right forefinger to touch his left eyelid. Merola duplicated the gesture.

Now they were protected.

BACKWARD

59. Arriving in Lune

The stolen medical ship landed on the grassy slope that defined the southern crest line of the Temz valley and the boundary of Lune. The ship's intelligence cycled the portal, and Merola, with Berzher's baton in its holster, Rydin, and Cinquemain stepped out into the fresh air and sunlight. From this elevation she could spot, across the river, in the northwest quadrant of the village, the tree that she called home.

"Can we make the first order of business getting me a new chassis?" said the intelligence at her hip. "I get seasick when you walk."

"To get seasick," Cinquemain said, "you would need a stomach—and an inner ear."

"No," Berzher corrected, "just a jury-rigged motion sensor."

"Yes, first thing," Merola told her intelligence. "You can pick out the entire tool kit." And then, to Rydin: "What are we going to do with the ship? It's contraband, isn't it?"

"That will be for the Troupe to decide," he answered. "However, I think there are only three possibilities: turn it over to Dottoressa Gerbus and the clinic for deep-time studies, return it to the ninth-millennium builders, or crash it into the sun."

"Did he say, 'crash into the sun'?" the ship's intelligence asked through the portal.

"Of course," Rydin went on, "returning the ship to Lore raises a problem—that uploaded personality software."

"Hey, you ordered that," Cinquemain protested.

"More like a question or suggestion," Rydin said.

"I don't want to 'crash into the sun,' " the ship said.

"We'll have to see what the Troupe decides," Rydin told the ship. "Close the portal, please."

The returning travelers started down the slope. Merola was wearing the clothing she had first worn to twenty-first century London: knee-length skirt, blouse and jacket, and pumps with stacked heels. The heels did poorly in turf and nearly turned her ankles when they reached the crushed-chalk pathways of Lune. She ended up taking off the shoes and walking in the grass along-side the chalk.

"You do understand that all of this was your fault," Rydin told her as they walked. "Don't you?"

"Berzher has explained to me about the baseball," she said. "But I still don't remember any of it."

"That's because you didn't follow protocol and failed to take an imprint before starting your mission."

"But Berzher could remember."

"That's because his brain processed imprints right up until his chassis was destroyed and his power inputs cut—which was *after* the baseball exchange but *before* the point in time that I ... corrected your first error."

"What did you do?"

"Made certain that Pinkus Boskin never heard of baseball."

"Did you kill him?"

"Oh, nothing so crude," Rydin said. "Cinquemain and I simply arranged that certain influences never surfaced in his life. What you do not know, you cannot covet. That eliminated not only your own temptation but also the probability of his contaminating other Jongleurs as well."

"That still didn't bring me home," she observed.

"No, because by then—and through the action of stealing the McGwire baseball—you had already attracted other attention. A trio of Flüchtlinge became so fixated on your mere existence that, apparently, any change in pre-existing circumstances, such as non-theft of the ball, could not shake them off."

"I never saw them," she said.

"But Cinquemain and I did."

"I killed one of them," the intelligence said.

"And did they send the Möglich after me?"

"Perhaps not intentionally," Rydin answered, "but we know the Möglichen sometimes follow them."

"So, the three Flüchtlinge blew up the toy store. That sent me to London and the Gill family's mirror-maze. And there the Möglich saw me and followed us back to the Devonian. What happened to my backup suit and ship?"

"And my chassis," Berzher added.

"Perhaps the Flüchtlinge were simply being thorough," Rydin said. "Perhaps the Möglich had already spotted you."

"So even though, by now, with your help, I have actually committed no breach of protocol—"

"Except," Berzher put in, "for neglecting that first neural imprint."

"—don't do anything like that again," Rydin finished. "Fortunately, we were able to resolve the situation without—"

By this time, they had walked through the outskirts of the village, penetrated the outer ring of treehouses, and switched through several branchings in the path. They had already passed a number of public benches, set out in sunlit glades, where citizens could relax in their idle moments. On the bench they were approaching a musician sat and sang a mournful song of love and loss, accompanying herself—for the person appeared to be female, although it was hard to tell—on a familiar nine-stringed mandolin. At the same time, she underscored the melody with chords from a squeeze-box concertina. The fact that this performance required one mouth and four hands, while the performer sat comfortably cross-legged on the bench, struck all three of the travelers at the same time.

Merola looked around. Other people were using the paths as well, and they were indeed all ... people. Two arms, two legs, normal placement and posture. One of them, the circuit designer who had recently improved the efficiency of her last liteship, greeted her.

"Why, hello, Mira Tsverin," he said. "Have a good flight?"

"Yes, um, thank you, very smooth, Mir Dustin."

"Always good to hear." He walked on.

This exchange had interrupted the musician, who paused, looked up at them, and smiled. The face was almost human, but the eyes were a fraction too widely set and had the vacant look that—in an earlier age, when such things were allowed to happen—suggested brain damage.

Merola smiled back.

The singer merely said, "Hmmm," and picked up her song again.

Merola, Rydin, and Cinquemain walked on in a state of shock. At the same instant, the two humans reached up and touched their right eyelids. Merola did not know what Rydin might be feeling, but the imprint did nothing for her.

"It could be some kind of mutation," he began when they were out of earshot.

"Not in a genome as thoroughly cleansed as yours," Cinquemain replied.

"Could it be a recessive gene?" Merola asked. "Something from—"

"Generally, recessive developmental coding will kill the fetus."

"Then some kind of parallel evolution?" Rydin suggested.

"Your antibody worked," she said. "Most of the time."

"Not a word of this to anyone," Rydin ordered.

"No," she said. "Way too much to explain."

"No Search reports with the Troupe."
"What about the Conoscenza?"
"For once, we let them go."
"Without retaliation?"
"On what basis?"
"Never mind!"

60. Arriving in London

The red-shirted Conoscenza staff member led Evgenya Uchelnaya personally back through the mirror-maze and out into the tiny antechamber behind shelves stuffed with cleaning supplies.

"Thank you for your participation," he said, almost mechanically. "Please remember your promise. Tessu Anastasis will contact you eventually about payment."

"Of course," she replied. And if she broke her promise and told anyone—who would believe her?

The man nodded and turned back through the glass that was not really glass.

Uchelnaya pushed on the insides of the cupboard doors, stepped down, and was standing in a hallway. The carpet of deep-blue syntholin and the overhead LED strip with its rainbow spectrum were the same, so it had to be the hallway that she had left so long ago—close to three months and a couple of trips across the galaxy—at least according to subjective time. She walked to the end of the hall, went down the stairs, and approached the registration desk.

The young woman standing behind it looked up and smiled. "Welcome back to Kreuzung Haus, gospozha! That didn't take long, did it?"

"Miss Gill?" Uchelnaya asked, groping for the first name. "Sabina?"

"Yes?" the young woman said simply. Her eyes, however, held challenges.

"How long was I away?" Uchelnaya asked—her second-choice question.

"From this reference now? Less than a day, about twelve hours, with leeway."

"And how long have *you* been here?" Her first-choice question.

Sabina Gill grinned. "Since right after you stepped off with your tour group, sometime in 2001."

"But that's more than two hundred—"

"Hush now," the woman cautioned. "Really, am I the most extraordinary thing you've seen recently?"

Uchelnaya considered the past three months, including the London she had visited that was no longer London. "No ... I guess not."

"Then let me arrange your flight—" The young woman stopped suddenly, her attention fixed over Uchelnaya's shoulder. Her pretty lips curled into a snarl.

Uchelnaya turned to look. Beyond the glass doors of the hotel, on the other side of the street, two men in leather smocks and baggy pantaloons were holding a third person wearing a brocade caftan against the wall. Uchelnaya did a double-take because the two men were using all four of the hands they possessed between them to accomplish this. The person being held was splayed against the brickwork, two arms pinned on one side, two on the other. The men were shouting hoarsely—heard only dimly through the glass. The victim was twisting feebly and turning its head one way and the other in confusion. One of the men kicked an instrument, a guitar with two necks and complicated fretwork, out into the street, where a ground vehicle ran over it.

Uchelnaya had a sick feeling that she knew all too well what was going on. "Are they robbing ... him?" she asked.

"More like harassment," Sabina Gill said.

"You should call the police."

"It isn't exactly illegal," Gill said cautiously.

"But you still don't like this ..."

"Even if it can't speak, the divina is not an animal."

"Divina? Is that what you call it?"

"Yes, of course. Don't you—?" Gill stared at her.

"We, ah, have another word in Russian."

"I see. ... Well, anyway. Your flight to Moscow." She pulled up a computer tablet and stroked it. "I can get you on the semiparabolic out of Heathrow at five today."

"That would be excellent. I'll be home for supper."

Uchelnaya wondered what she would find in Moscow.

———

After the Conoscenza staffer guided them to the linen closet and gave his final warnings, Rosalind Franklin and Francis Crick stepped out into the upper hallway of Carrefour House. They went down to the lobby and paused by the registration desk.

"What year is it?" Franklin asked the proprietor. She recognized him immediately. It was the same man, Sam Gill, who had been running the bed-and-breakfast back—back?—in 2001.

"It's 1955, Miss Franklin," he replied. "The same year as you left, just a few hours ago."

"Funny, it seems longer," she said.

"Travel has that effect." Gill smiled.

"Are there any charges for your services?" Crick asked.

"Why, no. All arrangements were made through Mr. Anastasis."

"May I offer you a gratuity then?" Crick reached for his wallet.

"Certainly not. I happen to know the salaries you scholars earn."

"But, please," Franklin said, "do take our thanks, to you and your family."

"With pleasure, miss."

Franklin and Crick walked out into the street and turned in the direction of King's Cross Station and the train back to Cambridge. Cutting through a park, they could see the trees were just starting to bud with spring— the same season they had left what seemed like months ago.

"Look, there's a squirrel," Franklin said, pointing. "I think it's a squirrel."

The gray shape, with a bushy tail as long as its body, scurried from branch to branch. Something about its movements was odd, or dislocated. It seemed to gallop with an extraneous bend in the middle of its sleek back, as if the poor creature has been injured. When the squirrel came to the end of an isolated branch, it launched itself and glided—front legs stretching forward, middle legs extending to the side, creating an arched airfoil of loose belly skin, rear legs thrusting backward—across the path in front of them to land on a tree forty feet away.

"You saw that, I'm sure," she said to her companion.

"With these two eyes," Crick said. "Though I don't believe it."

"Do you know what I'm thinking?"

"What, Rosalind?" he asked.

"We spent weeks catching those loathsome fish—"

"—and apparently all for nothing," Crick finished.

———

Mr. Charles Darwin emerged from the upstairs cabinet in Crossroads House and made his way down to the common room. It was still the same dark and ramshackle inn he had entered in 1862, before starting on his marvelous adventure. And there stood the innkeeper who last greeted him in 1862. It suddenly dawned on Darwin that this was the same man he was to meet so much later—in 2001, was it?—although now much younger, thinner, and with more hair.

"Mr. Gill?" he asked. "Samuel Gill?"

"Just Sam will do," the man said pleasantly.

"But you are still alive in, what, a century and a half?"

The innkeeper raised his eyebrows as if to shrug off the miracle.

"I understand," Darwin said. "This is another secret, isn't it?"

"Just so," Gill replied. "I take it you'll be returning to your place, Down House in Bromley? Will you go by way of our new Victoria Station?"

"Yes, but I'm afraid I'll need a cab to get there. I rode one in—"

"But they don't come willingly into the Dials, I know. Covent Garden is the closest you'll find a cab."

"I don't suppose it's safe to walk?" Darwin suggested.

Gill looked him over critically. "Not for a man of your age and station."

"Oh, dear."

"But not to worry. I'll have our porter, Felix, take you up."

Felix turned out to be a very strange young man. In the subdued light of the common room, Darwin saw a bulky body that appeared to be strong enough and tall, but the lad's face had the vacant eyes of a simpleton. Gill communicated with him by a complicated series of gestures, and Felix responded with a humming language devoid of words. When they went outside into the slums of Seven Dials, however, the full strangeness was revealed. As Felix opened the inn door and passed Darwin out with one pair of hands, tipping his hat as they went, he unfolded a second pair of arms from across his stomach and brandished a short club in one of these hands and a dagger in the other as protection against beggars, lurkers, and pickpockets.

"You seem well prepared," Darwin said.

The boy nodded at this and said nothing, while his eyes scanned the streets like a pair of lamps.

In Covent Garden, as Darwin settled into a cab, he offered Felix a coin for his trouble. The boy took it, stared at it, and dropped it on the pavement. Then he turned and disappeared into the Dials.

At Victoria Station, the new façade of brick and stone with its numerous dormers and ledges was already attracting colonies of pigeons. Most were the gray and mottled-iridescent birds familiar to every Londoner, but here and there Darwin could see a curious light-brown specimen. The difference was apparent when the strange birds took to the air, for rather than leaping and fluttering with one pair of wings, they counter-stroked with two, more like a dragonfly or beetle. The effect was a graceful, vertical, darting flight reminiscent of hummingbirds.

As he crossed the station concourse, it occurred to Darwin that he would have to learn biology all over again. The thought gave him a thrill. He was eager to find what amazements now awaited in his own garden in Kent.

61. Carrefour House

The London office of the Land Registry was a six-story building in red brick and sandstone at the southeast corner of the city's largest public square, Lincoln's Inn Fields, Borough of Camden. The building featured square towers at each corner that were topped with steeples of gray slate. Although built just before the Great War of the past century, it was vaguely reminiscent of the White Tower at the center of the Tower of London—but with more windows.

Late on a September afternoon in 2001, with golden light streaming through the trees, a young woman with equally golden hair crossed the square and entered the pillared doorway. She went to the counter in the public office and drew a sheaf of documents from her over-large purse.

"Yes, dear?" said the clerk, Agnes Mayhew, who had been with the registry for about as long as the building. "Can I help you?"

"I want to establish title to a piece of property," said the young woman.

"This would be the place then."

"Here is the original deed of land," the woman said, unfolding and spreading on the countertop a sheet of what looked like parchment, brown all through and flaking at the edges. It was heavy with wax seals and crumbling ribbons.

In the rounded uncials of an official medieval document—written in Latin, of course—Agnes could make out nothing except a date, a year: 1556. One of the seals affixing a ribbon looked as if it might once have borne the image of an inverted rose of five petals.

"I'm afraid I can't read this, dear. And our Latin scholar went out to lunch sometime in 1962."

"I have later documents."

"Please. It would help."

The young woman produced a veritable history trail, in parchment, vellum, and hand-laid paper, describing a property that began as a plot near a crossroads outside the walls of the City of London. It lay in the district now known as Seven Dials and currently fronted on Earlham Street. All of the later documents were in the family name of Gill.

"And to what use is the property put now?" Agnes asked.

"It isn't. There was a fire, a gas main explosion, early in the summer. The building was leveled, and the lot is now empty."

"Oh, dear. I am sorry."

"But these will help me establish ownership, won't they?" The young woman tapped the stack of papers.

"They will indeed—if you can prove your identity and relationship to this Gill family."

"Oh, but that's easy! My name is Sabina Gill." And the young woman pulled from her purse a driver's license, birth certificate, and British passport to prove it.

"Then we're in business. It will take a few weeks to issue a new title."

"That will be fine. I still have to get building plans approved."

"Although it's not my business, what are you building?"

"Oh, nothing pretentious! A little bed-and-breakfast, six rooms in front facing the street, seven in back overlooking the garden, and a little flat for us—my sister and baby brother—on the top floor."

"Sounds lovely, dear."

62. The Eyes of Envy

On the third day of the Conoscenza biological tour, having caught and sampled their fill of sarcopterygians, Rosalind Franklin and Francis Crick joined the other scientists in chasing dragonflies. The flying saucer had moved inland from the river by a distance Tessu Anastasis said was fifty kilometers, to the edge of a forest of fernlike plants. A miniature forest, three or four meters high at most, of green stalks and fronds without a leaf or bud in sight. But the flies were thickly swarming.

"Have you ever seen anything like this?" Franklin asked her companion.

She brought her net down on a specimen with a wingspan of twenty centimeters.

"Not in Devon," he said, "or wherever we're supposed to be."

"Actually, I think it's the west coast of North America. Or what will be."

Franklin pulled up on the back of the net, forming a little tent, to let the insect move about a bit. She considered putting her hand under, to touch the creature, but realized that she did not know whether the mouth could bite or the tail held a sting. Her field of study was physical chemistry, after all, not descriptive biology. Fortunately, the Conoscenza people had supplied tools for extracting DNA that would work through the netting. Now, if she could only find a vein ...

As one often does when concentrating, she sensed someone watching her. She glanced at Crick, but he had wandered away after his own dragonfly. She lifted her head and looked around. The rest of the tour members were similarly engaged. None was looking her way.

The feeling persisted, however, and it had now acquired a direction. Franklin's attention was drawn, almost telepathically, to the edge of the forest.

There her gaze was met by a pair of sunken, piggy eyes in a pale, shallowly concave face. The face was set well back in among the trees and shaded by the fronds near their tops. The being—whether animal or man, that was a toss-up—held the stalks apart with its paws or hands. With three of its four large, pale hands. And in the shadows just beyond those hands she glimpsed an iridescent shimmer, a ghost shape, that moved like water.

The eyes that had drawn her attention stared back. She could read in them confusion, hunger, envy, desire, and hatred. After three seconds of locked gazes, Franklin decided she could read every human emotion in those eyes—or else no emotion known to humans.

In the fourth second, counting slowly by chimpanzees, the creature blinked and disappeared. It simply vanished. The only clue she had that it ever existed was a gentle swaying of the stalks which, as it released them, swung back into place. But that might just as easily have been the breeze.

Acknowledgements

Every author works alone, usually in a closed room and often at night. Sometimes it feels as if we're sending messages to Mars by the dark of the Moon. If we have the opportunity to work in collaboration with another writer, then we can bounce ideas around, test them out before they become fixed on the page, and feel the reassuring pressure of another mind to keep us sane. On a solo book, a writer gets some of this contact and comfort from the efforts of a competent editor: at least the book goes off into the darkness after some other mind has first given it a thoughtful run-through. In the new world of ebooks, however, where the self-published author may be working without the safety net of a professional editor, we have to rely on the generosity of others.

With the supposedly finished manuscript of The Children of Possibility in hand, I was able to call on a circle of long-time friends and family members—all of whom have a professional oar in the writing and publishing business and who have taken an interest in my work. They agreed to read the manuscript and give detailed feedback. Their critical review, insights, and suggestions make this story the finished work it hopes to be. My heartfelt thanks to:

- **Patrick Larkin** (http://www.patricklarkin.net/)— former colleague from PG&E and my mentor in wargaming. Pat specializes in historical, military, and espionage thrillers. His novel *The Tribune* is the first of a series set in imperial Rome at the time of Christ, with a sequel now under way. He wrote two novels in Robert Ludlum's bestselling Covert-One series, *The Lazarus Vendetta* and *The Moscow Vector*. And earlier he coauthored with Larry Bond five novels of military fiction, including *Red Phoenix, Vortex, Cauldron, The Enemy Within,* and *Day of Wrath.*

- **Elizabeth Kern** (http://elizabethkern.com/)—another former colleague who also writes fiction. Her debut novel is *Wanting to Be Jackie Kennedy.*
- **Kate Campbell** (blogging at Kate Campbell's Word Garden, http://kate-campbell.blogspot.com/)—another former PG&Eer. Kate's debut novel is *Adrift in the Sound,* and I had the privilege of seeing it in draft and helping her with editing. Our email exchanges during the process will soon be published as "Between the Sheets: An Intimate Exchange About Writing, Editing, and Publishing."
- **George Calmenson**—another gaming friend who has a long career as a textbook editor and printer.
- **Robert Thomas**—my brother and a professional technical writer and editor, who has enthusiastically followed my books from the beginning.
- **Jessica Neasbitt**—my daughter-in-law, a published photographer, and a fair writer herself. Most recently, she has published original scholarly work on gender and cosmetic surgery.

ABOUT THE AUTHOR

Photo by Robert L. Thomas

THOMAS T. THOMAS is a writer with a career spanning forty years in book editing, technical writing, public relations, and popular fiction writing. Among his various careers, he has worked at a university press, a tradebook publisher, an engineering and construction company, a public utility, an oil refinery, a pharmaceutical company, and a supplier of biotechnology instruments and reagents. He published eight novels and collaborations in science fiction with Baen Books and is now working on more general and speculative fiction. When he's not working and writing, he may be out riding his motorcycle, practicing karate, or wargaming with friends. Catch up with him at www.thomastthomas.com.

Books by Thomas T. Thomas
eBooks and Paperbacks:
Coming of Age, Volume 1: Eternal Life
Coming of Age, Volume 2: Endless Conflict
eBooks:
The Professor's Mistress
The Judge's Daughter
Sunflowers
Trojan Horse
Baen Books and eBooks:
The Doomsday Effect (as by "Thomas Wren")
First Citizen
ME: A Novel of Self-Discovery
Crygender
Baen Books in Collaboration:
An Honorable Defense (with David Drake)
The Mask of Loki (with Roger Zelazny)
Flare (with Roger Zelazny)
Mars Plus (with Frederik Pohl)